KEVIN LAMPORT

A DIFFERENT WORLD

Many thanks to the usual suspects… Chad, Colin, Elyza, Jason, Monty, and Sara. And, of course, as always, Shona.

Thank you to the good people at Scribendi https://www.scribendi.com/ for their editing services.

Thanks to Damonza https://damonza.com/ for their professional cover art and formatting services.

This is for Molly Lamport

Cosmic Inflation – An explosive scaling-up of spacetime a tiny fraction of a second after the Big Bang. Some parts of spacetime expanded more quickly than others, creating "bubbles" of spacetime that then developed into other universes… the multiverse.

Multiverse – The hypothetical set of possible universes, including the universe in which we live. Together, these universes comprise everything that exists: the entirety of space, time, matter, energy, and the physical laws and constants that describe them.

The known universe has its own laws of physics, while other universes could have different laws, according to the multiverse concept.

"The past is a foreign country.
They do things differently there."

L.P. Hartley

PROLOGUE

Florida, October, 2022

"WILL WE SEE Ariel tomorrow, Daddy?"

Ray Albright swallowed a yawn and said, "I'm sure we will, Tinkerbell." He reminded himself to pay attention. Making the right mouth noises like he normally did when he wasn't too interested in a conversation, didn't work with Angie. She peppered everything she said with questions. From the moment she towed him down the jet-way into the wonderful Florida heat, chattering like an excited chipmunk the entire way, she'd barely slowed. She took after her grandmother in that respect—another lady who never stopped talking.

Six hours later she was still asking questions.

"Can we go on the Finding Nemo ride tomorrow?"

"I'd like a red apple on a stick, okay Daddy?"

Ray cut his eyes toward his wife in the passenger seat of their rental car. She was asleep, or conveniently feigning sleep, judging from the slight smile that played on her lips. Ray thought he might have faked sleep too if he'd been in the passenger seat instead of driving. He'd make Dawn pay for this trickery. Maybe he'd insist she go on that silly Small World ride two or three times in a row, just her and Angie, while he sat in the shade with a bag of peanuts and some icy lemonade. That plan came with its own risk. He'd have to listen to them both hum *that* song all afternoon.

Ray answered his daughter's questions patiently. "Of course, we can go on the Finding Nemo ride," and, "Maybe after lunch you can have a candy apple."

His answers seemed to satisfy her, and he thought his little blonde dynamo might finally be winding down. The pauses between her questions had grown longer, and when he looked at her in the rearview mirror, she sagged in her car seat and jerked her head up a couple of times as she fought sleep.

He spotted their rented condo poking up above the horizon, only a few miles down the road. Three traffic lights at the most, only one complete stop if he got lucky and caught the greens, and then he'd be done for the day. Ray blew out a silent sigh of relief. He was exhausted. Chasing a five-year-old around the Magic Kingdom all afternoon was harder than a full day at the office.

The three of them left Chicago early to reduce the stress of dealing with line ups, crowds, and the Neanderthals working security, not one of them with an ounce of common sense. Angie fell asleep the moment she sat down in the airplane, which probably accounted for the extra energy that carried her through the day. Dawn dozed the entire four-hour flight. He was the only one who hadn't napped. Now he was ready for some down-time. He wished he could bottle Angie's energy or tap it somehow. There'd be no late mornings this week. Not in Orlando with a five-year-old. There'd be no relaxing around the pool and no three-hour-long candlelight dinners, holding hands across the table with his wife.

Far from it.

Tonight they "dined" at a buffet where Disney characters mingled with the guests while they ate. Angie's eyes widened when they walked into the restaurant. She hadn't come close to eating her share of the twenty-dollar-a-plate buffet, although she collected three autographs in the autograph book she insisted Ray buy. He made a mental note to have a word with the daycare teacher who, bent at the knees and looking Angie right in the eyes, asked if she was going to eat supper with Snow White and the dwarves, thereby firmly lodging the idea in his daughter's head.

"Can we go in the swimming pool when we get home, Daddy?"

"It's very late, Tinkerbell. I think the pool is closed." He gave Dawn a second sidelong look, saw her smile with his answer.

Daddy? Is Mommy sleeping?" Angie's voice dropped to a very loud whisper. "Mommy, are you sleeping?"

Dawn said, "A little bit, my girl."

Ray reached across and patted his wife's thigh. He left his hand there and she smiled softly and he heard a low purr that sounded like happiness and contentment.

In the exaggerated whisper Angie said, "I like vacations, Mommy."

Dawn opened one eye, then slowly and lasciviously, she licked her upper lip. She grinned and Ray choked down a laugh because they both knew an evening of sweaty fun wasn't going to happen on an "Angie" vacation. "Yes, my girl," Dawn said. "I like vacations too."

Angie said, "What are we going to do tomorrow?"

One of her favorite questions. Ray said, "We'll figure something out, Tinkerbell." But first, a beer for himself and a glass of wine for Dawn, perhaps ten minutes of TV, feet up on the coffee table.

Dawn's eyes were closed again, but she must have sensed his glance. The same contented expression as earlier crossed her face. It filled him with warmth, and he thought he would have done anything in the world for that special smile. He wanted to brush the back of his hand across her cheek, so he could feel her softness and prove she wasn't a dream. He never got tired of looking at her.

He signaled, switching lanes. The condo was only half a mile away now, thank heavens. This was how Angie must have felt, just before she climbed into one of those preposterously big teacups. Anticipatory. He couldn't wait for the day to be done.

The stoplight in front of them—the last stoplight—turned from red to green. Ray didn't even need to slow his rented Ford Focus.

He thought about Dawn's suggestive lip-lick and wondered if there was some kind of Disney daycare of which they could take advantage. Park Angie in a big room with fifty overly stimulated children and spend a couple of hours enjoying some adult fun. It was a wonder Disney hadn't thought of it. When it came to making a buck, they covered most angles. Maybe the idea wasn't wholesome enough for them.

From the backseat, five-year-old Angie said in a voice that finally sounded tired and possibly a little condescending, "Maybe we'll see the *real* Tinkerbell tomorrow, Daddy."

It was the last sentence she ever spoke.

PART 1

CHAPTER 1

Florida, December, 2022

A LOW-SLUNG BMW sedan idled unseen in the back corner of an empty parking lot, away from the glow of the overhead streetlights. The dark tint on the vehicle's windows made the rainy, overcast night blacker than it really was. Three men sat in the car, one on the middle of the back seat, the other two comfortably ensconced in the front buckets. In contrast to the driver who waited in complete, sulky silence, the individual in the back couldn't shut up.

He said, "We ain't kids anymore, Eric. This is real. You nervous?"

Eric Dalrymple stared out the sedan's passenger side window without answering. He was keyed up for sure, but nervous? He wasn't certain. Possibly. Sitting motionless took all his effort. There was a weird hollow spot right in the center of his stomach like a bulls-eye, but he thought the feeling was excitement more than nerves. Nerves implied fear, and there was no way he'd admit to being afraid. Not to anyone, particularly Dom.

Dom said, without bothering to wait for a response, "You've gotta do this on your own."

This wasn't new information. Dalrymple nodded. He thought

Dom was the nervous one, the way the man yo-yoed on the edge of the seat making the plush leather squeak.

Chou was a different story. The little Asian wheelman was clearly feeling the pressure, fidgeting behind the steering wheel, fiddling with the stereo volume. Sniffing noisily. The dashboard lights cast a satanic red glow on the lens of his Killer Loop Sunglasses.

Dalrymple wasn't sure how Chou could see through the dark shades well enough to drive, and the incessant sniffing chafed his nerves like knuckles down a cheese grater. He didn't care for slopes in general, but he was starting to dislike Chou on a personal level. The Asian had loaded up on coke before they left. Blow sharpened his senses, he said. The chemical also made a guy paranoid. Dalrymple knew this and unease rippled his body. He didn't trust dopers. Fucking weaklings. He was happy to sell the shit, but he sure wouldn't use it and he didn't trust any fuck-wit who did.

Dom said, "We'll drop you off. Wait for you to get it done. You can't just scare him, though. You gotta kill him. That's how it goes. Freeze up, we're gone. Do it right, you're in."

Dalrymple nodded.

"You got your piece? Is it loaded?" Dom barely paused. "It's clean. No numbers. Don't drop it, though. We'll lose it later at the bottom of the lake. The cops will never find it."

Dalrymple turned away from his reflection in the passenger window and looked over his shoulder at his friend. Seemed like only yesterday he and Dom were punching kids out on the school ground. Stealing lunch money. Now his initiation was minutes away and Dom was running his mouth two hundred miles an hour, not saying anything Dalrymple didn't already know. They'd been through all the details, the procedure, a dozen different times. Dom's constant chatter was almost as irritating as Chou's sniffing.

"I got the gun," Dalrymple said. "I know the deal. Now shut up, would you?"

Dom slicked a long strand of black hair behind his ear. He

kept talking like he hadn't heard a word. "It might be a woman. Some hot-looking bitch. Don't matter. Pop her. Centerfold or not."

Dalrymple's fingers caressed the side of the pistol he held on his right thigh. "I said, shut up." His voice was flat as day old soda.

Dom stared at him. After a beat or two, he nodded. "Okay. You're ready." Making a statement, not asking a question. He slapped a hand on Chou's shoulder. "He's ready. Let's roll."

The Asian jerked as though shot.

Dalrymple guessed the coke-induced paranoia was kicking in.

Chou turned the stereo down and fired up the Beamer. He revved the engine and had to turn the volume back up for them to hear the music. When he pulled onto the road, the back tires squawked as they grabbed asphalt.

"Fifty-five," Dalrymple said before Chou had a chance to get up to speed. His tone didn't invite debate. "You're not at Daytona. No point getting pulled over for speeding, all the guns in the car."

Chou bobbed his head and drummed his fingers on the steering wheel in time to the rap music pouring out of the Beamer's speakers. Casually, as though it was his intent all along, he set the cruise control to fifty-five. The highway, a black and yellow ribbon, unrolled in front of them. The BMW's brilliant blue-white halogens lit up the night like two small suns in a galaxy of darkness. Sporadic raindrops pelted the windshield. The road was quiet.

Then, in the distance, a pair of headlights stabbed the night.

Dalrymple stiffened and had to force his muscles to relax into an unnatural calm. *Okay, maybe I am nervous.*

For the first time that night Dom sat quietly. His arms were stretched across the top edge of the back seat, his hands rolled into fists. Chou leaned forward in his seat, bracing himself in position with both hands tight on the steering wheel. A muscle twitched rhythmically in his jaw.

The approaching lights filled the Beamer's windshield. They

grew larger as the vehicle drew closer, until they filled the entire sedan. They did not vary in intensity—the driver did not blink his headlights rapidly between high and low, reminding Chou to dim the BMW's high-beams. Then it flew past in a cloud of mist, leaving the interior of the BMW dark once more. Nobody in the sedan made eye contact as the coiled tension wound down. Chou coughed quietly into the back of a hand. After a couple of seconds Dom leaned forward, a mad jocular grin on his face. He laughed and there was a touch of hysteria in the sound. "That was awesome."

Stress, like a knotted rope between Dalrymple's shoulders, loosened. He smiled. Dom had a way with words. The previous irritation with his friend disappeared.

They drove on, beneath a row of streetlights on one side of the road, past a strip mall on the other, all the shops locked up tight except for a late-night Chinese takeout anchoring one end. The tires were whisper quiet on the road. The occasional vehicle flew by in the opposite direction, but no one flashed their brights. So far it seemed the BMW's blinding high-beams hadn't offended anyone.

So far.

Chou entered a long sweeping curve. The strip mall disappeared behind them. In front of them a fresh set of headlights burned the night, two indistinct blobs in the drizzle covering the windshield. Seconds stretched like an elastic band. When the wipers cleared the rain away, the headlights sharpened. Doubled. One vehicle became two. The first vehicle, an ancient-looking Ford pick-up, drove past without incident. Whoever was driving the second vehicle wasn't as forgiving. He flashed his lights back and forth from high to low half a dozen times, making Dom shout, "That's the one! You shoot him, Eric. Don't matter who it is. Dead."

Chou stabbed the brakes, bringing the sedan to a stop on the shoulder. "Hey, man," he said. His voice was higher than normal. "That was a cop car."

"Don't matter it's a cop. The initiation don't change."

"Shut up. Both of you," Dalrymple snapped. He'd seen the Ford truck and right behind it the black and white. "Let me think about this."

"It don't matter it's a cop," Dom said, more insistently. "You still gotta—"

Dalrymple silenced him with a look and a hard, slicing motion of his hand. He wasn't about to mess up his initiation. He couldn't. Not if he wanted more responsibility. Not if he wanted to get away from pushing bags of crack and into more important jobs like collecting and enforcing. But, a guy didn't shoot a cop without due consideration. He rolled his head in a tight, quarter turn, and heard several satisfying cracks and pops. After several moments of careful thought, he said, "Follow him, Chou."

Chou stared straight ahead, avoiding Dalrymple's eyes. "I don't like this," he said. "Don't like chasing a cop."

"Follow him."

After several long, silent seconds Chou threw the sedan into an angry U-turn and stabbed the gas. The Beamer rocketed down the road.

Dalrymple focused on the taillights ahead of them. "Don't speed. And, don't get too close."

In front of them the light bar on top of the cop car came alive, scattering gems of red and blue light into the night.

"I knew it."

Dalrymple heard panic in the Asian's voice. How had the little slope ever become a wheelman? When the night was over the two of them were going to have a pointed conversation, Dalrymple decided.

"Pass him when he pulls over, Chou. Nice and easy. And, turn that noise on the stereo off. You call that music? I need to think." Dalrymple rubbed his chin. The dark red bristles scraped across the back of his hand. "The pig must have pulled the first guy over, the guy driving the pick-up truck." He spoke slowly, working it out as he talked. "We'll drive by, do a U-turn up the road a little way, sit there and wait. When the guy in the truck goes by, that means he's got his ticket. Pigs always sit on the side of the road for a few minutes afterward, wrapping up the paperwork. What not. I'll do it then."

He rested his arm on the door's windowsill and tapped his fingers slowly on the corner of the dashboard. Every inhalation and every exhalation came a little faster than normal, but each breath was even. Controlled. He thought about what would happen next—the murder of a completely unsuspecting stranger.

Killing an enemy, no matter how difficult the circumstances, didn't provide any particular mental challenge. For one reason or another, an enemy deserved a bullet. An innocent, on the other hand, a stranger picked out at random who wasn't involved in any way... Well, the physical challenge remained the same, but the mental challenge suddenly became enormous. Success validated his worth to the organization.

Dalrymple held his hand out in front of him, palm down. It didn't shake. He decided he wasn't nervous. Enemy or innocent, it was all the same to him.

Half a mile away the light-bar on the roof of the cruiser went dark.

Dalrymple raised the Beretta and pulled the pistol's slide back with his thumb and index finger. It slammed forward with an oily, metallic clang, chambering a round.

Here we go.

One dead cop coming up.

Initiation complete.

CHAPTER 2

MITCH REILLY'S LIFE stretched out in front of him in the same way a road stretched out in front of a person driving a car. His road was less traveled than the average, but the ride was essentially the same for everybody—you can see into the future a little bit, and now and then the surface gets bumpy but typically smooths out again, and now and then a curve comes out of nowhere that needs to be handled with more care than usual. On rare occasions the curve turns into an unexpectedly terrifying bastard of a hair-pin that keeps going and going and going… like the night Step-And-A-Half drank too much and Mitch got pulled over driving the man home.

It started much the same way as any other Friday night—beers after work with the rest of the crew, the first two going down fast, washing away the heat of the day and the thick taste of tar and roofing shingles sticking to the back of his throat. Then Step-And-A-Half switched to double Rye and Sevens. Mitch sighed and muttered, "Oh, man. I need a ride. You gotta get tanked tonight?" He pushed away what remained of his third beer and ordered a Diet Coke.

For the next couple of hours not much happened, except Step-And-A-Half became blind drunk, and Mitch pocketed his truck keys. Most of the others guys got fired up pretty good as well, Mitch buying the rounds because he knew they'd remember him with a thankful smile in the coming days, when he didn't show up for work.

He sipped his soda and watched them make less and less sense, feeling that strange blend of humor and impatience a sober person always feels in a crowd of dumb-ass drunks, a little regret in the mixture too. These were the last memories he'd have of these people. The ringing sound in the center of his brain had begun five or six days ago. The sound—the tinnitus—was like a mosquito trapped deep inside his head. Almost indiscernible in the beginning, intensifying as the week passed. Now it sounded like a dentist's drill, a shrill hum that meant tonight was the night, if history proved anything, that his life would change significantly.

For the eleventh time.

When Step started slobbering and looking for a fight, Mitch decided the time had come to run the man home and then drive himself to wherever he needed to go. Somehow Step would find his ancient Ford in the morning. He always did. If the search took a little longer than usual, well, Mitch wasn't worried. He'd be long gone by the time Step got around to being angry. Too bad really. Mitch would have enjoyed watching his buddy swear and fume and carry-on when he discovered his pick-up truck wasn't parked in his driveway.

Everything went according to plan until a police car lit him up, Mitch wondering what the hell? He was doing everything right. Watching the speed limit. Coming to a complete stop at every red light. He was in big-time trouble if the police officer was in a bad mood because he couldn't be locked up when the tinnitus peaked. It had never happened, not once in over a decade, but the dread living inside murmured, "It *could* happen," and sent worms of fear sliding across his skin.

Mitch rolled down the window. A warm wind puffed, blowing infrequent drops of rain the size of pebbles into his face. The air smelled damp and heavy. It felt like a monster of a storm was hiding just over the horizon. He watched in the truck's door mirror as the officer walked toward him and told himself, "Deep calming breaths. Be polite. Don't give him a reason to bust your balls."

He wished he'd shaved that morning, cleaned himself up, made an effort at looking presentable. Instead, when the alarm jangled, he deliberately rolled around hard enough to rouse Liv. He figured she'd go back to sleep when he left, so he didn't feel too guilty about waking her. They fooled around—Liv squealing in mock pain and outrage at the abrasiveness of his scratchy face on her smooth skin—and when they were done, there was no time to shave before he left for work. Now he regretted it. Sitting in what Step referred to as his "classic," more of a wreck in reality, with a police officer coming his way, Mitch thought looking a shade more respectable might have been a good idea.

The officer had a hard, no-nonsense face and a cop's typically stiff, authoritative bearing, but a fan of deep laugh lines at the corner of each eye gave Mitch the impression he *might* be reasonable. Mitch wasn't optimistic. When it came to police officers, his cup lay in broken chunks on the floor, never mind half-empty. His dislike stemmed from fear. When a man with a uniform and a Glock has the power to lock you in a cage, he doesn't have to understand the gray areas. The tinnitus meant Mitch spent a great deal of time in the gray areas—petty crime was a matter of survival.

The officer wore a flat-brimmed hat, the kind with the strap that clung to the back of his skull. He held a Mag-Lite in one hand, his fist close to the bright end, the long metal barrel over his shoulder. His opposite hand rested warily on the butt of his holstered pistol. He said, "You know why I pulled you over?"

"No, Sir."

"Your left tail light is burnt out."

The man's voice was conversational, amiable. None of the usual cop attitude. Mitch relaxed slightly. A dead taillight wasn't too significant. He had a halfway decent chance of driving away with only a verbal warning. He dangled one wrist loosely across the top of the steering wheel. He made sure he didn't bounce his leg or brush his hand across his goatee, down his unshaved neck. He said, "I didn't realize that. I'll get it fixed first thing." Looking the cop in the eye, showing he had nothing to hide.

The cop nodded. He shined the beam of the flashlight into the truck, panned it around the interior, across the backpack Mitch never went anywhere without. The beam landed on Step-And-A-Half in the passenger seat. "What's up with your friend?"

"Rye and Seven. A lot of Rye and Seven."

The cop nodded a second time. A whisper of a smile touched his lips. Disappeared. He pulled back a step, washing the flashlight across the Ford's rusty, dinged exterior panels. The beam slowed. Stopped. He frowned.

Icy goose bumps stippled Mitch's arms. The screech of the tinnitus rose like an air raid siren between his ears. He wanted to wince and clench his teeth and rub his ears against the pain. His mind leapt to the worst-case scenario—locked up when the tinnitus peaked.

Come on chief, let's go. I absolutely can't tolerate a delay. Not tonight.

He'd run before it came to that.

The cop said, "I need to see your license and registration, Sir."

CHAPTER 3

THE THING ABOUT shaving your head, Tony Carter discovered, was a guy didn't have time to get used to the feeling like he would have, had he gone bald traditionally, one follicle at a time. Even on a nice, early December day such as this, the warm afternoon breeze felt chilly on his scalp.

Something else he hadn't considered: shaving the top of his head where he couldn't see was difficult. Everybody knew head wounds bled profusely, but goddamn, he barely nicked himself. By the time he got the extra-large Band-Aid stuck to his scalp, he resembled a victim in a slasher film. The Band-Aid felt enormous up there (because it was), and Carter thought he most likely looked ridiculous rather than intimidating, which had been the point of the entire head-shaving experiment.

He kept his eyes moving as he walked through the park, until he spotted a man with the stocky build, wide flat face, and protuberant black eyes of a First Generation Regressive Individual—or derogatorily, Squat—sitting on a bench. With his legs crossed at the ankles and an arm outstretched along the back of the bench, the First Gen appeared relaxed. He licked the top of a huge ice cream cone, what looked like several different flavors stacked on top of each other and stared benignly into the distance at something he alone could see.

Carter adjusted his course and headed for the bench. When he got there, he sat down uninvited and said to his boss, "Afternoon."

"Something's different, Mr. Carter. Are you wearing contacts?"

Strange question. Deputy Warden Tyler knew he didn't wear glasses. Carter said, "Uhm, no, Sir."

"Did you shave off your mustache?"

"I never had a mustache."

The deputy warden faced him, fixing him in place with his bulging eyes. His huge slab of a forehead was creased in concentration. A moment later, he pointed an index finger straight up, shook it a couple of times and nodded like the answer had suddenly come to him. His long, sloping face took on an exaggerated expression of understanding. "I know what's different. You had your ears lowered."

Carter squinted at him.

"You got yourself a haircut, Mr. Carter. Why?"

Confused, Carter stabbed his tongue into the gap where an eye tooth used to live. Why did he get a haircut? Why does anyone get a haircut? He tried not to fidget under Tyler's unblinking stare. He said, "Why what?"

"What I mean to say is, why did you shave your head? You'll have to allow it to grow back. Aside from the Band-Aid, your appearance is far too intimidating for work. You look like, I don't know, a biker."

"That was the point." As an afterthought Carter added, "To look intimidating. Not like a biker," although, if his appearance gave the cons that impression, he wouldn't have tried to dissuade them. He'd actually been thinking more along the lines of a tough guy from the movies. Someone like Bruce Willis or Jason Statham.

"The inmates at Glades won't be fooled by your new look. However, the visitors—the lawyers, the social workers, the relatives—will see you exactly as you want to be seen. Intimidating. Wouldn't we rather have people believe we're respectable individuals? Firm, certainly, but compassionate and caring as well? Mr. Carter, we might be guardians to murderers and rapists but our job is to rehabilitate not to intimidate."

It was difficult to tell if the deputy warden believed what he was saying—a First Gen's simian features made reading their faces difficult—but based on how well he knew his boss, Carter suspected the man was being ironic.

Tyler's voice hardened. "Let it grow back."

"Yes, Sir."

They sat in silence again, Tyler with his waffle cone and the same contented smile as earlier, Carter growing more fidgety by the second, until he couldn't stand it any longer. He said, "What are we doing here?"

"You need to learn to relax, Mr. Carter."

"We could relax indoors, we gotta meet away from work."

Tyler swept an encompassing look from left to right. "You don't care for the park?"

"I like the park just fine but if we relaxed at a coffee shop, I could get a Clubhouse and beer. Or, the Landing Strip would be good. Even the shopping center. I could buy some groceries when we're done."

"I don't care for the strippers, Mr. Carter. The whole charade." Tyler shook his head. "The Landing Strip is expensive. The beer is what? Eight dollars a glass? I don't see the point. And, no offense, but Moderns aren't all that attractive. Perfect hair. Perfect breasts. Tiny asses, hipbones like knife blades. Mr. Carter, your kind are all too skinny. I appreciate something less obvious."

My kind? Coming from a First Gen, that was a strange thing to say. It almost sounded like Tyler preferred Squat strippers over Moderns.

Carter had never given that idea any thought. Now that it was out there in front of him, he couldn't see there being much of an audience for a Squat stripper. In general, a Squat was, well, squat. They had short legs and thick torsos. A Third Gen might put on an entertaining show, but it would be more of a circus act than exotic dancing. A Third Gen wasn't human, no matter what anyone said. First Gens though? They looked pretty much normal, bulkier than a Modern and maybe a little bit retarded, and that wasn't something anyone wanted to see, a bulky retarded stripper.

Did they?

Deputy Warden Tyler continued lazily licking his cone. Carter thought about how tasty a clubhouse would be, either as an early dinner or late afternoon snack, and he thought another strike against Squat strippers was all the hair. Squats—First, Second, and Third Gens, didn't matter which—were way, *way* too hairy.

He had to acknowledge, styles changed. He flipped through a fifty-year-old *Playboy* magazine in an antique store once. It seemed nobody in the early seventies, men nor women, knew how to work a razor. Back then questionable "grooming" must have been stylish and acceptable. Maybe one day thick thatches of hair from head to toe would become fashionable again, but he prayed it didn't happen. He'd run away screaming if he slid a girlfriend's panties down her thighs and saw that kind of carpeting. That much hair didn't belong anywhere other than a woman's head.

A hairy Squat stripper? Carter shuddered. It was a repugnant thought. He said, "My point being, we could have gone anywhere."

"I've got another appointment after you and I are done, Mr. Carter. A man who has a relationship with Mother Nature." He paused, then, "Did you compensate Colin McTavish appropriately?"

Carter breathed a sigh of relief. Finally, safer ground. Terrain on which he was confident and, apparently, the reason for the after-hours meeting. He answered, "McTavish is in solitary confinement. He expected that. I made sure he gets extra yard time. I turned the crappy programming off, so he's got decent television. I gave him some magazines. He's living better in the box than he was in general population."

"What about the individuals who assisted him?"

"I told McTavish, 'I can't look after your guys like I'm looking after you.' He said he understood. He'd square it with his guys."

Tyler nodded. "What about Sawyer?" Anger edged his voice.

"McTavish did good. Sawyer is in the infirmary. Broken nose, two awful shiners. A broken jaw. Two broken ribs." Carter laughed. "The best part? He's lying in the corridor bleeding and moaning, just a mess, and McTavish says, 'You right or left handed?' Sawyer spits out a mouthful of blood and a Chiclet or two and says, 'What?' So, McTavish asks him, 'You wipe your ass with your right hand or left?'"

Tyler frowned in distaste.

Carter didn't notice. Excited, he kept talking. "Sawyer, he doesn't have a clue. He says, 'Right?' One of McTavish's guys grabs his right arm, stretches it out and McTavish jumps on his hand. Broke three of Sawyer's fingers." Carter laughed. "Would have been worse if McTavish was wearing real shoes, not canvas Glades shoes."

Tyler's expression changed to one of approval. "Sawyer won't be agitating any more of my inmates? Won't be writing any more letters to Corrections about poor treatment and bad food?"

"Not anytime soon."

"Rabble rouser," Tyler muttered. Just as quietly he said, "We may have to turn McTavish loose on Joshua Parker, if the young man continues his uppity ways."

Carter kept his face blank. Calling Joshua Parker a "young man" was like mistaking a rabid Rottweiler for a fluffy poodle. Deputy Warden Tyler could believe in the homogeneity of Regressive Individuals and Moderns all he wanted, but when evolution misplaced a strand or two of DNA, and babies around the world were born more Neanderthal than Homo sapiens, several traits that made them decent human beings disappeared at the same time.

Joshua Parker was a First Gen who proved it every day.

Tyler pulled a bag out of his pocket. He hefted it up and down in his hand a couple of times before handing it to Carter. "The second thing I wanted to discuss... You can still unload this stuff?"

"No problem."

"Your guy doesn't know where it comes from?"

"He doesn't care."

"Remind him to keep it low profile."

"I will."

"I don't need some inmate's lawyer visiting my office, asking how his client's Rolex ended up in a pawn shop instead of the Inmate's Possession Bag where it belongs."

"I said I'll remind him."

"There's a lot in there. Several expensive watches. A few gold rings and a chain or two. Some diamond studs. The population in Glades Rehabilitation Facility increased significantly this month. I want to see," Tyler wobbled his head back and forth, "Three grand. You keep whatever's left over. Consider it a bonus. Arranging that thing with McTavish was good work, Mr. Carter." He turned away and looked into the distance. He lapped his ice cream cone.

Carter nodded. "Yes, Sir." Knowing the meeting was over, he stood. For some reason, he felt he had to say something before turning his back on his boss and walking away, so he asked, "Who are you waiting for?" He knew the instant the words crossed his lips that he was being presumptuous.

Tyler turned a laser-like stare on him.

A warm flush crept up Carter's neck. Tyler's unblinking stare, the lack of expression on his face, turned Carter's presumption into embarrassment. He nervously licked his chapped lips. His weight shifted from foot to foot. He tried meeting Tyler's eyes without looking away and succeeded for two or three seconds before he dropped his gaze.

Tyler said, "Not that my business is any of yours, Mr. Carter, but I'm meeting a man named Mr. Barnett. Interestingly, he shares the same last name as a person from my youth; a most disagreeable individual with whom I used to work." His face twisted into the same earlier expression of distaste. He waved his hand dismissively. "No matter. Barnett and I have a mutually beneficial working relationship. That's all you need to know—"

Which wasn't much, Carter thought.

"—now, get out of here. Let me enjoy my cone."

Gladly.

"See you tomorrow, Sir," Carter said. He walked away wondering what kind of scam the deputy warden and Mr. Barnett were running, whoever Mr. Barnett was.

CHAPTER 4

Britain, 1946

THE RAIN SLASHED down, falling in thick curtains from a sky so bloated and gray it appeared diseased. Wind gusted, sneaking into the tiny house through unseen cracks with random, desolate moans. Two men flanked the coal range in the room, deliberately ignoring each other. One man sat in complacent silence, a cup of tea in his hand, a thin smile on his face. The second man stood with crossed arms in front of a window sheeted with rain, staring out at the storm lashing his vegetable garden. He quietly hummed *Too-Ra-Loo-Ra-Loo-Ral*, one of those Bing Crosby numbers his wife never stopped playing on their gramophone, probably the last thing he heard before she stepped out earlier in the day. She had a melodious voice and enjoyed singing along when *Chattanooga Choo Choo* or *Don't Fence Me In* came on the wireless.

She enjoyed the picture shows too. She'd ask him, "Allen? Would you love me more if I looked like Ingrid Bergman?"

"Ingrid disna' hold a candle to you," Allen would answer. Then he'd make her giggle and say, "You looked like Ingrid, then maybe you'd want me to wear a hat like Bogie? I'm no' daein' that."

Allen thought trading in his dungarees for a hat like Bogie's might make him look a little silly. A little fancy; like the man sitting beside him in his crème-colored suit. His legs were crossed, his cup and saucer balanced delicately on his knee. His fedora, damp with rain, sat on the table. A tiny purple feather, the same color as the man's necktie, poked out of the hat band.

Fancy.

"We have a contract, Allen. It didn't end with the war," the man said.

He spoke in a deliberately patient and reasonable tone. A happy employee was a productive employee; it was important to give the impression he listened and cared. He took a slow sip of tea.

Allen glanced sideways. The seated man reminded him of a captain he served under in the army, a fastidious arsehole universally hated, an individual who thought himself better than everyone else with his perfect uniform creases and highly polished shoes. The man in his kitchen even resembled the captain. With that association in mind, it was difficult to remain civil, particularly given the decision he'd made. Allen's gaze returned to the window. He shuffled his feet. He told himself to be firm. He put some steel in his voice. "I'm no' daein' it."

The man swallowed the last of his tea. He placed the cup and saucer on the table and ran a hand down the length of his thigh, smoothing his slacks. He laced his fingers together and placed them on his knee, exactly where the tea so recently rested. "Why do you believe you have a choice? You cannot simply quit because you made it home from the continent alive."

Allen watched the rain. It wasn't much of a view but it was better than looking at the man beside him, this man with the fancy suit and ugly scar slicing down his forehead through his right eyebrow. In addition to the resemblance he shared with the arsehole captain, the scar further unsettled Allen. It drew his eyes. It made him stammer. Which was odd, considering the horrors he'd seen on the continent. He pulled the collar of his shirt away from his neck, the wool suddenly hot and itchy. "I dinna understand. Why blow up a bunch of miners? Lads only doing their job."

"I've explained this more than once, and in some detail." The man with the scar enunciated every word slowly and with precision. "With or without your help, the event is inevitable. It's the fallout that matters. The strife is what interests me." He forced a smile to hide his irritation. Every hobby had its frustrations, every career its ups and downs. He knew this. Explaining the same thing countless times to countless employees was definitely the "down" part of his job. It shouldn't have frustrated him, but it always did. "I'm not asking for anything different today than what I asked for in the past."

"Different times."

Comprehension crossed the scarred man's face. He nodded slowly. "I see," he said, his voice full of understanding. "The war is over and you imagine the violence is behind you, now your time in the military is complete." He paused. His tone became mocking. "It's not murder during times of war, Allen? The bombings were reasonable at the time, but now that peace is upon us, death has suddenly become abhorrent? Is that what you mean when you say, 'different times?' Is that how you justify the tasks you completed for me? You did it for God and Country?" He looked at Allen, eyebrows raised expectantly. "I'm interested. Tell me, please, how the war changed the laws of morality for you."

Allen flushed with shame. How was it this man, with whom he'd had only the briefest contact over the last ten years, could look inside his head and see his rationalizations? He said tightly, "Six bloody years of war. That's enough death for one world. I willna' be responsible for any mair."

"You were a little miner when we met, Allen. The noise inside your head was so loud, you couldn't form a coherent thought. Now you're such a sophisticated thinker, you can speak for the entire world?" The man with the scar shook his head in feigned astonishment. "Did we not agree, if I guaranteed you a comfortable life free of tinnitus, you would complete certain tasks for me? A favor for a favor." This was a currency the man with the scar used overtly, a currency human beings, no matter who they were, honored in a way that continually surprised him. How many people owed the bank money, had defaulted on a loan, had "forgotten" the five pounds they borrowed from a friend? Practically everyone. But, nobody allowed a favor to go unpaid.

He said, "I told you these tasks would be unpalatable. I said they were inevitable, whether or not you were involved. I was unambiguously clear on that point. What part did you misunderstand?"

"I was fourteen. I would have agreed to anything, just to make the noise go away."

"I opened a portal for you ten separate times. For all intents and purposes, *I* made it go away."

"It would have taken me to a portal. I dinna need ye to point the way."

"Very true. The tinnitus acts like a compass." The man with the scar nodded. "But tell me, if you acted without my guidance, where would you have ended up? Most people enter the portal, find a doorway in the darkness and then cross the Space Between into a different world. They don't get to turn around and come home. You realize that, yes? I made returning home possible."

Nonplussed, Allen said nothing. He didn't know where he would have ultimately found himself. He always entered the portal the scarred man created, the tinnitus always disappeared and then he always turned around and walked back out, returning to the spot where the scarred man waited. He finally answered, "You weren't being generous."

On this point, Allen was correct. Allowing him to return home was not an altruistic act. In 1936, with the world on the brink of war, allowing him to remain in his origin world, working in the mine with his shot-firer father, represented a future opportunity. Young Allen would grow from a boy into an adult. He'd learn how to plant charges and detonate explosives, and when the world began slaughtering itself on the beaches of Normandy and in the forests of southern Russia, nobody would notice an unexplained bombing or two. He could hide in a crowd of fighting men, impossible during times of peace, and when the scarred man needed him to do it again, he'd be close at hand.

"I'm no' killing anyone else." Allen continued, "For ten years, I did everything you asked."

"Six years, strictly speaking," the man with the scar corrected. "The first four times I opened the portal for you, I asked for nothing in return." He looked around the room, taking in the red and white checked tablecloth, the dishes stacked tidily on the shelves, the gramophone on the sideboard. He said, "I imagine you believe your neighbor's respect is something you earned on your own. Is it, though?"

A small smile of pride crossed Allen's face.

"I ask myself, why would Allen MacLean work so hard to become the community stalwart he is? The answer is obvious. You are assuaging your guilt. A good turn here balances out a bad deed there, yes?" He tilted his head and nodded slightly, his expression sympathetic. "I don't blame you, but I have to ask, would you have this comfortable life without our agreement?"

Allen said nothing. A gust of wind shook the house and rattled the windows in their frames. On the range, the kettle steamed.

The man with the scar could no longer contain his anger. He had an inkling of where the stubborn Scot was going with his sudden, unexpected refusal. "I'm waiting, Allen."

Allen's eyes shifted sideways. He nodded shortly and muttered a begrudging, "Aye. You made it possible."

The man with the scar inclined his head in thanks,

unconcerned the acknowledgement was coerced. He said, "Are you sure you want to throw it all away?"

The look Allen directed at the man with the scar was raw, free of everything except anguish and guilt but his voice was resolute. "I canny dae it any mair."

The man with the scar didn't immediately respond. He listened to the wind gust and the rain pepper the window. Eventually he said, "Nothing has to change, Allen. This will become a forgotten conversation between friends. Or, you can continue down the path you're currently contemplating. You have choices. Just so we're clear, there is going to be an explosion at Whitehaven. If not this year, then next. Miners will die, whether you're involved or not."

"I canny dae it any mair."

"If you're certain—"

"I am."

The man with the scar stared at the floor, tapping his lips with his finger. He sighed. "In that case our arrangement is over."

"That's it? You're not mad?" The words rushed from the Scot's mouth in a single, relieved gasp.

"What did you expect, Allen? I'm disappointed, but you're not the first who's decided to retire. You won't be the last."

"Then we're done?"

"Is that how a contract works? You ask for something and I supply it, no strings or complications? How does that benefit me? You get what you want. What do I take away from our relationship?"

Allen shook his head and shrugged, his relief so great he didn't hear or understand the agreement had not yet reached a complete conclusion. Instead, he thought about living without the sick, hollow feeling in his stomach, the unease that grew day by day with the knowledge that soon, the man with the scar would be back with another job. After the inevitable visit, Allen would build his bomb and plan his attack. When the bomb exploded, a whole different kind of sickness would fill him as he read about the dead and worried about being locked away for the rest of his life. He longed for a clean conscience and sleeping through the night, about a glass of Scotch, instead of the milk he drank to sooth the stomach ulcer.

The tinnitus was a disease, an inconvenience from which he'd never be free, but it was manageable. Next time it hit, he'd follow the sound to a portal on his own, without the scarred man's guidance. He'd walk into the Space Between, turn around when the tinnitus disappeared and walk back out, just as he always did, returning home to Agnes with clean hands…

His mind caught up to the scarred man's last comment—*what do I take away from our relationship*—and the happy thought stumbled. Suddenly, he understood there were shadows around the edges of this bright, unexpected freedom. A tingle of apprehension caressed the back of his neck. He said tentatively, "But, I can stay?"

The man with the scar ignored the hopeful inflection in Allen's voice. "Stay? In this sanctuary, I so generously provided? Don't be foolish. You'll go to a world similar to this one, to the back alley, or cardboard box you most assuredly would have ended up in, had I not rescued you ten years ago."

"What about my wife? This is her home too."

"Ah, yes. Agnes. Homely girl? Mousy brown hair? Kind of dumpy, if I recall. I don't consider matchmaking one of my better talents, but that introduction turned out well for you, no? Where is the lovely Agnes this afternoon?"

Allen faced him, thick callused fists clenched, both cheeks burning an angry scarlet. "Careful," he warned, fury in his voice. "She's visiting her mum."

The man with the scar was unmoved. He said, "When you kissed your wife goodbye this afternoon, it was for the last time. This is no longer your home; therefore, it is no longer hers."

"Maybe she can come with me."

"Am I not clear?" The man with the scar was all business now. "When you refused me the services I required, I did the same and took away that which I gave you. Agnes will be given two choices. Move or stay. If she stays, something unfortunate will happen. A fire, for example. Something tragic from which she won't escape."

Allen couldn't breathe. His legs went watery and the room spun. He grabbed the back of a chair for support. When his equilibrium returned, he said, "As long as she leaves the house, you won't harm her?"

"I have no quarrel with Agnes."

Allen let go a noisy sigh of relief. He could no longer live with being directly responsible for a continuous stream of violent death and heartache. Already he missed Agnes more than words could possibly express, but with her safety assured and his association with the scarred man at an end, he could hopefully rebuild and start over in a world in which he wasn't a murderer.

How many miners worked at Whitehaven? If he set his bomb, how many men would die in bloody, spectacular fashion? How many years of anguish would follow? How many months would it take before the scarred man returned, starting the cycle all over again? Allen understood the death toll would be the same with or without his involvement—the man with the scar made that perfectly clear—but at least he wouldn't be involved. It wasn't much, his conscience still prickled, but he could no longer be the cause.

Allen asked, "What happens now?"

"I need a moment to open a portal. Take the time to enjoy what remains of the afternoon. The storm is beautiful, no? Such a nice contrast from Mother Nature's sunny spring days."

"You're going to take me, then?"

"There's no other way." The man with the scar donned his fedora. He stood. His boot heels clonked loudly on the wooden floor as he strode to the door. When he opened it, the wind ripped it from his hand and slammed it into the wall with a boom. Rain blew into the house, forming a perfect wet arc on the floor just inside the entrance. He walked down the front steps and stopped beside the vegetable garden.

Allen watched him raise his arm and point into the gray nothingness of the afternoon. He turned away. He didn't need to see what happened next. He'd seen it before and it no longer astonished him. He let his eyes roam around his home. Maybe if Agnes knew that in leaving he was saving countless lives, at least for a time, his disappearance and the loss of her home would be more understandable and acceptable. But she would never know. He'd never told her what it was he did for the man with the scar. How could he? He wasn't a monster, but that's how she'd see him.

He considered leaving her a note, a short goodbye, but in the end, he decided the individual responsible for wrecking her life could explain. When the man with the scar told her to leave, he would manage her confusion and anger. Allen wiped his hands down his face, exhausted and incredibly sad. He sighed heavily and walked down the four steps out of his home for the last time, into weather as miserable as he felt inside. Within seconds his coveralls were soaked through, his muddy red hair plastered to his head.

The man with the scar stood beside the vegetable garden, hands clasped together at the small of his back. The gusty wind buffeted the fedora between his fingers. Beyond him, past the far edge of the garden where the rock dyke and the trees met, a black rectangle shimmered with oily translucence against the gray, foggy afternoon.

Allen forced one foot in front of the other, each step slower and shorter than the one before, until he stood hip to hip beside the man with the scar. Above the wind and the rain and memories careening around in his head, he heard a new sound, incongruous for the time and place. He cocked his head listening hard.

Too-Ra-Loo-Ra-Loo-Ral drifted toward him, a trick of the wind maybe, but after two or three lines he realized it wasn't the wind singing to him. It was the portal. Trembles shimmied up and down his spine and goose flesh pebbled his arms.

He held his breath in concentration, trying to capture the song so no matter where he ended up, he'd remember Agnes and the home they shared when he heard it again. They'd danced to this song, and *Chattanooga Choo Choo* and *As Time Goes By*, and others too. Friday nights with their friends at the community hall and often times when they got home, Agnes drinking Barr's Iron Brew and laughing, making her white dress swirl and her high heels click, her chestnut hair flying, not mousy or dumpy, but beautiful and happy.

He wept softly. "Maybe I could—"

With a single, abrupt shake of his head the man with the scar silenced him. "You said you were certain." His voice held a serrated edge. "You've become unreliable. I can no longer count on your commitment."

Allen looked at the portal. A wave of icy hot fear washed over him. His mouth turned impossibly dry, and that seemed ridiculous with the rain and tears soaking his face. He squared his shoulders and then walked toward the shimmering doorway, letting the tears fall without shame. His boots squelched on the saturated earth. *Too-Ra-Loo-Ra-Loo-Ral* grew louder with every step. The music should have calmed him and made him smile as it always did, but something was wrong. The song warped and distorted the closer he got to the portal. Instead of the piano and bells he should have heard layered beneath Bing Crosby's voice, he heard pleading screams; despair that wasn't his own.

The wind from the portal mixed and swirled and eddied, carrying the smell of something wet and recently dead. Bing Crosby grew fainter and the sounds of the lost and abandoned and desperate became louder, until their hopelessness soaked into his skin and became his weaknesses and failures. He staggered, throwing out an arm, searching for balance. Bile rose in his throat. He swallowed it down, the acidic burn stabilizing him.

At the invisible line on the ground where the portal touched the soil beneath his feet, he stopped. He'd stood here before. Ten times he'd looked into a portal just like this one. Ten times he'd entered it, waited a heartbeat for the tinnitus to disappear and then, ten times he'd turned around and returned home.

He blinked a couple of times, cleared his vision and took one last look at his home. Then he stepped across the threshold, into the portal's shimmering, haunted blackness.

As always, the black nothingness of what Allen thought of as "space" surrounded him in every dimension. It wasn't space, of course. He could breathe, and space wouldn't have supported his weight as the nothingness did, so where he was in reality remained an unanswered question. One thing of which Allen was certain: the discrepancy between nothingness and solid footing made his stomach roll and his head swirl with dizziness.

Sullen, heavy air roiled around him and plucked at his overalls and ruffled his hair. Water dripped and echoed, each plink like a note on an out of tune piano. Bizarrely, he imagined a cellar beneath an abandoned house, a dank, dark place where the Acid Bath Murderer might have hidden the oil drums in which he dissolved his victims. The screams were louder, the rancid stench stronger. Glimmering sparks, eyes maybe—diseased yellow and tortured crimson—stared at him and then disappeared. Something howled. It sounded like insane laughter; a slavering beast would come for him in the darkness, decaying meat between its teeth. Fingers caressed his cheek. Screaming, he jerked away, wondering if the dead hand belonged to a person as real as himself, or if it was a ghost trying to reconnect with the living. Terrified sweat trickled down his back and gathered at the base of his spine.

His breath came in spasmodic gulps.

He focused on a white rectangle in the distance. It would happen almost as fast as a memory, as it had so many times before. In the past, he "thought" himself back home. This time he needed to "think" himself forward, to the white portal so far away.

Allen's concentration splintered.

The portal in front of him, the portal to freedom, was shrinking. Fear turned to panic, fast and hot, burning a hole in his stomach, scorching his insides in an expanding wave of heat and nausea. He told himself to focus. The only thing that mattered was the distant patch of daylight that was *shrinking faster than he'd ever seen.*

He spun on his heels.

The man with the scar stood framed in the black doorway. His arm was out stretched, his thumb and index finger coming together in a pinching movement.

Allen cut a glance over his shoulder. The white portal was the size of a sheet of paper,

now an envelope,

now a postage stamp.

It disappeared altogether.

The scarred man's finger and thumb were pinched tightly together. He wore a grin on his face, an expression that seemed to ask, "Surprised?"

Now, Allen's only chance to escape was the portal back home, the one through which he entered the Space Between. As if he knew exactly what Allen was thinking, the man with the scar shook his head and laughed. He spread his arms welcomingly. Then he bent his elbows and brought his palms together in a peculiar, slow motion applause.

The portal shrank in concert. It halved in size, then halved again.

And, again.

"Allen?" he called. "I wasn't lying when I said I had no

quarrel with Agnes. But, you're not the only one who can break an agreement."

Allen's immediate and only thought was Agnes. His sudden fierce focus carried him to the edge of the Space Between, but he was ten years too late. The portal was already too small for him to escape through. It closed completely, sealing him inside the nonexistence that separates and isolates the infinite worlds. The darkness was absolute except somehow, inside his head, he saw an image: his home consumed in flames, and he heard the man with the scar say, "The future is inevitable, Allen. You can only move forward. You cannot move backward. It doesn't work that way."

In the vegetable garden, the man with the scar waited until the tangled, turbulent winds of two planes of existence faded away, and then he strode into the afternoon, humming *Too-Ra-Loo-Ra-Loo-Ral.*

He hated to lose an employee. It happened occasionally. The trick was turning an unfortunate situation around, turning lemons into lemonade, as it were. The question then became, how to best inform his remaining employees that one amongst them had been punished for breaking his contract.

CHAPTER 5

Florida, December, 2022

MITCH REILLY TOOK off his worn, shaped-just-right cowboy hat, and put it on the Ford's dusty dashboard. With the cop watching him, he leaned over and opened the glove-box, bumping Step-And-A-Half's leg as he did. Step jolted awake, mumbled a garbled, "The fuck?" then, after a snort and a gurgle, he settled back into his drunken slumber.

Mitch rifled through some dirty old road maps, a worn Ford owner's manual, a variety of nuts and bolts. He dropped a flashlight on the floor, just to get it out of the way.

Where were the insurance papers?

Son-of-a-bitch, he didn't need this. Not tonight. A cop staring at him out of eyes that seemed to know his secrets, the tinnitus making coherent thought close to impossible, the loneliness of leaving Liv washing over him in waves stronger than he'd ever felt.

He didn't need it.

He continued sifting through the junk in the glove-box until he found an oil-stained folder sandwiched between a couple of antique compact disks.

He handed the plastic folder out the window.

"You don't own this vehicle, do you?" the cop asked, saying it with emphasis on the "H". ve-HI-cle.

"No, Sir."

The cop flipped the folder open. "And, you're not Kelly Hunter, are you?"

"No, Sir." Mitch jerked a thumb in Step-And-A-Half's direction. "He is. He was supposed to drive."

"You been drinking too?"

"Diet Coke. When my buddy winds up there's no stopping him."

The same faint, fast smile as earlier tugged on the corners of the cop's mouth. "What's your name?"

"Mitch Reilly." To his own ears, Mitch's voice sounded even and stable. As it should have. He had years of practice sounding like everything was normal when nothing about his life was ordinary.

"I'll take your driver's license now, Mr. Reilly."

Mitch winced as the pitch of the tinnitus increased. Stress did that. The volume rose steadily as the days went by, but the pitch ramped up in tandem with stress. By day five or six, both were climbing side by side, the sound like the point of a spear in the middle of his back, making the need to move almost overpowering.

The cop's face hardened as if he suspected Mitch didn't have a driver's license, which wasn't the case at all. He had several sewn carefully into the lining of his backpack.

"In my pack," he said.

The cop nodded, his hand wrapped casually around the grip of his pistol.

Mitch leaned over and hooked his backpack off the floor. He fished his wallet out of one of the pockets, his current driver's license out of the wallet. It was clean, would show up in the DMV's database as being legitimate. Mitch Reilly was actually the name of an infant who died shortly after birth twenty-six years before. Mitch "borrowed" the baby's name and applied for a new birth certificate, explaining to the bureaucrat behind the counter that he lost everything to Hurricane Anne earlier in the year. His application was stamped without a second glance. He was just one more person in a long line of people who needed new papers. Natural disasters were great for that sort of thing. With a birth certificate in hand, he easily obtained a driver's license, as well as the rest of the plastic a person typically stored in his wallet.

He handed his license to the cop, keeping a carefully neutral expression on his face while the panicky knot between his shoulder blades cinched tighter. Hesitation, showing pain like he had a moment before, were inexcusable screw-ups, the kind of things that invited questions he couldn't answer.

A burnt-out taillight?

He'd been coasting, staying out of trouble for so long he'd become complacent. Now he was getting exactly what he deserved. He could have said, "No," to a night at the bar. He could have called a cab, instead of depending on a vehicle with bald tires and upholstery that smelled like a wet Springer Spaniel. Never once had he considered Step's ancient truck might leave him stranded or draw attention. With his time to slip only hours away, these details became critically important.

Too many mistakes.

The cop studied the license under the beam of his Mag-Lite. After several beats the cop said, "Don't move. I'll be back directly."

"Sure thing," Mitch said. With forced calm, he turned to the radio in the dashboard and twiddled the knob until he found Florida's Classic Country; just a guy without a worry in the world. Brad Paisley was in the middle of *Mud on the Tires,* perhaps one of Mitch's favorite songs, but even the good memories the song evoked couldn't slow his hammering heart or quiet the tinnitus. He dragged his hand down his face, tracing the outline of his goatee. His fingers found the Saint Christopher medallion Liv had given him. He wasn't Catholic, or even religious for that matter, but if the patron saint of travelers was out there somewhere, now seemed like a good time for him to present himself.

Liv's name filled him with a flood of guilt and loneliness. There was nothing he could do about leaving her—the tinnitus made it impossible for him to stay—but impossibility didn't make leaving easier. When he left her apartment that morning, he told her work would take him out of town for the next two, maybe three weeks, hating himself and the lie, even as it left his mouth. When he didn't return, if she checked with Step or the other guys from work, they'd tell her they hadn't seen him either. They'd say, it was like he dropped off the face of the earth, which wouldn't be too far from the truth.

He cut a glance into the rearview mirror. Still nothing happening back there. What was taking so long? If the cop didn't haul ass, there'd be no time to drive Step home. Mitch's only choice would be a straight line. He'd go directly to wherever the tinnitus took him, following the sound like pilots did back in the day when a constant tone in their headphones guided them to their destination.

The tinnitus gave him a prod. *Just go*, it said. *Follow the sound.*

Without conscious thought, Mitch eased in the clutch and tightened his fingers on the ignition key.

CHAPTER 6

"WE CAN ALL agree you suffered an immense tragedy, Mr. Albright. The untimely loss of a spouse can best be described as unexplainable, the loss of a child unimaginable."

Two guards escorted Ray Albright out of the courtroom, one on either side, holding him upright on legs unwilling to carry his weight, the heavy shackles around his ankles making full steps impossible. The judge's final speech followed him down the hallway like mad, echoing laughter in a haunted house. They marched him into a holding cell and helped him into a chair. Then they stepped back and flanked the door, all crossed arms and stern faces.

Ray paid them no attention. Memories consumed him— Dawn's unrestrained laughter, a sound that made everyone laugh with her, and Angie bouncing on his knee, wisps of her so-soft hair blowing in the breeze. The memory of little girl shampoo tickled his nose. He could see her mouth surrounded in a smear of chocolate ice cream, her tiny fist wrapped around the cone.

Unexplainable?

Unimaginable?

This was their entire epitaph? His wife and daughter rated one word each? Ray couldn't put his despair into words. There was no way of expressing his grief. One word certainly wasn't enough. Not for him, and not for a First Gen judge who sat there, pretending sympathy, pompously passing judgment before going home to his own family.

"However, you did not allow the System time to serve you. In your rush for vengeance—not justice Mr. Albright, vengeance—two additional families were destroyed."

Ray's lawyer walked into the holding cell. He opened his briefcase and removed a pen and a yellow legal pad. He put both on the table. His long, jowly face was heavily lined. Dark crescents underlined each eye. His exhaustion ran deeper than his appearance. When Neville Rollins settled into the chair opposite Ray, his flesh and bones seemed to sag and settle like leaves and sticks in a sack. He pressed his fingertips together. Finally, he looked Ray in the eye. "I'm sorry."

"Furthermore, you remain unrepentant. Although you cannot be punished for your attitude, the court finds it offensive."

"I had the right of way." Ray's voice was strained. He raised a hand to emphasize his point. The length of chain connecting the manacles around his ankles and wrists jangled, jerking his arm to a halt.

Neville said, "When an SUV broadsides a Ford Focus, the right of way is irrelevant."

In a much weaker voice, Ray said, "I had a green light."

"Without the traffic camera…" Neville shrugged. "The boys say you jumped the light. They were already there and couldn't stop. Anyway, none of that matters. We've been through this, how many times? A traffic accident is not why you're here."

"A jury of your peers judged you. It's my job to sentence you. Mr. Albright, I find your crimes particularly heinous. As is my right, I sentence you to death for the murder of Marcus Bell and Ross Scott."

"Doesn't matter? Of course, it matters. Those little animals got a slap on the wrist. I get the death penalty? I've got what? Sixteen months if you lose the appeal? My back is literally against the wall." Ray's voice rose. He knew he was taking his hopeless anger out on his lawyer. He was unable to help himself. "The traffic cam is broken, the little animal driving the SUV was drunk, and the judge is a Squat? It matters a great deal—"

"Right there." Neville slammed his hand down. The steel table clanged. The pen jumped. He stabbed a finger at Ray's chest. "That's the problem. The judge sees you as racist. You can't give him the idea, not even a sniff, that you're prejudiced toward Regressive Individuals." Neville's angry eyes left Ray's face. He looked over Ray's shoulder, shook his head and flicked his hand dismissively.

Ray glanced behind him in time to see a guard's face disappear from the small, mesh-lined window set into the steel door of the room. Obviously, the guard didn't like to hear yelling coming from an interview room, not when a lawyer was locked inside with a mad-dog killer. Ray knew that's how the System saw him. From the lowly court clerk to the high and mighty judge, everyone in the building knew he murdered two First Gen teens, and they condemned him without taking time to learn the details. Out on the street the everyday man probably saw him as a hero. Finally, someone stood up and said, "No more," and did what should have been done when the crime rate went stratospheric and the System reacted with tolerance. But, here in the courthouse, that wasn't the feeling.

It wasn't how his lawyer felt either, apparently.

Neville continued as if the guard hadn't interrupted him. In a lower voice, still laced with annoyance, he said, "Calling the judge a 'Squat' even in here, between us," he waved a hand randomly around the interview room, "is not appropriate. It sends the wrong message. It complicates my job."

Surprised at his lawyer's accusation Ray leaned forward in his chair and snapped, "I don't have a racist bone in my body."

"Not in the past, but now? I'm not so sure. The judge is

convinced you do. He's the only one who matters. You sat in his court room for days, nothing on your face. No respect. No deference. No regret." Neville's hand sliced the air with each point. "Maybe you were a million miles away, thinking about your family, but that's not what he saw. He saw contempt. And, you have to know he believed it was directed at him. Why? Because you killed two First Gen teens, and there he is, a First Gen judge passing sentence. No question he saw contempt." Neville shook his head. He smoothed his tie and the lapels of his coat, and when he spoke again it was as though he'd brushed away his anger with the palm of his hand. "What a mess," he murmured. "I don't know where we go from here."

Ray said nothing. He didn't like seeing his lawyer angry and defeated. He didn't like the clean yellow legal pad, free of brilliant, exonerating last-minute scribbles. He didn't like being called a racist.

But, was he?

He didn't see himself in that manner. He certainly considered himself "better" than the segment of society known as Regressives. When eighty percent of the population is better educated, has better jobs, and live a more stable home life, then that eighty percent is better than the remaining twenty. It seemed obvious. Did that make him racist?

How could it?

Racism, by definition, was the belief that one man is superior to another simply because of hereditary factors. Ray's opinion was based on solid, substantial, documented facts, not something as arbitrary as genetics. A person could get into long, circular debates about why one segment of the population was better than the other. Each side would have valid points, but Ray believed every argument had a bottom line. His opinion represented that quintessence.

Ray said, "What was it, Neville? Eighty, ninety years ago when things changed?"

Neville sighed. A resigned expression covered his face. "There are time stamps all over history. Opposable thumbs, the internal combustion engine, the silicone micro-chip. Pick one."

"You know what I'm talking about," Ray said. "Rick Parsons. Not engines or micro-chips. We studied him—"

"Yeah." Neville nodded. "I knew that's where you were going. But again, for the purposes of this conversation, Rick Parsons is irrelevant. He was born before our time."

"—we studied him in school," Ray continued as if he hadn't heard the interruption. "The world's First Generation Regressive Individual. What a title. How long did it take society to dream up something as benign as that?"

Neville leaned back in his chair. He widened his eyes, inviting Ray to speak then crossed his arms, putting a barrier between himself and the pending speech.

Ray didn't notice the contradictory body language, nor did he pause long enough for Neville to answer the question. "Before the title, before the moral majority and the left wing started preaching tolerance, before we were told to 'forget' how scientists described little Ricky Parsons, do you remember what they said about him? They said a baby missing a crucial strand of DNA was a genetic abomination. A mutation. A freak. Mother Nature must have hiccupped."

Neville said, "Long before you and I studied Regression in school, those words were discredited."

"The scientists were excited. A human being genetically regressing? Evolution in reverse? A living breathing Neanderthal? They were giddy! Remember? All the gaps in the human timeline were about to disappear."

Ray leaned forward. The restraining chains clanked. He was reaching the crux of the matter and he didn't care if Neville guessed what he was going to say. His lawyer wasn't looking a firing squad in the eye. "Then these First Gen abominations and mutations and freaks—scientist's words, not mine—started having children.

Suddenly, we have Second Generation Squats and nobody questions the radical drop in university enrollment, rising crime, or the fact that orangutans are wandering around dressed in suits?

"They aren't human, Neville. They're not like us; they're not Moderns. You can't expect them to act like they are. You can't give them driver's licenses and shake a finger at them when they fail to stop at a red light. Third Gens can barely talk. They certainly can't think."

Unlike him.

All Ray did was think and every thought came with slabs of guilt.

Guilt for the exasperation he sometimes felt when Angie did what five-year-olds do, make a mess at the dinner table or shout and whine in the grocery store line-up. Guilt for not remembering to say thank-you each time Dawn ironed one of his work shirts or slipped something special like a note or a chocolate bar into his briefcase when he wasn't looking.

Guilt for one thousand other little slights he'd never be able to fix. At that moment, Ray missed Dawn and Angie with a hopeless ache that was beyond describing. Every memory led to another and the pain settled into his body far deeper than a terminal disease. His eyes burned and the lump in his throat made talking impossible.

Neville said, "It wasn't Second or Third Gens who hit you. It was a couple of teenagers, joy riding in Daddy's Escalade. That was—"

"First Gen teenagers."

"—tragic."

Ray made to interrupt again, but Neville stopped him with a raised palm.

"I believe you would have acted in the same manner if the other car was driven by," he made air quotes with his fingers, "Moderns or Third Gens, either way. But I repeat, you are not here because of what *they* did. You are here because of what *you* did. You seem to think that if there was proof the teens blew the light, then the judge would have dealt with you differently."

Ray nodded. "Life. Not the death penalty. They were drunk. All I'm saying, there were extenuating circumstances."

"No, there weren't. There is no conspiracy. The cops didn't disable the traffic cam. Nobody paid the judge to look the other way. The System dealt with the teens—"

"They didn't get the death penalty, did they? They didn't get life in prison."

"They were juveniles."

"Drunk, First Gen juveniles who killed my wife and daughter, but here I sit."

"There's one difference, Ray. What you did was pre-meditated. In society's eyes, First Gens—those little Squat animals as you call them—are no different than you or I. They made a tragic mistake." He emphasized tragic. "You? You went to a pawn shop. The salesman remembered you. It's not every customer who asks for a gun that holds lots of bullets." Neville shook his head in clear astonishment. "If you already owned a pistol and simply shot them, the judge may have handed you life. Maybe. If he was feeling especially generous. But blatant pre-meditation as well as a perception of racism?"

Neville picked up his pen and began twirling it around his fingers. He shook his head.

"It's 2022, Ray. It took the better part of three generations for most Americans, not all—the KKK is still active for Christ's sake—to accept the idea that Blacks and Jews are no different than White Moderns from Oak Brook. The entire civil rights movement took a huge step back when Ricky Parsons was born. All the ground we gained after Rosa Parks? Gone. Why? Because people remember scientists using words like *abomination* and *freak*. Suddenly, Squats—damn I hate that term—are somehow less human—"

"Get over it," Ray snapped. "I'm getting the death penalty because a judge decided I'm thinking, 'Squat' rather than, 'First Generation Regressive Individual?' Tell me who's being prejudiced."

Neville sighed. "My point is, hate and intolerance haven't changed since 1955. The way it's dealt with it has changed a great deal. There are black politicians and Mexican bankers and First Gen judges and countless others who won't put up with a whiff of racism. Not only will they not put up with it, they've learned how to respond to it and how to fight back in a way that counts."

Overhead, behind a vent, a fan whirred quietly, cycling cool air into the room. It should have felt comfortable. Ray thought it had a stale, remanufactured odor. It seemed to catch in the back of his throat. He wondered if his senses were lying to him, or if the desperation tearing ragged chunks out of his soul, like a rat chewing on the soft parts of a homeless corpse, was preparing him for the future…

Twelve months in prison. Three months for the appeal process. One month on death row. And then a black hood and a pock-marked wall.

Earlier in the day, before the judge sentenced him, Ray thought he'd be okay in prison for the rest of his natural life, which probably wouldn't be an especially long time. The System struggled with daily fights, monthly murders, and semi-annual riots. It was common enough behavior in any prison but worsening in recent years with the increasing numbers of Second and Third Gens behind bars and a politically correct System that refused to acknowledge co-mingling created problems.

Eventually Ray said, "You remember what it was like back in eighth, ninth grade when everything, even Algebra class, turned you on? You're walking around in a haze because every girl in high school could be the next Playmate of the Year? That's when I met Dawn. I liked everything about her. We drifted together and apart. Together and apart. Every time we got together, I liked her more. I remember the first time I saw her. It's September, Indian summer. Can we say that now? I don't know anymore. Nobody was ready for classes. It was too nice out. Back then the girls were allowed to wear shorts to school. No uniforms back then. They were made of some kind of slippery, striped material, cut high on the leg, let a tiny bit of ass cheek peek out when they walked?"

Neville's pen went in circles. He nodded and smiled, a faraway expression on his face.

"That was the style at the time. White and blue or white and green. Whatever. All the girls wore them. Dawn's were red and did she ever wear them! You want to talk about time stamps? I remember the way she looked in those shorts like it was yesterday. I remember the first time I kissed her. It was like an electric shock. I remember the first gift she ever gave me."

"A watch, if I had to guess."

Ray gave him the thinnest of smiles, about all he could manage. He'd known Neville for years. His lawyer hadn't made much of a guess. "I still have it. I don't wear it often. She gave me other watches over the years. And then, you know, Angie—"

"Ray."

"—Angie came along and as much as Dawn was my matched half, Angie was more. I didn't kill those two boys because they were First Gens. I killed them because they didn't have the genetics to learn from their sins and the System wasn't going to punish them."

"I know, Ray, because I know you. Unfortunately, it doesn't matter." Neville slid his pen into an inside pocket. He picked his briefcase up from the floor, opened it and dropped the blank yellow legal pad into it. He met Ray's eyes. "The judge is going to write his report. He'll pass it along to the appeal judges. When the three of them are done with it, they'll affirm your sentence. We will lose. You need to prepare yourself."

CHAPTER 7

DEPUTY WARDEN TYLER licked his enormous ice cream cone and thought, *an individual who shares the same last name as a person from my youth.*

The words he used to describe Mr. Barnett when Tony Carter asked who he was meeting, and the only information he was prepared to give his subordinate. Tyler believed fences needed to stand between himself and his underlings. He had the big picture. He managed the details. They knew only as much as was required to do their job.

There was more to his reticent description than his arm's-length management style. He didn't discuss his personal business with anyone. A man was entitled to his secrets. On top of which, sharing feelings and emotions drew people closer. They tore down fences. They made a person appear weak and vulnerable, both of which were unacceptable for a man in his position. He had to be stern. Keeping eight hundred inmates obedient and placated was no picnic, particularly when sixty-seven percent were Regressive, mostly Second and Third Gens. First Gens didn't act noticeably different than Moderns, although Tyler was willing to admit (if only to himself), that being a First Gen made him biased.

…who shares the same last name as a person from my youth.

The words didn't define his utter hatred toward his first boss.

Years later he still heard the nasal voice, "If you can't handle the work, Tyler, I got ten resumes on my desk. People who'll get the job done," the man said while dragging his oily, thinning hair straight back with a plastic comb he didn't need. Twenty years after the fact, the memory still made Tyler's heart stagger. It accounted, at least partially, for the wound-up on-edge feeling he always experienced when meeting this new Mr. Barnett.

He crunched a mouthful of waffle cone and Chocolate Chip Cookie Dough and watched Tony Carter walk away. The gangly guard rubbed his shiny pink scalp with one hand while the rest of his limbs went in several directions at once. Tyler guessed Carter never stopped to consider how cold his head might feel if he went hairless overnight. The man was loyal but not the shiniest star in the night sky.

A sudden gust of wind blew through the park.

Shaking his head in mild exasperation, Tyler looked away from Carter, as if to find the source of the gust, and saw Barnett standing before him, like he'd been there the entire time and purposely hadn't shown himself until Carter disappeared.

Startled, Tyler pushed himself to his feet. He transferred his ice cream cone from his right hand to his left and reached out to shake, remembering too late that Barnett didn't care for that formality. He quickly dropped his arm. The usual feeling of dislike and nervousness filled him. Suddenly the ice cream didn't taste so good. He said in a rushed and buoyant tone he didn't really feel, "Mr. Barnett, how are you?"

"Sit, sit. Tyler. No need to stand on my account."

Tyler sat back down, as far to the left side of the bench as he could manage, convinced if he hadn't stood, Barnett would have given him one of his disapproving glares. Then he told himself to quit acting like an adolescent. He was a grown man, not a disobedient student standing before the school principle. He was a manager with an important job. What he did during his personal time was immaterial. There was no reason to feel intimidated and no reason to feel like a subordinate with Barnett; they were equals. "Where did you come from?" he asked.

Barnett waved the question away with a vague hand. "Nowhere important."

A response designed to imply exactly the opposite of the spoken word. Tyler gritted his teeth. He said nothing.

Barnett settled himself onto the park bench with a grunt. December wasn't an overly hot month, but beneath his sparse hair, his scalp glistened with perspiration. The scar that ran down his forehead through his right eyebrow was a shiny, white ridge on his flushed, red face. A swollen layer of fat drooped over the edge of his shirt collar.

Tyler kept the distaste off his face. He'd forgotten Barnett's slovenliness in the same way the man's physical appearance always slid from his memory. Even though this Barnett and his old boss—who Tyler had never forgotten—looked similar (not dead ringers but close enough for government work), Tyler couldn't have described him, had someone asked what he looked like.

Strangely at odds with Barnett's slovenliness was the man's impeccable suit. Nobody could doubt the quality of his wardrobe. Tyler figured someone else must have picked it out. Possibly a personal assistant. Who wore a burgundy tie with a crème-colored suit? Nobody. There was probably a cute, contemporary name for the color because nobody went into Macy's and asked for a crème-colored suit. They asked for Café au Lait, or Beeswax. Maybe Barnett had them tailored; he owned more than one. Tyler couldn't remember a single instance when the man wore anything else.

He couldn't remember the man but he sure remembered the suits.

He said, "Why are we meeting?" His nerve ends jinked and jumped, making his query sound brusque.

"Are you in a rush, deputy warden?"

"I don't see any reason why we can't get started," Tyler said, pretending his terse attitude was all about getting down to business. He hated, absolutely hated, not having something on Barnett, the same way Barnett knew too many details about him.

Barnett said, "Very well." He straightened his tie and brushed a hand down the lapels of his suit, across the thighs of his pants. He tapped his lips with a finger and his forehead creased in concentration. After this long charade of deep thought—Tyler wondering if the pompous ass thought he was fooling anybody with his elaborate ruminations— Barnett said, "How are things running at Glades Rehabilitation Facility?"

"We're almost at capacity and I'm understaffed," Tyler answered.

"Business as usual, then?"

"Fortunately, there's a course of new-hires about to graduate." Tyler sighed. "More unexplained sick-days, time-off requests, and late arrivals. And, let's not forget," he made air quotes and closed his eyes in exasperation, "the safety concerns."

In response, Barnett made an amused little noise and smiled. It struck Tyler as a faintly sardonic. "What?"

Barnett brushed the question away with a lazy swish of his wrist. He said, "Have any new prisoners come to you lately—"

"Almost every day."

"—who are possibly a little confused? Deranged?"

"They're all confused. Most don't understand, or pretend they don't understand, why they're in prison. They think the System screwed them."

"What I mean, do any of them act as if they came from somewhere else? Do they hear voices, or suffer from terrible headaches, or complain about the smells inside the facility?"

Tyler finished the ice cream cone. He rubbed his hands together, wiping off the waffle crumbs. It seemed Barnett had zeroed in on the reason he wanted to meet, so this question required more thought than the others. After several seconds he said slowly, "There are two like you describe. One who came to us approximately a year ago. At first, he was fine. His condition has deteriorated, particularly in the last two months. We've had to restrain him. He keeps clawing the sides of his head, ripping out his hair. In moments of lucidity, which are becoming increasingly rare, he says he doesn't belong here. He's not talking about Glades. He says strange things like, 'I need a portal,' and, 'I don't belong in this world.' Gibberish."

Barnett leaned forward, piggy eyes wide and excited. "Yes, yes. That is exactly what I'm referring to."

Tyler wondered if this greasy, eager excitement was something he could use. Was it something that would put them on an equal footing so he too had negotiating power, rather than always having to supplicate?

He said, "Another person came to us three, possibly four months ago. Initially he seemed normal, for an inmate I mean. But he's following the same pattern as the first individual. He becomes agitated more quickly than he did a month ago. He demands meetings and is very concerned about his continued incarceration. His objections aren't the standard inmate nonsense." Tyler paused. He frowned. His last sentence surprised him. It was accurate but until he vocalized it, he had never paid attention to the differences between this inmate's concerns and those of the remaining seven hundred and ninety-nine.

"What do you mean?"

"Most inmates go on about how they're innocent, or how the System screwed them. This individual's sole concern is what will happen to him if he remains locked up. He told me something in his head would break." Tyler snapped his fingers, emphasizing his point. "He would go insane. He'd become a shell. Alive but unable to function. I asked him to be more specific. He was unable to explain any further."

"This is excellent news." Barnett smiled a huge pleased smile, making the scar on his forehead bulge. "Tell me, Tyler, where were these men apprehended?"

"I don't recall where the first individual came from. The other fellow was apprehended in a local store called Eastern Ventures. The store was closed for the night, but he tripped an internal motion sensor. There was no forced entry. No indication how he got inside the store. The owner looked at the security camera video. The first view he had of the intruder was when he walked out of a freezer. He carried nothing but a duffle bag containing some personal items. If the security company hadn't arrived promptly, they wouldn't have caught him at all."

"No sign he was in the store until he walked out of the freezer?" Barnett bent forward again. His eyes nailed Tyler with a disquieting intensity. "You're certain of that?"

Tyler nodded. "Why's that important?"

"Go to this store. I want a padlock on the door and a chain link cage built around the freezer. If someone manages to open the door, they'll walk out of the freezer into the cage. Understand?"

"No."

The man with the scar flicked his hand indifferently. "You don't need to. Pay the store owner whatever he asks. If the scenario you describe happens again, there must be no chance for the individual to escape."

Tyler clenched his jaw against a rapid surge of anger. Barnett's hand gesture was both showy and demeaning. He was saying in silence, "My affairs are more important than yours. Furthermore, they don't concern you." The lack of respect infuriated Tyler. "No," he repeated. "I don't understand." He paused a beat. "If someone shows up in the freezer, how do I contact you?"

"You don't. My business interests will make contacting me next to impossible. However, I will return frequently, every two or three months over the next year. If someone else shows up in Eastern Ventures, tell me when I visit."

"The lock and cage will be expensive. This is a privately-owned facility. No association with Glades."

"I'll ensure you have the money you need to make the appropriate payments."

Tyler nodded.

They sat in silence. Tyler knew the meeting was over, that Barnett heard what he needed to hear, and had delivered the corresponding instructions. Now it was time for the awkward part of the conversation, the time when all his earlier arguments about *equals* and *professionals* and *mutually beneficial working relationships* fell apart and the angst simmering inside came to a full-fledged boil…

Payment.

On the ground between Tyler's feet several large ants had found the waffle crumbs he brushed off his fingers. He wondered if ants ate waffle cones with as much enjoyment as he did. Maybe they found them too sweet. Did they take them back to their mound and regretfully tell their little ant wives that waffle crumbs were all they could find today? Or did they bring them back with excitement and say, "Look what I found today!"

Without raising his eyes, he said, "All this extra work…" His voice was phlegmy and feeble. He cleared his throat, hating his weakness and hating the question he was about to ask and hating the answer the man with the scar would give. "How are you going to—"

"Compensation, Tyler?"

"Yes."

"I assume your tastes haven't changed?"

Tyler kept his eyes on the ground between his feet. He shook his head.

"For a job as important as this, I could arrange three new acquaintances. You could mix and match?"

Tyler didn't need to look up to know Barnett was smiling. He heard it in the man's voice. He felt his neck and ears flush with shame. At the same time his mouth dried and his breathing shallowed and excitement quickened his heart.

"Maybe a year or two younger this time, yes?"

Tyler's face burned. He shifted on the bench. He nodded vigorously, hating his eagerness but unable to control it.

Barnett laughed and then instantly turned serious. "Let me impress upon you, Tyler… This project is vitally important to me. I want to know about anyone who arrives in the grocery store in the manner you described. I will be extremely unhappy if this doesn't happen. Once they are in your custody, you *must* take a personal interest in their well-being. They are to be treated well. I won't tolerate anything less."

Tyler looked up, the intensity of Barnett's nasal voice drawing his eyes like a magnet.

Barnett stared at him. "If something, anything, unfortunate happens to an individual who comes to you via this Eastern Ventures store, I will hold you personally responsible. There will be serious repercussions. Your filthy little secret might become public. Thirteen-year-old boys, Tyler?" Barnett smiled an evil, threatening smile. "You'd end up incarcerated in the facility you currently manage. All the prisoners you presently guard will become your peers."

"Yes, Sir." Tyler's voice was barely a whisper. He hated this Barnett at least as much as he hated the old one from his youth.

"Now, I need to visit the two prisoners you described."

It was his day off but Tyler didn't bother objecting.

CHAPTER 8

USING THE TRUCK'S large mirrors, Mitch Reilly kept an anxious eye on the cop, the officer sitting under his cruiser's dome light doing who-knew-what in a molasses-slow manner. Fat rain drops hit the windshield and exploded, as if someone was plinking at it with a .22 rifle. Thoughts of Liv careened around inside his head, insisting he stay while the tinnitus screeched and warbled and demanded he move.

He did his best to ignore the sound. As much as this affliction he suffered through every twelve months wanted him to run, experience told him there was no need. He still had a few minutes, and running didn't make sense. Driving away with a cop parked behind him would put him in the exact jackpot he wanted to avoid: locked up when the tinnitus peaked. He forced himself to release the ignition key and remove his foot from the clutch pedal.

A calming technique Liv mentioned came to mind, something she learned in a yoga class, or a meditation retreat or a love-your-self seminar. With one hand on his belly just below the ribs, he inhaled a deep breath in through his nose and then released it slowly through pursed lips. She said he had to do it a minimum of three times in a row to be effective. The way he was feeling? He'd have to do it twice that many times.

He thought about her while he breathed in and breathed out,

already missing her New-age woo-woo attitude. She worked in a health food store, wore capris, and wanted to save the world one exotic hardwood at a time. Normally he would have rolled his eyes at a person such as this, but when she talked to him about her beliefs and convictions, she did so with a smile on her face that gave him permission to be a little less committed to the "cause" than she was. Their shared love of staying busy and getting outdoors more than compensated for the occasional lecture on the evils of gold mining in the Amazonian basin. Truth be told, he agreed with her. He just did so silently.

At some point, he'd read the first thing a person forgets about another, is the individual's face. The features soften and smear until there's nothing left. Hair and eye color stick around for a time, but quickly fade as well. Eventually, the only thing that remains is a soulless description: she's a blonde with blue eyes and high cheek bones. Wears lip-gloss, not lipstick.

Nothing but a featureless image and a dying memory.

It was a depressing thought.

Before Liv, when he was alone in an antiseptic hotel room, a stranger in a strange new world, she wouldn't necessarily have been the picture that sprang to mind had he wanted to warm up the night. That girl leaned toward trashy—dark roots, tall heels, a skin-tight dress. A flat stomach and large breasts. A timeless, familiar cliché. Ironically, That Girl didn't have a face either, but in her case, it didn't matter. In Liv's case, it mattered a great deal. Mitch wanted to remember everything about her: her intelligence, her optimistic viewpoint, her fast laugh, her skinny runner's body, and yeah, the shape of her face. Everything.

He realized he was bouncing his leg again and sliding the Saint Christopher medallion back and forth on its chain in frantic little jerks. Liv's breathing exercise hadn't helped.

He looked in the rear-view mirror.

Son-of-a-bitch chief, what is taking so long?

As if in answer to his silent question, the car door slammed shut behind him. Mitch turned the radio volume down, and reminded himself in a hoarse whisper, "Be calm. Be polite." In the mirror, the cop squared his shoulders and settled his hat squarely on his head. He dropped his hand to the pistol on his belt and then began a slow walk toward the F150.

Mitch rolled the window down while his heart did a nervous two-step high in his chest. He guessed everything was cool; the cop's gait was easy and relaxed.

"Mr. Reilly," the cop said, "you've got a nice clean record, young man. Keep it that way. If you're not done for the night, make sure Diet Coke is all you drink." He smiled and handed Mitch a ticket made out to Kelly Hunter, owner of a two-thousand-eight F150. "Give this to your friend. Make sure he gets his ve-HI-icle repaired." He touched the brim of his hat. "Have a safe night." He walked away.

Mitch sagged with relief. He swiped the back of his hand across his forehead and wasn't surprised to see it come away sweaty and trembling. He turned his attention to the ticket. One hundred and fifty dollars, plus a summons. Step-And-A-Half had to show up at the cop-shop in a week's time to prove the taillight was fixed. Mitch folded the ticket in half and stuck it into a cup holder. It stuck up like a bright yellow Oakland A's pennant. No way Step could miss it.

The pitch of the tinnitus faded to a low drone, the sound like a hive of bees on the far side of a field. The desperate urgency to move also dropped. Mitch looked at his watch and smiled sheepishly at all the unnecessary worrying. The cop had detained him at the side of the road for all of seven minutes. Nowhere close to the thirty or forty it felt like. He still had time to drive Step home and, although he'd never see his friend again, Mitch was relieved. He would have deserted Step in a heartbeat if the tinnitus told him he'd run out of time, but abandoning a friend wasn't how he wanted to leave this world.

He tugged the brim of his shabby straw cowboy hat down low on his head. He eased on the gas and worked the ancient Ford up to speed. On the radio, Toby Keith sang *Whiskey Girl*. Mitch turned up the volume until the speakers hissed and popped. In the rearview mirror, the cop sat in his car on the shoulder of the road, presumably finishing his paperwork. Farther down the road, behind him, another vehicle's headlights came on suddenly, those brilliant blue-white halogens that are stock on high-end European vehicles like BMWs.

Mitch dropped his eyes and looked forward into the rainy night. Everything behind him was history. He canted his head to the side—the wipers left a wide smear in the middle of the windshield's sweet spot—and he thought happy Liv thoughts, while he still could. It wouldn't be long before the tinnitus pushed her, and everything else, into the background.

On Florida's Classic Country, Toby Keith wrapped up *Whiskey Girl* and Tim McGraw started in about the good ole days, a song called *Back When*, a song Mitch enjoyed for its upbeat sound and reminiscent lyrics. He let his fingers drum the steering wheel in time to the beat, wondering where he'd be when the sun rose.

Chapter 9

AN HOUR AFTER the ride, Ray couldn't have described too many details about the trip to Glades Rehabilitation Facility.

Neville Rollins had left the interview room and two guards entered. With a hand under each of his arms, they dragged Ray to his feet and escorted him to a van parked inside a concrete garage. Inside the van, they secured the chain between his ankles to the floor and then slammed the twin doors shut. The side windows were blacked out. The only light in his moving cell came through the windshield, filtered to almost nothing by the bars separating him from the driver and the second guard in the shotgun seat. Without adequate ventilation the temperature rose quickly, thickening the stink of BO and fear. The ride took twenty-three minutes—for some reason they allowed him to keep his watch—and when the guards opened the doors again, Ray found himself looking out at a heavy rock wall of indeterminate height and width.

Brilliant white arc lights turned the evening's dusk into an abstract canvas of harsh light and black shadow. The rocks making up the wall were the size of kitchen appliances, the stone-work random and gothic, like an impregnable castle out of fourteenth-century England. Directly in front of him, an archway twice the height of a man broke the wall's ragged plane. A man stood in the archway with his feet well apart, a tall skinny individual backlit by a long, bright hallway.

One of the guards from the van and the tall skinny guy exchanged paperwork. The second guard unlocked the chain securing Ray's legs to the floor. He shuffled toward the archway, the chain clanking with each short step. When he drew alongside the tall skinny man, he paused and looked at him with enquiring eyes.

Tall-Skinny said nothing. He stared at Ray without expression. There was a purple slice of scab on top of his head, surrounded by sparse hair that looked like mildew growing on a tomato. His lips were badly chapped. He indicated the hallway behind him with a single nod.

Ray shambled forward on the painted concrete floor. Cameras in the corners tracked his progress with a faintly audible whir and blinking LEDs. With the gothic entrance to Glades behind him, the ancient castle impression vanished. Now the building was exactly what it seemed—an antiseptic government facility.

Panic struck hard and fast.

His vision faded around the edges. His breath came in shallow, rapid mouthfuls, the noise echoing loudly in his ears. His heart beat hard enough to hurt. He wasn't supposed to be here. He was a professional. A family man. He donated to charities, took his daughter to ballet lessons, and bought his wife flowers on Valentine's Day.

Behind him the van's rear doors slammed shut with finality, first one and then the second. Ray looked over his shoulder in time to see a steel door slide across the archway, sealing him inside the prison.

The white hallway tilted crazily. He stumbled. Crashed into a wall and dropped to his hands and knees. His stomach clenched. He thought he'd throw up, but he closed his eyes against the dizziness and swallowed the feeling. The stab of panic he felt when the judge sentenced him to death was nothing like this. In the courtroom, he felt it on the surface. It faded to unbelieving bewilderment as quickly as it arrived. Now reality was settling in and dread wrapped around every muscle and flowed like mercury through every capillary.

He wanted to rewind time, cancel his vacation to the asphalt hell of Orlando. If it were possible, he would have melted into another dimension, into another time and place. He wanted a newspaper and a Starbucks before work, and an Ardbeg when he got home. Most of all he wanted the warmth and pressure of Dawn's hand on his shoulder and Angie's tiny perfect fingers wound around his own.

"On your feet."

Ray wiped the water from his eyes. Tall-Skinny stood beside him, one hand holding the clipboard, the other resting on the grip of a weapon on his hip. The thighs of his dark brown pants shone, a cheap no-maintenance material recognizable as uniform fabric the world over.

Supporting himself with a hand against the wall, Ray staggered to his feet, very aware of the thousand-dollar suit he wore. Neville Rollins told him he needed to make a good impression in court. Ray had shrugged. He dressed well without thinking about it. Part of going into the office was a decent suit. Clients didn't want to see their financial advisor wearing faded jeans and a college sweatshirt. They expected to see success, because that meant they'd be successful too. There were several suits in his closet. The one he wore now just happened to be the one Neville retrieved for his court appearances. He'd left all of Ray's ties on the rack. Nobody wanted to see him hang himself before they had the opportunity to shoot him.

Tall-Skinny studied the clipboard. "Raymond Albright?"

"Yes," Ray said.

"Yes, *Sir*. In Glades Rehabilitation Facility it is always, 'Sir.'

That's rule number one. Don't forget it." He swiped his tongue across his lips and then said, "My name is Tony Carter. You can call me 'Mr. Carter' or 'Sir.' There are no other options." His voice was even and neutral, not friendly but not antagonistic either. "Standing at attention is rule number two. Any time you are waiting for Glades personnel to do something, or waiting to speak to Glades personnel, or interacting with Glades personnel in any way, you will stand at attention. Shoulders and ass against the nearest wall, hands clasped in front of you. That's rule number two. Don't forget it. All right?"

"Yes."

The scab on the crown of Carter's head bulged with sudden pressure. His face hardened. He swiped his tongue across his upper lip, leaving behind a shiny smear. "You trying to be smart? You will address me as 'Sir.' Didn't I make that clear?"

Ray mumbled, "Yes, Sir."

"I've explained rule number one and rule number two for three reasons. First, you just entered Glades so you couldn't possibly know them. Second, when you meet the deputy warden he will expect you to know them. Finally, it's my job so I have no choice." Carter's bored monotone changed. He grinned and stabbed the tip of his tongue through the gap between his teeth. "Whether or not you remember the rules is up to you. Quite frankly, I'd prefer you forget them. Punishing convicts is about the only interesting thing that happens around here."

Ray's body rippled with anxiety. What form of mistreatment did these punishments take? Were there varying degrees? Was it just rule number one and rule number two, or did other infractions incur punishments as well? He wanted to ask, he needed details, but Carter was droning on again, and Ray didn't think interrupting was the best idea.

"This is the last free advice you'll get. You're an inmate now. Guards are not your confidants, friends, or peers. We are here because every zoo needs a keeper." He pointed down the hallway. "Walk."

Ray walked.

At the end of the hallway he stopped in front of a door marked, "Processing." There was no door knob. No handle. No bell. No knocker. Ray looked from the door to Carter and back again. A scanner was attached to the wall. It seemed obvious it would open the door, but Ray had no idea how to work the thing and doubted it was his responsibility. He glanced questioningly at Carter.

Carter stared back, menace in his eyes. In an almost inaudible whisper he said, "Rule number two."

Ray hastily stepped back and pressed his shoulders and butt against the cold cinderblock wall. He clasped his hands together.

Carter raised his palm and pressed it against the scanner's glass face. A bar of light fell from the top to the bottom, scanning his hand. On the top of the device, half a row of LEDs turned from red to green. He unclipped the identification tag from his pocket and slipped it in and out of the scanner.

The LEDs turned red.

Carter cursed softly. He scanned his palm a second time. Working more quickly, he dipped his identification tag into the slot and this time all the LEDs turned green. The door clicked and slid sideways into the wall. He said, "Enter."

Ray entered.

The room he walked into was as white as the hallway behind him, undecorated and barely big enough for a desk and the First Gen who sat behind it. He wore the same uniform as Carter, tan shirt, brown pants with a red stripe. Ray's first thought was, *a Squat guard?* He hadn't expected that. For some reason, he assumed the guards would be Moderns, not Regressives.

The Squat's fingers were laced together, resting on an empty garment bag. Stenciled in white across the front of the bag were the words, Inmate's Possession Bag. A short stack of clothes sat on the desk beside a small selection of toiletries.

The Squat tilted his head and stared at Ray out of black eyes that protruded from beneath his long sloping forehead. He didn't blink. He said nothing.

Ray felt like a bug under a microscope.

Behind him the door clicked shut. Carter said, "Strip."

Ray glanced around the sterile room. Floor to ceiling cinderblock walls, two heavy steel doors on opposite sides—the one through which he entered and the one he'd leave through, he guessed—and in one corner a showerhead sprouting out of the wall like the branch of a tree. There were two faucets and, on the floor, a four-foot section of tile with a drain in the center. There was no shower curtain, no change room, and no privacy blind. The stink of Lysol wrinkled his nose.

Ray asked, "Where?"

The First Gen behind the desk spoke. "Mr. Carter, did you explain the protocols to Mr. Albright? The rules? Perhaps he didn't understand you."

The tone was patient, momentarily quelling Ray's barely contained fear. He flashed a tentative smile at the First Gen, hoping the man might respond with a reassuring word. He got nothing but a flat stare as an answer.

Carter said, "Yes, Sir. He said he understood."

Ray immediately realized his mistake. Rule number one. He was supposed to say, "Sir." He tensed. Dry mouthed, he held his breath. What form would his punishment take?

The First Gen's eyes bored into Ray, no spark in that unblinking gaze, just those dead, black eyes. "Mr. Albright, I'm a busy man. Glades houses eight hundred individuals such as yourself. We may or may not see each other again, depending on your behavior. If we do cross paths, I expect you to address me as 'Sir,' or 'Deputy Warden Tyler.' You've been told twice. Rule number one won't be explained a third time. Once you join general population you'll find these two reminders were exceedingly generous."

It sounded like he was expecting a, "Thank you." Ray tried but the words lodged in his throat. He mumbled, "Yes, Sir."

"Pardon me?"

Ray burned with humiliation. Louder, he forced out a reluctant, "Yes, Sir."

"Okay, to business," Tyler said. "Out there, in the world in which you used to belong, the bleeding hearts sip their lattes in overpriced coffee houses and say, 'Inmates are human beings. They have rights. They deserve a certain dignity. A certain respect.' Mr. Albright, I would debate most of that statement. In fact, I would go so far as to say those left-wing crazies are largely incorrect. When you chose to break the laws—"

"That's not the entire story," Ray objected. "You don't have all—"

The next thing he knew, he was on the floor while expanding waves of indescribable agony radiated away from his stomach. His eyes poured water and his lungs heaved for oxygen. He wrapped his arms across his mid-section gulping spasmodically, while fireworks of pain exploded with every inhalation and his mind screamed…

…*what in the hell?*

One moment he was explaining, his wife was dead. His daughter was dead. The System failed him. Yes, he'd snapped momentarily, but in killing those juvenile delinquent First Gens, he'd balanced an inequity.

The next moment…

He never saw Tony Carter swing his fist.

Several seconds later, gulping and drooling, Ray pushed himself from the fetal position to his hands and knees. Was this the punishment Carter referenced? Physical abuse? Beatings? Despite the pain, Ray was somewhat relieved. It could have been much worse. He looked up and met the deputy warden's eyes.

Tyler stared down at him with mild interest on his wide flat face, a hint of amusement on his lips. Ray suddenly knew something was "off" with the man, something other than being born a Squat. The patient, reassuring voice behind the desk was not meant to ease his stress. Rather, it was a reflection of the deputy warden's belief—his complete knowledge—that he was the one in charge. Anyone who stood before him was no more significant than a housefly trapped behind glass.

"Stand up, Mr. Albright," Tyler said. "For future reference, I don't tolerate interruptions."

Ray stood slowly, swaying on wobbly legs. He wiped the back of his hand across his mouth and dried it on his shirt. Never before had he experienced that kind of violence. He hadn't played hockey in school, had never been in a fight as a kid. Situations like this didn't come up in a financial planner's world. His skills were with people, reading them, understanding them, hearing what they were *really* saying when they spoke.

"As I was saying," Tyler said, "when you broke the laws of the land, you forfeited all your rights and dignities. You are not entitled to respect in this new life, as you exhibited none in your old life. Make no mistake, through your behavior you *chose* Glades Rehabilitation Facility. A jury of your peers and a judge didn't place you here. They simply agreed with the choice you made."

Tyler paused. He tilted his head. His black eyes narrowed, as if daring Ray to contradict him. "As physical beings, you and I are the same. Our differences are simple. I exist in the outside world. You do not. For you, the outside world is gone. When you entered Glades, everything that identified you as an individual disappeared, including your name. A computer generated a random number and renamed you," he glanced at his clipboard, "Inmate 66-780. Since nobody has ever left Glades and reentered the outside world without permission—escaped in other words—your former name is irrelevant. You are inventory. Nothing more. Is that clear?"

The overhead bulb cast harsh, bright light into every corner of the silent room. Ray kept his face sensibly neutral. He didn't understand the details like scientists did, but this Neanderthal deputy warden was one or two DNA nucleotides short of a full load. He might not want to admit it, but a microscopic deficiency in sugar and phosphate most definitely made him different than Ray.

Ray remembered a time years ago, before he entered grade school, when tolerance was nonexistent and First Gens and Second Gens (still too early in the planet's timeline for Third Gens), were thought of as "primates," not people. "Monkey" calendars were popular back then. His Grandfather had one hanging in his shop, *because if your Grandma won't let me have bikini girls on cars, then at least I can have humor.* The monkeys wore clothing—chimpanzees wearing coveralls in a garage, or nautical clothing beside a boat—always with a trite little quotation on the bottom of the page. As a child, Ray didn't understand the calendars. The logical part of his young mind thought the monkeys would have preferred swinging from jungle trees and eating bananas. His puzzlement ran deeper than these contradictions. Why did his grandfather wink and put a finger to his lips when Ray flipped through the calendar's pages, almost like he was letting Ray get away with something? Why did the wink make the calendars seem illicit, like the bikini girls?

Thirty years later he understood. Regressive individuals were certainly not chimpanzees, but when Ray looked at Deputy Warden Tyler, he saw a page torn from his grandfather's calendar.

The First Gen deputy warden glared, as if he somehow understood Ray's thoughts. "You're trying my patience, 66-780."

Ray grudgingly said, "Yes, Sir. Clear. I'm a number."

"To avoid future misunderstandings that result in disciplinary action, I will do you the courtesy of explaining two things that should already be self-evident." His elbows were on the desk, one on each side of the clipboard. His steepled fingers propped up his chin. He looked as though he were deep in thought.

Acting, Ray thought. Everything Tyler had said to this point and everything he was about to say, had been scripted and performed many times in the past.

"First, a rat will flee from a cat. Instinctively. Always. However, if it becomes cornered and cannot flee it will fight and ultimately die. A rat doesn't have the intelligence to realize it will inevitably lose a fight with a cat. Neither does it have the intelligence to show a cat the proper submissiveness, even if the cat was inclined to accept it.

"A dog, on the other hand, will roll over and present his belly to a stronger, superior species. Dogs aren't intelligent, but they're smart enough to understand that respect and submissiveness will prevent unnecessary violence." Tyler paused and shrugged. "Perhaps this is instinct and not intelligence. I don't know. I'm not a dog lover. It doesn't matter. The results are the same. The weaker species submits to the superior. Violence is avoided. The natural order is maintained.

"Presumably, although this is a debatable point and only time will be the judge, your intelligence leans more toward 'dog' than 'rat.' Accordingly, when you address a staff member at Glades you will roll over and show your belly, so to speak." He smiled as though they were sharing a joke.

A huge grin covered Tony Carter's face. The black gap between his teeth and the shiny smear of his tongue across flaky lips gave him a completely demented appearance.

"In short, 66-780, you need to remember your place. Is that clear?"

Ray nodded miserably. The judge was a Squat, the teens who killed Dawn and Angie were Squats, and now he was in prison looking at the death penalty, listening to a lecture from a smug deputy warden who was also a Squat. Nothing made sense.

Carter stepped forward, his fist drawn back.

Ray hastily retreated. "Clear, yes, Sir."

Carter looked disappointed.

Tyler said, "Now to the second point. In Glades, we say things once. If something is unclear, you may ask for clarification. But let me advise you, Glades staff can smell inmate bullshit the way a hound sniffs out a fox. Truthfully, it isn't that difficult, is it, Mr. Carter?"

Carter said, "No, Sir." He looked at Ray. "With some people, it's easier than others."

"True enough." After a brief pause Tyler said, "If you want to avoid disciplinary measures, I'd advise you to be convincing when asking for explanations. Clear?"

"Yes, Sir."

"Excellent. Now, do you recall what Mr. Carter asked you to do?"

Ray nodded weakly. "Yes, Sir. I remember."

"Then do it."

Something Ray once read came to mind—if an individual wanted to completely demoralize a woman, to leave her defenseless and fully at his mercy, he needed only to physically strip the clothes from her body. To achieve the same result with a man, to put him in the same submissive, demoralized state of mind, one forced a male to stand before other men and strip himself.

The difference was subtle. The result, and the effect, was identical.

When he read it, Ray understood the concept in a purely intellectual way. Now, in this brick room with two people who didn't know or care who he used to be, with what remained of his dignity and identity disappearing with every button he unfastened, Ray understood completely.

He tried to put himself somewhere else. He thought about Dawn and to his dismay found that too much tragedy in too short a time had drawn a translucent curtain between them. He couldn't see her face clearly. She'd grown foggy around the edges.

The best he could do was remember some of the good times they shared, and that wasn't enough. Not for this time and place. He thought of Angie's clean, little girl smell and her limitless energy, and that hurt worse.

With the deputy warden and Tony Carter watching, contempt on their faces, Ray stared at the wall out of eyes clouded with tears and shrugged out of his shirt.

CHAPTER 10

MITCH LEFT STEP-AND-A-HALF leaning comfortably against his front door. Mrs. Kelly Hunter had apparently locked up for the night, and Mitch wasn't about to waste time unlocking the door, carrying his drooling buddy inside, and then dealing with an angry, sleep-deprived wife.

Twenty minutes later, he drove Step's truck down a street eerily devoid of vehicles and people. The evening's drizzle had become torrential, lashing from the sky in heavy sheets. The wipers barely had time to sweep it away before it covered the windshield again. Mitch had seen this before. He suspected the horrible weather he invariably experienced on the days he slipped, was some kind of unexplainable cosmic protection that kept "normal" people away from a portal that was about to open.

The tinnitus was distractingly loud, as if the mosquito in his brain was panicked. It brushed its little wings against the inside of his eardrums and bumped into the back of his eyeballs in a futile attempt to escape. Mitch's entire skull itched from the inside out. He wanted to rub his ears and shake his head in an effort to get rid of the uncomfortable sensation. He resisted, knowing neither action would make a difference.

In the distance, a police siren rose and fell. An ambulance followed, lights and sirens awakening the night. Busy out there, Mitch thought absently, maybe a traffic accident. On a night like this, an accident wouldn't be too surprising. It might have happened on the highway he'd only just left behind. The wipers cleared the windshield. He spotted a splash of green neon hanging over the sidewalk, startlingly out of place in the monochromatic night.

The buzz in his head accelerated like an engine shifting into higher gear. Everything else about the night—the party with the guys from work, the citation, the traffic accident behind him—became insignificant. This was it, the place he would slip from this world into another.

He drove closer. The green smear formed itself into a shamrock.

Murphy's Pub.

Mitch nodded approvingly. He'd waited in worse places than an Irish pub. A shiver rippled through his body when he remembered killing an afternoon in a decaying sixty-six Firebird in the back of a farmer's field. Two hours reading a dog-eared Lee Child novel, waiting for the portal to open while the wind whistled through rusty bullet holes and smashed windows and the sound in his head grew so loud it stabbed the back of his eyes like the icicles hanging from the rotten upholstery. A long afternoon.

Mitch parked. Without much hope, he scanned the cab for anything he might put to good use in a new world. He scooped the loose change out of the cup holders. Money was different from world to world, and always in short supply during the first month or two. It had never happened yet, but he hoped one day when he slipped, it would be into a world in which he'd lived before and some saved cash would be incredibly helpful.

He scribbled an IOU to Step on a dirty Walgreens receipt and tucked it between the folds of the summons. He grinned. A summons, a hangover, and an IOU that would never get paid. All of it to go along with an annoyed wife clutching a page-long honey-do-list. Step was in for a real fun weekend.

Nothing else in the truck caught his eye. Things that seemed like a good idea often turned into dead weight, like the time he slipped with a flashlight, only to find the batteries in the parallel world were of a different diameter than the world he'd just left. He always restrained a smile when people spoke about loving their car, or not being able to live without their cell phone. There was no point getting attached to anything that was easy to replace. It was all just "stuff." Try losing a friend, a family member, or someone special like Liv every year, as regularly as sunset. Suddenly, an iPod didn't have a whole lot of value.

Mitch tugged the brim of his cowboy hat down, dashed across the street through the driving rain, to the entrance of Murphy's. Behind him another police car sped past trailing a white cloud of vapor and water, siren and lights going full blast. He ignored it. Whatever had occurred out there on the highway requiring the attention of an ambulance and all those cops no longer interested him, as harsh as that sounded. It was impossible for him to be anywhere other than Murphy's Pub.

He paused in the front door long enough to shake the rain off his hat and survey the room. It smelled like he expected, a not unpleasant mixture of beer and peanut husks. Sports clips and rock videos played silently on a scattering of televisions, both strangely at odds with the country music flowing from the jukebox. Where was Enya or Van Morrison, or at the very least, U2 in this so-called Irish pub?

On the other hand, thank God there was no Enya playing in this so-called Irish pub.

The only patron sitting at the bar glanced without interest in his direction then turned back to her drink. On the opposite side of the room, a foursome shot pool. Empty Budweiser bottles covered their table. The foursome filled the corner like they lived there. Mitch guessed on Friday nights they probably did. Why else would they be out on a night like this? Because, they always went out on Friday, and they were gonna have fun no matter how miserable it made them feel, bad vibes and terrible weather be damned!

He raked his hair into some kind of messy style with his fingers, then strode to the bar, boot heels clacking loudly on the well-worn hardwood floor, cowboy hat in hand. He dropped his backpack at his feet and leaned against the age-stained oak counter.

"Hey, brother," the bartender said, "What can I get you?"

Mitch studied the row of taps. "How about a Smithwick's?" When in Rome and all that…

While the bartender pulled his beer, Mitch cut a fast glance at the lone woman at the other end of the bar. Unlike the people shooting stick, she seemed out of place. She wasn't watching any of the televisions. She wasn't swaying or nodding in time to the jukebox. Not clock watching like she had a date or eyeing the door as if expecting friends. She just sat there, shoulders slumped, head down staring into her glass. Killing time. Waiting.

What he was doing too, Mitch thought, and if a person had to wait, Murphy's Pub was as good a place as any and better than most.

CHAPTER 11

Chicago, 1968

THE SUN PRESSED down out of a cloudless August sky, a dome of super-heated sheet metal that broiled Chicago's asphalt streets and concrete buildings. Most people left their doors open in hopes of catching a stray breeze, and they left their curtains closed against the heat glazing their windows. Cafés and coffee shops with air conditioning benefited from a surge in business. In one such café, a tinny version of *I'm a Believer* played on a radio behind the cash register.

A waitress wearing a mustard yellow dress and a white apron bristling with pens didn't hear The Monkees' song. Linda (stitched in red cursive on the right lapel), was far too busy to pay attention to the radio. For her, the music disappeared behind the drone of the exhaust fan, the sizzle of food on the grill, and the hiss and bubble from the deep fryer.

The man who Linda currently waited upon, did hear the song. He loathed it. He felt it lacked depth. It had nothing but a catchy tune to keep people interested. Arguably, simplicity may have been the secret of the song's success. That made sense. Time and time again humans proved they didn't have long attention spans. Including, it seemed, the DJs who worked in the radio stations. Over the last several months, other than songs by The Beatles, *I'm a Believer* was about all he heard on the radio, along with *Mrs. Robinson*, which he enjoyed and *Brown Eyed Girl*, which he was back and forth on. He enjoyed the guitar work but could live without the lyrics.

He wiped his hand across his sweaty forehead, over the ridge of a scar that ran through his right eyebrow, a sweat slick speed bump under the heel of his hand. When the waitress took away his empty glass and replaced it with a full Coca Cola, he nodded his thanks without looking at her and immediately took a long, hard pull on the straw poking out of the ice. He followed the noisy slurp with a quiet, appreciative sigh.

The bells above the door tinkled. A man entered the diner, along with a wave of heat. When the door swung closed with a second cheery jingle, the comfortable chill in the restaurant returned. The new arrival scanned the room through a pair of dark, wire-rimmed sunglasses. When he spotted the man with the scar, he started across the dining room, dangling his sunglasses off his wide leather belt. His bell-bottomed jeans flapped wildly around his ankles. He slid into the booth, making the red vinyl bench squeak. He looked at the man with the scar, the wry smile on his face partially hidden behind a thick black moustache.

He said, "Always with the suit and tie, man. You know it's ninety degrees out there? You're wearing a suit and tie?" He didn't wait for answer. "Sweetheart, over here." He waved at Linda. When he had her attention, he pointed across the table. "I'll have a Coke. Large. His tab." He dipped a hand into his pocket and removed a package of Marlboros, simultaneously dragging the ashtray toward him with the opposite hand.

The man with the scar touched his burgundy tie, centering the knot exactly. He didn't do it self-consciously or apologetically. He said, "I wear the suit because it possesses a timeless quality. I can fit in almost anywhere wearing clothes such as these. I've explained this before, Mr. Smith."

The first time they'd met, the man with the scar asked with skepticism, "John Smith? Are these your given names?" Smith had looked at him, eyebrows raised. He blew cigarette smoke from his mouth and nose and waited without blinking until the man with the scar hiked his shoulders and said, "Shall we get to business, then?" The truth was, as much as he appreciated the perfect anonymity of John Smith's name, he didn't care what his employees called themselves, as long as the jobs he assigned them were done efficiently and effectively.

In the Chicago diner, the man with the scar said, "I've mentioned before, I'd prefer you didn't smoke, yes?" It was a filthy habit he couldn't get used to, a stench that lingered and worsened with time.

The match between Smith's fingers flared. The stink of sulfur and burnt wood drifted across the table, followed by a cloud of cigarette smoke.

The man with the scar narrowed his eyes. With a scowl, he pretentiously waved the smoke away.

"Stay out of Grant Park," Smith said, after exhaling mightily. "Your fancy suit won't help you fit in there. You'll stand out like a sore thumb. People are mad. They might mistake you for a politician. Who knows what might happen?"

The man with the scar looked across the table at Smith's shirt, a hideous orange tie-dyed creation, open halfway down his chest. A silver peace sign medallion hung from a heavy chain around his neck and nestled comfortably in a tangle of black chest hair. The hair on his head was shaggy, unkempt, and hung well past his collar. Smith was right, the man with the scar thought. He wouldn't fit in.

"Why am I here?" Smith asked.

"As you said, people are—"

"Oh, hey sweetheart," Smith interrupted, quickly turning his attention to Linda, who'd reappeared with pencil and pad.

"What's on special today? You know what? Never mind. I'll have a hot turkey sandwich."

Linda nodded. She blew a quick gust of air from the corner of her mouth. Curly brown hair momentarily floated away from her face. She glanced at the man with the scar then back to Smith, eyebrows raised. "His tab?"

Smith smiled widely and winked. He turned his attention back to the other side of the booth. "You were saying?"

"The black man's assassination in April sparked unprecedented violence—"

"One of yours?"

"Sadly, no. Just good fortune for me. Anyway, I'd like to see the momentum continue. These political protests and anti-war demonstrations could easily turn violent."

"We're not about that, man. It's peaceful. It's a Festival of Life. Flowers and *Kumbaya* in the park."

The man with the scar said sharply, "It's about, 'Kill, kill, kill' and, 'Pigs are whores.'" He stared intently at Smith. He slowly shook a finger, as though reprimanding a small child. "Let me remind you, Mr. Smith, you're not *about* anything. Or, more accurately, you're about exactly what I tell you to be about."

This was the moment most employees began fidgeting—nervous finger-tapping or involuntary leg bouncing. They tried to hide their hatred and fear behind a thin veneer of nonchalance and defiance, but their eyes never landed on his face for long. The scarred man didn't care about their feelings. It was important to remind them that no matter how well he looked after them, they still belonged to him and were obligated to do his bidding.

John Smith, on the other hand, gave him a long, "Fuck you" stare. He inhaled deeply and then blew out a huge cloud of smoke, this time without turning his head, not so much directing the cloud but making sure he didn't direct it away from the scarred man either. He said, "Lucky for both of us, our interests align, huh?"

The man with the scar couldn't decide what annoyed him more—the lack of deference or the cigarette smoke. He chose to ignore the smoke and not for the first time, wonder about the lack of deference. If he'd thought to ask, and assuming Smith was willing to answer, he'd have learned that Smith saw him as a bully from the sixth grade, an ignorant hick who terrorized him for most of the school year. Smith remembered the bully with hatred but the associated fears had disappeared with adulthood, blunting the intimidation he might have felt when in the scarred man's presence.

The waitress arrived with the hot turkey sandwich. Smith said, "Far out, sweetheart. Looks good." He stubbed the cigarette out and immediately started eating. A thin tendril of smoke spiraled up from the ashtray.

The scarred man's jaw tensed. His eyes flicked from the still-smoldering cigarette to the drops of gravy clinging to Smith's moustache. Faintly disgusted, he turned his head and stared out the window. He hated this weakness in himself, as much as it could be described as a weakness. After all, he could "end" John Smith with little more than a thought, or punish him with the Space Between, as he had to others who flagrantly disobeyed him or decided they wanted to retire. But, that was an extreme measure. Smith was effective and reliable. People like him who were capable of travel between worlds were difficult to come by. He chose to tolerate his subordinate's annoying but ultimately harmless behavior.

Between noisy, sloppy bites Smith said, "You're thinking of what, another shooting? More riots?"

This happy and welcome distraction made the man with the scar smile. "Riots, I think. The outrage often lasts as long as that which follows an assassination, but it's difficult to catch the exact moment on camera. With the media filming the convention, we could easily have several minutes, even hours, of anarchy playing on loops on every television across the county. The disquiet, the unrest, it would be quite exciting, no?"

Smith looked up, through wisps of smoke still lazily twisting their way out of the ashtray toward the ceiling. He spoke thoughtfully to himself, quite unaware of the unrestrained anticipation in the scarred man's voice. "Chunks of concrete. Rocks. Even food. The convention ends on Thursday. There'll be 10,000 people on the streets by then. Maybe more. That fascist Daley has already called in the Illinois National Guard. The pigs are geared up with shields and gas." He looked back at the man with the scar. "It won't take much. I'll be at the front of the crowd. I'll wait for that one little moment when something goes wrong. It will happen on Wednesday or Thursday. Then I'll start throwing bricks."

"Don't get arrested."

"Once the fighting really gets going, I'll fade to black."

"It's much easier for me to aid in your escape if you're not in police custody."

Smith stood. He dropped his stained napkin on the gravy-soaked plate. He covered his eyes with his sunglasses. "You don't think I know how it works?" Then, he walked out of the café.

Light my Fire played on the radio, somehow apropos, the man with the scar thought. He pulled the ashtray toward him, tentatively, with the tips of his fingers. A grimace covered his face. He crushed the cigarette butt to death with the ball of his thumb. As disgusted as this made him feel, he also felt a rush of adrenaline and a buzz of excitement. The butchery to come would be a sight to behold. It might even show up in the history books.

CHAPTER 12

Florida, December, 2022

RAY HELD HIS shirt toward the tall, skinny guard.

Tony Carter stared at him. "Who am I? Your maid?"

Ray shrugged and dropped the shirt on the floor. He didn't like doing it. It was a nice shirt, but without a miracle at the appeal, he'd never wear it again. The judge was clear in his sentencing: *The firing squad.*

Carter said, "You may have got away with dropping stuff on the floor before, your wife picking up after you like a slave. But in Glades, we don't tolerate that."

Deputy Warden Tyler said mildly, "Settle down, Mr. Carter."

"Pick it up." Carter pointed to the black garment bag on the desk. "Everything goes in there."

Ray clamped his teeth together, suppressing rage that attacked him harder and faster than anything he'd ever known. Six months ago, his mood rarely tilted more than a degree or two away from even keel. He didn't get angry, which seemed like a good policy, but neither did he get excited.

Now though?

Now that emotional vacuum had been filled, amplified like never before, from the inexpressible way he missed his girls, to the complete satisfaction he felt when he shot the two kids who murdered them, to the doubt he was beginning to feel (given his current situation), about the rashness of that action. And, of course, to the body-trembling fury Tony Carter provoked by slurring Dawn. Ray gave the guard a hard, narrow glare. In the deep, prehistoric part of his brain, he promised to even the score, if the opportunity ever presented itself.

He unzipped the Inmate's Possession Bag, removed one hangar, and hung his shirt on it.

Tyler wrote, "Dress shirt, 1," on the inventory list attached to the clipboard.

Ray toed off his shoes, a pair of polished Rockports that were as comfortable as a lazy Sunday afternoon, then he slipped out of his pants. Down to his socks and underwear, Tyler dutifully recording everything on the clipboard, Carter kicked a two-gallon garbage can at him. It skittered across the floor.

"Socks and shorts in the trash. I don't want to touch them," saying it like he thought Ray might have spent a week schlepping through the Everglades without bothering to change. "Everything, Albright. Watch and rings too."

Ray peeled off his socks and dropped them into the garbage can. The concrete floor was cold on his bare feet. "I'm going to need my watch," he said, his voice as weak as jasmine tea. "For the schedule. Meals and such."

Deputy Warden Tyler shook his head regretfully, but when he looked at Ray his strange protruding eyes shone and sparked with excitement. He leaned forward. "What did I tell you about repeating instructions?" The composed, patient voice disappeared. "Mr. Carter, next time you ask 66-780 to do something and he questions you, remove the Taser from your belt and shock some obedience into him."

Ray's eyes jumped to the holster on Carter's hip. His earlier fear, which he had managed to control through the mechanical movements of the check-in procedure, rushed back like wildfire. He remembered horrifying media reports about unimaginable pain, even death, the Taser caused. Surely the guards weren't allowed to electrocute prisoners at will?

Carter's grin was back, larger than ever. "Yes, Sir," he said enthusiastically.

"I've warned you twice. I've cut you as much slack as I'm going to. Out there, in general population, you'll get neither courtesy. One way or another, you need to understand that. Orientation time has officially ended." Staring at Ray in the odd way he had, the deputy warden continued, almost as an afterthought, "You're doing time, 66-780. That's the only time that matters. You won't need your watch. You'll get used to the bells."

Ray unfastened the metal buckle of his TAG Heuer chronometer. He read the engraving on the back one last time. *Happy tenth anniversary. Forever, Dawn.* He dropped the watch into the sturdy, transparent bag Carter offered. Next came the ring on his right hand, the ring his grandmother gave his grandfather when they were married some eighty years before. He licked his knuckle, twisted the ring in circles, working it off his finger. He dropped it in the bag with the watch. He held up his left hand, showing Tyler his wedding band. "I'd like to keep my wedding ring."

Carter's hand dropped, found the Taser's grip.

Ray realized his mistake. As the weapon cleared the holster on Carter's hip, a red LED turned green and Ray thought, *palm-print safety.* He threw his hands in the air defensively, backpedaling. He slammed into the brick wall behind him. Panting shallowly, heart beating hard and fast, he managed a frantic, hoarse, "No!"

The smile on Carter's face expanded.

The Taser in his fist buzzed, or rattled, or vibrated. Ray wasn't sure how to describe it, but for a brief moment he was reminded of the sound a stick makes when dragged rapidly across bicycle spokes. Two wires flew from the "barrel" of the weapon, stabbing into his bare chest. Every muscle in his body tightened like band-steel, stretching him onto the tips of his toes, and it felt like someone was beating his spine with a two-by-four.

Unable to help himself, he screamed in unadulterated pain. Then he collapsed and his head bounced on the concrete floor. The rattling stopped. Blessedly, he felt nothing for the next several seconds.

When he opened his eyes, Carter stood over him licking his lips with the Taser in hand, the safety LED glowing bright green. He said, "We call that, 'riding the bull,' Albright. I think it's a rodeo reference, except those idiots have to hang on for eight seconds. You only have to go five. Piece of cake, right?"

Ray could hardly breathe. He said nothing.

Carter continued, "Now, you gonna play nice? If you are, I'll take the probes out of your chest. If not, I'll leave 'em alone and hit you again. Every five seconds until the battery goes flat."

"Yes, Sir," Ray said, in a husky whisper, remembering the correct lexicon despite the pain.

The probes were barbed, and it hurt when Carter plucked them out of his chest, leaving two bloody cuts behind. When he was done, Ray grabbed the edge of the desk and hauled himself to his knees, panting. He ached all over. He tasted blood and the side of his tongue was swollen and sore, where he bit it when the Taser's electricity hit him, he guessed. Under Tyler's impassive black eyes, he struggled from his knees to his feet, his legs like rubber.

A couple of years back—longer, pushing a decade now—he'd fallen off a ladder putting up Christmas lights a day after the snow flew for the first time that season, instead of the day before like Dawn asked. The fender of his car didn't slow him down much and he hit the driveway hard. The ladder came down on top of him, pile driving him into the asphalt. The next day he was as sore as he'd ever felt. Until today.

Carter said, "The nice thing about this," he held the Taser up so Ray got a clear look at it, "if I use both cartridges, it'll still work like a stun gun. I don't have to shoot wires. I just have to reach out and touch someone." He grinned his gap-toothed hillbilly grin. "Versatile. Okay, you remember I told you to remove your ring?"

Ray swiveled his wedding band around his finger several times, loosening it as though it were a nut seized on a rusty bolt. His eyes found the plastic inventory bag on the desk. He froze. He immediately forgot his current pain and misery. Seconds ago, the bag contained his grandfather's ring and his TAG Heuer. Now it was empty. The ring lay on the desk. The TAG was in Tyler's hand, the Squat inspecting it as though contemplating a purchase in a jewelry store.

Carter said, "Let's go, Albright."

The wedding ring bumped over his knuckle, the first time it had been off his finger in fourteen years. He held it tightly in his fist, remembering the day Dawn gave it to him. With an effort, he stepped forward and placed it gently on the desk.

Carter swooped in and snatched up both rings. After a few seconds of contemplation, he replaced the wedding band on the desk. He held Ray's grandfather's ring up to the light, studying the worn surfaces, every scuff and scratch a memory for Ray.

Ray didn't like seeing the Squat fingering his watch. Far worse was watching the hillbilly examine his grandfather's ring.

"Should polish up nice," Carter said. He glanced at Tyler with raised eyebrows.

The deputy warden nodded once.

Smiling, licking his lips, Carter slid the ring into his pants pocket.

Tyler dropped the TAG Heuer into the breast pocket of his coat.

Too astonished to speak, Ray stared back and forth between the two men. How naive was he? He hadn't seen this coming.

He could have given his jewelry to Neville, to store in the event they won the appeal. But, no. He decided to hang onto these significant symbols of his life, as if they'd somehow keep his memories sharp and poignant. Instead, every memory of Dawn and his grandparents would now have a footnote: *In addition to that which you've already lost, you allowed two more pieces of your life to be stolen.* Frustrated with himself, Ray didn't have a clue how to react or what to do next.

"How it works in Glades," Tyler said, "all personal items can be requisitioned. Every request comes across my desk. If I feel the request is reasonable and the inmate has conducted himself in a manner the administration expects, I have no problem granting the request. It's really quite simple. Obey the rules and you will be rewarded. You already know what happens when you choose the other path." He pushed Ray's wedding ring into the plastic inventory bag, folded the top over and sealed the adhesive strip.

Ray stared at Carter. All remnants of his earlier fear were gone, at least for the time being. "I want to requisition my grandfather's ring."

"What ring?" Tyler studied the clipboard. "I only see one ring listed on the inventory. A wedding band. It is in the bag, as you can see. Do you see two rings listed on the inventory, Mr. Carter?"

Carter made a show of studying the clipboard. "Nope."

Ray stood in front of the deputy warden wearing nothing but his boxers, his hands rolled into fists. He wasn't reckless enough to tackle Carter, and he wasn't going to leap over the desk and throttle the life out of the arrogant Squat warden, but suddenly he was angry enough to challenge them both without regard for the consequences. He leaned forward, planted both fists on the desk and glared hard at Tyler. "You and I both saw him put my grandfather's ring into his pants pocket."

"I didn't see anything of the kind."

"I want my watch."

"What watch? That's not listed on the inventory. Accusing Glades personnel of theft won't win you any friends, 66-780. Now, didn't Mr. Carter say, 'everything?' Lose the shorts." He dropped his gaze, making a show of ending the discussion. He signed the completed inventory list.

Slowly, staring hatred at the Squat, Ray peeled off his boxers, too angry to feel embarrassed or self-conscious.

Without looking up Tyler said, "Keep eye-balling me like that and you'll discover how I feel about silent insubordination." He pushed the clipboard across the desk to Carter.

Carter witnessed Tyler's signature then plunked the pen down on top of the clipboard. He spun it one hundred and eighty degrees and slid it toward Ray. "Sign where indicated."

Ray glanced at the inventory sheet. Not only was his jewelry absent from the list, he noticed his shoes hadn't been inventoried either. He crossed his arms. "I'm not signing that."

Carter smiled. He palmed his Taser. The red light on the side of the weapon turned green.

Ray sighed. There'd be no winning. One way or another, whatever he did, he was going to hurt, either physically or emotionally. The question was, which pain lasted longer? After a few seconds of thought he slowly, reluctantly picked up the pen.

He scribbled, "Daffy Duck," on the signature line.

Tyler glanced at the signature, glanced at Carter, nodded once.

A rattling sound, like a stick across bicycle spokes, filled the room.

CHAPTER 13

"QUIET NIGHT, HUH?"

"Maybe it's the weather," the bartender said. He avoided Mitch's eyes. "I seldom see it this slow." He slid a Murphy's coaster across the bar, placed the beer on it, then scooped a wicker basket full of peanuts out of an oak barrel. He pushed that toward Mitch too. "You want anything else, I'll be down there." He hooked a thumb over his shoulder toward the opposite end of the bar, as far from Mitch and the solitary woman as he could get.

Mitch forked over a twenty.

The bartender waved the money aside. "You're gonna be here a while, right?" He was already walking away. "Run a tab."

Mitch shrugged and pocketed the cash. He shelled peanuts, dropped the husks on the floor and washed the nuts down with shallow sips of beer. The best technique with Smithwick's was to drink it slowly enough to savor it, but fast enough to ensure it remained cold to the last swallow. A fresh glass of piss had more fizz than a warm Irish beer.

He sighed. This is what life came to every eleven or twelve months? Trying to make a beer last until the portal opened while a senseless collage of rock videos played on a television in the background? There had to be more. More what, he had no idea but he wasn't sure how much longer he could skirt the edges of the law

without finding himself in a jam from which he couldn't escape…
Breaking into low-end motels during the first month after slipping, just to get a shower and a decent night's sleep. Stealing food
until he scraped enough cash together to buy a real meal. Leaving
friends behind. Leaving Liv.

He shook his head, wondering about this rare bout of self-
pity. Usually there was an anticipatory feeling in the hours before
he slipped, the sort of feeling people experience before going on
vacation. He couldn't remember ever becoming maudlin before.
He desperately wanted to hear Liv's voice. Late as it was he
thought she might still be awake. He'd tell her how he left Step
leaning against his front door, slobbering on his shirt, just to hear
her laugh. Oh man, he missed her laugh. He'd listen to her talk
about her plans for the weekend, and maybe when he got back,
they could try out the new Thai place for supper?

There wasn't a pay phone in sight. This day and age everybody owned cell phones. Deep down, Mitch was relieved. Calling
would have been a mistake. He would have had to lie and pretend
everything was good. The added deception would have hurt her
further and ultimately increased his guilt.

At the opposite end of the bar, the lone woman stared
in his direction. Their eyes met and she instantly whipped her
gaze forward.

He caught a reflection of himself grinning foolishly in the
mirror behind the bar. He brushed a hand down his mustache
and goatee in an effort to wipe the grin away. Girls, ladies, didn't
check him out as often as he would have liked, but her furrowed
brow and studied look hadn't been a passing glance. He saw curiosity in her expression. Beer in hand, he picked up his backpack
and walked toward her. When a lady opens the door, it is only
polite to walk through. He had an hour or two. Might as well kill
it with company.

"Hi there," he said. "My name's Mitch." He dropped his backpack and stuck out his hand. "Mitch Reilly."

The instant she touched his hand the tinnitus intensified, like someone switching an amplifier from Off to On. A stabbing pain between his temples accompanied the sound. He flinched and sucked a startled breath in through his teeth. After a second or two the pain backed off and the noise stabilized. Two more volume spikes like that and he'd be talking a little louder, compensating for a noise nobody else could hear.

"Lindsay." She dropped his hand. "Are you all right?" Her face was all angles and points. She used L'Oréal, or some such product, to mask a mild case of acne mottling both cheeks and the bridge of her nose. She wore a silver necklace with links the size of dimes.

"Bit of a headache is all," he said. "I like your necklace."

She smiled before turning back to her drink. "Thank you."

"Mind if I join you?"

"Suit yourself."

Not real inviting but he figured, what the hell. They could chat or not, and if they didn't, he was leaving soon anyway. "Is there a story? Where'd you get it?"

"No story. I travel. I picked it up along the way."

"Where do you travel?"

"Places you've never been."

He tilted his head and narrowed his eyes at her abruptness. Under different circumstances, at the beginning of the year rather than the end, he might have hung in there, but not tonight. She trick-fucked him with her look of interest. That was fine, it happened now and then, but when a person measures life in twelve-month blocks, time is a commodity. Mitch Reilly didn't waste it.

"I've been a lot of places," he said. He downed the Smithwick's and grabbed his backpack from the floor. By the time he decided he'd only have one more beer before switching to Diet Coke, Lindsay was already a fading memory.

She touched his arm. "That was rude. I apologize. I'm not feeling well. Let me start again. My name is Lindsay. Lindsay Thompson." She waved at the empty barstool beside her. "Sit down."

"Seems like you'd rather be alone."

"Take a load off," she said with a small smile. "I won't bite again."

Her smile convinced him. All those angles and points smoothed out when she smiled and her face went from interesting to appealing. Mitch nodded once. He sat back down, absurdly wondering what it would take to make her smile more often.

Neither of them spoke. Out of the corner of his eye he watched her spin her empty wine glass between her fingers. She nibbled her lower lip. He stood the cardboard coaster on edge and tapped it up and down on the bar. He looked into his empty glass. Dried Smithwick's residue lined the sides in scummy white waves. They both stared at an array of hard stuff lining the wall behind the bar, studiously avoiding eye contact. Seconds stretched. He said, "The bartender isn't too attentive."

"You need to send up a flare to get his attention."

"What are you drinking?"

"Red wine."

"You ready for another?"

She nodded.

Mitch waved until the bartender couldn't ignore him any longer, then he ordered Lindsay another wine and a second Smithwick's for himself. The man took his sweet time and then rushed away a fraction of a second after delivering the drinks. It seemed the cosmic force that drew Mitch to the bar and repelled others, was working inside as well as out on the street.

Mitch said, "I'm not interrupting anything, am I? You waiting on someone?"

She shook her head. "No."

He looked at her backpack, so similar to his. "Is there a one-armed man chasing you?"

She looked at him. "What?"

"You're not, you know, a fugitive, are you?"

"No."

Not waiting on company. Not a fugitive. And, not a vagrant either, the same way he wasn't a vagrant. Sure, she carried a couple too many pounds and suffered a mild case of acne but she obviously cared about her appearance. Her hair was styled. She wore jeans that hadn't come from a thrift store and her wide leather belt matched her brown boots. Her top really crossed his eyes, some kind of soft, fuzzy material that clung to her chest in a distracting sort of way. Despite all that, she sat on her bar stool without company, in the same bar to which the tinnitus drew him. She felt superficially ill, just like him, and she was as indefinite about her past as he was when someone asked too many questions.

Suddenly, it seemed obvious. Lindsay was slipping too!

Was it possible?

He knew he wasn't the only person on the planet who slipped. He knew it without proof, the same way most people "know" they aren't alone in the universe. But he'd never actually met someone like him before. "Let me guess," he said cautiously. "You slip between worlds? You're waiting for a portal."

Lindsay inhaled sharply. Every muscle in her body tightened. Sitting perfectly straight she swiveled on her stool and faced him. She stared at him out of surprised eyes.

An incredible explosion of relief filled him. Loneliness, an emotion he hadn't known he was feeling until that precise moment, evaporated like a cold mist under a hot sun. She was like him. They could compare worlds and share hints and tips. They could walk through tonight's portal side by side, maybe spend some time together in the new world. They could look out for each other.

He wasn't alone.

He kept his voice even, restraining his excitement. "You do, don't you? You're waiting for the portal."

"How'd you know?"

"A couple of things pointed me in that direction," he said. "You've been here what, a year?"

"That seems to be the schedule. Every twelve months, or so."

"How do you know when it's gonna happen?"

"I get headaches and this uncontrollable need to be some place other than where I am. The headaches are mild at first. Then one comes that won't go away. That's usually a week out." She wrinkled her nose. "After that things start to smell."

Mitch said, "My nose gets sensitive too."

"Sensitive would be nice. What I get goes way beyond that. At first everything smells like an abandoned house. Kind of dusty and musty and run down. Plaster and old furniture. It's hard to explain." She shrugged. "Old. Like an antique store. It's not too bad until day four, then the stench really thickens. I kind of follow it."

Mitch nodded, thinking about the way the tinnitus ramped up on the fourth day and how he followed the sound. "I get that, only it's a noise in my head, not a smell."

"How does it work?"

"It's called tinnitus. It gets louder as the time gets closer. I go in a direction that keeps it from hurting. If I go off course, the sound changes and it hurts. The first time I heard it I was fifteen. My parents took me to the family doctor. He was baffled. He didn't know what caused it, and he didn't know how to stop it. I grew up figuring out how it worked."

"It's almost instinctual, I'd say." Lindsay's hand drifted unconsciously to a pimple on her cheek. "I get a few other hints a week or two before. The smell is the clincher. It gets worse when I go off course. It goes from old to rotten, like something has died—"

"Like inside the Space Between?"

She closed her eyes, shook her, head and blew out a frightened breath. "It's like the walls of the world are growing thin and the Space Between is leaching into this world."

An uncontrollable tremor shook Mitch's body. The darkness between the worlds terrified him. If forced to describe it, he would have said the parallel worlds were like soap bubbles blown through a child's toy, spheres of different sizes floating beside each other, some close together and some far apart. The space between them was a poisoned darkness. Filled with despair, bad memories, and the horrors ripped from a child's nightmare, it was another facet of the same cosmic force that repelled those who didn't slip. And, because it was so horrifying and a person naturally wanted to be anywhere else, it perversely aided those who had no choice but to traverse it.

Mitch had no way of confirming any of this but after slipping eleven times, he thought his suppositions made sense. Experience counted.

Lindsay twisted the stem of her glass. The wine became a burgundy pinwheel. "How different are the worlds for you?"

"The big stuff is the same, like the names of continents and significant historical events. It's the details that change. In the next world, this place will be Murray's. Or Mandy's." Maybe she'd never run into someone like him, and needed her experiences to square with his, but she nodded as he spoke, like she already knew what he was going to say.

She said, "Money is the easiest way. It's different—"

"—in every world," Mitch said, finishing the sentence at the same time she did. They laughed together. Once again Mitch enjoyed the happy look on her face. "You ever get back to the same world?"

"Once," Lindsay said. "Into the world I grew up in. My origin world."

"So, it's possible. I didn't know that. It's never happened to me."

"You know those ads they put up when the police have lost all hope? The ones for missing children you see on telephone poles and milk cartons?" A wistful, faraway look crossed her face. For a moment, he might not have been there. "I saw a picture of myself in a post office once. A school photo, taken just before I crossed the first time." Her voice was low and wistful. She shivered. "I was fourteen. I just walked away. I had to. At the time, it was all I could think about. And, the smell…" She said the last in an apologetic tone.

Mitch remembered how close he'd come to driving away earlier in the evening when the cop was checking his driver's license, the frantic urge to move that was almost impossible to ignore.

She continued, "After the first time, I thought about how I'd never talk to my parents again. They must have been so worried. Maybe they still are."

"You didn't look them up when you slipped back into your origin world?"

Her eyes grew misty. "A long time had passed. What could I say?"

Mitch didn't know if there was a correct answer. Her parents were probably desperate to know what happened to their little girl. Tracking them down and trying to explain would have been worth her time.

Lindsay read his face correctly. "Don't judge me."

He held up an apologetic hand. "I'm sorry," he said, telling her what she wanted to hear while silently promising himself to knock on Liv's front door without hesitation—for better or worse—if the right portal opened and led him back to her world.

Lindsay blinked several times. She shook her head. She swallowed the last of her wine and placed her glass down with exaggerated care. "I need something easier to drink. Maybe a lemon drop. Do you think our attentive bartender could make me one of those?"

Mitch shrugged. "I don't even know what it is."

"It's a kind of martini. It's a very popular drink. How do you not know that? What planet have you been living on?"

"Hilarious. Have your lemon drop. I'll stick with beer."

They talked and now and then they waved the bartender away from his tasks, and he reluctantly kept serving them, and they got pleasantly drunk. Then, by some unspoken agreement, they both backed off so the drunk stayed alive and floating and didn't become some wild, roller coaster party with deep valleys and mountain-top highs. The tinnitus thrummed like a guitar in the hands of an untrained child. Somewhere along the way Mitch squirmed on his stool, looking for a more comfortable spot. His thigh brushed beneath Lindsay's leg, and she didn't move away. Instead she shifted, almost imperceptibly, so the pressure of her leg on top of his increased. When they talked they lowered their voices and leaned into each other in a pantomime of privacy. Eventually she said, "I need to take a walk."

He watched her walk past the battlefield of debris the foursome at the pool table left behind when they finally waved the white flag on the night. He wondered if she was giving it a little extra for his benefit, because the silver crowns embroidered on the back pockets of her jeans wriggled just right. When she looked over her shoulder with a tiny smile on her face and gave him a bad-boy shake of her index finger, he didn't have to wonder anymore.

He studied the scuffed tips of his boots. He'd get new footwear in the next world. Tan scratches crisscrossed the weathered leather. The heels were worn down on the outside edges, which made him a pronator. Or, was it a supinator? He could never remember. He stroked his moustache and goatee and the toes of his boots seemed to disappear. Maybe it was the beer talking, but he liked Lindsay. After a couple of hours and a couple of pints, he wasn't the best judge, but waiting for the portal to open had never been as enjoyable. The question was, what happened on the other side? He liked the idea of travelling with her, at least for a time, perhaps a month, if she was willing. Having company, even for the first few days, when adjusting to the new world was most difficult, was something to look forward to.

Deep in thought, he didn't notice her return until she dragged a hand across his shoulders when she passed behind him. She'd reapplied her rusty-red lipstick and although his vision was a little foggy around the edges, he thought she may have teased her hair up a bit too. He said, "You look good. Dressed up and ready to go travelling."

She touched her acne-spotted cheeks. "You're sweet, Mitch. But I don't think 'good' is the best—"

Without warning the sound of bells jangling in his head intensified so loudly and so rapidly his eyes watered. Silver, striated light flashed around the shrinking edges of his vision. Pressure, like two giant thumbs, pushed on each eardrum. A grunt of pain slid through his gritted teeth. The air became electric and stunk of ozone.

Lindsay's face turned gray. Sweat beaded on her forehead. With a look of complete misery on her face, she smeared the back of her hand across the bottom of her nose. She moistened her lips with the tip of her tongue and closed her eyes. "I'm going to regret those drinks."

Hollow and distant, her voice sounded like it came from the far end of a tunnel.

The time to slip had come.

Mitch cut his gaze around the pub until he found the portal, partway down the hallway leading to the restrooms. Shimmering calm, flat like a swimming pool standing on edge, it filled the hallway, obscuring the exit sign hanging over the backdoor. He grabbed his hat off the bar and tugged the bent brim down low over his forehead. He picked his backpack up and straightened, every movement slow and deliberate. Side by side he and Lindsay faced the pool of black light. They linked fingers without premeditation. He said, "We roll."

Without warning, the heavy front doors to Murphy's crashed open, smashing into the wall on either side of the entrance. Police officers swarmed inside, firearms in hand, yelling.

Shock sobered him. Mitch remembered the armada of police cars that sailed past earlier in the evening, lights and sirens turned up loud. It looked like every one of them, plus a few of their cop buddies, had backtracked to Murphy's Pub.

CHAPTER 14

"INMATE 66-780, YOU'RE awake. Stand up."

Ray recognized Tyler's voice. His memory, along with his anger and dislike returned in a hurry. The Squat deputy warden had stolen his anniversary watch. Carter, the hillbilly guard, had pocketed his grandfather's ring, and tased him. Twice. Lying on the concrete floor with his eyes closed hoping it would all go away was tempting. Unfortunately, this was prison. He couldn't roll over, brush Dawn's calf with the tip of his toes for warmth and assurance, and then fall back asleep, secure in the knowledge the nightmare would be forgotten by morning.

Reluctantly, he opened his eyes.

A light in the ceiling, screened behind heavy wire mesh, shone in his face. Carter stared down at him from where he sat on the edge of the desk, arms crossed, his mocking smile filled with enjoyment. "Come on," he said. "On your feet. We're not done yet."

Ray rolled onto his side. His entire body ached, a pain so deep and complete he wondered if simple movement was possible and if it was possible, would gravity snap off his limbs when he stood? He sat upright.

Stood on wobbly legs.

Closed his eyes against a rolling wave of dizziness.

When he opened them again, both Carter and Tyler were

staring at him. The Inmate's Possession Bag lay open on the desk. It held his suit. The plastic bag containing his wedding ring hung on the clothes hanger hook, along with a yellow inventory receipt. His Rockports were nowhere to be seen. The Daffy Duck autograph was scribbled out. His name, Raymond Albright, was scrawled on the signature line, the result unlike his signature in every way. He hazily wondered who signed on his behalf— Tyler or Carter? With sadness, he realized it didn't matter. After they stood him against the wall, nobody remained in the world to claim his effects. If someone did show up, Neville Rollins for instance, the deputy warden would probably shrug and hand over his possessions without the receipt attached.

Tyler continued to watch him out of his bulging eyes. "Is there something you need to say, 66-780?" His voice was cold and hard.

Ray looked steadily back at the deputy warden, didn't see a hint of pity or concern, nothing other than cold detachment in the Squat's demeanor. He said, "No," and waited for Tyler's eyes to narrow, before adding a derisive, "Sir."

"Okay, Albright," Carter said. He sighed loud and long. "Turn around. Bend over. Spread those ass cheeks."

"What?"

"You think I want to look up your hairy ass?" Carter shook his head. "I don't like it any better than you do. But you're in Glades now. You'll get used to the pose." He laughed harshly. "Me? I'll go home and watch women's tennis on TV, or women's curling, or women playing darts, for that matter. Garbage yeah, but enough to burn the image of your naked butt out of my head."

"Mr. Carter," Tyler said, warning in his tone. Then to Ray, "We don't want you smuggling contraband into Glades."

Ray said desperately, "I've been in a guarded jail cell or a guarded court room for weeks. What could I possibly have stored up there that would interest you?"

Tyler's flat face remained expressionless. He stared at Ray without blinking. "Mr. Carter, have you ever had the privilege of watching an inmate ride the bull three times during the check-in procedure?"

Carter's tongue poked in and out of the gap between his teeth and then slashed across his chapped lips. "No, Sir. It would be a new record." He sounded excited.

Face burning with mortification, Ray turned around. He bent over, grabbed his backside with each hand and after a couple of seconds that seemed to last a couple of months Carter said, "Okay. Stand up. Shower time. Be generous with the soap."

Trying to ignore the audience, Ray faced the hot water spray and scrubbed like he hadn't showered in days. Some men didn't mind communal showers. Ray wasn't one of them. After a squash game, he'd wrap a towel around his waist, hit the shower—in and out in a hurry—then dry off and re-wrap the towel. The rest of the guys could wander around wearing nothing but flip-flops if they wanted. The only person he cared to shower naked with was Dawn. The idea of a shared shower in Glades, without the benefit of a friendly gym atmosphere, was beyond tolerable.

The dirty, violated feeling wouldn't wash away. Eventually he quit trying. He cranked the faucets off. Carter threw him a towel. Ray lunged for it, snagged it before it landed in the water pooling out the drain at his feet, and shot a glare in Carter's direction, guessing the man had deliberately thrown it short. When he was dry, Carter pointed at the thin stack of clothes beside the Inmate's Possession Bag. "Your new wardrobe. Get dressed."

Ray pulled a no-color T-shirt over his head, the white gone a million washes ago. He stepped into worn boxers, socks, and lastly a pair of orange coveralls. As he dressed, Carter talked, his bored monotone back.

"Laundry day is Wednesday. Take your dirty laundry and exchange it for clean stuff. You bring in one pair of socks for washing, that's all you're getting back in exchange. Ruin a pair of coveralls, rip the sleeves off for example, you'll earn yourself inmate punishment. Haircuts are done every day of the week except Sunday, alphabetically and without exception. When your name comes up you will be given a Number Two. There are no other options. Clear?"

"Yes, Sir," Ray replied without interest. His hair had been thinning for years. A Number Two wouldn't make a noticeable difference.

Deputy Warden Tyler jumped in and said, "In the short term you will be sharing a cell with inmate 34-008. Mr. Rufus Santos is a barbarian similar to yourself. You and he should get along fine." He held out Ray's copy of the signed inventory slip. "Keep this. It's your proof you have belongings you can requisition.

"Mr. Carter? Take 66-780 home. Be sure to explain the bells on the way."

For the briefest slice of time, hope flickered. Not Glades. Home. Towering summertime thunderstorms and blinding winter blizzards. Blistering July heat and bitter January wind. Ray would have traded a single month of crazy Illinois weather for the next sixteen months he'd spend in Glades. He would have traded a single week in Ass-Wipe-Anywhere if he could have spent it with Dawn and Angie.

Of course, Tyler didn't mean Illinois. Illinois wasn't home. Glades was home. Like a spark in the wind, the flicker of hope blew out as quickly as it appeared.

Not quickly enough. Tyler must have seen its brief glow on Ray's face. The Squat smiled wickedly. "Whoever said, 'Home is where the heart is,' has never taped a photograph to a wall in a Glades prison cell, have they, 66-780?"

CHAPTER 15

THE COPS CAME through Murphy's front door pushing a bow-wave of aggression, yelling, "Down!"

"Down!"

"Down!"

Mitch spun around slickly on the hardwood floor, putting the iridescent portal behind him. More cops? Twice in one night? Dealing with these guys was becoming a very bad habit.

"On the floor! Now!" the cop in the lead hollered. Behind him officers fanned out, checking booths, scanning dark corners, searching the rest of the bar, shouting, "Clear! Clear!"

Lindsay's gaze jumped from them to Mitch and back again. She clutched his hand in an incredibly strong grip. Her eyes were wide, her pointed face pale and confused and somehow sharper in distress.

"All clear," an officer shouted. He pointed at Mitch. "It's gotta be him."

The lead cop cocked his head. The lines beside his stony eyes deepened. "You," he yelled, leveling the barrel of his weapon at Mitch's face. "On the floor. Do it now!"

It's gotta be him?

What did that mean?

Beside them, on the other side of the counter, the bartender stood with his hands raised, eyes blinking in uncomprehending surprise. He dropped his knife. It rattled on the counter amongst the lemons and limes he'd been cutting into slices and quarters. On the other side of the room a beer glass plunged off the edge of a table. Mitch *felt* it shatter, the glass javelins reminding him of the night's priorities. He'd risk a bullet. He wouldn't risk missing the portal.

He lunged sideways, towing Lindsay toward the bar, ignoring her surprised scream. He swung his arm around her body and yanked her into him, holding her as a human shield.

The lead cop weaved sideways, the barrel of his weapon bobbing, the man searching for a clean shot, not finding it with Lindsay in his line of sight. He looked ill, his face pale and sweaty. He also looked determined.

Mitch grabbed the bartender's knife with his free hand. He held it vertically in his fist, the point only inches from Lindsay's throat. The hair on the top of her head tickled his chin. The flowery aroma of her shampoo tickled his nose. He mouthed into her ear reassuringly, "I've got you. Now fight me." He raised his head and yelled, "Back off, chief. I'll cut her."

The cop's jaw hardened. His lips compressed into a thin white line. He switched smoothly into negotiation mode, holstering his pistol and raising his hands. He pushed his palms toward the floor several times. "Take it easy," he said. "Nobody wants to hurt you. But know this: there's no way out. The back door is covered too."

"Yeah, right," Mitch said, sarcastically. The cop wasn't about to trick-fuck him on those two points. Every other officer in the bar had a pistol in hand, looking very much like they wanted to hurt him. And, if someone were behind him at the back door, he'd already be flat on the floor with a knee between his shoulders, wrists tightly cuffed.

"My name is Olson," the cop said. "Roger Olson. I just want to talk." The hard rage in his eyes contradicted his calm, even voice. He took a step, narrowing the gap between them. "Let her go."

Mitch flexed his fingers around the plastic handle of the knife, citrus juice dripping down the blade, sticky on his fingers. "Back off, chief."

"We can work this out. The lady doesn't have to be in the middle."

Mitch shuffled backward. His foot banged into a chair. He kicked it away. It hit the wall and toppled with a thud. Neither he nor Olson looked at it. The tinnitus warped and distorted the song coming from the jukebox, a familiar Faith Hill tune obscenely light for the situation.

Where in the fuck was the Irish music?

To Mitch's right, a cop pressed forward trying for a different, flanking angle. Mitch twisted slightly, keeping him in sight. He shook his head. Waggled the knife.

As if on cue, Lindsay screamed and clawed his arm.

Olson motioned the man back without taking his eyes off Mitch's face.

Another step and Mitch was in the protection of the hallway, the walls on either side pressing in on him reassuringly, all the cops stuck behind their leader now, in the open area of the bar. On a door to Mitch's right, the word *Calin* was painted above a stick figure wearing a skirt. The tinnitus screeched. The pain between his ears verged on unbearable. Twin rings of striated light strobed painfully around the circumference of his eyes. He kept moving, surprised he hadn't yet walked into the portal. It had to be close. He remembered seeing it only a few feet from where the hallway spilled into the main part of the room.

Another step, and this time instead of pacing him, the cop hesitated. A new expression took the place of the rage on his face. Confusion? Trepidation? Mitch guessed the portal's unnaturalness had shaken Olson's confidence. Either that or the unexplainable energy that drew Mitch to a portal and repelled those not meant to slip, was working on the cop. It was working on the other officers as well. The crowd had become ragged. One cop swayed, clutching the brass rail along the bar for balance. A second officer leaned over and propped his hands on his knees. The two farthest away stood motionless in stupid incomprehension.

A breeze, as if someone had opened a door to the rainy night, ruffled Mitch's clothes, the hair hanging over his collar, the cowboy hat on his head. He shambled backward, holding Lindsay tightly, feeling for the portal with the worn heels of his boots. Something sucked hungrily at the back half of his body. The need to move became uncontrollable. The brilliant sphere of white noise with which he had lived for the previous week broke into pieces and reformed into tormented screams of countless people who'd lost everything they'd ever loved. Mitch's throat tightened. He clenched his teeth, biting back despair.

He kept moving.

He crossed the razor-sharp line the portal formed on the floor and entered a darkness the light bulbs hanging from the hallway ceiling were unable to penetrate. The tinnitus ceased abruptly. The pain disappeared with it, but there was no relief. The tormented screams living in his head had moved. Now they surrounded him as if he were in a stadium full of invisible guests. He wanted to believe it was a trick, like the sound wind makes when it blows through bridge girders, but he knew it wasn't. He was listening to the voices of the Space Between.

Eyes stared at him through wispy clouds that floated by in the currents, eyes that accused him of trespassing, insane eyes of individuals hiding in the darkness. The stink of death and decay assaulted his nose, faded with the wind, only to grow rancid all over again. Pinpoints of lights blinked on and off in the distance. Portals possibly, or stars or other celestial bodies a mile away or a thousand miles away.

Mitch didn't know.

He stared across the top of Lindsay's head into Murphy's, seeing the bar in two-dimensions now, like an episode of *Law and Order* on television. The cops, the tables and chairs, the bottles, everything had flattened. Everything had edges, cardboard cut-outs that shimmered with polluted color. The neon Murphy's sign appeared to melt, the shamrock leaves dripping a continuous flow of molten green wax. Roger Olson wavered like a hitchhiker beside a highway on a hot summer day. He compressed his lips in what Mitch already recognized as an expression of decisive determination and then he pushed forward, as if the aberration in front of him didn't matter or was less important than apprehending his quarry.

Mitch couldn't understand his persistence. Why was he coming so hard?

He stepped deeper into the Space Between, dragging Lindsay with him. As the darkness wrapped around her, she doubled over retching violently. Mitch jerked his arm to the side before the knife in his hand cut her. She dropped to her knees.

Olson's hand blurred to his waist. When he raised it again, he held his pistol. His lips moved, but his voice blew away in the wind. The pistol bucked once.

Twice.

A third time.

The gunshots sounded like popping light bulbs. The first bullet hit the portal, shearing into the darkness, leaving a silvery, spiral tail in its wake. Mitch bobbed sideways. It flew over his shoulder. The second bullet followed a fraction of a second later. He leaned in the opposite direction, dodging it as well. There was no time to evade the third. It zipped toward him, carving a shimmering contrail, bright and beautiful, in the darkness.

Was this how it ended? A bullet in the back hallway of a want-to-be Irish pub? It wasn't the ending Mitch imagined. Not when he was so close to a different world. Not when there was so much left to do and so much left to experience. It didn't seem right. He saw Liv's face in exquisite detail. He remembered the way she smelled and tasted. He wondered where she was at that very moment.

For some reason, he saw himself standing at the entrance to Green Earth. He wanted to go in the store but hesitated, like he promised he never would. He looked over his shoulder with a nervous expression on his face. A man and a young girl, neither of whom he knew or recognized, nodded their encouragement. The man was thick around the middle and going thin on top. The lines around his mouth and across his forehead spoke of stress. The girl wore a black trench coat over t-shirt and jeans. Her eyes were ringed with heavy black makeup, making her face appear unnaturally white. She parted her wavy brown hair in the middle. The jewel above her upper lip looked like a red wart.

The vision changed.

Now the unfamiliar man was opening the door to Green Earth. He walked in with the girl a step behind. The familiar welcome bells jingled over her head as they crossed the store's threshold. Mitch could not see himself in this vision and an enormous feeling of sadness and loss filled him…

…and then vanished when the third bullet struck the palm he raised in useless defense.

The bullet slammed his hand backward, into his nose. He grunted in pain and a milky-way of colored stars burst behind his eyes. Blood stippled his shirt. He swiped the inside of his arm across his eyes, drying them. The lead bullet, still warm, nestled between his index and middle finger.

From her hands and knees, Lindsay looked up at him. Her face was the color of wet newspaper. Her eyes burned feverishly white in the darkness. Drool and vomit dripped from her lips. She gulped and her chest heaved. When she spoke, Mitch could only guess what she said. He dropped the lead slug, reached out and hooked his fingers around her thick leather belt, yanking her to her feet.

She nodded vigorously.

A quick scan and Mitch spotted the portal into the new world. The quality of the portal's blackness was different than that of the Space Between, like a rectangle of gloss black paint stroked over top of a flat-black canvas. He wished it were daylight in the new world, or if it turned out he was slipping into a building, a lamp or an overhead light would have made a nice easy target, but the perfectly straight lines framing the glossy new portal would work as well.

The Murphy's portal began to shrink, evenly from the outside corners, in toward the center. Olson disappeared from the chest up and the knees down. He reached into the opening. His arm flailed through the darkness in a vain attempt to grab something.

Unable to believe what he was seeing, Mitch watched him climb over the bottom lip of the shrinking portal. With one leg, an arm, and shoulder inside, his reach lengthened considerably. His scrabbling hand latched onto Lindsay's sweater.

She shrieked and swatted ineffectively at his arm.

He didn't release his grip.

Mitch curled his fingers into a fist and drove it into the cop's elbow joint. The cop's fingers loosened and Mitch heard a distant, shouted curse. Backpedaling quickly, he and Lindsay linked hands and swiveled. He concentrated, forcing aside all thoughts except how much he wanted to be *there*.

Side-by-side he and Lindsay crossed the Space Between and slipped through the glossy black rectangle that was a door into a different, frigid new world. The screaming voices ceased. The flashing, striated light around his eyes disappeared. Mitch pushed his hat back on his head. His breath huffed out in a white cloud. He armed the sweat off his forehead, already feeling his body temperature dropping in the cold, unknown environment. With thumb and index finger, he polished the Saint Christopher pendant and mumbled, "If you're out there somewhere, thanks." The medallion brought images of Liv to mind and he wondered what a good Catholic girl would make of something as un-worldy as the Space Between.

There wasn't much to see in the room in which they landed. The single overhead bulb cast very little light, leaving both ends of the narrow room dark. A ragged layer of hoar frost blanketed the walls to the right and left of the portal, before disappearing into the depths of the room. Opposite the portal, a row of stainless steel freezers lined the wall, reflecting the white ghosts dancing in the Space Between.

Lindsay said, "Mitch, look."

He followed the line of her pointing finger. His mouth dropped open in astonishment.

Olson had fully entered the Space Between.

"Son-of-a-bitch," Mitch muttered. What had he done to attract this kind of attention? Sure, he'd been sloppy, drawing more scrutiny than he should have, but nothing in his relatively short past warranted this kind of dogged pursuit. Who in their right mind would follow him into something so obviously unnatural? Nobody. Not unless they had a reason so overwhelming strong—

"He'll be stuck in there if he doesn't hurry, Mitch." Lindsay's voice was airy, concerned.

Mitch agreed. When he thought about becoming trapped in the Space Between, he did so in an abstract sort of way, the way a person thought about drowning on a sinking ship or being buried alive. It was conceivable but unlikely. Unfortunately for Olson, that abstract thought would become reality if he didn't hurry. As much as Mitch didn't care for police officers, he couldn't stand by and see Olson condemned to the Space Between.

Mitch yelled. He swept his arm in big come-this-way waves.

Lindsay cupped her hands around her mouth and screamed.

From his crouch, Olson looked at them, and then turned back to the Murphy's portal, presumably conversing with a colleague in the bar. Someone thrust a flashlight through the rapidly shrinking portal.

A sick feeling filled Mitch's stomach. In all things—forest fires, oil spills, nuclear melt downs—Mother Nature healed herself, given enough time. Mending a hole in her very fabric would be no different. He'd never seen a situation such as this but a dawning certainty filled him: the portal wouldn't stop closing when it met resistance.

Knowing his voice wouldn't carry, knowing his warning would come too late, he yelled, "Your arm!"

With shocking suddenness, the flashlight's beam rose and then abruptly fell. Olson recoiled, scuttling back like a crab on a floor that didn't exist. The beam of the flashlight shone into the black nothing, rocking back and forth in diminishing arcs,

nothing,

nothing,

then onto a hand and arm, the limb severed cleanly through the forearm.

Nauseated, Mitch closed his eyes. He opened them a moment later. The glossy, black rectangle that opened into the world in which he and Lindsay landed, began to shrink, drawing closed from the corners into the middle as the opposite portal had done seconds before. In the Space Between, illuminated by silvery ghosts and the single flashlight, Olson had become a bizarre shadow puppet, a light shape in the greater darkness.

Lindsay hopped in agitation, her calls increasingly shrill and distressed.

Mitch yelled loudly and gestured frantically. It may have been his imagination but when Olson finally decided he wouldn't be going back to where he came from, it seemed to take him a long time to cross, several seconds instead of the instant Mitch was used to experiencing. But, after that measurable moment of time, Olson climbed through, joining him and Lindsay in the glacially cold room.

The portal shut behind him in silent surety, leaving behind not the slightest hint that anything abnormal lay behind the wall through which they just walked.

CHAPTER 16

Arkansas 1991

THE SUN FELL quickly, as it always did in the middle latitudes, bruising the sky multiple shades of red and purple. Magnolia trees lined the street. The bright pink blossoms delicately perfumed the air. A light spring breeze ruffled the hair on the scarred man's head. There was a glower on his face, and he walked with long purposeful strides, deliberately oblivious to Mother Nature's picture show, as if the sensory spectacle somehow annoyed him. When he reached his destination, he climbed the steps two at a time and pushed through the double doors, entering a foyer as dreary as the exterior world was brilliant.

Muzak played quietly from hidden speakers, *Take My Breath Away* possibly, a song from the late eighties he recognized and thought he might have enjoyed at one time. The man with the scar liked music, but not Muzak. He wondered why humans did that sort of thing… continually took something that worked perfectly well and screwed it up for no apparent reason.

He signed in at the reception desk, his signature an untidy, illegible scrawl and then clipped his visitor tag to the lapel of his crème-colored jacket. After several seconds, a security door in front of him buzzed and then clicked.

He strode through.

A man in baggy white pants and a white button-less shirt met him on the other side of the door. He stared at the man with the scar through thick, wire-rimmed glasses, his face empty of all but a limited amount of intelligence, yet also filled with helpfulness and purpose. "I'm Jeffery," he said. "The patient you're here to see is in 109. If you'll follow me?"

Side by side the two men walked down a long, brightly lit hallway. The scarred man's shoes squeaked on the heavily waxed floor. Jeffery, who walked in perfect silence, said, "We all learn which shoes to wear. Rubber makes the most noise."

The man with the scar said nothing.

"You're with the police, a shrink? Sorry, psychiatrist?"

The man with the scar said, "The young lady I'm here to visit will be charged with murder. Involuntary manslaughter, at the very least. It is important to find out whether or not she is mentally capable of withstanding a criminal trial."

"She's better now than when she arrived."

"Is that right?"

"Maybe it's the tranqs."

Doors lined each side of the hallway. From behind them, the man with the scar heard sobbing, moaning, and pleading. In one case he heard high, hysterical laughter and in another a loud, single-sided conversation. From behind several doors he heard nothing at all. He wondered if people "lived" in the silent rooms, the occupants asleep or so heavily tranquilized they were incapable of making a sound. He was only curious in an off-hand sort of way. He didn't really care. The young lady in 109 was the only person who truly interested him. The hallway smelled like industrial-strength cleaning products. He guessed the rooms would have a more personal, more offensive stench—body odor and vomit and excrement—the sort of things for which industrial-strength cleaning products were intended.

"Here we are." Jeffery stopped in front of a white door with black numbers painted upon it, harsh and insensitive against the white background. He pointed at them, 109, in case the man with the scar had somehow missed them.

The man with the scar nodded at the viewing window. "May I?"

"Be my guest."

The window was small, the size of a hardcover novel sitting on edge rather than standing upright, more of a slit than a window. It was set into the door at eye level, the view into the room obscured by a panel. He slid the panel sideways and peered through the hatch.

The hospital referred to her as patient. "Inmate" was closer to the truth. She sat propped up in the corner, arms wrapped around her knees. A faded, oversized hospital gown completely obscured her shape. Her hair was cut into a sensible, low-maintenance mommy-bob. Thin and greasy, it lay plastered to her skull like a damp dishtowel. The sides of her face, from ear to ear, were streaked with long, scabby scratches.

"No straightjacket?"

Jeffery answered, "Until yesterday. But, like I said, she's calmed down."

"What happened to her face?"

"Her fingernails are all broken."

The man with the scar smiled slightly. Encouraging news. "Did she say anything when they brought her in?"

Jeffery nodded. "She kept screaming, 'My baby, my baby,' and, 'Make it stop. Make it stop.'" His eyes bulged with interest behind his glasses. "Do you know what that means?"

The man with the scar knew exactly what it meant. He contained his growing smile and shook his head shortly. "Not without speaking to her. I'd like to do that now."

"Administration told me to allow that." Jeffery pulled a single key out of his pocket. He reached for the door handle. "This key opens all of the patient's rooms. It's a safety procedure. One key."

The man with the scar gave Jeffery a cursory nod. He didn't plan on staying in this facility any longer than required. The protocols couldn't have interested him less. He put a restraining hand on Jeffery's arm. "Is the room monitored? Camera and microphone?"

"All high-risk patients' rooms are monitored."

"My conversation with her needs to be confidential."

"Like attorney–client privilege?"

"I'm not a lawyer, Jeffery."

"Doctor–patient confidentiality, then? You said you were a doctor. I remember now. That sort of thing happens in here all the time. Like on TV."

The man with the scar smiled vaguely. He hadn't said anything of the kind, but if that's what Jeffery remembered, it suited his purposes fine.

Jeffery said, "I'm not supposed to let high-risk patients out of their rooms."

"Very logical. You're being very diligent." The man with the scar paused. He tilted his head and tapped his lips with his index finger, pretending to think about the problem. "How about this," he said slowly. "Let her walk beside me the length of the hallway. It's monitored. I see cameras. The doors we came through are locked. There is nowhere for her to go. She's all of one hundred and fifteen pounds. I believe you said she was on tranquilizers. Probably a cocktail of other drugs as well. I doubt she's eaten a proper meal since she was admitted."

He didn't want anyone listening to the conversation he was about to have with the patient in 109. If someone heard what he had to say, there was no doubt in his mind he would be locked in 108 or 110, which was more of an inconvenience than a problem, but still something he preferred to avoid. He said, "How high a risk could she possibly be? For added security you can walk behind us if you like, just out of earshot."

Jeffery looked doubtful.

The man with the scar dropped his voice to a stern, confidential whisper. "Doctor–patient confidentiality, Jeffery. Our conversation must be private."

Jeffery finally nodded. "Walking in the hallway," he mumbled uncertainly. "I guess that would be okay." Moving slowly, he unlocked the door.

The man with the scar nodded his thanks. He turned and faced the room. The dry air stank of carbon dioxide and all the other offensive odors he imagined earlier. He wrinkled his nose. "Deena," he said.

She raised her head, looked at him out of eyes puffy and red.

"On your feet. We'll be more comfortable if we walk."

She didn't move. "Who are you?" she asked in a tone completely devoid of interest.

"I'm here to help you."

"You can't help me. I killed my baby." Tears filled her eyes and trickled down her cheeks. She dropped her chin. Her entire body shook.

The man with the scar waited, tapping his foot. When the shaking stopped and the gulping ended and the sniffles quieted, he said simply, "I know."

"His name was Ryan. He was only four months old. So tiny and perfect and helpless. I was supposed to protect him, but I killed him."

"I want you to tell me about that."

She looked at him, something in her scratched face other than despair now, a barely visible fire, a strong protective instinct for her dead baby buried just under the surface. "What kind of sicko are you?"

"You didn't mean to kill your son, did you? I want you to tell me what happened. On your feet. Let's go."

She looked at the floor. For several seconds she didn't move, then she hiked her shoulders apathetically and pushed herself up right, sliding her back up the wall. She snuffled loudly. She used her arm to wipe her nose then dried it on her shirt. At the entrance to her room she paused and looked in both directions, like a kid at a crosswalk. "Who's he?" she asked, staring at Jeffery who stood at the end of the hallway, arms crossed, feet apart, guarding the locked entrance/exit doors.

"Jeffery. He's the hall monitor. He makes sure everything in this wing stays in ship-shape condition. Forget about him. He is unimportant. Tell me what happened. Start, let's say, a week before your baby died. Start with the sound you heard."

The fire surfaced again and Deena gave him a sharp look. "How do you know what I hear?"

"I guessed. The sound is called tinnitus. Now, tell me your story. I won't interrupt again."

"I guess it was a week or ten days before Ryan—" She faltered and gulped. Tears brimmed once more, but she swallowed them down and continued. "—when I started hearing the noise. The tinnitus?"

He nodded.

"It was faint at first, but it got louder. Every day, it got louder. It was alive in my head, shrill as nails down a chalkboard. Near the end, it hurt. Everything stunk, like my nose suddenly started working one-hundred-ten percent. I got this feeling like I had to move. The sound guided me or directed me. When I walked out the front door it became muffled. It didn't hurt so much. When I turned around and went back into the house, it came back, harder than before."

The man with the scar walked beside her, treading softly to keep the soles of his shoes from squeaking too loudly and distracting her. He kept his eyes on the end of the corridor, lest she see the smile that crossed his face. She wasn't ready to see his happiness. Not yet. Very soon he'd tell her he wasn't a doctor or lawyer. He'd explain how he wasn't visiting the hospital in an official capacity, despite the lies he'd told and the paperwork he'd faked to obtain entrance.

But before he told his story, she needed to tell hers.

"Ryan," Deena said, "wouldn't stop crying. I wrapped him up and I went walking and I sang *Hush, Little Baby* to calm him. I followed the sound, just going in whatever direction dulled it. And then—"

They reached the end of the hall. Deena stopped talking. They turned around and started their slow stroll in the opposite direction. She was crying again, silently this time. The man with the scar wanted to grab her by the arms, look her in the eye, and tell her to pull herself together. The baby's death was inconsequential, an insignificant event in the world's great scheme of things. He restrained himself. She needed to cry, and she needed to talk. Prohibiting one and forcing the other wouldn't get him where he and Deena needed to go.

Her voice had risen and accelerated as she told the first part of her story. When she started speaking again there was nothing left but a quiet, dull monotone.

"—and then Ryan really started crying, almost screaming he was crying so hard. The noise was unbearable. I rocked him and at the same time the sound in my head went as loud as it ever was. I sang *Hush, Little Baby* and he screamed and I shook him, just trying to quiet him. My eyes were watering and it felt like white hot needles were stabbing my ears. I clawed my face, trying to rip out the noise." She seemed to sag into herself. "All of a sudden, the noise was gone. Just like that, it stopped. I was on my knees on the street barfing and Ryan wasn't crying anymore." She sniffled loudly. "I picked him up, and he was dead."

She crumpled against the wall and sobbed uncontrollably.

The man with the scar sighed with exasperation. *The boy is dead.*

Yes. I understand. Can we please move on? He didn't have children. His understanding of a young mother's despair was inadequate. That wasn't what brought about his impatience. Rather, it was the narrow view all humans held, that somehow the death of one tiny baby could fundamentally change their world until the end of time. It was ludicrous. Logically, everybody knew their time on the planet was limited, a grain of sand on an endless beach, in terms of age. So, how did an event that didn't affect people one city block away, take on such galactic importance, particularly when events that were truly galactic occurred in the universe every day? It was a question he couldn't wrap his mind around.

When the sobbing turned to infrequent gasps and gulps he said gently, "Except the sound isn't gone, is it? It's still there. Quiet, but deep in the background, yes?"

"How do you know?" This time Deena didn't sound surprised.

"I know things about tinnitus, Deena." He gestured with his head and they began walking again. "On a scale of one to ten, how bad is it?"

She seemed to think for a moment. "Two."

"Two is as good as it will ever get. It will never get better than that. You'll have to live with at least 'two' for the rest of your life."

"How do you know?" she repeated.

"I've met people like you before. A good many, actually. Many of them not as strong. Or stupid, depending on how you look at it."

She glared at him. "What's that supposed to mean?"

"You were right to say the sound guided you. That's what it does. That's its purpose. If you were smarter, you would have allowed it to guide you, like most people with your ability do. The fact that you overpowered it, resisted it until it passed, shows your strength."

For a while Deena remained silent, and the man with the scar allowed her time to think. Eventually, after a couple of more hallway laps, she asked, "Where would the tinnitus have guided me?"

"Specifically? I don't know. Initially, you would have found yourself in front of a door, of sorts. A portal. If you had walked through the portal instead of ignoring it, the tinnitus would have disappeared entirely. For a time. What you experienced, the tinnitus peaking and then disappearing, was the sound of the portal opening and then closing."

"You're not making sense."

He ignored the comment. He was making perfect sense, and very soon Deena would understand. He said, "Let me tell you what happens next. You will remain locked in a cell of one kind or another until the courts decide what crime you've committed. They'll decide if you're fully guilty or only partially guilty. Either way, you'll end up in another cell, paying penance for killing your baby. That entire process will take a long, long time. In the meantime, the tinnitus will return. Within months. Stress and confinement accelerate the cycle. You'll have to take my word on this. As I said, I know things about tinnitus. When it returns, what you described will reoccur. Because of your incarceration, you'll miss the portal a second time. The tinnitus will peak and fall off, but only to a 'five' on your scale. As strong as you are, I doubt you'll remain sane. Not with five between your ears for another full year." He tapped the side of his head with the tip of his finger. "The third time it happens…" He hiked his shoulders. "Probably not survivable."

"And, that's why you're here?"

"Smart girl. I can get you out. Probably within the week. I can get you to a place where the tinnitus can be managed. To a place where you can begin your life anew, outside of the box you're currently confined to, both literally and mentally. Does that interest you?" He hoped she'd find his question rhetorical. He wanted her. He had plans. An attractive young lady (once she cleaned herself up and ate enough to put a little beef on her bones), was exactly who he needed to skewer a handsome, charismatic up-and-coming presidential candidate. Nothing captured American's imagination or shook their political foundations quite as vicariously or violently as an extramarital affair.

She shrugged, as if his proposition was only mildly appealing, but the man with the scar noticed her step falter and he heard the hitch in her breath. She was undeniably filled with grief, but as he'd noticed earlier, she was also smart. It didn't matter if she believed him about the tinnitus and what would happen when it struck again. What mattered now was her understanding of the court case she faced, her continued confinement, and the inevitable punishment.

"What about my son? I can't leave him."

"Why not? He is no longer a factor. He is a memory."

"Bastard," she said, and then she said nothing for several, long seconds until she asked, "Why would you do this for me?"

The man with the scar smiled.

Deena shuddered. She turned away from him in a hurry.

He said, "Nothing is free, but I pride myself on giving people choices. You can stay here and face the consequences as I've described them. Or you can work for me. The only question that really matters is this: What does working for me entail? What will I ask of you in return for setting you free?"

Twenty minutes later, hands stuffed in the pockets of his crème-colored pants, the man with the scar walked down the entrance steps, into a warm, fragrant spring evening. His feet were light. He had a swagger in his step. He was humming, not a sugary version of *Take my Breath Away*, but rather, a cheerful rendition of *Hush, Little Baby*.

CHAPTER 17

Florida, December, 2022

RAY WALKED OUT of the Glades check-in room carrying everything he owned in the world—a pair of orange coveralls, six pairs of socks, six shorts, and two T-shirts. On top of the clothes was a small collection of prison-issue toiletries. On his feet, he wore a well-worn pair of canvas slip-ons with soft rubber soles. As he moved deeper into Glades Rehabilitation Facility and farther away from freedom, automatic lights in the ceiling blinked to life. Behind him Tony Carter doled out essential Glades information, occasionally interrupting his monologue to bark directions.

"You need any more soap, toothpaste," Carter said, "those kinds of staples, you requisition them. Every inmate gets an annual allotment. Run out before your year is up, you can buy what you need from the prison commissary." He pointed at the toiletries Ray held. "That stuff is like money in here, just like you see in the movies. Don't come crying to me if someone steals it. I don't care. You have a prison account. Glades credits it two bucks a day. If you work, in the laundry for instance, that can go up to a maximum of five dollars. You need more money? You better have someone on the outside who can top up your account. Stop here."

Ray didn't need to be told. There was nowhere else to go. The hallway ended at a locked door, the familiar scanner glowing with a line of red LEDs across the top. He waited for Carter to scan them through, looking back down the hallway at various administrative offices, closed doors and dark windows at this time of evening. Security cameras hanging from the ceiling twenty feet above his head, monitored everything that happened in the hallway.

"That was the last of my goodwill, Albright." Carter stared at him, that dangerous expression on his face, tongue slashing back and forth across his lips. His hand hovered over the Taser on his hip.

Ray stepped back fast, straightening and pressing himself against the wall.

Carter gave him a lingering, disappointed look then raised his palm to the scanner and dipped his ID card in and out of the slot. The lights turned green and the door slid open.

They entered a well-lit foyer with glass walls on either side. In front of him, behind another glass wall, was a room on a raised platform that made Ray think of an airport control tower. He guessed the view from the platform would be excellent, giving the individuals up there an unobstructed view through both the right and left windows, as well as down upon the entrance area where he and Carter now stood.

Carter said, "The entire facility is secure, but the door you just walked through took us from what we call a Level One secure area into a Level Two secure area." He waved at the guys in the tower. Two men waved back without interest. He said, "Those guys, sitting up there like pharmacists, are called Control. There are cameras all over Glades feeding monitors up there. Control watches the monitors. Any sign of trouble, they hit a button and the only bell you need to worry about goes off. It's a double claxon. You hear it, you've got forty-five seconds to get back to your cell. Your cell is the fourth level of security. Clear, so far?"

Ray nodded.

"I didn't hear you, Albright."

"Clear, Sir," Ray said wearily.

Carter pointed to the left of the tower. "Woman's detention wing is over there. Administration, infirmary, supplies, that sort of thing, are down the hall behind Control. We're going right, into the men's detention wing. The common areas in the men's wing is Level Three. The last place you're ever gonna see." Grinning, he pointed to a door centered in the glass wall to the right. "The next time you're outside of Level Three, we'll be carrying your worthless carcass out in a box."

The muscles in Ray's jaw worked nervously. The earlier argument, during the check-in procedure, before Carter tased him the second time, had taken away some of his hopelessness. It gave him the temporary impression that he was in control. Now though, he was a passenger again. Panic and desperation nibbled the edges of his sanity. He'd never suffered from claustrophobia but he was quickly beginning to understand the condition. The prison walls pressed in on him. The air seemed hot and thin, as if there wasn't enough oxygen in the room. An irrational fear of a slow, suffocating death filled his mind.

Carter scanned them into Level Three, talking the entire time. "These walls? Reinforced, bulletproof glass. Control has perfect visibility into the common area, but a convict can't get through to their side." He paused and then, sounding absurdly proud of the next statistic, he said, "You know how many people have escaped? None. Zero. You know how many people have tried? None. Zero."

"The deputy warden mentioned that," Ray said.

"Don't interrupt, Albright. Now, say you decided to try... I think you're too big an idiot to get past the electrified inner fence, but say you actually made it? Before you got to the outer wall, the German Shepherds will tear you to shreds. We only feed them four times a week."

Carter paused and looked at him, so Ray nodded because it

seemed to be what the man expected. His back was sticky with sweat. His scalp itched. "Is it always so hot in here, Sir?"

"It's not hot. Men's side is a constant sixty-eight, three-sixty-five. The women's side is seventy." Carter continued, "What I was saying, the outer wall is thirty feet high and impossible to climb. Even if you could scale it, which you can't, you'll never get over the top. There's no razor wire up there. A person can cut that stuff out of the way. And, there's no cement encrusted glass up there. A person can cover glass with an old mattress." He smiled. "No, the top is edged with a horizontal aluminum cylinder, like piping on a suitcase. Think about that. Six feet in circumference, you can't get your arm around it. Slick as baby shit too, nothing to grab onto. No toe holds." Carter still sounded as proud as if it was he who designed the impregnable prison walls.

Ray looked over his shoulder wondering if it got crowded down at this end of Level Three, with the woman's detention wing on the opposite side of the glass wall, but the Control tower was built to effectively block any view of the women's wing from the men's. They walked past closed doors inside the Level Three common area, the gym, barber shop, library and chapel before entering a new hallway with cells on either side. Snores and grunts, sounds of numerous sleeping people, floated through steel mesh doors.

Carter continued. "If you made it as far as the outer wall, and managed to Spiderman to the top, and somehow found a way to cling to the cylinder, there are marksmen spaced at regular intervals around the perimeter. They don't shoot to wound. The hole they put in you will be ten times bigger when the bullet comes out the other side. The upside of hollow points.

"Inside Level Three you can go anywhere you want. The yard. Gym. Library. Chapel, if that floats your boat. Just remember, that double claxon sounds, you've got forty-five seconds before every door in Level Three slams shut and locks. You're not in your cell when the guards come in to bust up whatever is going on, we're going to assume you're involved." He smiled. "Clear?"

"Yes, Sir," Ray said, remembering how much the Taser hurt.

Carter stopped in front of a door painted bright red and constructed out of steel mesh. "The cells are all numbered and color coded. Blue, green, yellow, and red. Two people per cell, 400 cells. This is you. Red 350."

Unable to help himself Ray said, "What's the reason for the color/number combination?"

"What?" Carter sounded surprised, as if this wasn't a question he'd heard before. "It's administrative. A way to keep maintenance, janitorial staff, and medical personnel from tripping on each other." He licked his lips and gave Ray a glare that was easy to interpret: *I'm done with Q and A.* "Anything else?"

"No, Sir." Ray waited a handful of seconds until it seemed Carter had relaxed and wouldn't tase him or club him with the baton hanging from the ring on his belt. Then he said, "What about the bells? You didn't tell me anything about the bells."

Carter said in a low, dangerous voice, "I told you about the double claxon. You'll get used to the other bells. You don't, you'll miss chow. By the way, you ate anything this evening?" When Ray shook his head, Carter laughed. "Too bad. I'm gonna burn a steak on the BBQ tonight. Wash it down with a cold Pabst Blue Ribbon. If I'm in a good mood tomorrow, I might tell you how it tasted."

He kicked a dented, discolored panel along the bottom of the door into Red 350. The door shook and clanged. He gave Ray another hard look then said loudly, "Attention, Santos."

Ray pressed himself against the wall, holding his small stack of clothes and toiletries in front of him.

Carter nodded his approval. He peered through a viewing slot in the door, the mesh too tightly woven to see clearly inside the dimly lit cell. After several seconds, he scanned the cell door open. It slid sideways on a track in the ceiling and another one set into the concrete floor. When it reached halfway, the lights in the cell automatically came on full bright. A man stood at attention against the wall of the cell. He stared straight ahead, his jaw thrust out in clearly defined annoyance. He ignored Ray and Carter.

Carter said, "Welcome to your new address." He made a sweeping after-you arm gesture.

Ray walked into the cell. He glanced at his new roommate, a tall guy standing there, his buzzed black hair smeared flat against his skull like he'd just woken up. His cheeks were mottled, his skin dark. If not Mexican, then some other South American country. His almost-fat belly hung over the waistband of his shorts. His tattooed arms were big but not sculpted, his knuckles all scraped and scabbed. He had some size, but he wasn't in great physical condition.

Ray turned around in time to see the cell door close behind him. At the halfway point the room lights dimmed. A moment later the door clanged shut. He heard two sharp clacks that he guessed were the latches snapping into place, locking him inside. He turned around in time to see his roommate stretch out on the bottom bunk. He said, "You're Rufus Santos?"

A grunt was all he got in response.

"Sorry we woke you up."

"Shut up, Albright."

Rufus had a definite Spanish accent, but not so heavy he was incomprehensible. Ray was relieved. He wasn't too good with accents. He had to work hard to understand British or Aussie accents, never mind foreign languages. He asked, "How do you know my name?"

"Carter."

"He's a piece of work, huh?"

"What I just say, man?"

Ray looked around the cell. It took ten seconds. A sink was

attached to the right side of the back wall, and to the left, a water-less toilet without a privacy screen, other than the edge of the lower bunk. Both the lower and upper bunks were integral to the concrete wall—no bed frames or springs or metal brackets that could be turned into weapons. Two cabinets without doors hung on the back between the toilet and sink. One was empty, the other stacked with clothes and lined with a neat row of books. A snapshot of a young girl protectively holding a baby was taped to the wall beside the cabinet with the clothes. Both children wore floppy hats and huge smiles. Their legs and feet were covered in sand. The baby clutched a squishy red ball between his chubby arms.

Rufus' children? Niece and nephew? Ray smiled. It didn't matter. Even in a place like Glades it was easy to feel good when a person looked at a photo of kids on the beach.

A glossy photograph of Sofia Vergara (also at the beach wearing very little clothing and a whole lot of sand), was taped beside the family snapshot. As good as Ms. Vergara looked, Ray preferred the family photo. It reminded him of Angie and his eyes clouded and he had to swallow a lump in his throat.

Rufus lay buried under a rough wool blanket on the bottom bunk, already breathing heavily. Ray placed his thin stack of clothes and toiletries on the shelves in the empty cabinet. He tilted his head and scanned the titles in Rufus' cabinet, running his thumb along the spines as he did. Lots of recognizable names from the New York Times best sellers list and surprisingly, for a "barbarian," as Tyler called him, a volume of poetry. There was also a heavy hardcover with a rip down the spine, obscuring the title. Curious, Ray pulled the book out but it was only an English-to-Spanish dictionary. He turned away, pushing it back onto the shelf as he did. He missed the gap from which it had come and it slipped and fell, hitting the floor with a loud, flat whap.

Rufus sat up muttered, something unintelligible. He seemed

to focus, found Ray and said, "Wake me up again, Albright, we gonna have a problem."

Ray mumbled, "Sorry." He climbed up the ladder to the top bunk and lay down without removing his orange coveralls. The thin plastic mattress squeaked. He stared up at the concrete ceiling. Surprisingly, the images that came to mind were not of Dawn and Angie but rather those of Marcus Bell and Ross Scott. He tried to push them away, tried to concentrate on his beautiful wife and angelic daughter but all he saw were the two First Gen teenagers, saw them as the kids they were, in their ill-fitting suits, just before he shot them. He saw them the same way he saw Angie, the same way any parent would look at their child.

"… *in your rush for vengeance—not justice, Mr. Albright, vengeance—two more families were destroyed…*"

Ray shook his head and tried blinking the image away. He didn't like seeing them as people. It was easier when they were Squat killers, two individuals who murdered his family. As hard as he tried, though, a voice he couldn't ignore kept whispering, *they were the instruments of Dawn and Angie's death, but they weren't killers. There is a difference.*

He slept restlessly, that version of sleep in which a person tosses and turns and his dreams are close to the surface. In them, steel doors clanged and Carter chased him with his crazy, gap-toothed grin and a rattling Taser, and then Angie was beside him, holding his hand, guiding him to safety, saying, "This way, Daddy," speaking in a guttural voice that sounded eerily similar to Deputy Warden Tyler's. When she swept her blonde, windblown hair away from her face, he saw a long sloping First Gen forehead, and the protuberant eyes of a Squat.

He sat bolt upright on the mattress, the back of his coveralls and his face wet and hot with nervous sweat, his breath coming fast. He had no idea how long he'd been asleep. He muttered a curse, wishing his TAG Heuer was on his wrist. After a few moments staring at the ceiling, letting his eyes get used to the dim light in the cell, waiting for his jack-rabbiting heart to slow, he dragged himself to the end of the mattress with his heels. He climbed down, remembering to step carefully, so as not to put his feet in the toilet bowl.

At the bottom, standing in front of the toilet, Ray thought about what would happen in the months leading up to his date with the firing squad. As farcical as it sounded, his main concern was boredom. He could see that coming. He was used to a full schedule. Typically, he met clients at the office between nine and five, but it wasn't unusual to meet them at their homes in the evening after their work day ended, or in a coffee shop over lunch because the location was convenient for both of them. No two days were the same. They were full and interesting and when work ended, he went home to a buzzing firefly of a daughter who didn't believe in relaxation. Boredom wasn't something with which he had much experience. How did a guy kill thirteen or fourteen hours a day locked in a cage the size of a janitor's closet?

And, the air in the place… sixty-eight degrees? Not a chance. Already his sinuses were dry and cracked.

He finished at the toilet and automatically pushed the flush handle. A rushing, roaring sound filled the tiny cell. He guessed it was some kind of vacuum system, instead of traditional tank and water, presumably more secure and less dangerous. No "accidental" drownings that way—

An enraged roar erupted behind him.

Instantly, Ray knew he'd woken Rufus a third time. He swiveled, an apology on his lips. He didn't have time to say the word before Rufus was on him, fists wrapped around the lapels of Ray's orange coveralls, lips pulled back in a snarl of rage, eyes swollen with sleep. He pushed Ray backward, slamming him into the wall between the toilet and the cabinets. Ray whoofed with the impact, more in surprise than pain.

"I hate getting woken up, Albright. Once is too much. I ain't going to put up with it three times in one night." He spoke quietly, probably to keep from waking the other inmates or alerting the guards.

For a second Ray was too shocked to respond. Then it occurred to him that he'd been pushed around, taken advantage of and demeaned the entire night. With Carter and Tyler, he had very little recourse. But, he didn't have to accept this kind of treatment from an inmate, someone with equal status to himself. More importantly, he knew he had to stand up for himself—take his lumps if that's what happened—but stand up for himself or live with being pushed around and objectified for the next year. He raised his hands, got both of them on the taller man's chest, and pushed. "Get off me."

It was like pushing a brick wall.

"You hear me?"

Ray said, "Get off me." He pushed harder. At the same time, he raised his knee fast and hard, trying for a groin shot to bring Rufus down, show the man he'd wouldn't accept being shoved. If they were going to share a cell, there needed to be some give and take. He was going to get up in the middle of the night. Rufus needed to get used to the idea.

Rufus twisted sideways. All the force behind Ray's knee hit him on the thick, meaty part of his thigh instead of the soft, vulnerable area between his legs. A crazed gleam filled Rufus' eyes. He pulled his arm back and hurled a clenched fist into Ray's face. Ray recoiled, instinctively snapping his head sideways. He saved himself a broken nose, but Rufus' fist smashed into his cheek. Ray's head crashed backward and bounced off the concrete wall. Lights sparked behind his eyes. His knees went weak and he staggered, flung out a hand and caught the edge of the clothing cabinet. His grip slipped and he swayed and dropped with a groan onto the floor.

"We understan' each other now?"

In the dim light of the cell Rufus was nothing but a huge silhouette towering above him. Weakly, as if it were someone else talking, Ray heard himself ask, "What?" He knew even as he spoke, he should have kept his mouth shut.

The blurry silhouette shifted, the right leg slashed out.

Agony blasted through Ray's head as Rufus' foot slammed into his face. Ray cried out, a hoarse, frightened yelp, knowing his voice wouldn't carry and if it did, nobody would pay attention.

Rufus stalked back to his bed.

Flat on the floor, Ray repressed a moan. He raised his fingers to his cheek and recoiled from his own stinging touch. The air across his broken lips sent cold bolts of pain needling into his brain. He swallowed a mouthful of blood and saliva. He probed at his teeth with his tongue and felt a fresh new pain as one of his molars wiggled in his gum. Nothing was broken, probably because Rufus wasn't wearing shoes. Ray thought about getting up but couldn't be bothered. Everything hurt too much and the cement floor was cold and surprisingly refreshing.

A bell shattered the silence. The overhead lights went bright.

Rufus swore loudly. He sat up on his mattress. "You couldn't wait ten minutes, Albright?"

Ray pushed himself upright, wincing as he stood. "What?" His voice sounded thick and wooly in his ears.

"You just had to take a leak. Couldn't wait ten minutes?"

"I guess I could have stayed where I was, hung it over the edge and pissed on the floor. You think you could sleep though that? How am I supposed to know the wake-up bell was going to ring? Tyler stole my watch."

"Better not happen again."

"I guarantee it will, so you better get used to it. What happens when a guy hits forty."

Rufus said nothing.

Ray asked, "What happens now?"

"Figure it out."

Rufus made his bed, pulled on his coveralls, used the toilet, washed his hands and face. Ray moved from side to side, trying to stay out of his way while the man went through his morning routine. Ray was gratified to see Rufus favoring the leg Ray had struck with his knee.

Maybe fifteen minutes later another bell rang and the cell door slid open. Already Ray was beginning to understand what Carter meant when he said, "… you'll get used to the bells." He said, "What's this?"

Instead of answering, Rufus backed up against the cell wall and stood at attention, so Ray did the same. A few seconds later inmates wearing orange coveralls began filing past, right to left in a neat, orderly line.

A voice Ray recognized called, "Santos. Albright."

Rufus walked out of the cell, turned left and joined the tail end of the orange line. With no idea what was happening, Ray followed. He glanced right and saw Tony Carter, the ultra-short hair on the guard's head nothing but black fuzz. A grin split the hillbilly guard's face and the black gap between his teeth looked like a bullet hole.

"You enjoy your first…" Carter's voice tailed away. "Happened to your face?"

Ray raised his hand, touched the cut on his cheek.

Carter barked, "Attention, Albright." Then louder, sounding more exasperated than authoritative, "Rufus, attention."

Ray closed his eyes for half a second, sighed softly and then backed into the wall and crossed his hands. He looked left in time to see Rufus' shoulders slump. The man came to a stop, swiveled ninety degrees and stood at attention, his back against the wall.

Carter said, "What happened to your face?"

"It's nothing, Sir," Ray answered.

Carter turned his glare on Rufus. "Did you see what happened to this idiot? How'd he get a black eye, a big goddamn bruise on his cheek? You have any idea how that might have happened?"

"No, Sir."

"No Sir what?"

"No, Sir, I didn't see what happened. Maybe he come into Glades that way?"

Carter said, "You trying to be smart?" He looked back and forth between Ray and Rufus several times. "You're one idiot convict aren't you, Albright? Not inside a full day, already you're making enemies. Okay listen up. Neither of you are getting break-fast until one of you tells me exactly what happened."

Rufus looked straight ahead, his face stony.

Ray followed his lead. Explaining what happened had no up-side, as far as he could see.

"Like that, is it?" Carter said. "All right, let's go. See what Deputy Warden Tyler has to say."

CHAPTER 18

THE SINGLE OVERHEAD bulb threw almost no light.

Mitch had no clue where the three of them had ended up, except they were probably indoors. He heard none of the typical outdoor sounds. No traffic. No wind. No barking dogs. The only sound was their collective breath, which seemed abnormally loud in the absence of all other noise. Cold air nipped at his ears and the tip of his nose. He felt Lindsay shiver beside him. He tightened his grip on her hand and she responded with a squeeze of her own.

"Something stinks," she said.

The smell was unpleasant but not overpowering. Mitch couldn't identify it so he chose to ignore it. He said, "Do you have a lighter in your pack? Or a flashlight?"

"No."

"What about you, chief? You got the flashlight your friend handed through? Or, hanging on that fancy tool belt you're wearing?"

"I've got a flashlight," Olson said.

His voice was subdued. He didn't sound like the same guy who burst into Murphy's shouting orders, pistol in hand. Mitch suspected that guy would reappear. It was his nature. The law enforcement profession attracted individuals like Olson. The training they received simply honed their aggressive, abrasive edge.

Clothing rustled and then a bright white orb flared to life. It panned quickly around the room, found Mitch and came to an abrupt halt, the beam shining directly into his face. Mitch raised a hand against the glare and blinked rapidly, clearing away the sudden red dots behind his eyes. He said, "Aim it at the roof."

The flashlight's beam didn't waver.

Olson said, "I don't take orders from you. You're under arrest. Move and I'll shoot you. I'm sure as hell done chasing you."

Unconcerned, Mitch shrugged. Within the next few seconds, Olson would begin to wonder what happened, and question where they were. A minute or two after that, he'd begin to realize he had no authority in this new world. Mitch would quickly become the least of his problems. Mitch said, "Fine, fine. I'm under arrest. You want to shoot me. Big tough cop. Point the beam at the ceiling. I'd like to know where we ended up."

Slowly, as if he wanted to know where they were as much as Mitch did, but didn't want to appear as though he were acquiescing, Olson tilted the flashlight until the beam pointed at the ceiling. With the light under his chin, his face was a devilish painting of dark shadows and orange highlights. His pistol was in his hand, pointing down along his leg. In the dim light, his shirt was covered with black spatters. Mitch hadn't seen exactly what happened in the darkness but his imagination filled in the details: Olson's friend handing the flashlight through the opening, the closing portal severing his arm, blood spurting...

Olson said, "Step away from the lady." He looked at Lindsay. Sounding less harsh, he said, "Miss, are you all right? Are you hurt?"

Lindsay tucked a little tighter into Mitch's side. "I'm fine. Mitch wasn't trying to—"

Olson interrupted her. "The police officer this guy killed was the best man at my wedding."

Lindsay stiffened. She jerked her hand out of Mitch's and side-stepped with a horrified expression on her face. "You killed a—"

"What?" Incredulous, Mitch's eyes jumped from Olson to Lindsay and then back again. "Of course not," he said. "What are you talking about, chief?"

Olson said, "We found him in his cruiser on the side of the road. A bullet in his head. Seventeen minutes after he wrote Kelly Hunter a ticket for a burnt-out taillight. I went to Hunter's house and spoke with his wife. According to her, you dropped Mr. Hunter off and then drove away like all the hounds of hell were on your tail."

"Was Step-and-a-Half lucid?" Mitch realized the nickname wouldn't make sense. "Was Kelly awake? Could he talk?"

"He was too intoxicated to speak. He's in police custody. When he's sober we'll question him. Now shut up. I don't need to explain anything to you." Olson slowly ran the flashlight around the room. "Where are we? What just happened?" His voice dropped. "Damn, I feel crappy."

Mitch almost felt sorry for him, this confident cop who typically handled most situations without effort, now way out of his element and struggling to deal with something he couldn't possibly comprehend. At the same time, he was grateful for the cop's stunned confusion. If he were under arrest back in the old world and the cop was following standard operating procedures, he'd be restrained, face down on the floor.

Tentatively, Lindsay asked, "Step-and-a-Half?"

She stared at him with a blank, neutral expression. Mitch guessed she was searching for an explanation, something she could grasp easily, before they got to the real issue—the dead police officer. He smiled, not happily or cockily but calmly and he hoped, reassuringly. He wanted to dial down her fear and find the comfortable place they'd shared earlier in the evening.

"His name is Kelly Hunter," he said. "Me and the guys at work called him Step-and-a-Half. We were roofers. This one time Step needed an air-nailer. I swung the thing to him; it was still hooked up to an air hose. When he grabbed for it, he stumbled on the incline of the roof. He dropped down for balance but his finger was already on the trigger. He drove a nail through his foot. He limped around for a week. Oh man, we laughed. The nickname stuck."

She gave him a single, cautious nod.

Olson said, "Shut up."

Mitch ignored him. He said quietly, "I don't know what he's talking about. You know how it goes, Lindsay. The tinnitus was bad. The only thing I could think about was getting to Murphy's. I didn't shoot anybody. I don't own a gun. Yeah, I got a ticket driving Step home in his truck," he hiked his shoulders, "but a couple of hours before I slipped? Come on. You know I wouldn't do anything to jeopardize that."

She nodded a second time and he saw her visibly relax.

"Third time. I won't tell you again," Olson said. "Shut up."

To Mitch's ears, the cop's confidence sounded as though it were slipping. He sounded blustery now, uncertain, yet trying to exert control for no other reason than that's what he did—acted hard, like he was the boss because he wore a uniform and carried a gun. "Listen, chief," Mitch said harshly, "you might think you're running the show but you're not. Nothing is the same as it was thirty minutes ago. When you walked through the portal, everything changed. All your cop buddies are gone. You have a family? They're gone too. Everything you knew is different. You're literally in a different world."

Olson stepped toward him until they stood chest to chest.

"Call me 'chief' like that again. Go ahead."

They glared at each other, for several tense seconds before Mitch said, "You're right. You're not a cop anymore. You're just an angry guy with a gun. If you want answers, back off and listen. I've been in this situation before."

Olson stared back, contempt on his face. "I know your kind. Petty criminals. Derelicts. You straddle the line between right and wrong, until you do something serious. Like shoot a police officer—"

"I didn't shoot anyone."

"—and that's when I show up. You act tough. I have to listen to your bullshit. I bust you anyway because all you're doing is putting on a show." He looked around the room. "I don't know where we are. I don't know what just happened. I don't believe this 'different world' baloney for an instant. Even if I did, I'm still an officer of the law and you're still under arrest." Without taking his angry eyes off Mitch's face, he reached down to his belt with his free hand and unsnapped a thick leather case. He pulled out a set of handcuffs, the chrome chain clinking brightly in the freezer's cold air.

Mitch made a small snort of derision. That was the thing with police officers. They never took time to consider anything but their own foregone conclusions. Well, Olson was about to find out that when Mitch said he'd do something, he did it. Living without a world to call his own for over a decade meant he didn't talk. He acted. It was a matter of survival. Did he want to eat a decent meal or garbage from a dumpster behind a restaurant? Sleep in a bed or under a bridge? Take a girl out for a drink, or watch them turn their noses up as they passed him on the sidewalk? He didn't wait for his situation to improve. He made it improve. Olson thought he was a talker? Well, Olson was in for a surprise. Mitch would drop him and restrain him with his own handcuffs.

A sudden rush of anticipatory adrenaline rippled through his body. His hands shook and his fingers tingled. He saw the angle, visualized his forehead smashing into Olson's face, and then he was moving, leaning back slightly, weight on his heels—

Lindsay put a hand on his arm. She said, "Boys, boys. I'm freezing. Wherever we are, we've got to get out. You can beat each other up later."

Mitch reluctantly allowed her to tow him back a couple of steps. He heard the clackity-clack of her teeth banging together and the tension came out of him instantly. He broke the staring contest he had going with Olson and looked at her. Concerned, he asked, "Lindsay, you all right?"

She looked back at him reproachfully.

Puzzled, he mouthed, "What?"

She leaned into him and whispered, "He doesn't understand."

"He doesn't want to. He's doing what cops always do. They get tunnel vision. Nothing outside their own little fish bowl matters."

"Hey asshole," Olson snapped, "I'm right here. I can hear you."

"You're right," she replied. "But, he's going to need time. It has to be confusing." She took his hand and gave it a firm squeeze. "Be nice. At least until we figure out where we are."

Mitch hesitated. Then he nodded once. "Okay." For Lindsay's benefit, he would make an effort. He'd exercise patience and try and work with Olson, at least until they figured out where they were and how they were getting out. For her benefit, he would be more understanding.

He most definitely would not be nicer.

Olson would see "nicer" as weakness, and Mitch didn't want to give the man an inch. Everybody knew what a cop did when given an inch. "Okay," he repeated. He straightened, breaking their conspiratorial huddle. "Let's see where we are."

With Lindsay standing beside him, they looked at Olson. For a couple of seconds, the cop didn't move, then he slowly washed the flashlight's beam around the room. The light cut a narrow swath into the depths of the rectangular space, giving them an impression of where they were, rather than details.

The wall through which they entered was behind them. In front of them, a row of side-by-side deep freezers lined the wall. Mitch turned and walked right. Under the flashlight's white light, he moved into the deep, dancing shadows he'd seen earlier. The bad smell was stronger at this end of the chiller. After several steps, he paused. Something hung from the ceiling.

On the wall beside him, Lindsay's shadow jigged nervously.

Peering into the gloom, Mitch took another cautious step and realized he was looking at slabs of meat dangling from the ceiling on sharpened re-bar hooks. Icicles of blood dripped from the bottom of the slabs, pointing down at frozen pools of blood on the floor. Fragments of white bone stabbed out of veiny pink flesh.

Olson said, "Not human, at least."

"How do you know?" Lindsay's voice wobbled.

"I've seen my share of traffic accidents and road kill, miss," Olson said, sounding confident, once again, almost friendly.

A reassured smile flickered on Lindsay's angular face.

Mitch said, "There's no door at this end." He did a one-eighty and walked quickly to the opposite end of the freezer. A steel door was set into the center of the wall. He pulled the sleeve of his denim jacket over his hand and brushed a thick coating of frost off the chrome handle. The cold steel seemed to slice through the fabric into his hand. The door refused to budge. He raised his hand to his mouth and blew warm air through his fist.

He pushed the handle and when that didn't work, he tried twisting it.

Nothing.

"Step away from the door," Olson ordered. "I'll do it."

Mitch stiffened. *What? I don't know how to open a door?*

Olson shouldered past him, pistol raised, Mag-Lite pointing

at the lock in the door's handle. His lips were pressed into a thin, hard line of determination.

Mitch grabbed his arm. "Whoa. Slow down, chief. You need to think before you start banging away in here."

"Take your hand off my arm."

Mitch dropped his hand, too concerned about bullets flying around in a locked room to think about the implicit threat in Olson's voice. "The door," he said. "What if it's bullet proof? In this room, the bullet will ricochet around like a racquet ball."

"Since when are walk-in freezers made out of bullet-proof steel?"

Mitch wiped his hand down his face. His goatee rasped. Summoning the patience he promised Lindsay he'd exercise, he said, "Listen to me. You're no longer in the world you knew. The rules have changed. You're probably right. Why make a freezer out of bullet-proof steel? But, we don't know for sure."

Olson flexed his fingers around the pistol's grip. He looked at the door and then at Mitch and his expression turned angry. "Enough with this different world nonsense."

Mitch raised his voice and kept going. "We don't know what's on the other side of that door, assuming the bullet goes through it. And, I'm betting you don't have more than two magazines, right? Thirty-four rounds? Something like that? You've already wasted three. You may need all that's left."

Olson said scornfully, "It's a nine mil. You can buy ammo by the crate at Walgreens."

Before he'd even finished speaking, Mitch was shaking his head. His tolerance was gone, as was his vow to be patient. "Listen, dumb-ass. There is no Walgreens. There might not even be nine-millimeter handguns in this world. They'll be nine point five. Or eight and three quarters. You don't know."

"Dumb-ass? I don't mind wasting one more bullet on you."

"Mitch?" Lindsay said, "We have to get out of here. I can't

feel my toes anymore." She was wrestling herself into a second sweater. A matching wool beanie lay on the floor beside her pack. From the floor where she kneeled, she glanced up at him. "I think you need to let him try."

Olson said, "I'm not asking for permission."

Both Mitch and Lindsay ignored him. Mitch said, "We don't know what's out there."

"We've got a better chance out there than in here."

"That bullet doesn't go through the door, it could easily kill one of us."

Lindsay nodded. "You need to let him try. If we don't get out soon, the cold will kill us. It's what? Ten Fahrenheit in here? Less? Either way," she shrugged and a small resigned smile touched her mouth, "Dead is dead."

Shivers rippled Mitch's body, controllable when he concentrated, but that wouldn't last. His toes tingled in his boots and his ears had gone numb. None of them would survive much longer in the subzero meat freezer. He let go of a sigh and asked Olson, "Any suggestions where we should stand? In case of ricochets?"

"In a corner. Cover your ears. It's going to be loud."

Both Mitch and Lindsay poked fingers into their ears. Olson stood to the left of the door and aimed at the lock. He squeezed the trigger. The sound of the shot bounced around the room but there was no angry whine of a bullet ricocheting off the walls. A round beam of light poked through a fresh hole in the door. Olson squeezed the trigger twice more and two more beams of light speared into the walk-in. He holstered his pistol and tried the door handle.

It refused to move.

Olson looked nonplussed. "What now?"

The question sounded as though it was directed at the icy air in the room rather than him or Lindsay, and Mitch didn't have an answer anyway. He knelt beside the triangle of fresh holes and peered through one, carefully avoiding pressing his flesh against the icy steel door.

"What's out there?" Lindsay asked.

"It looks like some kind of grocery store. Not like Safeway. The floor's plywood. It's all uneven. There's a chain-link fence or something a few feet in front of the door."

Olson said, "We're in a locked freezer with a fence around it? What the hell?" He shrugged. "If we can't get out of here, I guess it doesn't matter."

Mitch thought it mattered a great deal. He'd slipped in and out of all kinds of strange places—abandoned cars, condemned buildings, and one time, the landing of a stairwell in a parking garage. He'd never once slipped into a confined area, like where they were now. But, if the walk-in had been used as a portal in the past by someone such as himself, it wasn't difficult to imagine the chain link fence had been installed to contain the next person who did it. He was probably being paranoid but after a quick look at Lindsay's worried face, he guessed she was thinking the same thing.

He stood and shuffled several laps around the suddenly small walk-in, vainly trying to stay warm. The entire slip had been strange and unsettling, from the point when he first met Lindsay, to Olson's dogged pursuit, to their present confinement. He had no ideas or experience on which to draw that would help them out of the situation.

A creaking sound filled the freezer.

Mitch whirled. Then relaxed.

Lindsay held a deep-freeze lid open above her head with one hand. She looked at him. "Pork chops, I think." She let the door slam shut and lifted the next lid in the line. "Maybe steak."

Mitch said, "Shut the lid. You'll let all the cold air out."

She looked at him. Her breath puffed out in foggy clouds. In a passable imitation of his voice, she said, "Hilarious."

Olson said without conviction, "Shut up."

A retort was on the tip of Mitch's tongue, but the recognizable crash of a slamming door interrupted him. The sound came through the bullet holes, muted but audible. Voices and footsteps followed. He dropped to his knees and peered through one of the pinkie-sized holes.

Lindsay whispered, "Who is it?"

Mitch watched as a man rounded a corner on the other side of the chain link fence. He wore jeans and a black shirt with Eastern Ventures embroidered in white on the breast pocket. He spoke over his shoulder as he walked. Mitch pressed his ear to the hole.

"… didn't understand at the time. Put a padlock on a walk-in cooler? Build a chain link cage around it? Call if anything strange happens? What the Sam Hill? Well, something strange did happen. I'm doing paperwork in the office tonight and I hear gunshots."

Mitch stared through one of the holes and now he could see to whom the Eastern Ventures man was talking.

There were two of them, each wearing the white shirts, epaulets, and blue paramilitary cargo pants that security forces seemed to favor in every world into which he'd ever slipped. They stood with their chests out and their shoulders back, but it wasn't their uniforms or posture that made his stomach clench and his muscles tighten. It was the machine pistols each man had dangling from his shoulder on black webbed strapping. He stood. In a whisper he said, "Looks like the owner of the store and two security guards. Or cops. It's hard to tell. They have weapons."

"Cops I can talk to," Olson said. He glanced at his watch. "I gotta get you two booked, get home in time… What's wrong with my watch?"

"Is it digital?" Mitch asked. "Are all the numbers going crazy?"

"How'd you know?"

Mitch figured he'd answered that question three or four times already. He said, "I don't like the look of these guys. Something is wrong with their faces. They look like," he paused, knowing what he was about to say would sound nuts. "They look like monkeys. Monkeys wearing clothes." He shook his head. "I don't like this. Something odd is going on. If we're quiet, if they don't see the holes in the door, maybe they'll go away. With luck, it won't be long before an employee opens it up. Then we can get out."

Lindsay nodded in agreement. "I don't like anything about this either." She stood with her shoulders rolled over, arms crossed, hugging herself for warmth. The wool beanie was pulled down low on her head, covering her ears.

Olson looked back and forth between the two of them. "Yeah. Right." He slammed both fists on the door and yelled, filling the freezer with noise.

Lindsay's mouth opened in a horrified O of surprise. She looked at Mitch with huge eyes. It wasn't difficult to guess what she was thinking. Avoiding the authorities was paramount after slipping, when there was no credible reason for being somewhere they weren't supposed to be, when everything they owned hung from their shoulders in a backpack, when their wallets were empty and they had no legitimate identification.

He dropped to his knees and looked at the three individuals on the other side of the door. The Eastern Ventures employee fumbled through a huge key ring. The security guards flanked him, machine pistols aiming at the walk-in door. Mitch looked at Olson, too frustrated to be angry. "Nice going, chief. You've done us but good."

CHAPTER 19

STARING OUT OF a seriously swollen eye at a point six inches above the deputy warden's head, Ray stood at attention, nervously waiting for somebody to say or do something.

Deputy Warden Tyler gazed back at Ray without blinking. He made quiet slurping sounds and fiddled with a tiny cellophane candy wrapper. Finally, he said, "What happened to your face, 66-780?"

Out on the street, in the world Ray used to know, if someone had slugged him or kicked him in the face for being too noisy, he would have called the police and had the perpetrator charged with assault. If he could have worked it into a lawsuit, he would have done that as well. On the inside, the rules were different. There was no recourse, other than through the deputy warden. Since Tyler had already proven himself monumentally untrustworthy, Ray couldn't see a good reason to give the Squat any information. In addition, he thought staying silent might earn him a little respect with Rufus and the other inmates. He said, "Sir, I'm in the top bunk. I slipped climbing down the ladder."

"Really?" Tyler's eyes bored into Ray. He pushed the candy to the other side of his mouth. His cheek bulged. "34-008, is that what happened? Did 66-780 fall out of bed?" His voice dripped sarcasm.

Rufus said, "Sir, I was asleep."

Tyler waited. The silence stretched. Beside him Rufus stood without moving. Ray followed his experienced cellmate's example.

Tyler said, "I don't believe either of you. Therefore, you'll both be given inmate punishment. 34-008, stay where you are. 66-780, you're dismissed. Mr. Carter will escort you to the dining hall. We'll discuss your punishment at a future time. Shut the door on your way out."

"Yes, Sir." Ray did an about face and walked out of the office, pulling the door shut behind him, his stomach churning uneasily with the ominous threat of "inmate punishment" ringing in his ears. What did that mean? Almost certainly punishment in Glades would be worse than beatings or Tasers. They seemed to hand out that kind of treatment rather off-handedly. What did he have to look forward to?

Carter waited for him, leaning against the wall, one knee bent, a gap-toothed grin on his hillbilly face, as though he knew Ray was facing some kind of punishment and the idea pleased him immensely. "Take you to breakfast," he said, "although it's against my better judgment. Tyler's a softer touch than me, I guess."

Ray said nothing. He was still thinking about punishment, although the mention of breakfast took the edge off his anxiety. He hadn't eaten in twenty-four hours, not since they served him breakfast in the courthouse jail. His appetite had disappeared after the judge passed sentence. Food hadn't crossed his mind. Now though, with the mention of breakfast, physiological needs took over and his stomach rumbled noisily.

Carter said conversationally, "It's never good when someone screws up so badly the deputy warden needs time to think about the punishment."

Ray's step faltered.

A smile tickled the corners of Carter's face. "Don't worry, Albright. Ain't no big thing. You'll probably just go into the box."

He paused, drawing it out. "You know? Solitary confinement. A ten-by-ten room for twenty-three hours a day. You get an hour for exercise, outside in the cage, rain or shine." The hint of a smile turned wicked. "You get a couple of books in the box, and there's a television." He licked his smiling lips several times, enjoying himself, probably thinking he was ratcheting up Ray's fear. "How long you're in solitary, now that's the big question."

Visions of water-boarding and electro-shock vanished from Ray's imagination. Solitary didn't sound like any kind of fun, but if there were books and a television in there to help pass the time, it didn't seem like something of which to be afraid.

The aroma of frying bacon wafted down the hall, making his mouth water. He heard men talking. The dining room was close. Suddenly, the only question left in his head was if he'd still be able to chew with his mangled lips, gums, and teeth. He quickened his pace and forgot all about solitary confinement.

"It's not like the old days when the box really was a box, something you couldn't stand or sit in. Bleeding hearts think a week squatting on your haunches is too much like torture." They turned a corner, Ray one step ahead of the guard, and the hillbilly said, "Attention, Albright."

Ray slid to a stop in his flimsy Glades shoes and assumed the position against the wall. He surveyed the dining hall while Carter talked.

"How it goes, you start on the left side in front of the counter. Grab yourself a plate. See them stacked there? The tools are beside the plates. Grab yourself one package. Someone will be watching. Take two packages of cutlery and you'll find yourself in the box for a week. Walk along the counter, nice and orderly behind the guy in front of you, leading the guy behind you. Stop at the serving windows. You see them?"

Ray nodded. "Yes, sir." He saw the plates, the counter, the serving windows, and on the opposite side of the room, men wearing orange coveralls just like his, seated on benches at the tables.

"The cooks on the other side will spoon the groceries onto your plate. Once you've got your meal, you go right. Find the first table with an available seat. You don't pick and choose where you sit. First available. That's the rule. When you finish your meal, you bring your dishes and tools to the far end of the hall, show the guard. Then you can leave. Clear?"

"Yes, Sir."

"I should be getting overtime, the amount of talking I'm doing. Now go."

Under Carter's watchful gaze Ray paralleled the counter to the first serving window, a paper plate in one hand and a package of plastic cutlery in the other. A cook spooned scrambled eggs onto his plate. After two more stops he had bacon, hash browns, and toast, a plastic cup of juice in his hand and the package of utensils in his pocket.

He did exactly as Carter instructed. He turned hard right at the end of the counter and walked to the first table with a seat. Thankfully it was empty. He didn't want company and he didn't want to deal with whatever hazing ceremonies took place to newbies in Glades. It was coming. Of that he was certain, but for now the food on his plate was the only thing that concerned him. He bent over his breakfast and ate. By the end of the year runny eggs, limp bacon, and damp toast might not look quite as delicious as it did this morning, but it sure went down easy today.

A wide shadow fell across his plate.

He raised his eyes. The fear that ebbed and waned but never entirely disappeared, rushed back, filling him like glacier water.

Four individuals stood before him. Four Squats. Two First Gens and worse, a couple of Second Gens, all of them wearing hard faces, all of them staring at him with angry eyes. Up close the Second Gens looked much less human than the First

Gens. Evolution hadn't been kind to them or, maybe Second Generation Regressive Individuals looked exactly like Mother Nature intended. By today's standards though… Damned if they didn't look as though they'd stepped right out of the pages of his Grandfather's calendar—monkeys in a prison setting, dressed in convict clothing, only these guys wore orange coveralls rather than black and white stripes.

The calendar wasn't as funny as Ray remembered.

One of the First Gens stood in front of his three companions, staring down at him with a sneer on his face, a short guy almost as wide as he was tall. He looked as solid as a Jeep. Most of his hair was shaved tight to his head, nothing left but black stubble, but for some reason the Glades barber had left some of it unshorn. A fist-sized ponytail spouted out the top of the Squat's head and fell forward over his sloping forehead, covering his bulging eyes in long greasy strings like a worn-out dishrag.

Behind him one Squat massaged his fist like he was warming up for a prize fight. The other two had their arms crossed high on their chests. Ray had seen this pose before, usually in the gym change room after a game of squash, when one of the muscle-heads pretended to be checking his watch or taking a drink, and what he was really doing, he was flexing in the mirror, pumping up his arms in an effort to impress whoever was standing nearby. These guys were doing the same thing. They looked huge towering over him as they were, six hundred plus pounds of rage pressing in on him.

Several inmates watched with curiosity from nearby tables. Occasionally they glanced at a big Modern with a shiny white scalp and bushy Fu Manchu, as if waiting for him to react in some way. He sat slightly apart from the rest, elbows on the table, fingers laced. He'd torn off the sleeves of his coveralls and his huge, veiny biceps bulged. Motionless, he looked on with a mildly interested expression.

Ray wanted to turn and search for Carter, suddenly liking the hillbilly more than he had earlier in the day. He wanted to bob and weave on the bench, see if he could spot the second guard, the one at the exit at the far end of the hall. He wanted to jump onto the table and wave at one of the security cameras mounted high up in the corners near the ceiling. He wanted to run.

Any one of those actions would have made him appear weak, or worse, act like gasoline on the Squats' smoldering rage, so he did nothing but fork breakfast into his mouth. It tasted awful now, adrenaline and instant eggs coming together like poison in his mouth. He chewed slowly and manufactured an unconcerned inquisitive expression.

"You're Albright," the leader with the dishrag hair said.

Ray nodded.

"You're the killer. What I hear, you're a racist. Don't like Squats. Shot a couple of defenseless boys."

A surprising wrench of guilt twisted his stomach, making Ray shift on the bench. He remembered the way it happened, and yeah, they were defenseless all right, coming down the courthouse steps with their lawyers, big wide smiles on their flat faces after the liberal judge gave them harsh admonishment and community service.

Ray walked up the steps as they came toward him, and he pulled the pawn shop .38 out of his pocket and shot the first one in the face, then did the same to the second young Squat, both of them dead before the crowd on the steps started to scream. Defenseless all right, but no less defenseless than Dawn and Angie.

He said, "I just want to eat my breakfast." His voice was low and measured, keeping his nerves in check.

"We're defenseless." The Squat looked over his shoulder, right and left at his three buddies. "Maybe you want to try and take out four more Squats. Killlllller," stretching the word out, crooning it.

Ray picked up a strip of bacon. He popped it into his mouth

and chewed it into a mushy, tasteless pulp, the pressure on his loose tooth painful but, for the moment, insignificant. He wondered why it was okay for a Squat to call himself a "Squat," but when he did it, he was a racist. And, *why, WHY,* could nobody get it through their thick Neanderthal skulls, that race had nothing to do with killing those two boys?

On the opposite side of the table Dishrag had worked himself into a rage. Air whistled and buzzed in and out of his nostrils, stinking horribly of old food and nicotine and chunks of breakfast still stuck between his teeth.

Ray knew he needed to do something. But what? Talking wouldn't get him out of this. Ignoring them wouldn't make them go away. He'd seen movies and read novels and the hero always acted the same way in a situation such as this—hit the other guy first. Hit him hard. The hero would jump up, grab the leader by the ears and slam his face into the table. Or something along those lines. Something dramatic.

Ray remained glued to the bench.

He couldn't stand up swinging. The idea was much too foreign. He didn't fight. He analyzed situations, every situation, and his response was always considered, not a reaction.

So, what was his solution? Did he have one?

Defense.

It was the only answer he could come up with.

He would have liked a real weapon. The plastic knife would shatter against the Squat's slab of a forehead. A plate of scrambled eggs wasn't—

Dishrag slammed his fists into the table. Ray's plate jumped. The plastic cup of orange juice toppled, sluicing onto the table. "Hey, Killllller, I'm talking to you." The Squat leaned his weight on his knuckles, his sloping face only a foot away, staring through the curtain of oily hair.

Ray breathed deep, trying to slow his racing heart. He'd have to go the movie-hero route. He'd stand. Dishrag would straighten. He wouldn't want Ray leaning into him. It would make him appear diminutive, if only for a fraction of a second, so he'd have no choice but to straighten. When he did, when he was part way up, a little bit off balance, a little bit bent at the waist, that's when Ray would grab him.

Ray put his hands on the edge of the table. He pushed himself back, pushed himself upright, kept his weight forward, powering up through his legs, his heart high in his chest, pounding three times its normal speed, mouth so dry he couldn't swallow, terrified, knowing a beating or worse was seconds away, only some misplaced sense of pride compelling him to take it standing up…

"Is there a problem?"

Carter's voice.

Ray's gaze swung left. At the end of the table, the hillbilly and a second guard Ray didn't recognize looked on, Tasers in hand, the green LEDs glowing brightly. Ray looked back at the four Squats lined up in front of him. They glared hatred at him and trembled with barely contained tension.

Nobody moved.

From behind Carter, another voice said, "Albright's with me." Rufus Santos shouldered past Carter, holding a plate of breakfast. He sat down opposite Ray.

The tension bled out of the First Gen with the dishrag hair. He made a face then stepped back one pace. Behind him, the other Squats vibrated, faces red, veins in their necks and temples pumping. They turned and slouched away. Dishrag jabbed a warning finger in Ray's direction. "I'll catch up with you in a week, Killlllller."

His entire demeanor seemed to suggest his statement was a warning, but it didn't make sense to Ray. What would happen in seven days? Why a week, and not five days? Or ten? He shook his head slightly and exhaled a long, slow breath. He noticed the big guy with the bald head and the Fu Manchu tracking the crowd of Squats as they crossed the dining hall. Dishrag must have sensed Fu Manchu's scrutiny in the strange, extrasensory way Squats had. His step broke and he met Fu Manchu's gaze. "You got something to say?"

Fu Manchu looked at him with unblinking eyes. The faintly amused grin on his face widened.

Tony Carter snapped, "Get moving, Parker." Dishrag turned his angry stare on Carter.

Carter held the Taser against his chest and looked back, eyebrows raised. "Something you need to say, Parker? No? Then get out of here."

Opposite Ray, Rufus looked up from his breakfast and told Carter, "Me and Albright, we cool."

Carter nodded and walked away, none of the typical I'm-the-boss behavior Ray was used to seeing from the hillbilly. Rather, it was a cordial sort of vibe, similar to what he'd seen earlier in the day when Carter stopped him and Rufus outside Red 350.

Ray's breath came in short, bird-like sips. The shakes hit him. He rolled his hands into fists and planted them on the table, hoping his fear wasn't too obvious. After several seconds, when he felt like he could talk without trembling, he glanced expectantly at Rufus. The man looked back at him with a grin and Ray knew he hadn't hid a thing from his cellmate. He decided to acknowledge it, no point in trying to come across unaffected. He shook his head and said, "Jesus, this place." He heard the underlying hysteria in his voice and didn't care. He asked, "I'm with you?"

"I carry some weight in here," Rufus said. "You know who that was? The First Gen with the crazy hair, I mean?"

Ray shook his head.

"Joshua Parker. He's one of the main guys. Like, the boss of the Squats. You gonna have to watch out for him."

Ray looked in Parker's direction, caught the Squat and his

three friends eye-fucking him from the other side of the dining hall. "What's his deal?"

"Why's he inside? Assault. Aggravated assault. Assault with intent. He can't handle his alcohol."

"How'd they know me?"

"Cons watch a lot of TV 'cause there's nothin' else to do. You all over the news, Albright. Everybody in here knows you. Half the population wants to shake your hand. You just met the other half."

"Who's the guy with the Fu Manchu?"

Rufus looked over his shoulder. He nodded a respectful hello, then turned back and faced Ray. "Colin McTavish. A lifer. He seen it all in this place. More than once. He got a following too. He leaves everybody alone for the most part. Expects the same courtesy. He don't like Parker. Word is, he's gunning for the Squat. He just waiting for the right time."

"What's the right time?" Ray was trying hard to understand how a person decided what the right time was to go "gunning" for another individual.

"Probably when Parker isn't surrounded by all his frien's." Rufus changed the subject. "You're waiting for your appeal."

It was a statement more than a question, no real way to respond so Ray nodded and said nothing. He wondered why Rufus had sat down, how he'd managed to chase the Squats away so easily, why Carter seemed to treat him with more respect than he did everybody else.

Rufus said, "They always affirm the court's decision. The appeal process is a joke. You're on borrowed time."

"I know."

"And, you're going to the box for lying to Tyler. Probably a week."

"You're not?"

"They gonna transfer me to death row soon. My sentence was

affirmed a few weeks back." He shrugged. "Tyler didn't see much point putting me in the box."

"What did you do?"

Rufus stared at him, nothing but pockmarks on his dark face.

After a couple of seconds Ray understood. "It's not an appropriate question in here?"

A slight nod and then Rufus said, "How's your eye?"

It was Ray's turn to shrug.

"We're sitting here friendly like," Rufus said, "But you wake me up three times in a night again, you're getting another one."

"Like I said, I get up in the night. Twice for sure. We can work it out. I'll be as quiet as possible. Won't flush. But, I have to get up and you have to deal with it."

"Won't have to worry about it for a few days. You'll be in the box and I'm gonna be—"

Ray didn't want to hear about Rufus' pending fate. "Why am I 'with you' Rufus? Why are you sitting with me?"

"You stood up to me. Not very good, but you did. Then with Tyler, you kept your lip buttoned. I give you full credit for that. He knows what happened. Tyler is smart for a Squat. But you didn't say anything…" His voice faded away and then he picked up where he left off. "I'm one of those guys who'd shake your hand. A world with two less Squats is a better world. I'm gonna put the word out. Let people know how you handled yourself today. You come out of the box, maybe you have a new roommate. Someone who ain't gonna be able to run Parker off when he comes head hunting. But there will be other guys who'll make sure you don't have to go against four or five Squats at the same time. Even dead, I'll carry some weight in here. For a little while, anyway."

When Parker comes head hunting.

Like it was a foregone conclusion. Something else to look forward to. Fear shimmied up Ray's spine. He wondered how long a guy could be afraid, how long he could live with anxiety and nervousness. Hopefully it would turn to weariness and acceptance, although the way he felt right now, that seemed unlikely.

"Understand, Albright, you gotta fight your own battles. When Parker comes, you gotta deal with him. Only you. Don't hold back. Get barbaric. Hurt him bad. Someone else will handle his frien's."

Ray pushed his plate away, his appetite gone. Breakfast used to be an enjoyable event… Angie "cooking" eggs or waffles, Ray cleaning up after her, listening to her chatter about subjects that were important to a five-year-old. Now, over breakfast, he was listening to someone tell him he'd probably not die when one group came for him because he'd have protection from a different group, people who thought he'd done the right thing, shooting the teens.

The entire situation was… Ray didn't know how to describe it. He was grateful for the protection certainly, but the gratitude shamed him. What he'd done shouldn't have brought him status. His crime was his alone to deal with, however he saw fit. Unfortunately, it seemed to belong to everyone in Glades. The infamy or popularity of his actions made both the death of his family and the death of the teens, far more terrible than they already were.

He absently grazed the tips of his fingers over his swollen right eye, thinking hard, coming to the realization that the situation was out of his hands, and there was nothing he could do to change it. He said, "Rufus, why did Tyler say we'd discuss my punishment at a future time? Everybody seems to know I'm going to solitary."

"It's a head game, man. He just want you to sit around worrying." He lined up the three pieces of plastic cutlery on his plate for inspection and disposal. "Let's get out of here. Try and enjoy the day, before they lock you in the box."

Part 2

"If an injury has to be done to a man, it should be so severe that his vengeance need not be feared."

Niccolò Machiavelli

CHAPTER 20

MITCH REILLY WALKED down the corridor inside Glades Rehabilitation Facility, half a step ahead of a guard named Christopher Tanner, unsure where they were going and debating whether or not he should ask. After only five days in Glades he already knew the guards loved an opportunity to play with the Tasers on their belts.

Five days of incarceration and already worried about what would happen if he was stuck inside Glades next time he had to slip.

All thanks to Roger Olson.

The dumb-ass couldn't keep his mouth shut, and the next thing Mitch knew, the manager of the Eastern Ventures store had opened the walk in freezer and he, Lindsay, and Olson were looking into the hollow end of two machine pistols, and the uncompromising eyes of the security guards who held them. Mitch couldn't remember ever being as furious. Rage at the hopelessness of the situation and rage at Roger Olson for refusing to keep his arrogant cop mouth shut.

He cut an inquisitive look at the young guard and decided it was probably safe enough to ask an innocent question. Christopher seemed like a decent enough guy... for a screw.

Screw. In his considerable travels, Mitch had never heard the word used as a slur. As he'd never been incarcerated, he supposed it wasn't something he needed to know. Now he was imprisoned and under the control of a group of people he didn't care for, he was pleased to have the new term in his mental dictionary. It satisfied the negative feelings he held for cops, security personnel of all ilk, and the guards in Glades, without being insulting enough to warrant a tasing if it squeaked out in conversation.

He said, "Where are we going?"

Christopher ignored him.

Mitch raised his voice. "Who is it I'm meeting?"

"How would I know? And, why would I care?"

"Dick," Mitch muttered.

Christopher barked, "What was that?"

"Think! I can't *think* of anyone who would be visiting me."

Christopher fixed him with a long, knowing glare. After several seconds, he said, "You're meeting a guy named Taggart. Deputy Warden Tyler calls him Barnett. I don't know why. Taggart is a strange dude. He always wears an awful crème-colored suit and a burgundy tie. He reminds me of a neighbor we had when I was a kid. A total asshole. I hated him." Christopher's face scrunched up in apparent confusion. "That guy's name was Taggart too."

"What's he look like?"

"I really don't remember. When I think about it, I see my old neighbor." Christopher still looked puzzled. He shrugged it away and then touched his forehead above his right eye. "He's got a big scar right here. I remember that."

Mitch had never met anyone named Taggart or Barnett and after that kind of vague description, he wasn't any closer to guessing who the man was or why he'd be visiting. But, with nothing else happening in the daily, monotonous prison routine, he welcomed a change.

Christopher said, "Stop. Attention."

Mitch backed into the wall and crossed his hands in front of him, Glades protocol instinctual already. Looking over the screw's shoulder, he read the sign attached to the door in front of which they stopped: Self-Termination Monitoring Room.

What did that mean?

Christopher rapped on the door twice quickly and then a third time. Without waiting for an answer, he scanned his palm and dipped his keycard into the slot. The light bar turned green and the door slid sideways. He glanced at Mitch, dropped his gaze as though he was nervous and twitched his head sideways. He mumbled, "Enter."

Mitch stepped through the door and automatically stood at attention a second time.

A counter was attached to the wall in front of him as well as to the wall on his immediate left, forming a capital L, the short part of the letter in front of him. Above the counter, the walls were lined with several flat screen televisions. Deputy Warden Tyler leaned against the right-hand wall, the empty wall, with his arms crossed. His prominent black eyes drilled Mitch with anger and resentment.

A second man sat on a roller chair in the crook of the L and fiddled with a remote control, presumably the remote for all the televisions. The scar Christopher mentioned was a prominent white ridge running down the center of the man's forehead through his right eyebrow. He was tall, trim, and tanned. His fingernails were manicured and possibly coated in a clear polish. He looked like a game-show host. Mitch didn't know too much about expensive clothes, but he guessed the burgundy tie cost three bills, the crème-colored suit an easy grand, if money was relative to the world he left almost a week ago.

In the same way the man with the scar reminded Christopher of his old neighbor, he reminded Mitch of someone from his past, although he couldn't immediately put his finger on who that person might have been.

"So, you're Mitch Reilly," the scarred man said in a smooth baritone that was perfectly in tune with his good looks. He smiled, his square jaw revealing two rows of gleaming white teeth.

"Yes, Sir."

He kept his eyes on Mitch. "Tyler?" he said, in a much less friendly tone. "Leave us. Ensure we're not interrupted."

Tyler's lips thinned. His wide, First Gen face flushed and his eyes narrowed. "Sir," he said quietly. He pushed off the wall and shouldered past Mitch, far closer than required for the size of the room.

The man with the scar continued to stare at Mitch with an expression of mild curiosity. When the door closed, he said, "Sometimes Deputy Warden Tyler forgets who is in charge of this facility." He waved a trivializing hand. "Not your concern, Mr. Reilly. Office politics. I apologize." He hooked a second chair out from beneath the counter with the toe of a shiny black loafer and kicked it in Mitch's direction. It rolled on smooth, silent wheels until it bumped into Mitch's leg.

"Have a seat. Make yourself comfortable. You've been inside what, about a week?"

"Yes, Sir."

"What do you think of the Third Gens?"

Mitch wasn't sure how to answer so he settled for, "I wonder if prison is the best place for them?"

"They're animals. A zoo would be better. Or, we could fence off a big parcel of Florida and charge people to hunt them, like an African safari. The problem is, Florida real-estate is too expensive to make that profitable." For a moment or two, he looked disappointed. "Too bad. It would be fun, yes? I take it you've never seen them before, people like them, I mean?"

Surprised despite himself—it wasn't often people in authority made such inflammatory remarks—Mitch took a couple of seconds before responding. "No, Sir."

"That means you're getting farther away from your starting point." The man with the scar abruptly changed subjects. "I imagine you're wondering who I am?"

The hairs on the back of Mitch's freshly shorn scalp stood up, warning him to be wary.

…you're getting farther away from your starting point…

Who was this man, this stranger, and what did he know? His statement suggested he had knowledge of slipping, which wasn't problematic necessarily, except, where did his knowledge come from and why had it put Mitch in his sights? He answered cautiously, "Yes, Sir. I am wondering who you are."

And, I'd like to know what this is about, and if it wouldn't be too much to ask, why are you talking to me?

"You may call me—"

Without warning, in mid-sentence, the scarred man's voice no longer existed externally. Mitch heard, "Mr. Cole," but he heard it as a thought, rather than a spoken word. He flinched like he'd been slapped, the sensation so odd, and the name… Not "Barnett," as the deputy warden referred to him, nor "Taggart," as the young guard referred to him.

Cole.

A name from his past. A name he hadn't heard since high school. Back then Cole taught science, and you either understood the subject and he liked you, or you didn't and he dealt with you using sarcasm and insults. Mitch preferred letters to numbers, literature to physics; the dislike between teacher and student was mutual.

He studied the man opposite him, and the earlier sense of familiarity solidified. He saw his science teacher, the resemblance not identical, but close enough when he combined the man's appearance and name. Like a squirt of gasoline on dying embers, his old dislike ignited hot and red, no different than thirteen years ago in an eighth-grade science class.

A brief, knowing expression crossed Cole's face—the barest hint of a smirk—almost as if he knew his name would illicit this kind of reaction. As fast as it arrived, it disappeared. He said, "For all intents and purposes, I'm the warden of this facility. Actually, I'm the warden of several facilities." Now his voice came the normal way, externally, outside of Mitch's head. "In that capacity I stay very busy, as you can imagine, which explains why you haven't seen me before today."

"Yes, Sir."

"For today, in this room, I think we can drop the formality. Would that be all right with you?"

Mitch nodded.

"Excellent. There's no reason we can't relax and interact like equals." He didn't give Mitch a chance to respond. He said, "The deputy warden brought you to my attention. Your arrival at Glades was unconventional, was it not? He thought, correctly, that I might be interested in hearing about it."

"Sir?"

Cole's tone instantly sharpened. His eyes narrowed in anger. "You're not stupid are you, Mitch?"

"No."

"Then drop the act for both our sakes. You're a traveler. You don't belong in this world. You're in Glades because you came through a portal and failed to adequately explain how you ended up inside a locked walk-in freezer."

"There were three of us in there. It wasn't just me."

"As I understand it, Roger Olson tried to speak for you all. I interviewed him an hour ago."

Mitch frowned and tensed with irritation at the mention of Olson's name.

Cole laughed. "No love lost between you and Mr. Olson?"

Mitch gave his head a single, short shake. "The guy is all mouth."

When the freezer door opened, Olson had started yapping, trying to convince the monkey-looking security guards—people Mitch now understood were First Generation Regressive Individuals—that he was law enforcement and therefore somehow exempt from detention. The First Gens weren't in a listening kind of mood. He, Lindsay, and Olson were unceremoniously hand-cuffed and driven without explanation directly to Glades.

Cole said, "Mr. Olson told me how you used the young lady as a hostage to aid in your escape from the other world. He said it was clear your only goal was getting through the portal. Nothing else mattered." He paused and smiled his friendly game-show-host smile. "Don't be embarrassed, Mitch. Your actions weren't cowardly. I know how it is when the tinnitus rings." He paused a second time and then continued. "Olson doesn't interest me. Sixty seconds with him, and I knew you were the traveler amongst the three of you. The actions he described and the expression on your face prove me correct, yes?"

Mitch nodded again, slowly.

Close enough.

It seemed Cole had jumped to a hasty conclusion. He hadn't considered the idea that Lindsay slipped too, or that Olson had described what he thought he saw, without the benefit of all the facts, which wasn't too surprising for a cop. Mitch decided to keep Lindsay's affliction to himself, at least until he figured out what Cole wanted.

"Tell me about it," Cole said, his voice oil-slick smooth.

"What do you mean?"

Cole's photogenic good looks vanished. He slammed his fist on the counter, making the remote-control jump. "Tell me," he yelled. "Tell me what I want to know!" Panting heavily, he wiped the saliva off his lips with the back of his hand. "Are you deliberately trying to annoy me, Mr. Reilly? Neither of us have time for that, young man. You need to understand, I can turn your fortunes around or I can make you wish every day was your last. Do you believe me?"

Mitch was inclined to believe him, partially because of his sudden apoplectic rage but also because he seemed to know about slipping. "Yes, Sir. I believe you."

"Then quit trying my patience. Explain how you travel."

Mitch started slowly. "I call it slipping, not travelling. The first time it happened I was fifteen years old. It happens every year, roughly. I have no control over it."

Cole leaned forward hungrily, his friendly mask back in place. Only the livid white scar betrayed his outburst.

"I find a portal and walk through it, or into it, I guess. When I come out the other side I'm in a different world."

"Yes, yes!" Cole said, excitedly. He held the remote control tightly in his hand. All his fiddling and casual action had disappeared. "Tell me Mitch, how do you know in which direction to go?"

"The tinnitus guides me." Mitch hesitated before vocalizing something he had no way of proving. "I think portals exist all over the world. The tinnitus takes me to the closest one. That's the only thing that makes sense. It explains why a portal is never too far away when I need it. Something about me interacts with the portal I'm nearest to, and when the time is right, it opens. If they just opened randomly, everybody would know about them, and that's not the way it works."

Cole nodded several times. "Very good, Mitch. There are other pointers. Nausea. An over heightened sense of smell—"

Like what Lindsay experienced.

"—but tinnitus is the most common compass." Cole's focus switched. "How old are you, Mitch?"

"Twenty-six."

"You've travelled, excuse me, you've slipped eleven times. Have you ever slipped into the same world?"

"I don't even know if it's possible." Mitch lied easily and without qualm. Until he met Lindsay, it wouldn't have been a lie. Even now he wasn't certain why he held back, except for a nebulous feeling that giving Cole more information than necessary would not be in his best interest. The scarred man's excitement was almost voyeuristic.

And, Cole had sought him out for a reason that hadn't yet revealed itself. Until it did, Mitch figured he'd play the long game.

"Oh, it's possible, Mitch. It's not common but neither is it uncommon. The fact that you haven't is interesting, don't you think?"

"Sir?"

"How many worlds are there, Mitch?"

Mitch slumped back in his chair. He wiped a slow hand down his face, feeling his goatee's bristles, wondering why Glades personnel hadn't insisted he shave it off when the barber gave him the tight number two. He'd shave it off himself. He thought the goatee, combined with his essentially bald head, made him look ridiculous, like some dumb-ass biker or moronic action-movie star…

Like exploding fireworks, an idea burst in his head. It had something to do with Cole's last statement. Mitch stared at the ceiling, pretending to think about the number of worlds there might or might not be, and instead took a handful of seconds to pin down the beautiful, optimistic idea, before all the sparks blinked to nothingness. Cole said slipping into a world in which he'd previously lived was not unusual. Lindsay slipped into her origin world, inadvertently proving Cole's assertion. Mitch had long believed something about him interacted with portals he was close to, as he just explained. Lumped altogether these facts and suppositions meant…

Had he figured out how to make his way back to Liv?

Cole rattled his fingers tips on the counter. In a dangerously low voice he said, "Mr. Reilly?"

"I don't know how many worlds there are," Mitch said. "I've never given it much thought. I just go where the portal takes me."

"We can agree on twelve, wouldn't you say?"

Mitch agreed. There were at least twelve—his origin world plus the eleven different worlds into which he'd slipped.

"What if I told you the number was infinite, each one of these worlds differing slightly from the one next to it? Differing in subtle ways, from the basics like money and clothing to the big elements, like evolution and genetics. Imagine for a moment a picture of an atom in a child's textbook. There's a tiny ball at the center called the nucleus, which is the origin, the beginning of everything. Stemming from the nucleus are two spheres. The proton and the neutron. You've seen those diagrams, yes?"

Mitch pictured the textbook diagrams. "I've seen them."

"Imagine those three spheres are three different worlds, each connected to the other by those little stems. Stemming away from each globe is another one. Branching from those, three more. How many times could you do that? If you were to draw it on paper for instance?"

"How long is a ball of string?"

"How long is a ball of string! Excellent answer. Inaccurate, however." Cole chuckled. The sound seemed manufactured. "I agree it is impossible to pin down the string's length because the ball could be as small as a marble or as large as a boulder. Either way, there's always two ends. A more precise answer is, infinite. There are infinite worlds." He barely paused before saying, "How do you like it in here?"

Mitch shot him a dead flat stare.

Cole held both palms up near his shoulders. "I apologize. Allow me to re-phrase. What is the worst part about being here?"

Mitch didn't have to think about the answer. When the tinnitus restarted, he'd have to slip. But, there was no escape from Glades as far as he could tell, and no way of negotiating a release. Most everyone in the prison was only one exit ramp away from insane, so telling the deputy warden he'd go insane too, if he weren't released, would do no good. "I don't know when I'll get out of here. Nobody tells me anything. But I can't be locked up when the tinnitus hits."

Cole's smile turned wicked, once again fracturing his polished mask. "Tell me why," he said in the same hungry whisper as earlier.

Mitch was certain the man already knew the answer but judging from his earlier tantrum, he wanted to hear the words. "I can't explain for sure, but something in my mind would break." He pointed at his temple. "I'm afraid the tinnitus would never go away. Each time I missed a portal it would get worse until I went crazy, but somehow, inside my head I'd know what was going on. I'd also know I couldn't do anything about it." He shrugged. "I'm guessing. But it makes sense, considering how powerfully the tinnitus pushes."

Cole's wide smile was an evil spit-slick snarl. "You'd be a homeless waste of oxygen within three years." He pushed the remote control back and forth with the tips of his fingers. "On the outside, if you missed the portal three times, you'd have the freedom to walk around collecting aluminum cans and jabbering to yourself. Making normal people uncomfortable. That freedom takes some of the crazy away. Not all of it, but some. Locked in Glades, the crazy has nowhere to go. It's trapped in the same cell as you. Inside Glades, I'd be surprised if you lasted a full two years, never mind three."

In what Mitch was beginning to recognize as a habit, Cole suddenly changed the subject. He said, "Have you seen this particular room before?"

"No."

"It's the Self-Termination Monitoring Room."

"I don't know what that means."

Cole picked up the remote, studied it for a moment then pushed a button. One of the flat screens flickered to life. "Suicide watch, Mitch. But that's an ugly word, so…" He hiked his shoulders. "Inmates often become suicidal. It's not uncommon. You know that, right? We don't want them to kill themselves. Not before we have a chance to execute them, so we monitor them from this room." He nodded at the screen. "Look."

The picture wasn't high def. It didn't matter. The individual in the room was plainly visible. Webbed belts restrained his legs, torso, and arms to a gurney. His head was turned to the side, held immobile with a strap across his forehead. Thick clumps of hair were missing. A wet stain discolored his coveralls at the groin. The mattress near his mouth was soiled and something viscous dripped into a pail on the floor.

Horrified, Mitch jerked his gaze away, putting the monitor behind him. He swallowed drily.

Cole laughed at his reaction. He had a happy smile pasted on his scarred face. He said, "No audio. I apologize."

"Why are you showing me this?"

"Why indeed?" Cole thumbed the remote and the monitor went black. "That image bothered you, yes? There are others like him in Glades. One of them stabbed a fork in his eye. Another smeared feces all over his cell. He refuses to use the prison restrooms. They share your ability. I could have saved them, had I known about them."

Ability or affliction? Point of view was an incomprehensible thing.

Mitch whispered, "Oh, man."

"That's you if you don't slip."

"Oh, man."

"What would you say if I told you, I can show you a way out?"

Hope bloomed like a spring flower, but Mitch held it in check. "Nothing is free."

Cole offered up a half-assed shrug that contained no regret or sympathy. "Everything precious and valuable is dear, Mitch. Whether you're locked inside Glades or not."

The dislike and distrust Mitch felt for Cole turned to full-on loathing. "I don't have anything. No way of repaying you."

Cole wobbled his finger back and forth, pointing at himself and Mitch in turn. "What did we say about being stupid? You travel. Slip. There aren't too many individuals like you. Thousands, yes. Tens of thousands? I don't think so. I employ as many of you as possible. I need people with your talent."

"For what?"

"One thing at a time. The answer to that question is third on the list. First is the contract. A simple gentleman's agreement. I'll ensure you walk out of Glades a free man. In exchange, you'll work for me for the rest of your life."

Mitch opened his mouth, but Cole held up a hand, stopping his objections before they began.

"I believe in choices, Mitch. If you don't like the terms as I've described them, then by all means, remain here as a guest while the bureaucrats decide what to do with you. It's entirely up to you. Let me warn you, they have no experience with someone who appears," he snapped his fingers, "out of thin air. Your case confuses them. Their decision will be a long time in coming. Should I go on?"

Mitch realized he wasn't being offered a choice. Not really. The only question was, how expensive would the contract be? He supposed almost anything trumped pissing himself while tied to a gurney. "Go on," he said weakly.

Cole nodded. "Second: I don't expect you to work for free. People aren't at their best when they are coerced but not rewarded. You'll be given a generous compensation package. I could explain, but what's the expression... A picture is worth a thousand words? Would it be okay if I showed you?"

Mitch had little doubt about his "compensation package." It would be nothing more than a way of keeping tabs on him once he left Glades. It was enticement as well, in case the images on the monitor hadn't been enough. Cole had to balance the horrific with something equally as wonderful.

Cole didn't wait for an answer. He rose to his feet. He stood perhaps three feet away from the empty wall in the suicide room. He tilted his head and pointed his finger at the ninety-degree angle where the floor and wall met. His eyes narrowed and his square jaw hardened in concentration. A tiny curl of acrid smoke twisted toward the ceiling and a black dot appeared at the joint. It looked exactly like he'd pressed the tip of a lit cigar against the wall or reached out and stabbed a hole in the painted cinderblock with the tip of his finger.

Astonished and suddenly, unaccountably terrified, Mitch wet his lips.

Cole slowly and steadily raised his arm, his pointing index finger vibrating. Starting at the black dot, a vertical line drew itself on the wall. When the line had grown to the height of an average-sized man, Cole changed direction and drew a short horizontal line. Then he moved his quivering index finger downward, sketching a third black line. The three lines formed a door's unmistakable shape. Outside their perimeter, the gray cinderblocks looked as they always had. Inside the rectangle, something black and featureless had taken the cinderblock's place, something that resembled a silken sheet. It had depth and Mitch thought if he reached out, his hand would keep going and his searching fingers would never touch the shimmering cloth.

Cole's concentration was extreme. His arm moved horizontally now, from right to left, returning to his starting point.

With sudden clarity, Mitch knew he didn't want to be in the room when the four lines connected and the indistinguishable substance contained within became… what? He pushed himself away from the wall with rubbery legs until he bumped into the counter and there was nowhere else to go. A small noise of panic slipped from his throat. Was the door into the suicide room locked? His eyes leapt to the scanner.

All the LEDs burned a prohibitive red.

The black lines connected.

Agony detonated inside his head. He howled and clutched his face as a brilliant silver scream of tinnitus exploded and expanded, threatening to rupture his eardrums and spear the back of his eyes. For several excruciating heart beats, it stole his breath, and when the air came back to him, it tasted like salt and smelled of the ocean. The silver scream faded quickly, leaving him feeling small and insignificant, like a single leaf in an infinite forest and he wondered how one sense could simultaneously become so many, and then the sound was gone entirely, leaving nothing behind but an echo only he could hear. His eyes watered and his head thrummed. Trembling, he cracked open his eyes the tiniest amount. He found himself squinting at a gleaming rectangle that looked exactly like the portals he'd seen every twelve months over the last decade.

The man with the scar grinned at him. "Open sesame," he said, and waggled his eyebrows. "Impressive, no?"

Mitch stammered, "Is that aberration my way out?"

Cole rocked his head from side to side. "Yes and no. On the other side, you'll find your compensation package. Why don't you take a look?"

Mitch looked at the portal and then back at Cole, his liquid gaze a silent question.

"What you'll find on the other side is as real as anything in this room. But it's only a bubble pushing into another reality. I didn't create a portal for you to escape through, just a space big enough for you to see the possibilities. Now go. Take your time. Enjoy. I'll wait here. I can entertain myself while you're gone." He picked up the remote and aimed it at a monitor.

Mitch turned his head away, but not before he saw a man wearing a straitjacket and diapers, vomit in his lap.

CHAPTER 21

IN HIS DREAM, Ray Albright sat on the floor with dozens of brightly colored Lego blocks between his splayed legs, sticking them together exactly as his young daughter directed. Angie had a plan, elaborate and, as far as Ray could tell, indecipherable. She prattled on and occasionally Ray managed to get a word in, replying without the condescending lilt so many adults used with children. Her current focus was some young singer, a fresh-faced teen who graced the covers of all the magazines, an "artist" with a slick haircut and zero talent. When Angie paused, he said, "You know, a very famous band wrote a song about you once."

With her yellow sundress splashed on the floor around her and a Lego block in each hand, she looked up at him and asked if it was the adolescent sensation on the magazine covers.

Ray laughed. "No. The band I'm talking about has talent." He told her they made music for over forty years and the lead singer had great big lips. "The band is called The Rolling Stones. The song about you came out on an album called, *Goat's Head Soup*."

She wrinkled her nose. "Yuck."

"Yeah, yuck, but the song is great. It's called *Angie*."

She looked at him out of eyes wide with interest. "Like me?"

"Just like you. And, I happened to find a copy of the CD in a second-hand store the other day."

"Oh, get it, Daddy, please. Let's play it."

"I don't know." Ray pursed his lips and furrowed his brow, pretending to think. "You might not like it. It's not like the young kid you're listening to."

"Please, Daddy. Please. Pleeeeeese!"

Ray's heart feels as though it might rupture with the expression of awe and astonishment on her face. He dreads the day she won't be so innocent, or so easily pleased a song has her name, or filled with fascination that he knows as much as he does. In the bright glow of his daughter's wonder, tears fill Ray's eyes. He blinks them away and wakes with a sob in his throat, knowing something is different.

Something was different.

Ray swabbed away his tears with the back of his hand. Through eyes narrowed to nickel-width slits, he scanned the box and realized the only detectable change was the quality of the light inside his cell. It was brighter. Warmer. It stung his eyes. For the last week, twenty-three hours a day, he'd sat in solitary confinement, surrounded in a weak wash of sunlight that dissipated as it passed through the skylight and dispersed as it traveled down from the ceiling. By the time it hit the floor it was no longer strong enough to illuminate the corners. His single exercise hour happened randomly, sometimes in the middle of the night. More Glades head games he figured. The first time it happened, Ray asked a guard on the other side of the chain link and barbed wire, "What time is it?"

The answer he was given was both intelligent and informative: "Half past fuck-off, shit-tard."

After seven days, fresh new light was a welcome change, even if it took a minute or two for his eyes to adjust.

"You ready to play nice with others, Albright?"

Ray peered toward the sound of the voice and saw Tony Carter's tall, skinny silhouette leaning against the door jam. The fuzz on his head had filled in during Ray's week in the box. Still far too short for any real style, it poked out in every direction like a horse hair blanket. After seven days of solitary, Carter wasn't the first person Ray would have chosen to visit, but even the hillbilly was a welcome break from the saccharine television programming set on a thirty-minute loop.

Carter said tiredly, "Seven days in the box, you're already crying? Pathetic. You've gotta toughen up."

Ray knew his next thought was absurd in the extreme, but it was also undeniable: *he's not into it*. Tony Carter wanted to give him a hard time, probably thought it was expected of him, but he had just air-mailed in his taunt. There was no real feeling behind it, no depth.

Ray said, "Nice hairdo. Sir."

"You want another week, Albright? That what you want? One word from me is all it will take."

"No, Sir."

"On your feet. Let's go"

They walked in silence and when they reached Red 350, an unreasonable bubble of pleasure made Ray smile. He thought he'd talk with Rufus, ask if he could borrow one of his bestsellers, and then he was going out to the yard. He planned on parking himself beside the running oval, in a warm spot on the two-tier bleachers. He'd watch the inevitable game of hoops and listen to the muscle-heads grunt and throw dumbbells around, and perhaps he'd even crack open Rufus' novel. After a week in the box, he wasn't going to take a beautiful day for granted.

Carter said, "You're home. My job is done. Don't bother me again." He swiveled and walked away and in doing so, popped the fragile bubble.

Rufus wasn't inside Red 350, something that could easily be explained, but the man's possessions were gone too. Instead of a squeezed tube of toothpaste and half a bar of soap, a new collection of lightly used toiletries was lined up on the shelves, packaged and precise as though fresh from the pharmacy. The children-at-the-beach photo was gone. The only part of Rufus that remained was the glossy, curled-at-the-corners photo of Sofia Vergara.

Ray poked his head out of the cell. "Mr. Carter, Sir?"

Carter stopped mid-step. His head dropped to his chest and his shoulders slumped. Ray heard him release a long, tired sigh. When he turned around, he did so unenthusiastically. He raised his head and looked Ray in the eye. His usual mocking expression was nowhere in sight. In its place, Ray saw something surprising—weariness and possibly sadness. Suddenly Ray understood: Rufus told him he was being transferred to death row. He hadn't said when, but he'd hinted it would happen sooner than later.

Ray didn't want it to be true. He wanted Carter to give him a different answer…

He's in the library.

You're a worthless convict, Albright, and I don't have to talk to you.

Sofia Vergara stopped by; they're getting busy in the infirmary.

Any nonsense would do. Anything but the truth.

Reluctantly, Ray asked, "Where's Rufus? Where's his things?"

"He's gone."

"But, where—"

"He's just gone, Albright," Carter said, in a voice leaning on sympathetic. "You've got a new roommate now. A guy who checked in five days ago." He turned and strode away.

Ray called after him, "Who's the new guy?"

"Some idiot named Mitch Reilly. He's talking to the deputy warden right now. You'll meet him soon enough."

CHAPTER 22

FROM HIS CHAIR in the suicide room, Mitch tilted his head and studied the portal, trying to figure out how he was being trick-fucked.

Was it the same as the portals he was used to, despite the way it had come into being? Would it take him to a new reality, as Cole said? Would it strand him in the Space Between? He shivered, and gave Cole a side-long glance, hoping to see a hint or clue in the man's manner that might answer these questions. Cole didn't return his look. His eyes were glued on one of the monitors and the earlier unrestrained smile of enjoyment was back on his face.

Mitch looked at the portal. He frowned. His only choice was Cole's deal, and that deal started with the portal. A gurney, webbed strapping, and an endless mad scream weren't really alternatives. There was only one way to answer his unanswerable questions. He stood, sucked in a couple of deep nervous breaths and stepped into the iridescent blackness.

The odd sensation of standing on nothing gave him the usual feeling of vertigo. Clouds of swirling silver ghosts swam past, and the screams of the lost came to him on the wind. He found the portal that led out, concentrated and in what felt like a fraction of a second, he was on the other side.

All feelings of foreboding melted into the twilight surrounding him. In the quiet openness of this world, far removed from the constant noise and confinement of Glades, an almost unnatural feeling of serenity filled him. The earlier smell of the ocean explained itself; under a gentle breeze, water slapped cement pilings. A yacht, moored to the dock upon which he stood, glowed sleekly beneath a white wedge of moon. Beyond the yacht, pebbled with the reflection of a million stars, lay the ocean, empty and endless in every direction.

Mitch immediately understood his compensation package. Even for a literal individual, the symbolism was obvious. He was looking at freedom—freedom from Glades, but more. He was looking at a distant horizon and the potential to drift in any direction he wanted, whenever he wanted, in comfort and without restriction, for the first time ever.

"It looks fast." The feminine voice—smooth, cultured and British—came from behind him.

Mitch flinched and did a fast one-eighty. After a second or two he said, "You startled me. Who are you?"

"Sorry about that. I'm Heather."

Which wasn't really an answer, but then again, his question had been pointless. So naturally, he asked another, knowing the answer before the words crossed his lips… *the only place she could have come from was the portal…*

"Where did you come from?"

Heather smiled. The expression accentuated her cheekbones and deepened laugh lines at the corner of her eyes and the sides of her mouth. It came fast and easily, and suggested happiness and an enjoyment of life were her default setting. Her eye-teeth were a tiny bit large and a little too pointed. She was tall, not a waif, and she filled out the evening gown in all kinds of entrancing dips and hollows and curves and rises. Pebble-like nipples topped large breasts and strained the slippery fabric. When she fluffed the mass of high-lighted blonde hair off her shoulders to let the breeze cool her neck, Mitch saw dark roots amongst the waves.

She hooked a thumb over her shoulder toward the portal and said, "Back there. Do you like the boat?"

"Do you come with it?" He immediately winced and wanted to apologize, but she stretched out a nicely toned arm, offered her hand and threaded her fingers into his. Her touch was soft and warm and it made his heart do a cheerful little two-step. She answered him seriously, perhaps the only way to respond to such a preposterously lame line.

"If you want. Everything you see represents possibility. If you don't like the ocean, this boat could easily be an RV or a motorcycle."

And, by extension he understood, *if you don't like me, you'll be introduced to someone you will like.* So far though, he liked her just fine. He said, "I'm Mitch. Mitch Reilly."

"I know who you are."

"Why are you here?"

"He asked me to come."

"Cole?" Another foolish question. Seemed he was full of them tonight. He said, "Where are we?"

Heather shrugged. "We're at the beginning, Mitch. This place is the opposite of the turmoil and stress you've known your entire life. History doesn't exist here. From this world, you can move forward, on your terms, without the influence of countless other agendas."

Not exactly true. Cole's liberty wasn't free. He wasn't giving all this away for free.

Her somber tone disappeared. Her wide eyes sparkled with interest and excitement. "Let's look at the boat."

"You sound like a *Price is Right* model."

She laughed. "Sure, why not?" She made the familiar arm gesture and said in recognizable game-show patter, "This thirty-eight-foot Beneteau comes fully equipped with two..." Clearly not a person afflicted with overwhelming self-consciousness, she cracked up and laughed with unembarrassed pleasure. "I can't do it. I can't do the impression."

"It wasn't terrible," Mitch said, this lady dressed for an evening out confusing him, taking away some of the smarter things he might have said.

"Come on, let's look. It's beautiful. Kind of romantic too, don't you think? A boat on the water. The night and the stars."

He said nothing.

"What?" She slapped his forearm lightly. "Don't tell me you're afraid of an itty-bitty word like 'romantic.'"

"Maybe a little."

"I didn't think big tough biker types were afraid of anything."

He wiped his palm down his goatee. "I've been meaning to shave it off," he said, a trace defensively.

"Okay."

There was laughter in her voice and when he looked, the sparkle in her eyes and the mischievous grin on her face let him know she was teasing him. He couldn't help smiling along.

She pulled gently, and together they walked the length of the dock, her hip bumping against his, raising the hairs on his arms and shortening his breath. Her gown rippled like water with every step. He smelled a trace of cedar and bluebells and rose. There were questions he knew he should ask—she never did explain where she came from, for instance—but the answers seemed unimportant, and as quickly as he thought of the questions, they blew away in puffs of warm wind.

Heather said, "All we need is music and wine to make the evening complete."

"I'm more of a beer guy," he said. "But I get your meaning."

"Budweiser though. None of that self-important micro-brew, right?"

In her high-class British accent, Mitch wondered if she

understood the contradiction. "A can of cold domestic and I'm happy. And, a steak on the grill."

"I prefer wine, but a steak on the grill?" She closed her eyes and moaned enthusiastically. "Nothing better. What about the music? I'll listen to just about anything except pop. Awful earworm songs. They have no substance."

"Can't argue with that." He shrugged. "I listen to old country. Brad Paisley. The guy is a genius with a guitar."

"Not old. Classic," she said with a smile. "I love Brad Paisley's vibe. He doesn't take himself too seriously. Irreverent is the word, I think. *Southern Comfort Zone* always makes me cry. Do you play?"

"Badly. After the first time I saw him in concert, I took lessons. They didn't stick."

"I'm sure you're not as bad as you think."

He was inexplicably happy that Heather guessed he was a better "musician" than he suggested. He had a weak, ten-song repertoire but didn't own a guitar of his own—too large and cumbersome to slip with—so he couldn't practice as much as he would have liked.

As they walked, he dragged the fingers of his free hand along the hull of the boat, the gel coat glassy and smooth under his touch. He raised his fingers to his mouth and tasted the salty residue left behind from the last time the yacht sailed. Suddenly, the differences between where he was half hour an ago and where he was now, became a staggering assault. "This isn't real," he mumbled, knowing it was, knowing too that everything around him existed in the same way a set on a stage existed. Reality and fiction simultaneously. He understood what Cole meant when he said he'd opened a bubble into another world.

They stopped walking and Heather faced him. "What am I, Mitch? A hallucination? In an infinite number of worlds, is it so hard to imagine the freedom you crave with the woman you dream about, doesn't exist?"

The water washed the hull of the boat and the ropes securing it to the dock creaked. In the distance, a seagull squawked. Heather waited in silence, giving him time, he supposed, to think about the vastness of her question. His thoughts, however, were much closer to home. Already his attraction to her ran deeper than her appearance. He liked the way she switched off her casual attitude and turned serious when the weirdness around him edged toward overwhelming. How did she know he needed that moment of seriousness, and how did she know the ensuing silence would be neither awkward nor strained? Finally, he said, "How did Cole know I'd like..." His voice trailed away.

"How did he know you'd like me?"

He nodded, relieved he didn't have to say the words.

"I don't know." She shook her head. "He makes things happen. He's a facilitator. That's one of his jobs. He knows happy people do better work. He knows me. He knows you. He had an idea we'd get along. Like Match Maker dot com. Seventeen points of compatibility. He wasn't wrong, was he?"

"I don't think so."

"I'm glad."

"Heather? What is it he wants me to do?"

A shadow crossed her face and sadness filled her eyes. She put a hand on his cheek and stretched up on her toes and softly kissed his lips...

...and son-of-a-bitch he thought his heart would beat out of his chest, the little two-step a distant memory now...

"I'm sorry, Mitch. That's not something I can explain. You'll have to discuss it with him." She released his hand and walked down the narrow bridge leading from the dock to the boat. Somewhere in the back of his head he remembered it was technically called a "gangplank," as if that mattered or made any difference at this particular time. When she reached the deck of the boat, she turned and faced him. In a voice that held the same fun as a few moments ago, she said, "Tonight is not about work."

She started to sing the chorus to *Southern Comfort Zone*, swaying in a way that made him think of gently rolling waves. "You probably tell all the girls you don't like to dance, right?" She flashed her playful grin. "I bet I could talk you into it."

With the tips of her fingers, she brushed the gown's straps off her shoulders. It dropped to her waist, hung for a second and then whispered down her legs, past a red gemstone nestled comfortably in her navel. It puddled around her ankles, nothing left now but two insubstantial strings on each hip holding a miniscule pair of white panties in place. She beckoned with a crooked index finger. "Dressed like this, I might get cold. Come and warm me up."

The mischievousness was gone. In its place, he saw a third facet of her personality, a blend of seriousness and fun that told him their time together was important and it mattered but it could be silly too, and if either of them got tangled and tied up in sheets, or experienced a foot cramp, or dinged an elbow into the headboard, laughing together was equally important.

Mitch released a low primitive groan. Without conscious thought, he walked toward her on watery legs, nothing in his mind but Heather and the yacht, all polished wood and gleaming stainless steel. Inside he knew he'd find a stateroom with mirrors, supple fabric, dim light, and cool sheets. And Heather would be energetic and willing, a fantasy come to life.

She came forward to meet him, the heels of her shoes clicking on the fiberglass deck of the boat, the sound as sharp as snapping fingers...

...snapping fingers...

Mitch paused mid-step.

Not much made sense on this night, but really... high heels on a rough-hewn dock? On smooth fiberglass? On polished teak? He blinked a couple of times, as if trying to clear his eyes of dust or smoke or some other contaminant.

This compensation package—his mind said it with heavy

sarcasm—was too much. An extravagance such as the Beneteau might have been perfect for someone else, particularly if the future he faced was as bleak as Mitch's. But, aside from having to slip every twelve months, Mitch was content with an empty horizon and the meager belongings he carried in his pack. Perhaps he'd simply grown used to the lifestyle, such as it was, but other than the first few weeks when he had no money and no place to live, he enjoyed seeing what lay around the next curve in the road.

And, Heather... She was certainly the girl of his fantasies, and he sensed with time she might become more than that, but in the here-and-now, she wasn't the girl of his dreams. There was a difference. When he dreamed, it was Liv who came to mind and what it might be like to spend the future with her, without the hindrance of an expiration date.

Once again Cole had jumped to a hasty conclusion. He oversold. Rather than convince Mitch, this compensation package only raised the level of his earlier skepticism. What did Cole want that warranted a payment this rich?

Mitch knelt in front of Heather and picked up her dress. The fabric smelled of her woodsy, flowery perfume. He straightened, his eyes slowly traveling the length of her legs until they came face to face with the thin film of white silk and the soft mound beneath. His breath came in jagged hitches. He fought a near impossible urge to hook his thumbs under the strings, slide the panties off the rise of her hips and pull her into him.

Instead, he pulled the dress up, covering her. As much as he wanted to feel her softness and hardness, to taste her and smell her and listen to her murmur his name, he held back. It wasn't nobility or loyalty. A guy didn't say, "No," to a fantasy in favor of a dream, not when the dream had little chance of becoming reality. Rather, an intuitive certainty told him that saying "Yes," meant Cole would own him from that moment forward.

"I'm sorry, Heather." His voice rang raw with disappointment and desire. "Put your dress on."

The first hint of self-doubt he'd seen filled her eyes and showed in the way she nibbled her lower lip. In a whisper she said, "It's not me, is it?"

"Oh man. It's not you, Heather. It's definitely not you." He swiveled and walked the long walk back to the portal before he changed his mind. He crossed the Space Between, landing in the suicide room moments later. It was empty, but Cole hadn't bothered to turn off the monitors. They were alive with horrific visions of inmates in straitjackets or restraints, of padded walls and unidentifiable stains. Again, the contrast between where he was now and where he'd just come from was extreme and, Mitch guessed, quite deliberate.

The portal shrank rapidly, from the outside corners into the middle. Within seconds the rip in reality healed itself. The only traces of the world Mitch had left behind were memories—the smell of the salt chuck, the soft buzz of the wind and waves deep inside his head, and regret that he and Heather hadn't.

CHAPTER 23

THE MAN MITCH knew as "Cole" and Deputy Warden Tyler knew as "Barnett," sat in a gushy leather chair on the business side of Deputy Warden Tyler's desk—Tyler's rightful side—and studied the insides of his eyelids. Occasionally he tapped his lips with a contemplative finger. Tyler sat opposite him in the rigid chair meant for guests and in a passive-aggressive rage, loudly slurped hard candies. He didn't like being a subordinate in his own office, something of which Barnett was aware, and something about which Barnett didn't give a fuzzy rat's ass. There were more important things on his mind. Like the manner in which Mitch Reilly walked away from his compensation package.

It was maddening.

It made no sense, particularly given the young man's short-term future and the fact that he was a person who moved in straight lines, curious to see what lay over the next horizon. He was a drifter. Cole (Barnett) believed this of Reilly after their first and only conversation. The proof of his belief lived in the fact that Reilly never ended up in the same world twice. Cole also believed Reilly when he said he didn't know if returning to a previous world was possible. Straight lines meant each successive portal spit him out a little farther away from his starting point, into a world slightly different from the one he left behind. One difference on top of another logically meant he was getting farther away from the beginning, not closer. The idea he could go back probably never entered his mind. Had he been a home-body who moved in circles, there was a halfway decent chance he'd have looped back and ended up in a world in which he lived before, possibly even his origin world. In that case, the freedom Cole had shown him would have looked much different.

But, Reilly wasn't a home-body. He was a drifter.

He should have jumped—leapt with both feet and a yell of elation—at the wide-open freedom the yacht represented. Picturing Heather sunning herself on the front of the boat wearing nothing but a smile and the bottom half of a very small bikini, should have sealed the deal. Unfortunately, like so many travelers, Reilly was determined to do it the hard way. Now Cole had to find a different pressure point, which was also a pain-in-the-ass. Not impossible, but time-consuming: a different means of manipulation required an adjusted train of thought…

…a train of thought Deputy Warden Tyler interrupted, noisily crunching the hard candy in his mouth.

Barnett (Cole) opened his eyes and looked down. The three lower buttons barely held the fabric of his shirt together against the rhythmic rise and fall of his belly. A faded orange stain, spaghetti sauce maybe, discolored his otherwise white shirt. He adjusted his burgundy tie, hiding the ugly spot. Then he met Tyler's gaze, the First Gen staring at him out of his protuberant black eyes, his expression both impatient and irritated.

In his nasal voice, Barnett said, "You want to get down to business?" He shrugged up his eyebrows. "Is that it, Tyler?"

Tyler said nothing, just kept giving him the hard, unblinking stare, which might have worked well on the inmates, probably intimidated most of them, but Barnett knew Squats didn't blink much anyway. More importantly, he had hundreds of years of practice dealing with people who wanted to prove they couldn't be pushed around. It wasn't difficult shattering that illusion. He said, "Are the three boys I arranged meeting all your needs, Tyler?"

Tyler deflated and dropped his eyes to his shoes.

Barnett allowed himself a thin smile. "What about here in Glades? Two months ago, you mentioned a class of new-hires. How are they working out?" He twined his fingers together and rested his hands on the rise of his belly. He told himself to listen (and care) to the litany of complaints the deputy warden was about to unload. Tyler frequently needed to be reminded of his subordinate status, but along with discipline, a good supervisor needed to keep his employees on side by pretending to listen and care.

"Christmas is coming," Tyler mumbled without looking up. "It's a bad time of year in a prison. Everyone gets antsy. They know what they're missing on the outside."

"Stop playing the carols over the PA system."

"A psychologist assured me that, at a low volume, the music provides a positive, soothing message."

"Is that the reaction you're seeing?"

"Not really."

"Stop playing the carols."

"The carols aren't the problem," Tyler said sharply. "We're at capacity. It's crowded. It gets on people's nerves. There's hourly arguments and daily fights. This time of year, what with sick days and holidays, we're always understaffed. One class of new graduates won't make any difference."

Barnett had already lost interest. He said, "I need to see Mitch Reilly's Inmate's Possession Bag."

"Why?"

"Now, please."

Tyler stood with a loud, long sigh. He reached across his desk and pushed a button on the intercom. He told whoever answered to have Tony Carter bring in the bag. After hitting the disconnect button he said, "What's going on with Reilly?"

"Last time you asked that question, I refused to answer. Why do you assume I'll answer this time?"

Tyler said, "Last time he wasn't an inmate in my facility. Now he is."

"Why should that make a difference?"

Someone knocked on the door. One second later it swung open and Tony Carter walked in with the bag slung over his shoulder. When he saw Barnett his face blanched and his step faltered. He recovered quickly, marched forward and lay the bag on the desk, smoothing it out lengthwise before stepping back and shooting a hopeful glance at the door out of the room.

"Stay where you are, Mr. Carter," Barnett said. He looked back and forth between the two men on the opposite side of the desk. "You haven't pawned any of his belongings, have you?"

Carter flushed.

"Relax," Barnett said. "In most situations, I don't care. But, in Reilly's case it might be important."

Tyler said, "Nothing is missing from Reilly's bag. Nothing is missing from Roger Olson's or Lindsay Thompson's bag either. Given your interest in anyone who came out of the Eastern Ventures store, I thought special care should be taken with their belongings."

"Very wise, Tyler." Barnett paused. He washed a palm across his head from front to back, felt the greasy ridge of the scar, and then wiped his hand dry on the fabric of his shirt beneath his arm. "Mr. Reilly is being uncooperative. Since he is an inmate in *your* facility, as you say, can I count on you to make him more malleable?"

Tyler gave him a blank look.

"I want his spirit in the sewer. Ride his ass. Wear him out. When I meet him in a week's time, I want him begging for a change."

"I can make his life uncomfortable if that's what you're asking. What about the other two? Olson and Thompson?"

"I have no interest in them."

Tyler's thick black eyebrows came together above his bulging eyes, his wide face narrowing into a frown. "They were brought here per your instructions. They weren't arrested by 'real' police. They aren't in the system. If you aren't interested in them, why are they here? They're taking up space and draining resources."

"Get rid of them." Barnett shrugged. "It makes no difference to me. Reilly is the only one I care about."

Tyler turned to Carter. "You know inmate 52-203, correct, Mr. Carter?"

"Mitch Reilly. Yes, Sir."

"Find a reason to tase him. Then throw him in the box for a week. He'll be ready for a change by the time he's released."

"Yes, Sir."

Barnett held up a hand. "Hang on. That solution is not nearly imaginative enough." He tapped his lips with his finger. After a moment of thought he said, "You're going to release Olson and Thompson, correct?"

"If you don't want them, I don't want them," Tyler said.

"Before you do, ensure Reilly knows they're being released—"

"Olson and Reilly aren't friends. They can barely tolerate each other, as far as I can tell."

"I realize that," Barnett said. "But, friendly or not, I suspect it would be demoralizing for the young man to discover they were released and he was not, no?"

Dutifully, Tyler and Carter nodded in unison.

"Don't tase Reilly. Tase someone he's close to. A hard-case like Reilly shakes off such treatment. He gets angry and banks it. Ultimately, he becomes less pliable. Hurt one of his friends, on the other hand? Far more effective than hurting the man himself. After that, give him some time in the box to think about it."

Tyler said, "He's only been in Glades five days. I doubt he's friendly with anyone."

"Watch him," Barnett said. "See who he sits with. See who he talks to. By the end of the day you'll have an idea. If he's a complete loner and there's nobody, tase his cellmate. Chances are good Reilly will bond with that individual before anyone else. Do it before lights out if possible, and make sure Reilly sees it happen. It's more impactful if it happens in front of him, rather than him hearing about it second hand." He looked at Carter. "Go."

With an expression of relief, Carter nodded and left the room in a hurry. The door slammed shut and Barnett said, "Is there anything else on your mind, Tyler?" *Listen and care.*

Thankfully, the deputy warden shook his head so Barnett said, "In that case, give me the room."

"It's my office."

Barnett waited in silence until Tyler stood, pivoted and walked out, muttering a not quite silent curse just before the door shut behind him.

Barnett (Cole) smiled his thin smile.

He withdrew Mitch Reilly's worn and dirty backpack from the Inmate's Possession Bag. One by one he removed the items it contained. Sunglasses, a bottle of aspirin and a bottle of allergy medicine, a couple of old pocket books with inscriptions from Mom and Dad on the blank pages. He opened the wallet and studied two photos contained back to back inside a plastic folder, milky with age. One photo was a sepia-toned snapshot of an older couple standing in front of a cruise ship. Cole dismissed it with barely a glance. The second photo was far more interesting. It was a professional grade portrait of a young lady wearing a black cap and gown. He studied it for several long seconds before sliding it out of the folder and reading the message on the back, three short, loopy sentences written in an obviously feminine hand.

Yay! Finally done! Luv, Liv!

She dotted the I in her name with a tiny heart.

Cole put the photo on the desk in front of him and tapped it a couple of times with his finger. He allowed the smile to widen. He fanned the pages of both books until a birthday card fell out of one and a Valentine's Day card fell out of the other. Both cards had notes inside, written in the same loopy handwriting as on the back of the graduation photo. As well, each card contained a photo of the same young lady. In one, her blonde hair was tied back, away from her face. She wore athletic clothes and a huge smile. Sunglasses sat on top of her head and a large medal hung around her neck on a wide, striped ribbon.

Cole mumbled, "Sporty." He flipped the photo over and read aloud, "Thanks for all your support. Luv Liv." Again, she dotted the I with a heart.

In the second photo Liv hugged the hood of a raspberry red car that twinkled in the sun. She wore the same happy smile and the same sunglasses, only this time they covered her eyes. On the back of this photo she'd written, *My first baby! Luv, Liv.*

"It seems there's a young lady in Mister Reilly's life." Cole pulled the backpack to him. All he needed was a starting point. A hint. One way or another, Mitch Reilly would work for him, whether the young man liked the idea or not.

"Where does the lovely Liv call home?" Cole asked the empty room.

CHAPTER 24

RAY WATCHED TONY Carter turn a corner and disappear. A sudden heaviness pushed down on his heart, surprising him. In the mere hours he'd known Rufus, the man had slugged him in the face, and threatened worse. There was no reason to feel this depth of sadness, except Rufus was the first human connection he made when he was admitted to Glades. Rufus protected him and gave him begrudging, albeit misplaced, respect. Possibly these were reasons enough, Ray didn't know, but he was certain his unhappiness was real.

He stared down the length of the empty hallway, until it made no sense to do so any longer, then swiveled and entered Red 350. He plopped onto the lower bunk with a heavy sigh, propping his elbows on his knees and cupping his chin in his hands. As punishment, he wasn't sure if there was any value in solitary confinement. It definitely gave him time to think, although his lie to the deputy warden (the transgression that landed him in the box in the first place), never crossed his mind. Instead he thought about Dawn and Angie, and he thought about the drunk teens who killed them, and he wondered if their families were suffering like he was.

His eyes roamed around the tiny, gray cell. Stripped bare of all comforts and decoration, the room offered nothing hopeful or positive. How had he ended up in this place? Justice had not been served. Vengeance had been, but the gratification he should have felt never materialized. Without the relief of justice or the satisfaction of vengeance, what had he achieved?

Dawn and Angie were gone. The teens were gone. Rufus was gone. Each of them left a rip in the fabric of the universe when they "left." In Angie's case, someone who was young and innocent and pure, the rip was enormous. It was smaller for Rufus, but in both cases, it wasn't something that could be mended. The proof lay in the deep, aching sorrow he felt for Angie's loss, and the more surface-based sadness he felt for a cellmate he barely knew; sorrow and sadness that would never go away.

Gradually he became aware of the buzz of human activity—a clanging steel door, the high notes of a distant television, indistinct voices that came from nowhere and disappeared into the same place, the scuff and whisper of footsteps on polished linoleum, growing louder and then fading...

...except one set of footsteps didn't come and go.

The light coming through the open cell door disappeared.

Ray washed his hands down his face, hoping to wipe away some of the grief and guilt he knew he wore like stage makeup. He raised his head and met the eyes of an individual he'd never seen before, a big guy with a fresh number two and a dirty blonde goatee, a guy with thick forearms and wide shoulders that filled the doorway.

Hands on knees, Ray pushed himself upright with a grunt. "I guess you're Mitch Reilly?"

"I guess I am."

"Carter told me you lived here now. You joined us five days ago?"

Mitch said, "Seems longer than that." He tilted his head and narrowed his eyes. "Do I know you? You seem familiar, like I've seen you before."

"I don't think so," Ray answered. "I've got a good memory for faces."

"You're sure, huh? On the outside with a young girl? Brown hair, too much eye makeup? A jewel in her face, above her lip?"

"Don't know anyone like that. Sorry." Ray shook his head. "Something I've been wondering about, Mitch. Who checked you in? Was it Carter and Tyler? Did Carter tase you?"

A grin that didn't extend to his eyes flashed fleetingly across Mitch's face. "Twice. And, he sucker punched me too."

"Same with me. Must be part of the whole check-in procedure. Written on page ten of their manual, something like that. Tase each new inmate twice. Sucker punch him once."

"Carter will get his."

"Tyler's the driving force."

"I know. But, that gap-toothed dumb-ass enjoys his job a little too much."

Ray managed a weak smile. "He certainly does. If you want a piece of him though, the line is long." He paused. "It was good to meet you. I'm heading outside." He thought he'd get a book from the library, there were plenty to choose from, and then proceed with his original plan. He'd sit in the sun and read because it was calming and reassuring and sometimes getting lost in a good book could soften the edges of all those unrepairable rips.

"You could use some sun."

"It's nice out, then? I've been in solitary for a week."

"Isn't it always nice in Florida?" Mitch absently rubbed an ear. "I haven't been outside today. I just came from a meeting with the warden."

On his feet now, ready to leave, Ray paused. For the sake of saying something he said, "Tyler?"

"Not him. I'm talking about the head guy. Cole."

Ray perked up. The conversation had suddenly gone from ordinary to interesting... new facts and information. New data to chew on for a few minutes. When a person counted minutes—boredom making him wish they ticked by faster and a date with the firing squad making him wish they lasted longer—every one of them mattered. "I didn't know there was someone other than Tyler."

"I got the impression Cole isn't around much. He's definitely the boss, from what I saw. He slung orders and everyone hopped to."

"What did he want with you?"

"It's a little hard to explain. I don't belong in here—"

Ray interrupted him with a noisy, dismissive blast of air. "Eight hundred inmates. Not one of them belongs in Glades."

This time when Mitch grinned, he did so with depth. Ray caught a glimpse of the person he was on the outside, a young guy who was quick to smile, who didn't look as rough around the edges as Ray first imagined.

Mitch said, "I know how it sounds. But, I'm not from around these parts. I was arrested…" he hit "arrested" hard with sarcasm, "… under a strange set of circumstances. This Cole guy says he can get me out."

"What's the problem? Why are you still here? If you have a chance to get out, take it. Go."

"There are conditions. Cole wasn't specific about them. I think he wants me to stew for a while, so when he sees me again, I'm more eager to accept his terms."

"They do like their head games in this place," Ray said. "They're going to execute me in a year. I can't think of a single condition that would prevent me from doing what this Cole guy wants, if it meant I'd get out of here before then."

"They're going to execute you? Why are you in general population, not on death row?"

"A jury found me guilty, but my sentence hasn't been affirmed."

Mitch looked confused. "What?"

"You know," Ray said impatiently. This wasn't a subject he liked talking about. "My file has gone to three judges not connected to the original case. They look it over and decide if the I's were dotted and the T's crossed. If they were, they'll affirm my sentence. That's when they move me to death row." His voice faded to nothing. There was an expression of complete incomprehension on Mitch's face. Ray said, "You don't know how the system works?"

"I told you, I'm not from around here."

"The point is, technically I don't belong on death row yet. And, if it was me, I'd get out if I could."

"This Cole guy, there's something not right about him. I might be better off inside." Mitch vigorously rubbed one ear. "The noise in this place, it gets inside your head."

I might be better off inside? Quite a statement, Ray thought. He said, "It's like living beside a busy road." He waved a hand in the air above his head. "The drone disappears after a while."

Mitch traced the edges of his goatee with his thumb and forefinger, looking more worried than convinced.

CHAPTER 25

MITCH SAT ON the second tier of the bleachers alongside the track, panting. He swabbed sweat out of his eyes with the heel of his hand. "I ran the track twelve times. That's three miles."

Ray asked, "How long is a half marathon?"

"A little better than thirteen."

"Miles?"

He sounded incredulous, a little like Mitch sounded when Liv first told him about the half marathon she planned on running in February.

When it came to her sport, she spoke a foreign language, as far as Mitch was concerned. She talked about her long Sunday runs, her split times, her best half and she tried talking Mitch into running with her. It was all a little baffling. He smiled at her and said, "I don't think so. I might chase you, looking like that in those tights. That's the only running I'm doing."

She got a kick out of that, said something sarcastic about how sexy she must look after ten sweaty miles.

"Ten miles? You're not gonna make it out of the house. Go put on some high heels."

"High heels and running clothes? That doesn't make sense."

"It doesn't have to," he told her.

Now that he was on her side of the fence, talking the runner's talk as though he was an experienced athlete, never mind the three miles nearly killed him, he thought she would have enjoyed seeing him wheezing, soaked in sweat. He'd need every day of the next two months to train if he wanted to run his half on the same day as Liv ran hers.

Ray said, "You're going to circle the track fifty-three times? How will you keep count?"

Mitch didn't answer immediately. His eyes were on Roger Olson, the cop steaming toward the bleachers through shimmering waves of heat, long steps across the well-groomed grass in the center of the track. He looked like he always did. Determined, angry, and abrasive. He weaved through the weight lifters and skirted the edges of the basketball court where Colin McTavish, captain of the "skins," directed his team with precision. Skins might have been a liberal use of the word. Mitch couldn't see a single man on the court who wasn't inked, some of them enough it appeared they were wearing shirts. McTavish's back was covered in a leering blue skull, the size of which made Mitch wince. He didn't care for needles and guessed the tattoo would have taken the artist days to draw and color.

Mitch said, "When the time comes, the half will take me two hours. Maybe longer. I'll do it between breakfast and lunch, before it gets too hot. Hopefully there won't be any double claxons." He fully expected Glades' administrators to ring the double claxon just to wreck his race, but maybe they'd prove him wrong. "You can keep track for me, you don't mind? After the first five laps, I'll lose count."

Ray shrugged. "Why not." He dropped his eyes to the pages of his book. "It's not like I have anything better to do that day. When are you planning on running it?"

"February." He didn't know why running his race on the same day Liv ran hers felt important. Maybe it was just a way to stay connected to her a little while longer. He was doing his best to keep her memory close but, confined in Glades, it felt like the distance between them was growing. He wasn't sure how that was possible, considering she existed in a different reality. On the outside a guy could throw himself into his work, or drink himself into a coma, or get obsessive with a hobby—anything to keep his mind busy until the loneliness shrank to something manageable. Inside though? There wasn't enough to do and when the memories came, the distance increased.

Olson came to a stop in front of them, grass stains on the toes of his canvas shoes. He planted his fists on his hips. Staring hard at Mitch he said to Ray, "You, bookworm. Get lost. I need a word with Reilly."

Ray looked up in surprise. Then he nodded, folded the corner of a page over and made to stand.

Mitch dropped a hand onto his shoulder, gently holding him in place. "His name is Ray. He's not going anywhere." In the five days they'd been inside Glades, Mitch and Olson had barely spoken. Mutual animosity kept them apart, which suited Mitch fine, but if Olson wanted to change the status quo, slinging orders around wasn't the way to go about it. It wasn't something Mitch felt he needed to put up with. "You got something to say, chief, you can sit your ass down and be sociable or you can take a walk."

They stayed that way for several seconds, staring at each other, neither of them backing down until Olson finally shook his head. With a look of contempt on his face he said, "You know what? Forget it." He swiveled and stormed away.

"Hey chief?" Mitch called after him, "Don't go away mad. Just go away."

Olson's shoulder's tensed and his step broke. Mitch thought he might turn around and they'd end up exchanging more than harsh words, but after the slight hesitation, Olson kept walking.

Ray asked, "What's his problem?"

"We were arrested at the same time. He doesn't like me

because he thinks I'm a criminal and therefore a leech. I don't like him because he's a cop, which means he never gives anyone the benefit of the doubt. I probably wouldn't be in here if he listened, kept his mouth closed when I asked him to."

Olson was halfway across the mid-field when he skidded to an abrupt stop. He shook his head. Suddenly animated, he spun on his heels and came striding back, chin thrust forward, hands clenched into fists.

Mitch put what he hoped was an innocent, enquiring look on his face.

Olson said, "You have to make everything difficult, don't you? You can't help yourself." He sat down on the second tier, an arm's length away. "I guess you figure I'm responsible for this." He waved an arm from right to left, a gesture that took in all of Glades Rehabilitation Facility. "That if I stayed quiet we wouldn't be here?"

"I've walked through portals eleven times, chief. I've never been in jail before. Not once. You're the one who can't help yourself. You're always talking. Carrying on like you know everything, even when you don't know jack. Now and then you ought to listen. We would have made it out of the freezer just fine. So, yeah, I blame you."

"We would have froze to death."

"Maybe. Maybe not."

Ray said, "Portals?"

Both Mitch and Olson ignored him.

"I don't belong in prison. I'm an officer of the law. I put losers like you away."

Mitch wearily scrubbed a hand down his face, remembering he needed to shave off the goatee. He said in a worn-out voice, "I know. I'm a loser, you're the good guy. You've never sped. You've never blown through a red light and then flashed your badge to make the ticket go away. You've never punched some drunk in the mouth just because the uniform meant you'd get away with it."

Olson raised his voice. "I don't belong in here. I want out."

Mitch made a show of scanning the yard, turning his head slowly from one side to the other, taking in the inmates between himself and the fence-line. "Nobody else wishes they were on the other side? We're in prison. Or didn't you get the lecture during check-in? Getting out isn't on the agenda."

"You mean the, 'How many people have escaped lecture?'" Olson said. "Of course I got it. What are they going to tell us? Breaking out is easy?"

Mitch said nothing.

"Cops and corrections," Olson said. "Two different careers, but there's some overlap. We both have training in human psychology. The guards like to rattle on about how it's impossible to break out of Glades. They believe it absolutely. They look at the wall, and say, 'Escape is impossible,' because nobody has ever done it. They're so proud of it, they've become complacent. Think about this," he tapped his temple several times with his index finger, "The wall is the least logical way out of here. Look around. Really look. While your boyfriend—"

"Ray."

"—reads, and you waste time running laps, you know what I'm doing? I'm looking for weaknesses."

Mitch laughed, certain Olson was trick-fucking him, but something in the cop's expression cut him short. "You're serious?"

Olson gave him a short nod.

Escape. Mitch let the thought hang there for a moment, enjoying the fantasy of putting Glades in the rear-view mirror, of being long gone before Cole returned for his second visit. Despite the heat of the day, cold goose flesh crawled up his arms. His mouth went dry.

Cole.

The man wielded impossible power. The way he crafted a portal so casually still made Mitch shiver. Witnessing that would have fractured most people's minds, would have fractured Mitch's, if he hadn't seen identical portals before. It made him wonder what else Cole could do, if the man applied himself. Worse, with that kind of power in the tip of his finger, what could he possibly require of Mitch? Why did he need someone who could slip, when portals and their use was something with which he was so obviously familiar?

Mitch looked across the yard, through the chain link fence to the outer wall with the impossible-to-climb roll of aluminum at the top. Screws with rifles stared down from the guard towers while slobbering German Shepherds slept in the shady spots beneath. It wasn't just Cole that made him nervous. When he tilted his head in just the right way, he heard a faint mosquito-like buzz he shouldn't have heard for another eleven months. Hopefully it was only his imagination. If it wasn't... With an effort he controlled a second, stronger tremor. He said, "You want to sit here and dream about escaping, have at it. I have one or two real problems to think about."

"That's right. I forgot. It's all about you."

Mitch blew out a frustrated puff of air. "You only think you know me. Why are we talking?"

"In less than a week, I think I've found some holes. It's part of my training. Observation. Tactics—"

"Yeah, yeah. Psychology. You're brilliant."

"Guards develop bad habits over time. Shortcuts and complacency are weaknesses that represent opportunity. If I can get us out of here, can you..." Olson paused, stared at the ground and when he eventually spoke again his voice had changed. He sounded uncertain, even frightened. "That opening, through the freaky dead space—"

Mitch rolled his hand several times. He glanced quickly at Ray, who held his book in one hand, a finger marking his place. His eyes were narrowed, his forehead wrinkled into a question.

"Can you get to another one?"

Mitch said, "I can get to one. But it's not as easy as saying, 'Open sesame.'" *Unless your name is Cole.* "There's a little more to it than that."

Ray said, "What are you guys talking about?"

"I'll explain later, okay Ray?"

"Fine. Later. I don't know about this freaky dead space stuff, but it doesn't matter, does it? There are cameras and guards all over the place. Dogs. Electrified fences. Come on."

Olson looked at him with disdain. "Before you became a menace to society, what did you do?"

"Finance."

Olson's eyebrows came together in concentrated thought. A small smile flitted across his face. "Finance. You probably have some money hidden away. Maybe a lawyer who can access it?"

Ray shrugged.

"That's a 'Yes.' Now I'm glad Reilly insisted you hang around. It solves a big problem."

Ray said, "What's that?"

"Neither Reilly nor I are from around here. We don't have any cash. No contacts. No resources. Nothing." He looked around quickly. He lowered his voice. "Until now I couldn't figure out how to bribe a guard."

Mitch laughed. The sound and the emotion were genuine. Despite the preposterousness of the fantasy, the conversation had lifted his spirits, but talk of bribing a guard had moved the discussion into the realm of absurd. "Oh man. Here we go."

"Look, despite what you two losers think, there aren't cameras all over the place. There are some, but they're strategically placed, under Level Three doors for instance. Guards aren't all over the place either. They run a skeleton crew at night. During the day there are more, but they can't be everywhere at once. The ones on shift are easy to figure out."

He nodded toward Christopher Tanner, the young guard standing on the sidelines making sure the basketball game didn't get overly rough, inmates forgetting sometimes that basketball was supposed to be a non-contact sport. "Him, for instance. He'll give you the benefit of the doubt. He'd probably ask 'Why' before pulling his Taser. A person can use that hesitation." He pointed at Tony Carter. The gangly screw was on the far side of the yard, walking in their direction, a couple of screws Mitch didn't recognize a step in tow. "This red-neck loser, I bet he can be bribed. Does he know you, Ray? Why you're inside? Does he know you have money?"

"Everybody in this place knows me."

"A reputation," Olson muttered. Louder he said, "That means you're as big a lowlife as Reilly. But, with a guy like Carter, that can work for us. Okay, all you have to do is float something out there. Say, 'The library in here is garbage.' Say, 'I'd pay just about anything for an iPod with some audio books on it.' Leave it at that. Within a few days, I guarantee Carter comes back to you and says something sideways, like, 'How much is just about anything?' Now you've got him. It's a negotiation now. One thing leads to another, and when the time comes and we need him to look south instead of north..." Olson hiked his shoulders. "I'm not saying this will happen soon. Months not weeks, but I've got an idea that will get us out of here."

Mitch clocked Carter's progress. A tingle of apprehension squiggled up his spine. The gangly screw wasn't just patrolling. He and his colleagues were coming with purpose. Mitch tilted his head, pointing with his chin. "Carter is inbound," he whispered.

Olson continued in a rush, "This place is like a small city. They do laundry. Cook. It needs regular maintenance. Supplies come in through doors. They don't use a really tall ladder. They don't throw Glad bags full of trash over the wall." He rose and started walking away.

Carter stopped him. "Not another step, Olson. Stand at attention." He stabbed a finger in Mitch and Ray's direction. Belligerence radiated off him in almost visible waves. "You two, attention."

Mitch stood slowly, looking at Carter with uneasy curiosity.

Carter said, "Roger Olson, Deputy Warden Tyler needs to see you in his office. Apparently, you and Lindsay Thompson have been given your releases." He pointed at one of the other guards and said, "Take Olson. Go." He turned his attention in Mitch's direction. His tongue slashed across his lips in a happy, horrible grin that contained much more than simple pleasure.

Uneasy curiosity turned into foreboding. Mitch understood Carter's pleasure. The gap-toothed red-neck would undoubtedly enjoy seeing Mitch's distress as he watched the only people he knew stride toward freedom. But why did the screw's face contain anticipation too?

CHAPTER 26

TWO QUESTIONS SPRINTED through Mitch's head…

What did Carter's predatory grin mean, and why were Olson and Lindsay being released, but not him? For the tiniest part of a second, Lindsay's name reminded him of the enjoyable evening they spent in the Irish bar, which led to his next thought: he wouldn't see her again, wouldn't be able to thank her for the idea she inadvertently put in his head…

…*I can get back to Liv's world…*

…and her memory needled him into motion. He said, "Sir, may I have a word with Roger before he leaves? We're friends. We were arrested together."

Olson's mouth dropped open like a well-oiled hinge. His eyes widened into unbelieving Os. Just as quickly, he erased his dumfounded expression. Mitch hid a brief smile. Olson was an arrogant dumb-ass cop, but he wasn't stupid. He knew something was up. There was no circumstance in which Mitch would refer to him as a friend.

Tony Carter seemed just as confused by the request, as if the irregularity of the situation was unknown and therefore, how he managed it was also unknown. He opened his mouth but nothing came out. Mitch took advantage of his uncertainty.

He strode toward Olson with his hand out thrust. Olson took

it without reluctance, playing along even though his eyes were narrowed into a silent question. Gripping his hand tightly so he couldn't pull away too quickly, Mitch said softly, "I think you're a grade A dumb-ass. If you listen for once, maybe you'll prove me wrong." He held Olson's gaze. "Lindsay is like me. She can find a portal. Now hug me. Pretend like you mean it."

They embraced and while they slapped each other's backs, Mitch whispered, "Tell her to find the same portal she used when she entered your world. She'll understand. I think that's how you backtrack home. Whatever happens, don't let these Glades' assholes find out she's like me."

Carter found his voice. "Okay, very touching. Olson, get moving."

Mitch watched Olson walk away, doing his best to lasso the loneliness and helplessness blooming inside. *Why them and not me?* The hum in his head ticked up a notch, into something he could no longer deny. It wasn't the wind or ambient prison noise. It was tinnitus, and it was back, eleven months too early. He'd have to slip much sooner than he expected, just as Cole predicted.

Mitch suspected the scarred man was behind Olson and Lindsay's release. He was demonstrating his power. His fingerprints were all over it: *Neither Olson nor Lindsay can slip, therefore they are unimportant. You, on the other hand, can slip. If you want out of Glades, you only have to agree to work for me.*

"Why not me?" Mitch asked, convinced he already knew the answer.

"You want a week in the box?" Carter barked. "Is that it? Keep it up. Keep shooting me that pissed-off look."

Ray said mildly, "It was a simple question, Sir. No disrespect."

Carter's chapped lips pulled back from his teeth, the anticipatory grin amplifying into a wicked smile. "Was I talking to you, Albright?" His arm flashed down to the Taser in the holster on his belt. His hand curled around the weapon's polymer grip and the red LED turned a festive green. A familiar rattling sound filled the air and Ray screamed in agony and dropped like someone had scythed away his legs.

The loneliness and helplessness turned into scarlet rage, shoving Mitch to the front of the "Get Carter" queue. He knew he was being baited and this moment was the reason for Carter's evil smile. That knowledge was not enough to stop him. He drew back his right arm and threw a fast, hard jab into the center of Carter's face.

The screw's nose crunched beneath his fist.

Carter howled first in surprise and then in agony. He dropped his Taser and fell to his knees. Tears filled his eyes. He clutched his face with both hands, blood seeping between his fingers.

The second guard raised his Taser in both hands, his stance wide and balanced, his eyes narrowed in perfect concentration. The rattling sound filled the air a second time and almost simultaneously Mitch collapsed, quivering and screaming uncontrollably.

He regained his breath slowly. Over his own heavy panting and the subsiding waves of pain, he heard Carter say, "You broke my nose." From behind his hands, his voice was nasal and muffled. "You're going to the box for a long time, Reilly. I'll be retired the next time you see the light of day."

CHAPTER 27

GREEN EARTH.

A health food store with *Sounds of the Ocean* playing softly in the background and the aroma of whole foods and exotic spices flavoring the air. A store crowded with herbal medicines, sugar-free candy, incense, and sustainably grown coffee. A store with a sporty blonde clerk wearing khaki capris and ASICS running shoes, walking toward him with a welcoming smile. The tag on her Green Earth T-shirt told the man with the scar her name was Liv.

He returned the smile, and although it was directed in the young lady's direction, it was all his and not meant for her at all.

"May I help you find something, Sir?"

They locked eyes. He saw the usual, slightly confused expression of recognition flicker across her face. Her smile faltered. She recovered and the genial look returned as quickly as it disappeared, although now he saw caution on her face. If he hadn't been watching for the change, he might not have noticed it, but after more years than he cared to count, her reaction was familiar and easy to interpret. He wondered who she saw when she looked at him.

A militaristic piano instructor from early childhood?

Maybe the popular boy in the ninth grade, the one who hadn't spared her a second glance?

Perhaps he reminded her of a stepbrother who teased her, or an uncle who enjoyed bouncing her on his knee, holding her steady with overly familiar fingertips?

Anyone of those possibilities was enough to improve his already jovial mood. He said in a gracious and genuine tone, "Yes, you may, young lady. Where might I find the melatonin? I have such a terrible time sleeping at night." Lying in such an inflated fashion amused him. When he slept, he did so like the proverbial baby, without a single concern grating, or even tickling, his conscience. He wondered sometimes, when a rare, reflective mood passed over him, if he had a conscience. He couldn't remember ever feeling remorse or guilt or sadness.

Rage yes. Happiness certainly.

And, at the culmination of a job, when all his schemes and manipulations merged, he experienced mind-blowing euphoria that went way beyond paradise, or whatever else an individual defined as supreme bliss and perfect felicity.

But, he never felt shame or sorrow.

Liv nodded and said, "Melatonin is over here. We have several varieties." She crossed the shop and stopped in front of a shelf crowded with small bottles.

He followed her on silent feet. When he stood less than an arm's length behind her, he said, "Do you enjoy working here?"

"It's a good job. Is there a particular brand you prefer?" Her long pony tail swung wildly as she turned her head and glanced over her shoulder to answer him.

She started at his proximity. A small squeak of surprise flew from her lips. She took a half-step back, putting as much distance as she could between the two of them. He held back a grin and said, "No preference. Whichever one you think would serve me best."

While he waited for her to select bottles and read labels, he thought about how easily he'd found Liv Steves. It only took an hour and some patience before he discovered all of Mitch Reilly's secrets, or as many as the man carried around with him in his ratty old backpack. Reilly had hidden several driver's licenses and small amounts of paper currency in the lining of the backpack's rear panel. The cash narrowed the search down to four different worlds. The driver's licenses put him in the correct area of those worlds. Reilly seemed to prefer the southeast corner of the United States. The greeting cards, the license plate on the shiny new car Liv was hugging in the photograph, a business card, and random scraps of paper in Reilly's wallet, supplied the final clues.

"Sir?"

He shook off his reflections in an instant. "Yes?"

"What about dosage?"

"What do you recommend?"

Her gaze slid across his face and then dropped to the label on the bottle in her hand.

"If you've never taken melatonin before, you should start small and work up."

Her voice contained no inflection. She was saying the right words, but her face had gone carefully blank. He didn't yet see hatred or fear. They would come, as foggy memories and tenuous connections sharpened. Given time, the only person she saw when she looked at him would be the person from her past whom she loathed the most. Unfortunately, he wasn't going to be around long enough to effect that change upon her. He was only visiting Green Earth for leverage.

"That seems like good advice," he said with a nod.

Of his four choices, Liv's was the third world he visited. It helped he was already familiar with all four. He monitored dozens at any one time, particularly those in crisis. Happily, in the last several years, Liv's world was one of those in which human-induced problems were accelerating exponentially. Had she been a child of the fifties, sixties, or seventies, he probably couldn't have used her as leverage. During those three decades, her world had rotated on a relatively stable axis, political unrest and regional wars notwithstanding. Human suffering had reached a certain pinnacle and then leveled off after the Second World War. The inexorable problems associated with rampant globalization, overpopulation, and environmental disasters (his gin, tonic, and ice), had yet to begin.

Globalization as an ideal was wonderful and as a reality, atrocious. It eroded the exact lifestyle humans worked so very hard to construct. Without exception, it destabilized every world in an infinite number of worlds. He'd seen it countless times. A human's instinctive need to procreate conflicted with their innate need for personal space. Cultures did not integrate. They clashed, no differently in the fifteenth century when Europeans, with their diseases and missionary zealots, crossed the ocean and landed on the shores of the Americas, to today when the sand-monkeys in the dessert terrorized those in the enlightened West, in an effort to force them to buy their abhorrent beliefs.

Humans were superb at acknowledging the mistakes of the past. They did an abysmal job at preventing them from happening again. The world, any world, did not improve as time passed, despite experience, ever-increasing knowledge, and technical advancements. On a small scale, a person's lifetime for instance, this should have been obvious to even the most inbred mouth breather. All he had to do was read a newspaper once a month and compare stories.

On a large scale, had the mouth breather lived for two or three centuries and somehow been given the ability to see one of the other worlds, he would have witnessed today's problems compounding, becoming the catastrophes of tomorrow and the death of the future. Even he would understand the imagined utopia of the future was impossible to attain.

The scarred man couldn't create aberrations, or as he preferred to call them, miracles. He couldn't kill a world out of hand. It needed to be on the correct trajectory; he needed momentum on his side. And, he needed tools in his toolbox—globalization, over-population, and environmental disasters.

Liv's world was low-hanging fruit.

She said, "Can I help you find anything else?"

Such professionalism, he marveled. Such effort! And, in such a menial job. "Not today," he answered. And then, because it pleased him to see her so uncomfortable, he pressed her into another conversation. "It seems to me this would be a good store to work in. It gives people hope, yes?"

"Sir?"

"I mean to say, between SUVs filling the air with carbon and humans using the oceans as a septic tank, everything else that's going on, it must feel good to sell products that help the environment and are consumer friendly."

"I like to think we make a difference."

She smiled widely, surprising him. It seemed he'd stumbled onto a subject she was passionate about, something that shielded her from the uneasiness he provoked in her.

"If everybody changed their habits just a little bit, the positive impact on the planet would be enormous."

He covered a laugh of derision with a cough. *You poor, naive young tree-hugger.* His work took him from one corner of the universe to the other, from planets so young the cosmic fog still shone translucent under a new star's hopeful rays, to old teetering worlds like this one, where the polar ice caps were melting and the jungles that provided oxygen to every living thing on the planet were being razed. And, mankind's best solutions? Innumerable rock-star charity concerts, hemp clothing, hybrid vehicles, and hotels that did "their part" by churning out paper flyers by the tens of millions to inform guests they only washed the sheets and towels every three days, in order to protect the environment and save the planet.

Ludicrous.

He shivered with delight. "True, true," he commiserated. Then he faked a deep, concerned sigh and said, "But, is that enough?"

Liv said, "Oh, it's not. There has to be political will to change. Right now, it's mostly talk. I've got a bachelor degree in political science. I'm working on my master's. When I graduate, things are going to change." She blushed.

He chuckled because he knew he was supposed to, this adorable girl, this future politician who had the good grace to acknowledge such an enormous statement about her role in the planet's future, as if political will and good intentions were enough. Adorable. Little wonder Reilly was smitten.

The silence between them stretched, and he saw Liv's body stiffen with the same uncomfortable rigidity as earlier.

"Here's your melatonin." Now, her smile was thin and brittle. "Would you like to join our loyalty program? It's free and after you've spent one hundred dollars you get five percent off your next purchase." She spoke fast and did not meet his eyes, obviously anxious to get him out of the store.

He waved a negative hand, then watched as Liv, who hadn't waited for his answer or seen him wave her off, whipped a wallet-sized membership card out of the till and scribbled the date and her signature on the Green Earth associate line. She dotted the I in her name with the familiar tiny heart. She handed it to him, and he took it with a thanks and a smile.

"May I have two?" He had no specific reason for wanting two cards, but he liked giving himself options. Two of most things was generally better than one. He said, "Just in case I forget one at home, or in the car. That sort of thing."

"Certainly." She gave him a second card, complete with the

tiny heart signature. "Combining them is not a problem. Just don't lose one. Green Earth doesn't hold a record of your credits."

"This will be extremely useful," he said and for the first time that afternoon, he wasn't lying.

CHAPTER 28

MITCH LAY ON his back with his eyes closed, enjoying a sudden silence, dreading the sounds that would take its place. The music was on a loop, a very short loop, making it easily the worst part about the "entertainment" in solitary confinement. The inspiring literature could be ignored, as could the subtle-as-a-hammer-to-the-temple television programming, but there was no escaping the never-ending harmonies of the pan flute that filled every corner of his cell. It was all designed, ostensibly he guessed, to help re-program an offender. To help mold him into a gentler, more caring person. Someone, in other words, who wouldn't end up in the box. Mitch considered it torture in disguise. He wanted to smash the speakers with a baseball bat.

Strangely, the silence stretched.

He opened curious eyes. The program on the television was correct. The loop hadn't changed. A doe and a fawn stood in a meadow thick with grasses and wild flowers. Their tails flicked lazily. Their ears twitched. The camera zoomed in and focused on the doe's soft, moist eyes, huge and filled with love and pride. The only thing missing from this calming scene was the music that typically reached a crescendo when the fawn dipped her nose into the grass for a mouthful of whatever it was deer ate.

A new sound had taken the music's place.

Breathing.

A tall, dark shadow leaned on the wall to the left of the television.

Cole, of course, returned as promised, looking polished and trim in his crème suit and burgundy tie, looking exactly as Mitch remembered, although he was no longer certain who he remembered. Was it the science teacher of his youth, or the individual he'd met less than a week ago, the man with a scar over his right eye?

Were they the same person?

This idea kept popping into his head and his rational mind dismissed it every time. After eleven different worlds, the two Coles couldn't be the same person. But when Mitch thought about the meeting in the suicide room, he only ever "saw" his science teacher.

Cole looked around, taking his time although there was nothing in the box that required any great concentration. He absently fluttered a small rectangular business card across the fingers of his left hand. Finally, his eyes landed on Mitch and he said, "Need I ask how you're doing, Mr. Reilly?"

The eighth-grade hatred, no longer softened and rounded by time, swelled. Mitch said nothing. How did the dumb-ass think he felt?

"You broke Mr. Carter's nose. He has two black eyes! It must have been a good punch. Nicely done. I don't care for Mr. Carter. I feel as though he's always working an angle." He shrugged. "Not unlike me, but I'm not sneaky about it. My agenda is always front and center. Maybe that doesn't make a difference. I like to think it does."

Mitch didn't regret dropping Carter. Neither was he proud of it. The only thing that felt important now was the tinnitus and the fear that filled his fragmented sleep with oily, slithering blackness and screams he knew came from the Space Between. He guessed he had five days, at the most, before everything Cole had shown him in the suicide room came true.

Cole continued, "Heather is quite a sight, no?"

Mitch smiled. Heather's long legs, flat belly, and inviting eyes definitely were a sight, but he remembered the infinite sky and the endless ocean with more clarity and longing. As quickly as the smile appeared, it vanished. The compensation package was big and extravagant and almost certainly would not redress the tasks Cole would require of him. Mitch answered, "A bit much, wouldn't you say?"

"I'd say we all need a refuge and someone to talk to when the world's weight presses down upon our shoulders." He paused. A contented look crossed his face, as if he were imagining his own sanctuary at the end of a long, hard week. Then his expression changed to one of seriousness. "Last time we spoke, I offered you a way out of this world. Listen to me for fifteen minutes now and in thirty, you'll be free of solitary confinement. Consider it my way of saying, 'Thanks for listening.' If you agree to work for me, you'll be out of Glades within the week." He nodded and raised his eyebrows encouragingly. The business card buzzed back and forth across his fingers.

"Terrific," Mitch muttered. He caught flashes of blue and green, a pattern on the card he knew he should recognize but couldn't with the relentless, high-pitched whine thrumming between his ears and this man he disliked so intensely destroying his concentration.

"Come now, Mitch. Don't be that way. 'Tis the season, and all that…" Cole tined his fingers through his coiffed hair. A trace of impatience crept into his voice. "The tinnitus is back, yes? Stress will do that. Time is running out. Disappointing for me. Catastrophic for you."

"No thanks to you." He couldn't meet Cole's eyes, and there was a sulky whine in his voice that every eighth-grade science teacher would recognize, a sound Mitch hated for its weakness but couldn't control.

"I should leave then? If that's your wish, I will. As I've mentioned, life is about choices. Before I do, consider this… If I go, you'll never see me again. There'd be no reason for me to return. By this time next week, you'll be drooling down your chin and pissing in a diaper. Totally worthless."

"You exaggerate."

"Are you sure?" Cole slowly tilted his head from side to side, as though carefully weighing the options. "We discussed this. I thought we agreed, the cerebral effects of missing a portal will be different in here. Accentuated, is the word I'm looking for. Why not hear my proposal? Look at it this way, what else are you doing today?"

Mitch gave him the smallest of nods.

"Excellent," Cole said. "May I sit?"

Without waiting for an answer, he slipped the business card into the breast pocket of his coat and plopped down on one end of the bed, leaning against the wall and crossing his ankles. Without much choice, Mitch scooted sideways, moving as far away as he could comfortably maneuver. Cole was right. He didn't have anything better to do.

Cole said, "In human terms, a planet's life is infinite. In reality, they are born and they die. Not unlike you and I. Well, you. Me not so much." He paused, perhaps waiting for Mitch to ask what he meant, but only silence filled the room, so he continued. "A brief history…

"Somewhere, out there in the vastness of space, gas and dust collect and, under the influence of gravity, combine. They become increasingly larger and heavier. Dust becomes boulders. Boulders become proto-planets. This is birth. A planet in its earliest stage. If a planet is born in close proximity to a sun, the planet's death is assured. A sun is nothing but an endless nuclear explosion. When a sun collapses into itself and fusion forces it to expand again, the resultant red giant consumes the planet. This is death.

"What does this mean to the average person? Nothing. I mean, so what? It took a billion years for gas and dust to become a planet and in the end, it's nothing but a useless rock floating in space. It serves no discernible purpose. In a few million years, when the planet is consumed by the red giant, nobody will care. Nothing significant was lost because nobody knew about it anyway."

Cole shifted closer to the wall, correcting his slouch. For a moment, his manner became reflective. "The universe's essential essence—never-ending change—continually destroys the very thing it creates. Interesting, no?"

Mitch grunted non-committedly, unsure if he agreed or understood, not without having more time to consider the statement.

"Am I boring you, Mitch?"

"Not at all." Cole's smooth, game-show host baritone was the ideal voice for lecturing, and this science lesson was more interesting than anything Mitch had listened to in high school. He was curious to see where the scarred man was going with it. Something significant was coming. It had to be or Cole wouldn't have sat down in the first place. Mitch wanted to know how it pertained to him. He said, "Keep going."

"It's *essential* you understand that when something is alive—something as small as an amoeba or as large as a planet—there is a life cycle." He sketched an arc in the air with the edge of his hand. "Beginning to end. Time is not unlimited. It might take minutes or eons but no matter what happens, death is assured."

"The circle of life. I get it."

"Excellent. Let's consider one of these worthless space rocks, one of these planets we've been discussing. It's out there in the boundless, ever-expanding universe, so many millions of light years away that not even the most brilliant astronomers of our time, are aware of its existence. Imagine this planet is similar to earth. It has a sun and a moon and water and the exact atmospheric balance of nitrogen, oxygen, and carbon dioxide. Imagine further, that somewhere between cosmic dust and red giant, the changes acting upon this planet spawn—"

"Life."

"Yes, Mitch. Life. Suddenly, this planet is no longer a worthless piece of granite. Rather, it's a world. If a red giant were to consume it, we'd be discussing the death of not only a planet, but the extinction of every living thing upon it. Everything that made it a world. Early in the life cycle, it would only be single-celled microbes that perish. Seemingly unimportant, yes? But as time went on and the world changed and life forms evolved and became more complex..." He hiked his shoulders. "Billions of lives. A little more significant, wouldn't you say?"

Mitch nodded at both the abstraction and obviousness of the statement.

"Changes occur more rapidly in an old world than in a young world. Proof? Earth is roughly 4.6 billion years old. Earliest life arrived 4 billion years ago. Earliest humans 100,000 years ago. The peak of the first humans' technological intelligence was a stick that felt good in the hand. In less time than a blink of an eye, in terms of the earth's age, we've evolved from beating our enemies to death with clubs, to bombing them into oblivion with nuclear-tipped cruise missiles."

Cole's pace accelerated with what Mitch recognized as contained excitement.

"It takes millions of years for a sun to collapse, expand, and turn into a red giant. At five hundred and fifty miles per hour, two Tomahawks can destroy a city in hours. A couple of dozen would render the United States extinct in days. That's where we're at today. It's safe to say the extinction of a world is much closer than a red giant, no?"

Mitch nodded tentatively, not enjoying the direction the lecture had veered.

"These hypothetical worlds we're discussing should concern

you, Mitch. These impossibly faraway worlds filled with nuclear-tipped Tomahawks, these worlds on the verge of extinction, should be your utmost concern."

Cole had finally reached his point. Death and extinction. Mitch still couldn't see how it pertained to him, but tremors rippled his spine, and his arms were scaly with gooseflesh. He scrubbed a hand down his bristly face, felt it tremble slightly on top of all the whiskers. "Why?" he said in an uneasy whisper. "Assuming they even exist, why should they concern me?"

"They most definitely exist and they should concern you because these are the worlds you slip into and out of."

CHAPTER 29

"*WHAT DAY IS it?*"

"*Tuesday.*"

"*Nooooooo, Daddy. Is it Christmas?*" *Only she couldn't say it correctly, and it came out,* "*Chris-miss.*"

"*Not yet, Tinkerbelle. Two more sleeps.*"

Angie fidgeted on his knee. "*Then Santa Claus comes, right Daddy?*"

"*Have you been a good girl? All year?*"

Momentarily still, she seemed to think about it. Her huge eyes grew wide with seriousness. "*Yes,*" *she said, nodding vigorously.* "*Pretty good.*" *Twin barrettes shook loose, until they dangled from the tips of her fine blonde hair.*

"*In that case, Santa Claus will come.*"

She squirmed and Ray held her lightly, to keep her from toppling off his knee. Her grandparents always wanted to cuddle her. They'd squat down and greet her with wide-open arms, "*Come say hi to Gram and Grandad! Don't you look pretty in your dress?*" *Shooting Ray and Dawn critical eyes over Angie's shoulder the entire time. They didn't approve of a sun dress in the middle of winter. But, at five years old, Angie was already a lady, headstrong and particular about her appearance.*

She said, "Do you like my dress, Daddy? It's green and red for Chris-miss time."

In the distance a bell rang. Oven? Doorbell? Telephone? Ray didn't know. He ignored the sound. "It's a beautiful dress," he said. "You're my beautiful girl."

He smiled at his daughter and wondered how something so small could be so vital, so close to perfection without any experience or practice. Life had not left her with so much as a blemish on one tiny limb. Neither cynicism nor hypocrisy had tainted her fascination with the world. Moments like this, when she was calm and serious, filled him with optimism. If he protected his daughter, sheltered her and prayed nothing ever changed, how could the world not become a better place? When she slept with her face on his shoulder and her heart beating against his chest, he figured she was as close to a miracle as the world would ever know.

He heard the bell again, louder this time. Angie wriggled. She couldn't sit still for long, not for grandparents' cuddles or serious talks about Santa Claus. "What are we going to do today, Daddy?"

With a hand under either arm, Ray lifted his daughter from his knee and plunked her on the floor with a thump. She ran toward the clanging bell, impossibly fast on her short, five-year-old legs, so fast she'd shrunk to the size of a dot in the time it took him to blink.

She disappeared entirely.

Ray awoke with a jerk and gurgle of surprise. The novel he'd been reading dropped off his knee and hit the floor with a flat slap.

"What are we going to do today, Daddy?"

Angie's favorite question. He blinked several times, clearing his mind of sleep and his eyes of tears, listening as the final chimes signaling the midafternoon head count faded to nothing. Carter told the truth during the check-in procedure. Except for the occasional random headcount, the daily routine never varied, making his TAG Heuer redundant. Life in Glades was nothing but one long, never-ending day.

Sighing heavily, he put both hands on the back of the pew in front of him and dragged himself to his feet. He left the chapel and plodded down the corridor toward Red 350.

This was the worst part of the day. The time between noon and lights-out stretched toward infinity. With nothing much to do, he spent a great deal of time napping. All the extra sleep meant he never went all the way under, to the deep, unconscious place where dreams didn't happen. As a result, he remembered them. Often, they brought him and his family together again, and for a time, he was happy. Then he woke up and remembered Dawn and Angie were gone and the happiness dissolved into apathetic despair.

Pathetically, he still craved the dreams.

When he couldn't nap any longer, he read. The best place for this was the prison's chapel. It was cool and quiet, a calming place where he didn't feel so sad and alone. He couldn't understand why the chapel gave him a lift. He chalked it up to the natural awe and wonder every person feels when they enter a church. In a place like Cologne's High Cathedral of Saints Peter and Mary, a place steeped in history, it was the rare person who didn't feel the touch of something otherworldly. Even a church like Westminster Abbey, with its endless parade of tourists, left a person speaking in whispers and wondering why they were suddenly aware of an unfilled part of their being. For some reason, Glades' chapel worked the same way, despite the CCTV cameras and guards who routinely poked their heads between the swinging entrance doors, to make sure nothing untoward was happening in God's house.

"What am I gonna do today?" Ray muttered.

Take a shower?

Shave?

Exchange clothes at the laundry?

He blew out a derisive puff of air. He wouldn't bother doing any of that. What was the point?

Someone shouted, "Attention."

Ray and the rest of the inmates lining the hallway straightened and clasped their hands. Two guards counted heads, noting the conspicuously empty spot in front of Red 350 where Mitch Reilly should have stood, their smiles and nods of approval making it clear they were pleased he was locked in the box.

Ray smiled. He wished he'd seen the punch that broke Carter's nose. At the time he was riding the bull with a 50,000-volt wire stuck in his chest, so he missed it. By the time he became aware of what was happening around him, Mitch was on the ground doing the funky chicken and Carter was kneeling beside him, wailing in pain, blood squirting out of his nose.

Ray's smile widened. If there was ever a guy who deserved it, Carter was that person.

Ray assumed his tasing was the final straw for Mitch, but it felt good when the other inmates told him Mitch didn't hesitate. Apparently, he slugged Carter in the same way an older brother might have gone after a bully on the playground. The Taser's wires hit Ray, Mitch's fist hit Carter.

Before all that happened though, there was the nonsensical conversation between Mitch and Olson. Ray didn't feel quite as good about it. Discussing weaknesses in Glades' defenses was one thing. Olson was correct on that score. The number of cameras was limited, as were the number of guards, many of whom were young and didn't carry themselves with a veteran's confidence. But the freaky-dead-space stuff they talked about made no sense and the fact they were discussing it in such a matter-of-fact manner made Ray deeply uneasy.

Mitch said he'd explain it later. Ray planned on reminding him.

In the meantime, he'd been thinking about escape.

…this place is like a small city. They do laundry. Cook. It needs regular maintenance. Supplies have to be brought in and trash has to be taken out…

The orderly line-up of inmates disintegrated around him. Ray turned slowly and entered Red 350. He sat on the edge of the lower bunk, elbows on knees, chin cupped in his hands. He knew Olson's idea was fragile, the likelihood of success minimal. However, if he concentrated and remained optimistic, it might be interesting. In his previous life, he made his living as a financial analyst. Not the same as a cop or security consultant, but there were similarities: collect data, study it from different perspectives, search for the upside and the downside. Finally, make a decision based on all the information.

Unconsciously, his spine straightened. Olson gave him a starting point. Ray only had to see where it took him. When they released Mitch from the box, it might be nice to tell him he'd done more than sleep. It might be nice to say he looked into some of those ideas Olson mentioned. Ray was aware he was searching for approval, the way a younger brother does with an older sibling. He was also saying, "Thank you," in a subtle, roundabout way. He didn't really care. It gave him something to do.

Next time Angie asked, "What are we going to do today," he'd answer, "We're going to look for a way out of here, Tinkerbelle."

CHAPTER 30

…THESE ARE THE worlds you slip into and out of.

Before Cole finished speaking, Mitch was shaking his head. "Impossible. I cross the Space Between in an instant. I don't cross the universe."

"That's exactly what happens, Mitch. You cross the universe. It doesn't happen instantly, despite the way it feels. It takes a measurable number of seconds, depending on which world you're slipping into." Cole paused and his eyes narrowed. He tilted his head. "Have you never asked yourself where those worlds exist?"

"Not really," Mitch said. The truth was, he left one world, crossed the Space Between, and seconds later, arrived in another. That was all. He assumed the worlds existed in close proximity to each other like soap bubbles blown through a child's toy. He never gave any thought to where the bubbles existed. Since he had no choice but to slip, it didn't seem to matter.

Cole made a surprised kind of exhalation. "Fascinating. I thought that would be your first question. The universe is everything, both boundless and expanding. I'm curious; if you're not slipping to some other point in the universe, where did you think you were going?"

His tone of voice changed as he spoke, into something Mitch hadn't heard in years but immediately recognized. His mind side-slipped and he found himself back in the classroom with an unwelcome, molten panic souring his stomach.

I don't know the right answer.

I can't say, "Bubbles."

I don't get the concept…

…and he KNOWS I don't get it, and he's going to call on me anyway, and I'm going to sit here in a stupid kind of haze, with a blank look on my face and the eyes of the class staring at me impatiently, because even if I did know the answer, panic has stolen my words.

"Did you think the worlds were stacked on top of each other, like units in a condominium, invisible to everyone but you?"

"I didn't think that," Mitch mumbled, staring at the top of a desk that didn't exist in the box but did in the classroom, a desk worn from decades of service and abuse, *chipped along the edges, two wobbly legs, hearts drawn in old ink, faded initials contained within, proclamations such as Kiss RULES and Kiss SUCKS scratched into the wooden surface.*

"You've never given any thought as to where you go? It's only the time it takes to get there you don't understand? Is that it, Mr. Reilly?" Not Mitch any longer, but, Mr. Reilly. "After everything we've talked about, I find it incredible your only hang-up is that one irrelevant detail."

"It's not irrelevant," Mitch flared in the same mewling, defensive whine as thirteen years before. "Crossing the universe should take billions of light-years. It takes seconds." Thoroughly humiliated, flashing back and forth between the present and the past, he said with as much conviction as he could muster, "I thought it was the same world…"

I can't say, "Bubbles,"

"… just different planes of existence," which he realized didn't mean anything, other than it may have somehow explained how quickly he crossed the Space Between, as well as the similarities between the worlds.

"Planes of existence?" Cole's mocking tone was gone. Now he sounded genuinely perplexed. He tapped his lips with his finger. For several seconds, perhaps a full minute, he said nothing. When he spoke again, he did so contemplatively, giving Mitch the impression he was considering an idea that had never crossed his mind.

Cole said, "The movie industry has given us the idea that any species, other than humans from earth, must look distinctly alien. Think, *Independence Day* or the cantina in *Star Wars* or Klingons. I suppose if there are other planes of existence, the so-called multiverse, that is a conceivable hypothesis. A completely different universe *could* spawn a completely different species, and their appearance might look significantly different than we do.

"However, in this universe," he pointed at the floor several times, "that assertion makes no sense. Five minutes ago, you and I agreed that given the same conditions, a planet similar to earth was not only possible, it was probable. That being the case, the human species here is going to look like the human species there."

Mitch said, "What about the Squats?"

"Humans, Mitch. They're missing essential nucleotides of sugar and phosphate. But they aren't aliens, no matter their appearance or actions. Perhaps, if we kept going, deeper and deeper into the universe, we might see similar changes in a greater number. But, they're still human.

"As for the time it takes to cross an expanding universe, the portal compresses time and space. I can neither answer how it happens nor why. It just does. Take my word for it. Or not. I really don't care, insomuch as what you believe doesn't change the outcome of our discussion."

Mitch looked at him blankly.

"Oh, for... You're not making this simple are you, Mr. Reilly? Okay... When someone says, 'She lost her spirit,' or 'Her memory haunts him,' or any other such nonsense, it is not always teenage dramatics. Sometimes it is actually true. That energy, if you will, is out there in the universe. When the portal forms and compresses time and the space between the world you're leaving and the world you're slipping into, it necessarily gathers everything between those worlds, including those energies. Hence, the concentrated malevolence you experience in the Space Between. The wind you feel is the difference between two world's atmospheres, and the vacuum of the Space Between, trying to equalize."

"Simple, right?" Mitch said.

Cole shrugged, the sarcasm apparently lost on him. He said, "Now, will you please stipulate, how you slip and where you go—another plane of existence or a world on the opposite side of the universe—is largely irrelevant. What is relevant is the world in which you land?"

Mitch pushed himself to the edge of the mattress and then stood. Like a caged cat, he paced from one end of the box to the other a couple of times, finally stopping with his back to the wall, arms crossed. "Oh man," he muttered.

Cole closed his eyes, pressed his palms together and dipped his head as though in prayer. "Thank you," he said. He opened his eyes. "Carrying on then… I recently had business in a world you'd be comfortable in, should it happen that you travel there. Early in its life a meteor seven miles across struck this particular world, creating the Gulf of Mexico. It struck with enough force to wipe out most life forms. Significant, yes? However, the planet recovered. Life in its simplest form grew and evolved. As time passed, tsunamis wiped out countries. Volcanoes melted islands. Earthquakes turned continents into oceans. These cataclysmic events continued for millions of years, changing and aging the planet. Apes evolved into Homo sapiens, or God created Adam and Eve, if you go in for that sort of thing. Basically, the human element was introduced and the life span of the world shortened considerably."

Mitch nodded. "Yeah, yeah." They'd talked about the planet's shortened lifespan and he knew about the apocalyptic meteor. One struck the earth in every world he'd slipped into. He first learned about it in school, long before he left his origin world. He remembered it because it killed all the dinosaurs—as a kid he loved dinosaurs—and that had made him sad. An event of that magnitude didn't change across worlds, although where the meteor hit varied from one world to the next.

In Liv's world, the meteor had in fact, created the Gulf of Mexico.

"Eventually, in 1914—"

"World War One began. I know this stuff."

"You *think* you know your history, Mitch. But, you're only correct to a certain degree, aren't you? History is a moving target for a person such as yourself. I'm almost done. Bear with me and in a moment, I think you'll see where I'm going with this.

"The Great War wasn't a *world* war in the truest sense of the term, was it? But, the ball was in play. The earth was finally beginning to shrink, at least in a metaphorical sense. The first war's successor, particularly the end… 83,000 people dead in Hiroshima in an instant. Two days later, 35,000 more in Nagasaki. Within four months that number doubled! Two bombs!"

These were not unfamiliar facts. Every grade schooler knew about the atomic bombs. In Mitch's origin world, they landed on Tokyo and Osaka. In one world in which he lived, they wiped out Yokohama and Sapporo. What stole his breath and stiffened his posture, was the names of the cities Cole had so casually mentioned in his (to this point) obscure history lesson. As far as Mitch knew, the only world in which the bombs levelled Hiroshima and Nagasaki, was the world in which Liv called home.

If history was a moving target as Cole said, and his lecture was a bullet, then why was he always hitting Liv's world?

The tinnitus returned like an inhuman scream. His breath

burst out in a gust of surprised pain. His legs went watery, and he slid down the wall until he sat on the floor with his elbows on bent knees, palms covering his ears. As the pain eased, he remembered the blue and green business card Cole slipped into his pocket. It looked suspiciously like a Green Earth loyalty card.

Had Cole taken it from his wallet? Possibly, but another option popped into Mitch's head—Cole might have visited Liv's world and found her at Green Earth. Why would he do that? Mitch couldn't yet see where Cole was going with all his talk about death and extinction, but it seemed Liv's world factored into it somehow. He swallowed dryly and asked, "Why are you telling me this?"

"Everything in a world stores energy. Everything. Waves in the ocean. Tectonic plates in the earth. Countless kilowatts are stored as heat in the liquid core of the planet. Most interesting to me is the seven kilowatts of energy every single human body is capable of producing, until it doesn't because it is dead. Not so much you say? Seven kilowatts multiplied by a population of seven billion is a big number. When a world dies, that energy has to go somewhere. Physics, Mitch. Energy doesn't disappear. It has to go somewhere."

"Where? Where does it go?"

"Exactly. Where does it go? In all things, there has to be balance, doesn't there? Coke and Sprite. Two sides to the same coin. Yin and yang. Action and reaction. Where would the universe be if I weren't here to help maintain balance?"

"What are you talking about?"

"I absorb all that energy and redirect it. When the earth trembles, I turn the tremble into an earthquake. Thousands die. I soak up all those thousands of kilowatts and store them, not unlike a capacitor, until a tropical storm spins through the Caribbean. Then I cup my hands and blow, and the stored energy turns a tropical storm into a class five hurricane."

A growing feeling of dread made it difficult for Mitch to breath. "What do you want from me?" he asked, barely recognizing his own voice.

"Many worlds have one foot in the grave. They simply need a nudge. A helping hand to hurry them along, and I can't be everywhere at once. Neither am I especially suited for some of the tasks that ensure destabilization.

"You can't force a volcano to boil over, but in matters of humanity, well… In the case of the First World War, for instance, in the coffee shops and bars, when the Bosnian Serbs' rhetoric wound up, someone had to say, 'Kill the Archduke.' Someone had to keep Gavrilo Princip focused and supply the gun and the opportunity. The sand-monkeys flew jet aircraft into skyscrapers. Before that happened, the idea had to be conceived, planned, and financed. Do you know who shot Kennedy?"

"Nobody knows."

"I know," Cole said, with absolute certainty. "He worked for me. If you really want to know what came first, the chicken or the egg, I can show you." His eyebrows bounced up and down several times. "Impressive, no?"

Mitch said nothing.

Cole's smooth baritone changed from the contemplative lecturer to that of a supervisor, laying out the day's chores. "You will become a facilitator. You'll join hundreds of others who work for me, in dozens of different worlds. I'll assign you a task in a world that is racing toward its own demise. An assassination. A bombing. Something. You will perform the task, accelerating the inevitable. Once you've completed your task, you will walk through a portal I create and find safety with Heather on your yacht. If you'd prefer someone other than Heather, that can be arranged. You will live in freedom and comfort until I need you again.

"Remember, death in all things is assured. Feel no regret or remorse. These worlds are on their way out. All you're doing is hastening the end." He stared at Mitch intently, without blinking. "Where I concentrate my energies is up to you." He leaned forward, dropped a wink and said in a conspiratorial whisper, "This world, right here, is circling the drain. When evolution reverses itself, something is drastically wrong. Should we put an end to it?"

Appalled, Mitch said, "Why me? I don't belong in prison. I'm here by accident. Get one of the crazies in here to do it."

"Excellent question. Two answers. You'd think asking a criminal to help destroy a world would make sense, yes?" He shook his head. "That's not the case. I've tried. First Gens have too large a chip on their shoulders to take orders. Second and Third Gens aren't smart enough. Inmates are generally weak-minded and egocentric. They are unpredictable, unstable, and uncontrollable. Life is all about them. That's why most of them are in prison in the first place. It's difficult to reach the same kind of agreement you and I are hammering out when a person only cares about himself."

"What you're saying, you can't put them under your thumb without some kind of leverage."

"You say potato, I say... Well, you know. The second reason is, I need someone who slips. A normal person—"

"I'm normal."

"Don't be obtuse, Mitch. You know exactly what I mean. The same force that draws you to a particular time and place, repels people who don't slip. I'm sure you've seen roads and rooms empty as your time approaches. The weather grows worse, driving everybody into the safety of their homes. People near a portal feel unaccountably ill."

Mitch nodded his agreement.

Cole continued, "A normal person can no more travel between worlds and remain healthy, than you can stay rooted to one and remain healthy. It happens occasionally, as you saw with Roger Olson, but it can't happen routinely. If they slip, they will break, just as you will break if you don't." He shrugged. "I need someone who won't break."

Mitch said, "Why destroy entire worlds? To what end?"

"Why does a river run downstream? Because it must." Cole shrugged. "Same with me. I have to. You see me sitting here, well dressed and handsome, but I present myself to you in these clothes for two reasons. One, it amuses me to do so, and two, I am balance. I am energy and power and force. I can't show you that in a way you could possibly visualize. When two tectonic plates push against each other, you see the result, not the energy, power, and force that cause the destruction. They are invisible. I am that energy, power, and force. I do it because I must, for the same reason the wind blows and the earth rotates and the sun shines. There is no other choice.

"However, there is one difference between the river and myself." Cole smiled. "After thousands of years and hundreds of worlds, I grew tired of doing nothing but sitting on one side of the scale. I mean, how often can a person turn a tropical storm into a class five, before boredom sets in? I asked myself, 'What if I went bigger? What if I absorbed it all?'" His lips were moist and his eyes burned with the fervor of a fanatic.

"To answer your question, I've learned what it feels like to kill a world and absorb all the resultant energy. In terms you can understand, the death of a world is like winning the Super Bowl every day of the year. It's the first velvety sip of a fifty-thousand-dollar Macallan. It's a never-ending supply of your favorite ice cream. It's a tequila drunk with two insatiable porn stars, a bottle of Viagra, and a clear head in the morning. It is a life-long friendship and perfect love. It's all that and more, all at the same time, and with every world that dies, the resulting energy I absorb only intensifies the feeling. It's unbelievable, and I can't get enough."

"Who are you?" Mitch said in a low horrified whisper.

"We're past names, aren't we? I am everybody and nobody.

I'm everything and I'm nothing at all. I'm not the beginning, but I'm most certainly the end. When the world wobbles on its axis because of human or environmental factors, I'm the one who gave it a gentle push."

"You're the Devil," Mitch said in the same unbelieving whisper.

Cole's jovial mood disappeared. He blew a dismissive gust of air through his lips and flicked his wrist, waving the suggestion away. "You don't believe in that jibber jabber, do you?" He dipped a hand into his pocket. When he withdrew it, he held Mitch's Saint Christopher medallion. "Take it. Believe in its power if you want, but if you need something to believe in, I suggest you start with what's transparent." He spread his arms to the side, palms up and looked around the cell, as if to say, "Here I am, as real as the room in which we sit."

"Mother Nature is a little more translucent than I am, but still easily verifiable. Don't believe me? Take a walk in the forest. Every sense is alive. She's right there with you. I've met her, by the way, and let me tell you, she's the snotty bitch in the front row, the one who raises her hand before everyone else in the room. I can't begin to tell you how much it pisses me off when people give her credit for earthquakes and tsunamis. I'm not out there painting colorful autumn leaves, am I?"

Mitch said nothing. If this bizarre aside had a point—he expected it did as Cole seemed to favor the long, strong sales pitch—then the question was rhetorical and would be answered in due time.

"Take a further step in the same direction," Cole continued, "and we've arrived at the opaque place in which the Devil resides. You could make the argument that hell exists for the individuals we saw in the suicide room, but did the Devil put them there and is God going to rescue them? I don't think so." He shook his head. "I've read the bible cover to cover, several times. It is nothing but a series of short stories penned by the best writers of the time. I met a few of them. They were interesting people, but no different than any other author you'd find on the New York Times list of best-selling fiction." He gave an unimpressed shrug. "Do you know how many times they mention the boogey-man in the basement? Fifty-seven. That's it. The bestselling book of all time, a book over thirty percent of the world's population uses as a roadmap to life, only mentions the worst case fifty-seven times. Yet people choose to believe in the Devil and his heavenly opposite without being able to confirm either one with so much as one of our perfectly tuned senses.

"I understand many people need something to blame for their misfortunes and something to thank for their bounties, so in their cases I can give blind faith a pass. You, however, know better. You've met me, Mitch. I'm right here. So, don't insult me by calling me the Devil."

He clapped his hands once. "Enough talk. The world we spoke about earlier… Its time has come. I'm going to drop the West Coast of North America into the Pacific Ocean. The 'Big One,' as it is referred to, is finally going to happen. I'm going to level the East Coast from the Keys to Cape Breton with hurricanes that will make Wilma look like a pussy. The African continent will suffer the worst drought it has ever seen.

"While I'm busy with these 'natural disasters,'" he made air quotes and grinned a sly, malicious grin, "you and others will facilitate day-to-day operations. One country will shoot a passenger jet out of the sky. The sand-monkey's terror attacks will reach critical mass. In response, an incompetent and unintelligent president will launch the Tomahawks. In Asia, a paranoid dictator with nothing to offer, will sink one of the West's submarines. At the same time, an Eastern European leader will ethnically cleanse his country.

"Between the natural disasters and the man-made pressures, the world will reach a breaking point. The third great war, a truly global conflict, will begin and quickly go nuclear. The largest cities will be vaporized. Famine and poisoned water will kill untold millions. The few who somehow manage to survive, will burn under a sun no longer buffered by the ozone layer. How do I know this?" He raised his eyebrows enquiringly but didn't wait for an answer. "Because, I've seen it all before. Many times."

He shivered in anticipation. "This will all happen with or without you. You can be part of it and then escape to your sanctuary, or you can quickly go insane in solitary confinement. Choices, Mitch."

Mitch had finally heard enough. "Get out of here with your choices. Fucking psycho. Don't bother coming back. I'll take my chances."

"Psycho?" Cole cocked his head and tapped his lips with his index finger, miming heavy thought. "As in psychotic? I don't think so. I think you mean sociopath." He paused. "'Fucking socio' doesn't have the same ring though, does it?"

He pushed himself off the mattress, stood and rolled his shoulders, settling his coat on his frame. He swiped both hands across the sides of his head, smoothing his hair. "I said if you listened, I'd get you out of the box. I made that guarantee and I'll make it happen as a gesture of good faith. You need to think about this conversation in a less-confined environment." He fastened the buttons on his jacket. "Just don't think too long. The tinnitus won't allow that kind of time."

He took a step toward the door, then swiveled. He plucked the business card out of his pocket. He looked at it, smiled and then dropped it. The card fell crazily, fluttering toward the floor like a butterfly with a broken wing.

With hypnotic attention, Mitch stared at it.

"I bought some melatonin in a health food store," Cole said. "Quite worthless. The clerk though… Blonde, skinny, pretty in a plain sort of way, was extremely helpful."

CHAPTER 31

COLE WALKED OUT of the box, feeling hatred radiating off Mitch Reilly like the heat off a sunburn. Ignoring it wasn't difficult. The sun rises in the east and sets in the west—after countless years a man just gets used to certain things. The difficult part was having the whole, "future-is-inevitable," conversation for, quite literally, the ten-thousandth time. Keeping that irritant off his face took a little more effort.

He paused in the hallway with his back to the box, showing Reilly he was unconcerned and in no rush. He adjusted his burgundy tie and brushed a palm down each sleeve of his crème-colored coat, waiting for the cell door to slide shut behind him. When the magnetic locks clacked into place, his controlled calm disappeared. He shook his head and blew out a frustrated, noisy sigh. There was a moment or two in the box when he almost screamed, "Her world is next!"

Of course, this was to be avoided. Leverage, rather than blunt force, was a better approach. Let him think about it for a while. Stew on it. Let him visualize Liv's world as a worthless rock covered in a layer of radioactive slag. Reilly would make the right choice. Eventually he'd be able to justify it in a way he never could, had he been forced.

Cole strode down the hallway, annoyance prickling him like

bugs skittering over his skin, making him feel like he needed a shower, like he needed a couple of Advil for his aches and pains. For a second, he considered leaving Reilly locked in the box, watching him as he would a bug under a microscope, while his mind ate itself alive. A little payback for all the unnecessary irritation.

He shook his head. Travelers.

He made a mental note to speak with Tyler. The deputy warden would have to keep a careful eye on Reilly, keep the young man out of harm's way and prevent him from hurting himself if he delayed in making a decision too long, and the tinnitus became too bad.

Deputy Warden Tyler was a perfect example of an individual who only cooperated because of leverage, an individual who kowtowed in his presence and fought him in his absence.

Employees.

Maybe he'd tell the inmates about the perverted Squat's fondness for young boys. Cole didn't care which way the man's perversions ran, not after witnessing the debauchery of the seventeen hundreds, but watching inmates tear Tyler's limbs off one by one, would make for an entertaining afternoon.

He wouldn't do that either. Tyler was useful. He had captured a traveler, after all. Quite likely he would do so again.

Cole had the same problems (and then some) as every manager everywhere. Employees showed up late, didn't show up at all, wouldn't leave their cell phones alone, were rude to customers—the list was endless, but handling the likes of Mitch Reilly and Deputy Warden Tyler, and the rest of his employees across infinite worlds, created problems exponentially higher than those of the average manager. Just once he would have appreciated a little understanding, or at the very least, some sympathetic cooperation. He didn't think that was too much to ask. But, it never happened. It was always, "I can't do this…" or, "I can't do that…" and then he had to use intimidation and apply leverage.

Employees.

Travelers.

At the end of the hall he turned left and entered the monitoring room. His eyes jumped from flat screen to flat screen until he found the one displaying Reilly's cell. He said to the guard watching the screens, "You were watching, yes?" He didn't know the young man, nor did he care when the individual averted his eyes and answered in a voice strung high and tight with jangly nerves.

"Yes, Sir."

"But not listening?"

"No, Sir."

"Tell me, what did Mr. Reilly do when I left the room?"

"He put on a chain, first thing. Then he picked something up off the mattress." He paused a beat and then said in a shaky voice, "They aren't supposed to have personal belongings in the box, Sir."

"You're being very diligent, young man. But, in this case, we'll permit Mr. Reilly his trinket." He allowed himself a tiny smile. If Reilly hadn't guessed during their meeting, the Green Earth loyalty card should have made it clear which world was on the top of the Next to Die list.

Or, not.

The list could be changed. He thought he made that clear too, when he suggested this world was standing on the brink. If Reilly quit acting like a truculent grade schooler, they could kill off a different world and precious Liv's would see another day.

Cole watched the monitor intently. Reilly stood in the center of the box, staring at the loyalty card between his fingers. Slowly his head rose. His gaze lasered into the camera high in the corner, eyes hard and black.

Cole said quietly, without a trace of triumph, "Turn on the audio."

The young guard's trembling fingers hit a switch.

Soft static hissed out of the speakers, followed by Reilly's voice. "Cole? You mother-fucker? You listening? I'll do it. I'll work for you."

The kid working the control panel blinked and jerked back reflexively. His hand flew to the audio switch, snapping it to the Off position.

Cole gave a small laugh. The irritable, jittery feeling wasn't quite as noticeable as a few minutes before. He patted the guard's shoulder reassuringly. The kid stiffened under his touch.

"I've been called worse," Cole said. "May I tell you something interesting? Before the mid-twenties, 'mother-fucker' wasn't even an expression. If you called someone a mother-fucker in nineteen-twenty, that person would have looked at you in confusion rather than offense."

"Really?"

A non-committal answer, but Cole understood the kid had to say something. "I'm a student of history, young man. Believe it or not, what you just heard was a good thing."

CHAPTER 32

THIRTY MINUTES AFTER Cole left him in the box, a screw escorted Mitch back to Red 350, saying, "I don't know why they let you out. You've got some juice, I guess. Nobody's happy about what you did to Carter."

Mitch heard the screw's anger, saw him toying with the Taser on his belt, clearly anxious to use it on a prisoner who had the audacity to strike a colleague, and he said, "Yes, Sir," and nodded politely.

"Up to me," the screw said, "you'd go the full three months."

"Yes, Sir," Mitch said.

The screw gave him a long, "First-chance-I-get-I'll-mess-you-up," stare.

Mitch didn't care. He'd take hard glares all day long if it meant he didn't have to listen to another minute of the sugary music or inspirational messages on the television in the box.

He climbed the ladder to the top bunk, lay down and stared at the ceiling, with the tinnitus buzzing and stabbing, making his eyes water and his vision striate around the edges. The intensity was familiar, but the speed with which it returned—days instead of the usual year—worried him. He'd have to slip soon, especially if he didn't find a way of controlling the fear and stress. Cole said he'd have him out of Glades within a week. Mitch figured it would have to happen sooner. Five days was closer to the mark.

It was easy to guess how it would go.

Cole would show up late on the fourth or fifth day. He'd know the best time, in the same way he knew so many unknowable things. He'd apologize for the delay with a smile in his eyes that contradicted the words on his lips. By that point, the tinnitus would be practically unbearable. Mitch would curse himself for being weak and needing a portal so desperately. He'd beg Cole to create one like he had when he created the sanctuary.

"Calm down," he whispered. "You're not helping yourself."

"You're out?"

Mitch jumped slightly, the voice surprising him. He turned his head on the pillow and swept his gaze down to the side.

Ray stood in the doorway, his forehead furrowed into a question. He took a couple of steps deeper into Red 350 and then leaned back on the wall. He folded his arms over his chest. "Word was, you'd be gone three months."

"I got lucky."

"What's that mean?"

Mitch took a few seconds to answer, not really in the mood to talk with the tinnitus ping-ponging around his head, but he told himself to be patient. Ray seemed like a decent guy and there was no point alienating someone with whom he had to live. "Remember I mentioned meeting the warden? I agreed to…" His voice tailed off. He took a deep breath, held it, then released it slowly. It took a great deal of effort to complete the sentence. "I agreed to work for him."

"What does he want you to do?"

"Nothing I want to talk about."

Ray nodded. He shrugged off the wall, took three steps across the cell and a moment later, Mitch heard the weight of his body hit the lower mattress. Relieved Ray hadn't pushed the issue, he turned his attention back to the loyalty card between his fingers. Liv had signed the card and dotted the I with a tiny heart, as she usually did. He missed her like never before. The guilt over leaving her without an explanation was a physical, all-over ache. He knew some of it existed because of where he was and the predicament he was in, but there was more to it than that. The threat against her world and the threat against her were colossal contributing factors.

He could save her.

At the expense of another world, and the billions who call it home.

It was either her world or another if he believed Cole.

Why wouldn't you believe him? After everything the King of Lies showed you (if that's who he is), and everything he said, do you really need proof?

Mitch shuddered, imagining the form "proof" might take. Cole would tell him to pick a place. Haiti, for instance. He could hear the smooth, game-show voice, the precise way Cole put sentences together…

"Poor. Impoverished. A small population who take, take, take but give nothing in return." A reasonable shrug. "They're used to hurricanes in Haiti. You want proof I am what I claim to be? I'll hit Haiti with a class five. You pick the date."

Psycho. Socio. Whatever.

How could he stop the man? Was it even possible? Saving Liv might be the best outcome in an untenable situation, a move that wasn't entirely altruistic because in saving her, he saved an entire world.

At the expense of another world, and the billions who call it home.

Ray's voice drifted up from the lower bunk. "I was thinking about the stuff Roger Olson talked about?"

Mitch ignored the question in Ray's voice, hoping his cellmate would get the hint and remain silent for a little while longer. His head buzzed and the molten panicky spot in his stomach burned. He muttered, "Dumb-ass," hoping the arrogant cop and

Lindsay were hundreds of miles away, preferably as far from the Sunshine state as it was possible to travel.

"I think there's something to what he said," Ray continued.

Mitch didn't care if Olson made it, but he liked Lindsay. He enjoyed both their evening and meeting a person who shared the same affliction as himself.

"He was right. I have access to cash," Ray said, then, "Mitch? Are you awake?"

Mitch held a sigh in check. He said, "I'm awake, Ray. I've got a bad headache is all."

Ray rushed on, speaking quickly, like he had an idea to sell. "I think Olson was onto something."

"What are you talking about?"

"I started looking around, seeing what he saw. I started figuring out how much garbage eight hundred inmates generate in a day."

"You want me to tie you up in an Extra Strength Glad?" Mitch was a little flippant now, wondering about Ray's excitement but not particularly interested. "Toss you out with the rest of the trash?"

"I think that's what Olson was getting at."

"You don't think someone considered that possibility already?"

"Maybe. Maybe not. Maybe they didn't have the idea. Maybe they did but didn't have bribe money. Things change. What's right today is wrong tomorrow. He was right about the other things he mentioned. It will take some investigating and some planning—"

"How long?"

"I only have about a year left. We'd have to make it happen before then."

"Good luck. I got five days. Can you figure it out in five days?"

"Of course not," Ray exclaimed, dismay weighing down his voice. "One of us needs to get a job in the kitchen, for what I have in mind. That's where most of the garbage is generated. That alone could take weeks. Longer maybe."

"Sorry, Ray. I can't help. I don't have the time. Doesn't mean you shouldn't keep after it though."

"What do you mean five days?"

"Cole will be back inside a week. I don't want to work for him, but in five days I'll have no choice."

"Why?"

Mitch stared at the ceiling. They shared a silence that grew from seconds to minutes. Ray finally broke it. "Do you believe in God, Mitch?"

Mitch said nothing.

"I was in the chapel earlier. It's nothing much, but you still get that feeling, like you would in a real church. It got me thinking about Dawn and Angie."

Mitch thought the chapel had very little to do with Ray's memories. He said nothing. It didn't sound like Ray was talking to him, on top of which, two theological conversations in one morning was one too many for a guy who only went to church because his girlfriend liked him to accompany her.

"I shouldn't have killed those two Squats. I couldn't do it again. I'm not sure how I did it in the first place."

Everybody in Glades knew Ray's story. Mitch doubted there was a Modern in the place who didn't want to shake his hand. Personally, Mitch wasn't sure if he agreed or disagreed. He didn't have any experience with Squats and he wasn't sure whether that should have made a difference one way or another. He said, "Seems to me you've got some stones you didn't know you had."

"I don't know about that but look where it got me." Ray paused. "They say when a child dies she goes right into God's arms. It's because a baby is innocent. She's never sinned. She doesn't know the word or the concept. A five-year-old would go right to God's arms too I think, assuming heaven exists. I need to get out of this place, try and make amends. I'd like my baby girl to see me do that."

"Olson talks too much, Ray. Getting out isn't on the agenda." Mitch felt a stab of guilt. This wasn't patience. Maybe, just maybe, carrying on a decent conversation with a decent kind of guy, would take his mind off his own crappy predicament.

He took a breath and released it slowly. He put his hands together behind his head and crossed his ankles. In a friendlier tone, he said, "Growing up I knew one thing about church. It's where a guy went to meet a really bad, good girl. That only worked once for me, so I suspect it's mostly bullshit. I learned a little more of The Truth from Liv. Not enough to convince me one way or another, but today I'm a little more receptive to biblical concepts than I was before. If you think heaven exists for your daughter, then I'm certain she's there, holding your hand right now. As for making amends, I don't think that's possible. Moving forward doesn't cancel the past."

Now, please leave me alone. Or, if we still need a way to kill all this boredom, we could get away from complex topics and discuss simpler subjects—redhead or brunette, electric or acoustic—that sort of thing.

Like a terrier on a pant cuff, Ray wouldn't let it go.

"You're certain?"

"Certain is a strong word. But, this Cole guy? He's real, and he's evil. He claims he isn't Satan. I'm not sure I believe him. Given some of the things I know and the way he acted and some of the things he said, I'm not just making noise. I'm open to possibilities."

After a long silence, Ray said, "You met Satan?"

CHAPTER 33

IN A PRISON full of whack-jobs, Mitch was coming across as a different kind of crazy, which shouldn't have surprised Ray, but it did. If nothing else, he could read people and he usually got it right. But, when someone tells you he's met Satan in the flesh, that's when you have to admit your judgment hiccupped.

Mitch didn't answer—Ray didn't expect he would—so he kept a careful monotone and repeated himself, louder this time. "You met Satan?"

He heard a long, loud sigh from the upper bunk. "Let's walk," Mitch said.

They left Red 350 and headed outside. Ray shrugged out of the top half of his coveralls and tied the sleeves around his waist as they moved into the sun. The guard towers wobbled in the afternoon heat waves. The chain link fencing was a hazy mirage. Overhead, the endless blue sky taunted him, telling him if not for the razor wire and dogs and guards with their guns, he could walk in a straight line forever.

Beneath that big sky, Glades felt like a very small place.

The basketball game was as intense as usual. Under a shiny layer of sweat, the grinning skull tattooed on Colin McTavish's back appeared to be alive. The skull's good eye winked and the arrow through the other eye bobbed a sardonic hello. Ray couldn't understand why the hideous caricature fascinated him. He tore his eyes away and followed Mitch toward the bleachers.

They skirted the gym, giving the lifters plenty of space. The Squats glared as they passed, all clenched fists and threatening faces. Ray nervously searched for Joshua Parker, but the angry First Gen was nowhere to be seen. The Moderns didn't interrupt their workout with even a glance in their direction. That was the difference between Squats and Moderns. Moderns fought if they had to, or if they were provoked, or if they had something to prove. It usually didn't take much to get them going. On the other hand, a Squat's fist was in mid-swing before the fight even started. It took nothing to wind one up, zero to full blast in three seconds, then fists flew and blood splattered and the guards rushed in with their Tasers and batons.

Despite the heat, a shiver rippled up Ray's back. The unpredictable explosions of violence no longer scared him to the same degree as they had when he first became an inmate, but he doubted he'd ever get used to the mayhem.

They found a spot on the bleachers. Ray sat down and leaned forward with his elbows on his knees, chin on his fists, waiting in curious silence. Mitch met Satan? Obviously, an exaggeration, but he wanted to hear the story.

Mitch's face was drawn and tired, his eyes bloodshot. He sat down on a riser one lower than Ray, leaned back and propped himself up on his elbows. He stretched out, crossing his long legs at the ankles. He stared into the distance. The pose reminded Ray of a habit Dawn had when she wanted to discuss an embarrassing or difficult subject. She'd ask him to cover his face with a towel or T-shirt, or she'd snuggle up behind him so they were both staring at the same wall. Somehow the lack of eye contact made it easier for her to say whatever she had on her mind.

Mitch took his time. "I have this disease? Affliction? I don't know what to call it. What happens every twelve months is…"

He told his story concisely and clinically and Ray listened without interrupting. When he finished, Ray said slowly, "To sum up… There are countless worlds. You have a condition that allows you to travel between them using portals. I can't see the portals because they deflect people who don't share your condition. Cole destroys worlds. He finds people like you to help him. People like you help him because they are pressured into it. He does it for the rush, for lack of a better word, and he rewards you to take the sting away—"

"A reward makes the next time easier."

"—and unless you help him, he won't spring you from Glades. Your condition will deteriorate. You'll go crazy or lose your mind, or something. In the meantime, he'll go ahead and destroy your girlfriend's world."

Mitch cut him a sidelong glance. "You're a quick study, Ray."

Ray squinted into the harsh, mid-day sun. He didn't have the heart to laugh or scoff. He could have said, "Fine, don't tell me the truth," but he didn't have the energy for that either. Mitch's story saddened him, coming as it did from someone he'd pegged as a person grounded and direct. Again, he wasn't surprised. Glades wore a person down. It chipped away at everything that mattered. All a person could do was find his own mental escape. Colin McTavish played basketball obsessively. Ray had decided to map the guards' habits and routines in hopes of finding a weakness. Mitch apparently escaped into a fantasy that had become more genuine than real life.

With nothing meaningful or insightful to say, he asked, "Can I slip too?" He knew the answer. It had to be, "No." Anything else and Mitch would have to invite him into his delusion and somehow prove it true.

"You want to come with me?"

"Doesn't seem like a bad idea."

"For people who don't normally slip, Cole told me it might

256

mess with their heads, the same way it messes with mine if I stay. But, yeah, it will work once. At least it did for Olson."

Ray chuckled, a quiet resigned sound that lacked humor. He was unsure of what he was laughing at—Mitch's impossible story, or himself for the absurd guilt he felt for asking a question that would take him farther away from Dawn and Angie. Still keeping it light he said, "You sound quite insane. You know that, right?"

Mitch stiffened. An annoyed red hue climbed his neck.

Ray instantly regretted his statement. "I apologize, Mitch. I didn't mean anything by it."

After a beat, Mitch said through gritted teeth, "Nobody believes me. It's why I stopped telling anyone. It's why I didn't tell Liv." He stood. "It's lunch time." He walked away, joining the loose procession of inmates heading indoors.

Ray followed, jogging every other step in an effort to keep up, analyzing Mitch's anger. Why anger? A more suitable response would have been a strong defense… "No, no. It's true. This one time I slipped, and almost didn't make it…" Building the story, adding details, making it more believable. Instead, Mitch lay down the facts as he saw them and figuratively shrugged when Ray questioned him… "Believe me or don't. It's up to you."

That was how a person acted when they *weren't* spinning a tale.

Side by side they entered the clamor of the dining hall. From the kitchen, on the other side of the chrome counter rails, a grill sizzled and an exhaust fan whirred. Christmas music, piped in through the public-address system, filled the gaps in all the various conversations. The room smelled of bacon, the sweat of a few hundred inmates and stale, over-cleansed air hissing from the air conditioning vents.

Ray plucked his sweaty T-shirt away from the small of his back and then grabbed a tray and a plate. He shuffled forward steadily, clutching his tray at the front corners, pushing the back edge into his belly. The disposable cutlery reminded him of all the garbage that had to be trucked out of Glades every week.

Mitch mumbled, "I hate this song."

Ray followed his irritated gaze to one of the overhead speakers mounted high in the ceiling. He didn't actually mind *Jingle Bell Rock*. As far as Christmas songs went, it was one of the better ones. "What's wrong with *Jingle Bell Rock?*"

"We're supposed to 'get into the spirit'? Christmas music is supposed to make us all happy 'cause it's the holiday season?" Mitch's voice rose and took on a honed and dangerous edge. "I didn't like Christmas music on the outside. I sure as hell don't like it on the inside."

The inmates surrounding them glanced in their direction and then quickly averted their eyes. The ones ahead of them pushed forward. The ones behind lagged back.

Ray knew the drill. Create some space. If tensions worsen, get your back against the wall. Maybe, with luck you don't get caught in the middle when the commotion starts. If it turns chaotic, get back to your cell, but don't run because sprinting attracts attention, and the guards don't care who they electrocute with their Tasers. In a fight, they put inmates down indiscriminately, which typically meant a person was out of his cell when the double claxon sounded. That was good for a week in the box and often a second tasing. Misfiring neurons made a guy slur and drool and stagger when he regained his feet and, presumably, appear threatening.

The sudden rush of adrenaline shortened Ray's breath. His heart galloped in his chest and the rapid thumps echoed in his ears. He discreetly patted the air with his palm. "Easy," he said. "It's just a song. It doesn't mean anything. Let's just eat, all right?" He shot a glance across the dining hall, hoping the Squats hadn't seen or sensed the sudden tension.

No such luck.

A mixture of First, Second, and Third Gens sat spring loaded on the edge of their chairs. Joshua Parker stared at him wearing open hostility on his face like war paint. Ray remembered the Squat's crooning taunt, *"Maybe you want to try and take out four more Squats. Killlllller."* The dish-rag fist of hair dangling off his forehead looked more intimidating than Ray remembered. He wondered if Parker was tuned into him specifically, or if Squats somehow felt the tension as a subtle increase in atmospheric frequency, in a similar way a fly tastes the air with its legs. He thought it quite likely. Maybe a primitive kill-or-be-killed strand of DNA had compensated and grown stronger when the Squats backslid down the evolutionary ladder.

Still trying to blunt the dangerous edge of Mitch's mood, he said, "At least we're eating a little better. Right?" Long-timers said food improved during the Christmas season. They also said inmates' tempers shortened in December. Everybody missed their families. If they didn't have loved ones on the outside, they missed the good cheer that came with the silly season. Ray wasn't sure he believed the thing about the food. He hadn't tasted much difference from meal to meal. On the other hand, scuffles and raised voices were commonplace.

Mitch said nothing.

Ray waited, until Mitch nodded, a barely noticeable twitch of his head. His face was carved in granite, his black eyes hard and empty but this silent acknowledgement was enough. The inmates surrounding them visibly relaxed. Someone said, "Hey man, way to put Carter on his ass!" There were smiles and fist bumps. Someone whispered a subdued, "Hoo-ah!" The line re-tightened. Everybody shuffled forward. *Little Drummer Boy* pa-rum-pa-pum-pummed out of the speakers.

Ray put a hand on Mitch's shoulder, giving him a gentle shake. "We're all good now, right?" If a guy spooled up over *Jingle Bell Rock*, he certainly wouldn't get behind *Little Drummer Boy*.

Mitch nodded.

The urge to duck and run faded. Ray blew out a relieved breath. If the proverbial shit had hit the fan, he wouldn't have gone anywhere. He couldn't have. Not with his only friend standing front and center. That truth terrified him. An inmate at the epicenter of a fight always took a beating or a tasing. Sometimes both. Ray preferred the tasing. It hurt like crazy but didn't leave lasting effects. The batons broke bones and caused concussions.

He reached the front of the line and thrust his tray across the counter, into the pass-through. The first server dropped two pieces of dry toast on his plate.

Ray side-stepped.

A second server slid two fried eggs off a rubber spatula onto the toast.

Ray looked at his plate. The yolks, an unhealthy ochre color, were cracked and dry, reminding him of desert hard-pan. The whites glistened with grease, edges burnt and curled. The meal didn't look good. It didn't smell good. Ray knew it wouldn't taste good.

He shuffled sideways.

Four strips of burnt bacon landed on his plate. They didn't waste food in Glades. No reason leftover breakfast bacon couldn't be used in an egg sandwich at lunch. He sighed. The last decent meal he'd eaten was months ago, almost too long ago to remember. Angie's delight at the Disney buffet made him and Dawn smile. The food was forgettable, but he remembered the meal fondly.

A stern voice said loudly, "Mitch Reilly! Move it along."

The tension threading through Ray returned in a single heartbeat.

Shane Wilford—the guard who monitored kitchen staff— glared at Mitch from the opposite side of the pass-through.

Wilford. One of the worst. A guard who loved cracking skulls, an ex-pro football player, gone to seed. He liked telling anyone who'd listen that he'd broken his front tooth during a game, when he was called up for the final two contests of the regular season.

He had the broken tooth capped in gold, presumably so nobody ever forgot this outrageous claim.

Ray doubted Wilford's story, if for no other reason than he disliked the guard. He hoped an inmate had broken the man's tooth and had scars on his knuckles to prove it.

He cut his eyes to the left.

Mitch hadn't moved. He was giving his lunch plate the same blank, thousand-yard stare Ray had seen on the bleachers. Ray guessed Mitch wasn't seeing the eggs or the toast or the burnt-to-a-crisp bacon. He was seeing life before Glades, another world that included a cute blonde named Liv.

Wilford pulled the baton from the loop on his belt, the motion un-tucking his sweat-stained shirt. He held the baton vertically and tapped it against the outside of his leg. Toast crumbs clung to his bushy mustache. The gold tooth shone wetly. "I won't say it again, Reilly," he said.

Mitch blinked. He looked from his plate to Wilford. His eyes narrowed.

Ray's heart hippity-hopped in his chest. He muttered, "Oh, no," then louder, he said, "Mitch—"

"You call this lunch?" Mitch said. His voice sounded hollow, as though it came from the bottom of a deep bottle. He leaned over the counter and flipped the food off his tray. The server's eyes widened. He recoiled reflexively, dropping his bright, tangerine spatula. Fried eggs and greasy bacon splattered his stained apron. Mitch's plate bounced off his chest, dropped, and clanged on the metal counter like a bell signaling the first round of a championship fight.

When Ray thought about it later, he remembered it as the exact moment a shit-storm the likes of which he'd never seen before, and would likely never see again, began.

PART 3

*"A person is smart. People are dumb,
panicky dangerous animals."*

Kay (Men in Black)

CHAPTER 34

FOR TWO, PERHAPS three seconds, nothing much happened.

Then everything happened at once.

The inmates in the breakfast line, those who were closest and saw Mitch flip his tray, reacted first. They dropped their own trays on the counter's chrome rails and most left the dining hall in a hurry. Those who remained behind, gathered around Colin McTavish near the south exit, waiting to see what would happen next. The guard at that exit, the young Christopher Tanner, ordered them to leave. They ignored him. Christopher didn't press the issue. Instead he raised a Walkie-Talkie to his lips and called for backup. Simultaneously, Joshua Parker and a crowd of Squats stood, pushing their benches back as one. The sound was like a chainsaw symphony, collapsing the moment of stretched calm in the dining hall. It didn't matter the commotion in the lunch line had nothing to do with them. They were simply obeying their nature.

David Dawson reacted at once. Leaving the north exit unguarded, he strode toward Parker, drawing the Taser from his holster as he moved. In a voice that filled the room he said, "Sit your ass down, or I'll put you down."

Parker stepped forward to meet him, his stocky torso rigid, both fists clenched so tightly the veins in his arms bulged. A pack of Squats clustered behind him. "We don't got nothing to do with this," Parker said in his deep, guttural voice. "Why you threatening us?"

The guard and the inmate glared at each other. Neither moved. The smell of burnt bacon floated on the air. Overhead, *Little Drummer Boy* continued to play.

Beside the gate into the kitchen, Ray's eyes flicked to the speakers in the ceiling. Everybody had their own reasons to hate *Little Drummer Boy*. Ray thought it sounded vaguely militaristic. Minus the words, it reminded him of the melancholy military records his grandfather used to listen to, marching tunes that accompanied young soldiers as they trooped to their deaths. He held his breath, wondering who'd blink first, Parker or Dawson.

He should have kept his eyes on Shane Wilford.

Every time Wilford read a memo from the human resource department saying inmates were human beings and as such deserved respect, he thought, *my ass*. Convicts were no better than dogs, and everybody knew a dog needed a regular whipping, to ensure the stupid mutt remembered who was boss. If a con had obeyed the rules, he wouldn't be in Glades in the first place. He wouldn't need to be reminded—in the most convincing way possible—that prison was punishment.

Rehabilitation?

My ass.

As a target, he liked the collar bone. One well-placed blow and a collar bone shattered and a con dropped, screaming on the floor. It was a painful, debilitating injury. The beautiful thing was, a broken collar bone wasn't life-threatening. As long as a con didn't die, nobody cared how many broken bones he suffered.

He surged forward. Anticipation and exertion turned his jowly face an unhealthy scarlet. His belly, spilling over his belt, wobbled and bounced. Hopefully, he thought, he'd collect a bruise or two in the imminent fight, something he could parlay into a sympathy fuck when he got home. Cynthia didn't put out as willingly as she did when he was in his ball-playing prime, but he'd weaken her knees. He'd describe how he, against overwhelming odds, was the one guard who ended a fight before it descended into full-fledged riot. He'd brag for months how he put Mitch Reilly, the shit-stain who broke Carter's nose, into the infirmary with a cracked skull. Reilly deserved a little extra attention, after what he did to Carter.

He swept his right arm back. The baton came up, over his shoulder. His lips parted beneath his mustache, the gold tooth turning his predatory smile into the strangest of snarls. He swung like he was throwing the game-winning pass in the final seconds of the fourth quarter.

Frosty the Snowman took over from *Little Drummer Boy*, merrily telling everyone to have some fun before he melted away.

Mitch saw the baton coming. He flinched and rotated left, planting his weight on his rear foot, leaning back at the waist. The baton flew past his face, whistling with speed, washing wind across his cheek. He rotated in the opposite direction and slammed his breakfast tray into the side of Wilford's head.

It hit with a dull, ineffective, thunk.

An expression of surprised anger, rather than pain, covered Wilford's face.

Mitch dropped the tray. With his feet firmly planted, he swung through his waist and drove a looping right hook into the side of Wilford's head, with all the weight and momentum of his upper body behind his fist. It was a good punch, possibly the best he'd ever thrown. He felt the impact all the way to his shoulder.

It should have put Wilford on the floor, but two hundred and sixty pounds of muscle-turned-fat doesn't drop easily, not after taking body blows on the gridiron from guys twice Mitch Reilly's size.

The ex-football player staggered and grunted. His eyes glazed. A ribbon of blood dribbled down the side of his head. Like a sailor in heavy seas, he swayed and rocked in small, dizzying circles. The baton dropped, clattered on the floor, and his hand rose and touched the side of his face. His fingers came back bloody. He blinked and shook his head like a wounded Sasquatch. Then he smiled. "You're in a world of hurt, little man," he said.

He snatched the Taser out of the holster on his belt.

CHAPTER 35

OVERHEAD, THE CHRISTMAS music played. In the center of the dining hall the two guards stood opposite Parker and the Squats, every man poised as if at the start of a race. At the south exit, Tony Carter and Ed Porter, the back-up guards Christopher requested, pushed through McTavish and the group of Moderns, into the hall. The three guards paused while the most experienced among them, Carter, assessed the situation. Then, he started issuing orders.

He told McTavish and the Moderns to return to their cells, told them if they didn't he'd personally speak to the deputy warden about their noncompliance. He pointed and Ed Porter headed for the north exit, the door Dawson abandoned on the opposite side of the room. He pointed again and Christopher Tanner strode to the middle of the dining hall and stood shoulder to shoulder with Dawson, facing Parker and the rest of the Squats.

Satisfied, Carter nodded…

…and then caught sight of Mitch Reilly over near the kitchen.

He went rigid with rage. His face turned red and his swollen eyes glowed a livid black against the strip of white bandage holding his nose in place. He licked his lips, pulled his baton from the loop on his belt and marched toward Reilly, slapping the club up and down in the palm of his hand. Hatred twisted his face like melting plastic. He hadn't forgotten who broke his nose and gave him the matching shiners.

Colin McTavish ignored Carter's instructions, just as he'd ignored Christopher. He seldom went to his cell when a screw told him to, and he never went when the double claxon sounded, which had become a bit of a joke. The screws thought he enjoyed solitary. Why else would he stay out when the claxon rang? He didn't—nobody enjoyed the box—but opportunities presented themselves when discipline fell apart in Glades. Today McTavish's priority was an uppity First Gen. Word had come down from above, all the way from the top. A primate was causing trouble. He needed to be reined in.

In the thirty-five seconds it took for the normally disciplined dining hall to disintegrate into chaos, Ray hadn't moved. Stiff with numb disbelief, he clutched one of the serving counter's chrome rails and watched wide-eyed and open-mouthed, as Christopher Tanner and David Dawson, clinging to control with ragged fingernails, stared down the group of Squats.

Shane Wilford's Taser was in his hand, his gold tooth dominating his savage grin. Mitch, palms up defensively, was backpedaling directly toward an apparently unhinged Tony Carter.

Ray's stupor finally crumbled. He shouted.

The warning came too late. Carter swung his baton. The blow caught Mitch across the lower back and his knees gave way. He flopped forward, blowing out a blast of air in sudden, painful surprise. His face slammed into the floor, driving his teeth into his lips. Blood drooled from his mouth onto the worn and stained linoleum.

Wilford barked out a satisfied laugh. The safety light on the side of his Taser glowed a bright, Christmas green, but he made no effort to point the weapon. Instead he nodded encouragement at Carter. "Hit the shit-stain again," he ordered.

Without thinking, Ray dived for the baton Wilford dropped.

Rising to his knees, with both hands around the handle, he swung for the nose-bleed seats. The blow caught Wilford across both legs. Ray heard a sickeningly loud, but somehow satisfying crack, when the guard's right shin snapped.

Wilford's eyes bulged. He screamed a high, shrill shriek of agony and dropped like a sack of cement, in exactly the same way all the inmates he'd beaten in the past, had fallen to the floor.

Carter faltered with his own baton raised. His eyes narrowed in momentary confusion then quickly refocused. He slashed his tongue across his lips the way a black mamba did the moment before it struck. His breath whistled nosily in and out of the gap between his hillbilly teeth. "Albright," he said, his voice pinched and congested. "Two losers in one day. I'm going to enjoy this."

Ray dropped the baton and grabbed Wilford's arm. The weeping, whimpering guard still clutched his Taser. Ray wrapped his hand over Wilford's, swung the weapon around and squeezed the trigger. The gun buzzed its telltale rattle. The thin, electrified wires shot from the barrel and hit Carter in the chest.

He collapsed, screaming and convulsing as he rode the bull.

Ray dropped Wilford's arm then dried both shaking, sweaty hands on the front of his T-shirt. Nauseated at what he'd done— if anyone deserved a beating it was Wilford, but at the moment it felt too close to shooting the teens—he grabbed Mitch by the collar. Pushing with his heels, he slid on his butt across the floor, dragging his friend under the dining hall serving counter. Hopefully they'd be invisible there and avoid Parker and the rest of the Squats' attention. Exertion made him pant and gasp. A painful lump was lodged high in his throat. He thought it might be panic, or fear, and he hoped it wasn't a heart attack or something more serious, and he hoped the fight was over…

…and, it might have been, but Joshua Parker had just seen a prisoner "win," and now Wilford and Carter were disabled, which meant there were two less guards in the dining hall.

…and, it might have been, except for the Squats' inherently violent nature, and the chip the size of a cedar shingle they carried on their shoulders.

…and, it might have been had McTavish and the Moderns returned to their cells as they were ordered.

But none of that happened.

Instead, when Wilford screamed, Christopher Tanner glanced over his shoulder. In that second of lost concentration, Parker roared and if there was any doubt about his primate origins, they ended right there. He sounded like a beast in the jungle. He lunged. Bellowing, the rest of the Squats followed on his heels. Snarling and spitting like rabid animals, they overwhelmed Christopher and Dawson. Howling in desperate terror, swinging their batons in random, ineffective slices, the two guards vanished beneath a flurry of fists and feet.

At the south exit, McTavish smiled. He looked at the faces of the men in the group and stroked his Fu Manchu. Just like on the basketball court, he led and everyone followed. "There are five guards in the dining hall," he said. "We're going to grab at least two, before the primates kill 'em. Knuckleheads don't understand hostages are more useful alive."

This wasn't some kind of do-gooder mission. Typically, McTavish wouldn't have pissed on a guard if the man was on fire. Guards and inmates were as compatible as crocodiles and antelope. What he wanted was a distraction. He'd gone to the box many, many times waiting for a distraction. A riot qualified. A hostage crisis upped the ante.

He said, "Don't bother with Wilford. The primates can kill that sack of shit, for all I care. Get in. Grab two. Get out." Heads nodded. Faces filled with excitement, but McTavish didn't see expressions powerful enough to send a group of Moderns in against opponents whose first instinct was to fight.

He needed to see rage.

He singled a man out from the crowd, a guy named Brent who naturally was known as "Bent," after a parking lot fight behind the sawmill where he worked left him with a permanent limp.

McTavish spoke quickly. "A primate takes your promotion, Bent? Fucking affirmative action. What were you supposed to do? Did the cops take the baseball bat out of your truck, or did you have it chromed and framed?"

Chuckles and smiles from the crowd. One of the Moderns slapped Bent on the shoulder, a sympathetic atta-boy.

McTavish found another face, a man who avoided the Florida sunshine obsessively, a guy who was more terrified of skin cancer than he was of the firing squad. He said, "Pasty, a primate banged your sister? You tired of buying your little niece bananas on her birthday?"

Noises of commiseration and anger now—anger because they all knew it was repugnant for a Squat and a Modern to mate, so Pasty's sister must have been raped, probably twice, maybe ganged.

McTavish ignored the unhappy murmurs. He didn't buy any of this bullshit. Bent was a lazy prick who didn't deserve a promotion. By most accounts, Pasty's sister and the First Gen she married were insanely in love and as thrilled with their baby as any new parents would be. He knew them all. He knew their stories. Every knucklehead he was speaking to was in Glades for a reason, didn't matter the excuse or rationalization…

…but as motivation this kind of inflammatory crap was incredible.

He found another face. "A Squat busts into your home, steals your stuff, and you're the one in prison? Lighter fluid and a cigarette butt was too good for that primate."

And, another, "… six rounds to the chest? No way that was overkill. You want to make sure what goes down stays down, right?"

They laughed and shouted. The sound grew strident as

it pushed farther away from normal good cheer and closer to hysteria.

McTavish sped up, until all the faces looking at him were hard with fury. Finally, he said loudly, "Get in. Grab two guards. Kick the living shit out of a primate if you can, then get out."

They yelled their approval and McTavish yelled over them, "Go, go, go!"

The Moderns charged with howls of bloodlust, every imagined slight perpetuated by a Squat in the forefront of their minds. They flew into Joshua Parker's mob with uncontrollable fury and the Squats met them with primeval glee. Nearby, David Dawson lay broken and forgotten. Beside him, Christopher Tanner lay crumpled and unconscious, blood dripping from his nose. In their battle lust, the Squats completely forgot them, as well as the rest of the guards in the dining hall, just as McTavish expected they would.

Two Moderns darted out of the rioting crowd and sprinted toward the kitchen. They hoisted Tony Carter to his feet and hustled the bewildered screw toward the south exit. A third Modern grabbed David Dawson beneath the armpits, lifted him into a fireman's carry, and he too headed for the south exit.

Beneath the serving counter, Ray leaned against the wall and watched the brawl with rapt attention. He'd completely forgotten Mitch. At some point, the final notes of *Frosty the Snowman* ended and as if to counter Frosty's earlier good cheer, Elvis Presley started singing a mournful *Silent Night*.

"Ray," Mitch said. He hawked a glob of saliva and blood on the floor. "What's going on?"

Ray looked at his cellmate. "You okay?"

"I'll be pissing blood for a couple of days." Mitch struggled to sit up. He winced. His face blanched. "He hit me hard."

"I took care of him for you," Ray said, distractedly. His attention was on the fight. "McTavish and some Moderns are fighting the Squats."

Against the ferocity of the Squats, McTavish and the Moderns drew back slowly. The moment McTavish saw his Moderns and their hostages disappear through the south exit, he thundered, "Enough!"

The Moderns turned and ran.

For two full seconds the Squats did nothing except stand in stunned surprise. A full-scale retreat was unexpected. A Squat didn't know how to run from a fight. Two seconds gave the Moderns time to escape through the south exit and kick away the bench that held the door open.

Panting, chest heaving with exertion, Parker swept the fist of black hair away from his forehead. He picked up a forgotten baton. His calculating eyes swept the dining hall. The south exit, to which the cowardly Moderns had run, was apparently locked. Beneath the kitchen serving counter, Albright sat beside an inmate Parker couldn't see well enough to recognize. He was tempted to stalk over there and start swinging the baton, watch teeth hit the floor, but Albright could wait. First, he needed to see if this fight could be turned into something bigger. His eyes swung to the north exit and landed on the single guard at the door, a newbie frozen in place with dumb shock. Their eyes met and the guard's catatonic expression changed to fear.

Parker pointed and slung orders. Several Squats ran toward the north exit.

Ed Porter knew he didn't have a chance of controlling or slowing the Squats running in his direction. He held his shaking hand against the scanner and dipped his keycard into the slot. The LED turned green. He grabbed the handle and threw the door sideways. It opened fully with a ringing crash and rebounded fast. Before it closed, he thrust his arm into the gap. The door smashed into it. He felt no pain. He shot a frightened glance over his shoulder. The only thing on his mind was escape, before he ended up like Christopher Tanner, a bloody heap on the floor.

Over the PA system the double claxon finally sounded, interrupting *Silent Night* mid-sentence. Guards and inmates alike knew that every door in the Level Three area would lock in forty-five seconds, isolating every room from each other. Violence would be contained to the smallest possible space. If Ed Porter had shut the door fully and watched the LED turn red, he might have stood a chance. He did neither. He raced down the corridor without a backward glance and the Squat leading the charge behind him easily caught the door before it clicked shut.

Joshua Parker smiled. He wondered why the officer working Control didn't sound the double claxon earlier. Surely, he'd seen the fight on his monitors. Maybe he hesitated a few crucial seconds, hoping his colleague would escape from the dining hall. Maybe lots of reasons; they might even become clear at some point but whatever they were, Parker didn't care. He'd have a third screw as a hostage in seconds, an unexpected bonus over and above Wilford and Christopher. For what he had in mind, extra hostages were ideal. Extra hostages were leverage.

Parker was certain the screw working Control wouldn't disable the security system now all the doors were all locked, not for a single guard and definitely not for a crowd of rabid Squats. He was just as certain he could change Control's mind with leverage. Leverage would give him access, and with access—Parker trembled with anticipation—he'd be all over Glades, into the areas an inmate was normally banned: admin offices, the armory, the infirmary, maybe even the women's pens. His mouth dried at the thought of the drugs locked in the infirmary and of the female prisoners only a few doors away, helpless in their cells.

He shot a wistful glance in Albright's direction. He couldn't wait to fuck the Killllller up. But, Albright was second on his list of priorities. Bending Control to his will was first on the list. He started issuing orders.

When Parker started talking, a second short calm, like

a pregnant drop of water on the tip of a faucet, ensued in the nearly empty dining hall. With the music turned off and only one muted conversation taking place, the big room was eerily quiet. The crowd of Squats nodded attentively as their leader spoke, and then they started to grin.

On the floor in the middle of the dining hall, Christopher Tanner lay sprawled like a dead star fish on a sunbaked beach. Whimpering and blubbering, Shane Wilford had somehow dragged himself to a spot in a corner at the opposite end of the serving counter from Ray and Mitch, possibly hoping he'd put himself in a good defensive position. Beneath the counter, Mitch and Ray sat side by side, Mitch in a pain-induced fog, Ray with no idea what he should do next.

The look of hatred Parker knifed across the hall in his direction sent a spike of fear burning through Ray's system. His hand involuntarily tightened around the baton. He was alone. There were no guards left. Wilford was out of commission, as was Christopher Tanner. Porter had run. The Moderns had kidnapped Carter and Dawson. When Joshua Parker came for him, Ray would be on his own. He'd fight, clobber as many Squats as he could with the club, but there were just so many of them. He was a dead man walking.

This thought made him remember how far he'd fallen in the last several months. For some reason, he saw his kitchen with the gingerbread moldings up in the corners painted a horrible yellow Dawn insisted on, something he accepted because if she wanted it, that was good enough for him, and if Angie wanted a gold-fish named Mr. Bubbles—always "Mr." for some reason—with blue marbles in a bowl on the counter, that was also good enough for him.

Now?

He was in some kind of gladiatorial arena, sitting beside a most-probably delusional scrapper who maintained he belonged in a different world, and he was going to go toe to toe with a segment of society he'd done his level best to avoid most of his life.

"Deep breaths," Mitch said. "In through the nose. Out through the mouth. When they come, we'll take Parker together. Full on, one hundred percent. Don't hold back. That might be enough. Sometimes you take out the leader and it's all over."

"How can you be so calm?"

"Not calm. Mentally prepared." Mitch paused. "Whoever's working Control took his time hitting the button."

"Or, the system malfunctioned. But, that seems unlikely."

"I guess it doesn't matter. Everything is locked now."

Ray nodded, his attention split between Mitch and Parker.

Most of the faces surrounding Parker wore smiles, but a Second Gen spoke up, possibly questioned his leader or said something derisive. In an unexpected blur, Parker swung his club. Blood misted the air. The Second Gen toppled like a tree in the forest. He spasmed twice. His heels drummed the floor. Then he lay still. Parker picked up where he left off, the interruption less important it seemed, than a mid-sentence belch during a friendly breakfast conversation.

Then, as one, half the Squats turned and ran toward Christopher Tanner. The young guard had regained consciousness. Sitting up on the floor, he looked perplexed and then terrified as the mob overwhelmed him a second time. They dragged him, toward the kitchen. Christopher fought back silently, digging the heels of his boots into the floor, leaving black rubber skid marks on the linoleum. He freed an arm and drove his fist into a Second Gen's face. The Second Gen dropped to his knees. Hands flew to his face, blood squeezing between his fingers. The other Squats laughed. One of them kicked his bleeding friend in the ribs as he walked by, making him wobble and then topple onto his side. They all laughed some more.

Parker watched with satisfaction. The leverage he required

started with the short and brutal task he'd given his followers. When they were done in the kitchen, he would open negotiations with Control. If Control refused to unlock the Level Three doors, Parker would up the ante, using the guard who'd fled into the corridor. If Control still refused, Parker would use Wilford and get more persuasive. He couldn't imagine having to raise the stakes a fourth time—Control would fold—but if required, Parker would move to whoever was sitting beside Albright. He'd kill them all on camera, one by one, if need be. Control *would* unlock the doors.

After which, Parker planned on finding Raymond Albright. Albright thought he could kill two Squats and get away with it? He was wrong.

Parker forked his index and middle finger, pointing them back and forth between his eyes and Albright a couple of times. He mouthed, "I'll be back, Killllller." He smiled nastily when Albright's eyes widened. Then he jogged for the north exit door, and the corridor where some of his Squats had overwhelmed a doomed Ed Porter.

CHAPTER 36

"WILFORD, YOU MORON," Ray said, quietly so as not to alert the small host of Squats who dragged Christopher Tanner into the kitchen. "You didn't lock the gate when you came for Mitch. What else did you leave unsecured?" He rose to his knees and peered over the counter.

In a thin, weak voice, Wilford said, "I won't forget this, Albright." He sat in the corner, leaning into it with one shoulder on each wall, his good leg straight, the other bent at a crazy angle. His face was beaded with sweat. "You're history. I'll come for you."

Without looking at him, Ray said, "I'll out run you."

In the kitchen, the Squats held the struggling guard upright against the food preparation counter. Two of them, one on either side, held Christopher's arm securely in place on top of the counter. A Third Gen lumbered forward with a meat cleaver in his hand. Christopher's petrified eyes were huge. "No, no, no…" he repeated in an increasingly piercing voice.

The dread in Ray's chest bloomed like a strip of reel-to-reel film melting in a projector. Panting shallowly, he sank back down until he was sitting beside Mitch. He stared straight ahead.

Mitch said, "What's going on? Why'd they take him in there?"

"They want his hand."

There was a thunk and a terrible scream. A second later, the Squats boiled out of the kitchen, laughing and cheering. One of them held the gory half of an arm aloft. Drops of blood marked a trail across the dining hall as they ran for the north exit.

"Oh shit. I should have…" Ray's voice grew shrill. He couldn't help it, he couldn't get enough air. "Those fucking animals, they just…"

"Nothing you could do." Mitch's face was hard and expressionless. His fists, resting on his thighs, were white with tension.

Ray knew he was right. He didn't care. Overwhelming guilt filled him. Guilt for not helping the young guard—even though there was nothing he could have done—and guilt for being so deliriously happy it wasn't his arm the Squats chopped off. He swallowed a deep breath or two and managed to string a sentence together. "I don't get it. Why? With the system disabled, the handprint won't unlock the doors."

"Use your head, Ray. A colleague gets his arm chopped off? That's not something Control sees every day. It might convince him to unlock the doors. If he does, the Squats got a hand and Christopher's card. Now they can go anywhere."

For several seconds, Ray said nothing. "We have to help him."

"What's that now?"

"Christopher. We have to do something. He's one of the good ones."

Mitch grimaced and rubbed his lower back. He stared longingly at the open dining hall door. He cursed softly. "I guess he's okay, for a screw. Give me a hand," he said. He stretched out his arm.

They found Christopher prone on the kitchen floor. What remained of his arm lay in an expanding pool of blood. Frozen in revulsion, Ray could only gawk. Beside him, Mitch mumbled, "Oh, man." A beat later he said, "We need a tourniquet."

Ray looked at him.

"A tourniquet, Ray. Take off your T-shirt."

Ray still had the arms of his coveralls tied around his waist. Mechanically, he peeled off his T-shirt and handed it to Mitch, who wrapped it around what was left of Christopher's arm, just below the elbow.

"Check the grill," Mitch ordered. "See if it's hot. Turn the gas up as high as it will go. Make sure it's clean. Use the scraper."

Following Mitch's instructions, Ray turned both knobs clockwise to the stops. Working quickly and efficiently, he scraped oil and food remnants from the back toward the drip-tray at the front of the grill. The flame beneath the sheet metal hissed and food and grease residue burnt away as it heated. The whirring fan in the smoke hood hungrily sucked up the coiling tendrils. Heat rose in waves. Sweat covered Ray's face and scalp. His bare chest glistened.

"Help me lift him up."

Side by side, they wrestled the unconscious guard to his feet.

"Now what?" Ray said. "You're not thinking about..." His voice faded.

"You want to do a good deed? This is the only way. He'll bleed to death before medical help gets here. Take his arm."

Ray's stomach flip-flopped. He couldn't swallow. His mouth was dust dry and his throat didn't seem to work. He wasn't sure he could keep himself from puking all over the grill, but he did as Mitch asked and took Christopher's arm. He lined it up so the bloody, dripping stump was perpendicular to the grill. The crimson droplets burned off, the stench nauseatingly bad. Ray clenched his heaving stomach and then, with Mitch supporting Christopher's body, he pushed the bloody stump squarely onto the gleaming, super-heated grill. The flesh burned and sizzled and smoked. Unable to control himself any longer, Ray spun away and threw up in the sink.

"I guess that will be enough?" Mitch asked, uncertainly, perhaps rhetorically.

Ray didn't answer. He didn't know the required length of time it took to properly cauterize the ragged stump of an arm using a grill typically meant for scrambled eggs and fried pork chops, any better than Mitch did. It wasn't something that ever crossed his mind, never mind something he stumbled over during his day-to-day routine. He sluiced a mouthful of water into his mouth and spit the slime and drool into the sink.

Silent Night began mid-sentence, where it left off when the double claxon first rang.

Ray's eyes flashed up to the speakers in the ceiling. He said unbelievingly, "Control unlocked the doors."

"That's not supposed to happen," Mitch said, stating the obvious. When he spoke again, he did so with a hopeful inflection, almost as though he didn't realize he was talking aloud. "We could be looking at a window of opportunity."

Ray heard Mitch talking, but he wasn't listening to what he said. His mind wouldn't let go of Christopher's horrific wound. He said, "With the doors unlocked, we could take Christopher to the infirmary."

"I doubt Olson was onto anything specific," Mitch said. "Fucking dumb-ass. But let's assume he was. This might be the time to take advantage of one of those weaknesses he talked about."

Ray said, "We can't just prop him up under a camera and hope Control sees him."

"It's unrealistic. I get it. The chaos won't last long. Reinforcements will arrive soon. Supervision will be restored. Between now and then, though? We're in the middle of an unprecedented situation. It might take them longer than usual to understand and control it. If there was ever a chance to escape, this might be it."

Ray finally heard and understood the words coming from Mitch's mouth. "You can't be serious. Where do you think you'll go? At least Olson had a rudimentary idea. You haven't done any analysis or come up with a shadow of a plan."

"If you don't look, you don't see, Ray."

"What does that mean?" He raised his voice and said firmly, "Take a side, Mitch. I'll take the other. Whatever you're thinking, an extra five minutes to the infirmary won't make a difference."

Together they carried Christopher into the dining hall. Ray stooped long enough to snatch up the baton he'd dropped earlier. He wasn't sure if he'd be able to use it as he had on Wilford, but if he had to protect himself or Mitch, he liked the idea of having a weapon. With Christopher between them, he and Mitch followed the trail of blood drops on the floor to the north exit.

Behind them Wilford called, "Where are you taking him?" The guard's voice became a desperate plea. "Albright? Reilly? You can't just leave me. I can't move. What if they come back?"

Half carrying, half dragging Christopher's unconscious body, they climbed over the bench the Squats had jammed in the door and entered the hallway. At the far end, a lone individual in a guard's uniform, sat slumped against the wall, forearms on his knees, head hung low. The sounds of destruction poured through the open doorway beside him.

"They'll kill me," Wilford wailed.

Ray said loudly, drowning out his plaintive cries, "I just read a novel. One of the characters had his hand bitten off by a dog. Or maybe it was a barracuda. I don't remember. Anyway, he had a weed whacker prosthetic. He carried around a pocket sized can of WD40 to keep it working right."

"That's sick."

"The book was funny."

"I don't think Christopher is going to want a weed whacker for a hand," Mitch said.

"Where is everybody?"

"They're wrecking things. This is a riot, Ray. I'm going to take advantage of it and get ahead"

CHAPTER 37

THE KEYCARD AND palm-print security system had not mal-functioned. Except for a fifteen-second lapse in standard operating procedures—what would later be determined as human error on the part of two junior Glades guards who shouldn't have been working alone—the system performed exactly as designed.

Only minutes before Mitch and Ray cauterized Christopher Tanner's arm, Jimmy Hilroy scanned the monitors in Control and noted with satisfaction (and not just a little relief), that everything in Glades Rehabilitation Facility was operating calmly and correctly. The dining hall was busy, most of the inmates lining up in an orderly fashion for their mid-day meal. Some remained in the common area watching television or playing cards. Others remained outdoors.

All very ordinary.

Which was good, excellent in fact, after all the warnings he'd received during training about how his job boiled down to hours of boredom interrupted by seconds of terror, thanks in a large part to the Squats who were too violent and unstable to live on the outside, this according to the instructors, who were all Moderns.

Jimmy nodded happily at the normalcy. He retrieved his lunch bag from under the counter. Inside he found a variety of Tupperware containers, enough food to last three days instead of his twelve-hour shift. Jimmy's girlfriend enjoyed cooking. There were always leftovers. She said she didn't want him to go hungry, even though he told her he did nothing to generate an appetite in Glades. He suspected there were ulterior motives in Bree's willingness to act like a homemaker, now they were sharing a nice apartment and he had a good job with a full benefit package. He didn't really care. He liked having her around, ulterior motives or not. She had a large heart and she was a fine cook.

His gaze drifted from monitor to monitor. One guard in the dining hall was pointing his baton at a crowd of Squats. In the ten days since training ended, Jimmy had seen that more times than he could count. He frowned in mild consternation, uncomfortable with the apparent discrimination. He hadn't witnessed Squats acting any worse than Moderns, despite what the experienced guards told him to expect. Yet, the guards didn't give the Squats an inch. It was no wonder they occasionally went nuclear.

His fingers found a folded piece of paper in his lunch bag. Bree's note read, "Enjoy your day! From the one who loves you best!" He smiled and a warm, pleasant flush filled him.

The good feeling nicely cancelled out the apprehension he felt at the beginning of his shift. Junior guy on the seniority list, he knew he'd be working during the Christmas season, but he wasn't supposed to be alone. Every guard was supposed to have a partner. Unfortunately, senior guys had holidays at this time of year. If they didn't, they were calling in sick. Either that or admin was understaffing on purpose, and Jimmy didn't believe they'd deliberately understaff. Whatever the reason, when he showed up for today's shift, there weren't enough guards to go around. The duty officer decided Control was the best place for the lone man. The rest of the guys would spend their time in Level Three with the inmates, working in close proximity as usual.

Jimmy liked working Control better than spending his time inside Level Three. He didn't consider himself timid, but to a fellow with a degree in criminology, an idealistic view that everyone deserved a second chance (and sometimes a third and fourth), and who had absolutely no previous exposure to criminals of any kind, the inmates were an intimidating bunch.

Jimmy tossed his clip-on tie over his shoulder and bit into his sandwich. A yellow stream of mustard squirted onto his shirt. "Damnit," he mumbled. He swiped the condiment with a napkin. Little rolls of paper peeled away and clung to his shirt, smearing the mustard. He dribbled some water from his bottle onto his shirt and tried again. The stain grew larger. "Damnit!"

He scanned the monitors...

...and froze solid in his chair, even as his heartbeat accelerated like a fighter jet.

The dining hall was bedlam.

A skirmish was unfolding near the kitchen. A mob of Moderns and Squats were kicking the hell out of each other in the center of the hall. Two guards Jimmy didn't recognize were down, and although the monitors were monochromatic, there was no mistaking the black liquid that dripped from one of the guard's faces and pooled on the floor. Near the north exit, Ed Porter stood catatonically—he and Jimmy were hired on the same day—with, apparently, no idea what to do next.

"Get out of there, Eddy," Jimmy whispered, his palm hovering over the red, lockdown button. He wanted to hit it—standard operating procedures dictated this was the time—but he hesitated, hoping Porter would get to safety on the other side of the door, before all the locks slammed into place and the keycard system deactivated.

Porter didn't move.

Three Moderns suddenly darted out of the middle of the fight. Two picked up Tony Carter. The third hoisted a guard Jimmy didn't recognize into a fireman's carry. All three did a fast shuffle to the south exit. A second later the remaining Moderns abandoned the fight and followed them at a dead run. For two full seconds, the Squats they'd been fighting looked around in apparent bewilderment.

Jimmy exhaled heavily. It appeared everything was over, nothing worse than a story to tell Bree when she asked how his day went. Something other than the usual, "You know," response…

…but as he watched, a First Gen picked up one of the fallen guard's batons. He tossed his head, flipping a long mop of dark hair away from his eyes.

Joshua Parker.

He surveyed the dining hall, spotted Porter near the north exit and aimed the baton. Several Squats broke into a sprint. Porter finally moved. He spun in place, threw a panicked glance over his shoulder, then dashed through the open door into the corridor.

Jimmy slapped the lockdown button. "Shut the door, Eddy," he whispered. Porter was loud and outspoken, the class clown, fun to hang around with, but Jimmy wondered in silence if the man had taken his training seriously enough. Hopefully he'd remember the only thing that mattered at this point—containment. It was drummed into them during training, something Jimmy thought impossible to forget. Hit the button. All the doors in Level Three lock. The keycard system quits functioning and the violence is contained to the smallest possible area.

Containment.

Porter didn't slow long enough to shut the door behind him. The Squat leading the charging pack caught it before it slammed shut. Barely slowing at the bottle-neck the narrow doorway created, the Squats surged out of the dining hall into the corridor leading to the common room. They raced down the hallway, swarming the unlucky guard. For a second before he disappeared, Porter's wide, terrified eyes met Jimmy's in the monitor. His mouth opened in a noiseless scream that pierced Jimmy's ears like needles.

In a different monitor, a small group of Squats dragged a

struggling guard into the kitchen. Jimmy gave this scene very little thought; his attention was on the hallway.

The Squats hauled Porter to his feet. In the monochromatic monitor, his face was brilliant white and streaked with black lines that could only be trickles of blood. They pushed him toward the door at the end of the corridor. One of them grabbed his arm and tried pressing his hand to the scanner. Porter resisted and a Second Gen put a huge, hairy palm on the back of his head and slammed his face into the cinderblock wall. The second time the Squat raised Porter's hand to the scanner, he didn't resist.

The door did not unlatch. Jimmy wondered if the Squats expected it would. Despite popular opinion, he didn't believe they were less intelligent than Moderns, but maybe he was wrong.

Without taking his eyes from the monitors, he grabbed the telephone. Thinking hard about what he'd say, he hit a speed-dial number, connecting directly to Emergency Services Dispatch. He asked for the anti-riot team. The fight had not been contained to the smallest possible area—the Squats had jammed one of the heavy benches into the door at the north exit and made their way into the hallway—but the damage was not significantly worse than it would have been had he pushed the button fifteen seconds earlier. The most important thing was, Level Three was secure, therefore Glades was secure.

"Response" came after "containment." The anti-riot team would muster quickly and formulate a plan. That entire sequence might take forty-five minutes, maybe as many as ninety. Much depended on the situation. The textbook was not specific because it couldn't be: a riot was never the same as the one that came before it, nor the one that came after. For the most part, however, everything was unfolding exactly as training suggested it would. There was comfort in knowing the book was accurate.

In the corridor, the crowd of Squats gestured angrily at each other. Two of them stood chest-to-chest, hands bunched. One yelled while the other shook his head with an unyielding set to his jaw. It wasn't difficult to guess what they were arguing about.

What are we going to do now?

An impatient Third Gen hurled his fist into Porter's stomach. Porter dropped like a bag of dirty laundry. The Third Gen kicked him three times in succession. Porter flung his arms over his head and curled into the fetal position. Jimmy winced and moaned each time the Squat's foot struck his friend.

The Squats who disappeared into the kitchen ran across the dining hall into the corridor. The entire group huddled. After a couple of seconds all but one drifted back, leaving a First Gen staring into the camera. A black clump of hair poked out of his otherwise bald head and cascaded down over his eyes. He vigorously criss-crossed his arms back and forth.

Joshua Parker had Jimmy's full attention.

The dispatcher on the other end of the telephone said, "Hilroy, what's happening? Stick with me. Keep talking. I need the play by play for the anti-riot team."

"It's Joshua Parker. He's got a guard. Ed Porter," Jimmy stammered. "Parker is waving at the cameras. I can't tell what he wants yet."

Parker stopped waving. He jabbed a finger at a Third Gen, who lumbered forward, raising a huge, muscled arm. Hair like fine wire poked out of his knuckles, partially obscuring the amateurish blue numbers tattooed on his fingers—2012—possibly the date he became a Glades' inmate. Jimmy didn't know or care. It was the kitchen cleaver in the Squat's hand that caught his attention. Parker reappeared, smiling nastily. He pulled something out of the open front of his coveralls and thrust it toward the camera, as the Third Gen had done with the cleaver.

Jimmy leaned forward, peering at the monitor through narrowed eyes, unsure of what he was looking at.

And, then he understood.

It was a human hand, an arm, severed cleanly just below the

elbow, the white bone in the center visible against the black flesh surrounding it.

With an inarticulate yelp of horror, Jimmy recoiled. The phone fell from his hand. Scrambling feet pushed at the floor as he rolled himself away from the screen. His chair struck his bottle and water gurgled onto the floor. A wheel rolled off the platform and the chair toppled, dumping him onto the floor, before somer-saulting down the tower's short staircase. Jimmy's hip hit the edge of the top step. He yelled again, this time in pain. He bounced to his feet panting, eyes jumping from the chair at the bottom of the stairs to the monitors on the other side of the platform. His scalp and back were slick with sweat. For several seconds, while his heart pounded raggedly, he did nothing.

The crazy Squat had chopped off someone's hand.

Whose?

Probably the guard they'd dragged into the kitchen.

But why?

With the doors locked, a palm print was good for nothing. If Jimmy didn't reactivate the system—something SOPs forbade him from doing—the Squats could steal keycards and hack off arms all day long. They'd still be stuck in the hallway with nowhere to go.

He stared at the monitors, seeing black and white shadows flicker at him, rather than actual images. The blood loss would be catastrophic. Whoever lost his arm would almost certainly die. If he didn't, he'd be horribly maimed. Jimmy blinked away a hot rush of tears, angry or sympathetic, he wasn't sure. Veteran guards would have asked, "You're surprised? It's what a Squat does. It doesn't have to make sense."

With a dry mouth and a churning stomach, he stood his chair up, sat down and rolled himself back to the monitors. He heard his name being repeated, a small electric sound coming from the telephone receiver on the floor. He picked it up and slowly described the silent horror show.

Two Squats held Porter face down on the floor. A third stretched his arm out and stood on it, one foot near the shoulder, the other near the wrist. The Third Gen with the cleaver knelt, raising the weapon. Bristly hair stuck out from his ears and cheeks in crazy, unkempt tufts, making him appear more beast than human. He licked his lips and slobber dripped from one corner of his mouth. Anxious for the go-ahead, his beady black eyes were locked on Parker's.

The wicked smile on Parker's long, sloping face didn't change. He put the chunk of arm back into the open front of his coveralls and then held both of his hands up to the camera. All ten fingers were splayed. He folded one finger into his palm.

A second later he did it again.

In training Jimmy learned how to identify a suicidal inmate. He'd been given self-defense lessons and taught how to search for contraband. He'd taken a course on how to talk with an inmate so as not to harm the individual's self-esteem. One thing training did not cover was how to manage an enraged Squat who, in seven seconds, would chop off a friend's arm using a stolen meat cleaver.

Six fingers now.

What did the textbook say about that?

Parker folded a finger into his palm.

Five seconds.

If Jimmy hit the button, the entire Level Three section of the prison became accessible again. Inmates would swarm through it, into the common rooms, the smaller offices, the gym, library, art room, chapel. Angry and without supervision, they'd probably wreck everything on which they put their hands. Unpopular inmates would end up beaten or dead when the cell doors unlocked. But, unless the rioters smashed through the reinforced glass window, they wouldn't breach Level Three and gain access to the less secure Level Two area.

Jimmy had three seconds left.

The Third Gen lowered the cleaver slowly, pressing it onto

Porter's arm, lining up the critical slice. A thin line of black appeared. Porter struggled. The Squats held him firmly.

Jimmy was certain of only one thing. If he didn't unlock the door, Porter would lose his arm. Jimmy didn't think he could live with the guilt. He'd never be able to look Eddy Porter in the eye again. He'd never laugh and shake his head at the man's clowning around. Every smile would be strained. For a while he'd overcompensate and offer to help around Eddy's home, mowing the lawn or painting the trim, that sort of thing, but as time passed he'd find more and more reasons not to go by his house until the only time they saw each other was accidentally, maybe the hardware store on a Saturday afternoon. Eddy would joke about how lucky he was, getting a full (disability) paycheck without putting in a day's work and they'd laugh together, but it would be a thin, artificial joke.

All he had to do was unlock the Level Three doors, the ones that were typically unlocked most of the time anyway. Nobody would die and Porter would keep his arm.

Two seconds.

His hand hovered over the button. How many times had he been told during training that Glades was secure, how nobody had ever escaped, how an inmate who entered Level Three never left, how the increasing levels of security meant the keeper was always in control of the zoo?

Countless times.

Parker folded the last finger into his fist.

Jimmy slammed his hand on the button. They wouldn't breach Level Three. Not before the anti-riot team arrived. *Silent Night* picked up mid-sentence where it left off.

Parker plucked the severed arm from his coveralls. He placed it against the scanner and dipped his stolen keycard into the slot. He pushed the door open and held it as Squats ran into the common room, cheering jubilantly.

Jimmy raised his eyes from the monitors. He didn't need the

television screens to see what was happening any longer. From his raised platform, he looked through the reinforced window into the Level Three common area, as Squats charged across the room like the leading edge of a debris-filled tsunami. They yelled as they came, an incomprehensible roar of success and then slid to a silent halt, as if the glass barrier confused them.

Nothing happened immediately. Then the crowd started pounding the glass with their fists, making the window boom. The yelling began again, shouts that grew in volume and rage. The crowd parted. Six inmates carried a table between them. Using it like a battering ram they smashed the corner of it into the window. They backed up and did it again. And again. More inmates joined with chairs and tables of their own. Initially they were unorganized but it only took a minute before everybody was smashing something into the window at the same time, backing up, repeating.

The purported shatterproof window spider-webbed. The inmates let out a triumphant roar and redoubled their efforts. With ominous cracking sounds, the spider web grew. A Third Gen carried a forty-five-pound plate out of the indoor-gym. He swung it into the glass with a roar of effort. A corner of the table punctured the glass with a noise that sounded like winter ice breaking under foot. Wires inside the glass snapped with audible pings.

Jimmy's eyes widened in terror. It wouldn't take long now, probably only minutes to create a hole big enough through which the enraged Squats could crawl. He clutched the phone with a hand white with strain. When the dispatcher said, "For your own safety, get out of Level Two right now," Jimmy ran, leaving all thoughts of benefits and a contented girlfriend behind.

He scanned out of Level Two. Unlike Eddy Porter, he ensured the door locked behind him. He sprinted out the front doors, slowing only when he reached the steps down to the Glades Rehabilitation Facility parking lot.

CHAPTER 38

MITCH AND RAY headed toward the sounds of destruction in the common area, hauling the unconscious Christopher Tanner between them. Ray had Christopher's good arm over his shoulders. Mitch, on the other side, did his best to avoid bumping the guard's freshly cauterized arm. From the dining hall behind them, Wilford's voice alternately shouted obscenities and pleaded for help.

Mitch avoided meeting Ray's eyes in case he had a crisis of conscience and decided to go back and help the unpopular guard. The entire situation was a bad joke. How could he be helping one screw, completely ignoring another, and simultaneously disregarding his own predicament? He should have been capitalizing on the confusion and searching for an escape avenue out of Glades.

With Christopher's dead weight slowing them, the corridor stretched out like a treadmill. What should have been a short trip to the infirmary felt as though it were taking an inordinately long time. They shambled forward step by step, eventually pausing beside the screw Mitch spotted earlier from the opposite end of the hallway. Sounds of destruction continued and voices babbled exuberantly. Mitch tossed a glance into the common area, but the angle was wrong and he was unable to see what was happening at the opposite end of the room.

The screw on the floor raised his head and looked at them out of uncomprehending eyes, his pupils like huge, black bullet holes. Tears and snot shone and blood dripped from his nose. He had a mouthful of broken teeth, some of which punched through his lower lip, turning his mouth into a swollen snarl.

Ray, sounding shocked, said, "What happened?"

Mitch thought the answer was obvious and didn't matter one way or another. He didn't wait for a response. He said, "There's another guard in the dining hall. Shane Wilford? He's alone. He's hurt. You might want to get down there. With the doors unlocked, inmates will be coming out of their cells."

The screw stared at him vacantly.

"Strength in numbers and all that," Mitch said.

The screw remained motionless.

In the common room, glass shattered. A jubilant cheer rose like a wave. Behind the racket, like a back-beat, the tinnitus whined and stabbed and hummed and probed. Mitch couldn't delay any longer. "Let's go, Ray."

They walked the final few feet and entered the common room and came to a second, unintentional halt.

Ray muttered, "Wow."

They were alone at this end of the room. At the opposite end, inmates had smashed a ragged hole through the window separating Level Three from Level Two. As best as Mitch could tell, Control was abandoned. He saw no sign of administrative or support staff, and no Glades' personnel trying to prevent the destruction.

As he watched, inmates enlarged the hole using furniture and exercise equipment like scrapers to clear away shards of glass that clung to the window frame. Then, as one they threw aside their tools and poured through the opening into Level Two, an area most never expected to experience again, after their initial admittance into Glades.

Mitch said, as much to himself as Ray, "So much for reinforced."

"They like to brag, but I guess the system has never been put to the test," Ray said.

With a small smile, Mitch glanced across Christopher's inert frame. "They were a little overconfident, wouldn't you say?" The smile vanished. "Nobody's going to be in the infirmary."

Ray nodded once, as though he'd already come to the same conclusion. He said, "What choice do we have? We can't just dump him."

Excited voices rose behind them. Mitch looked over his shoulder. An orange mob of inmates strode toward him, men who'd returned to their cells when the double claxon rang but vacated them again when Control unlocked the doors, he assumed. He nervously looked into the corner at a CCTV camera before remembering there was nobody sitting in Control to put Glades back into lockdown. He hated crowds. Individually, people were fine, but in a crowd even fine people lost their minds, and convicts were not fine people.

He said, "What do you say I carry the club for a while, Ray?" He wasn't sure if Ray felt the danger, but if one of these amped-up individuals took exception to the way they were helping a screw, things would get out of hand in a hurry. Ray tended to think too much. If someone came at them, he'd never swing in time.

With a look of relief, Ray passed the baton across Christopher's body, taking more care than necessary to avoid shaking or jostling the injured guard. Mitch liked him for that. He wondered about the contradiction, this guy who exhibited sensitivity to a virtual stranger but who'd bought a gun and executed two Squat teenagers. They shuffled forward, the toes of Christopher's boots dragging along the concrete floor like a sea anchor.

The last of the inmates in front of them clambered across the sill where the shatterproof window used to separate Level Three from Level Two. Voices rose in excitement as the inmates behind them saw the opening. Mitch's eyes jumped from side to side, as they rushed past. He made sure to avoid eye contact. No point in diverting attention away from the hole in the glass. He tightened his grip on the baton. "Let's keep moving."

Predictably, an inmate he didn't recognize jogged past, glanced sideways and then slowed to a walk. He said, "Why you crackers helping a fucking screw?" He swatted the man beside him on the shoulder. "Look at these crackers helping a screw." The two of them stopped. The second man shot a hungry glance at the hole, then shoulder to shoulder, he and the first man faced Mitch.

"Beat it. Just keep going," Mitch said. Two inmates didn't worry him much. What made him nervous was the others who might be tempted to get involved. He gave them hard eyes and held the club up, hoping he looked more intimidating than he felt. Fucking crowds. "You got him, Ray?"

"Yeah."

He stepped forward, letting Ray take Christopher's weight. If the two guys came at him, he'd feint one way, swing the club the other way and put whoever was closest on the ground. Yell his head off at the same time—jack himself up and maybe startle the remaining attacker.

That was the plan, anyway.

The second man tilted his head, appraising Mitch through narrowed eyes. He gave the hole a longer look. He shrugged. "Who cares?" He did a one eighty and ran for the window. The first man jabbed a finger at Mitch. "You and I ain't done," he said, and then hurried after his friend.

Mitch called after him, "Anytime you want."

Ray muttered, "Jesus, this place."

Bent and broken furniture lay discarded on either side of the hole. Reinforcement wires dangled. "Watch your feet," Mitch said, feeling pebbles of glass on the floor through his thin-soled canvas shoes. He stepped through, spikes of glass on all sides making him tread carefully, and then he and Ray gingerly maneuvered Christopher through the opening.

Several inmates ransacked Control, most likely searching for anything that would give them access to the bounty they'd surely find in all the locked rooms, as well as prisoners in segregation and, most probably, the female's pen on the opposite side. They'd be looking for a way to access Level One as well. If they breached those doors, Glades would no longer belong to the authorities.

A crowd of women stared open-mouthed through the window that kept them locked in their own Level Three area. Mitch saw four female screws looking on from the periphery with pale, strained expressions. Their tan shirts and brown pants with the red stripes were almost invisible in the sea of orange coveralls. He didn't know why the guards allowed the female prisoners to watch. Maybe it was easier and less dangerous than trying to herd them back to their cells. He was glad Lindsay was gone. She didn't need to see this, and she didn't deserve to be part of it.

On the control platform, the top of a file cabinet swayed and rocked like a skyscraper in an earthquake and then toppled with a ringing crash. He smelled something burning. Two laughing Squats rushed out of an office, wisps then clouds of smoke, following them.

Without warning the overhead sprinklers came on in an intense spray.

Mitch sucked a startled breath in through his teeth when the cold water hit him. It poured off his head and rolled down his neck, sheeting his back. For a few seconds, it felt refreshing compared to the hot, oily sweat of a few minutes earlier, but soon his coveralls and underwear were saturated and uncomfortable. He scrubbed his free hand across his face, brushing the water from his eyes. Dumb-assess. Even though their cage had suddenly grown to include Level Two, they were still locked inside. Did it make any sense to light the cage on fire?

Walking cautiously on the rain-slick floor, they carried Christopher past bloody inmates with glassy eyes and blank faces. They passed one who might have been dead, lying beneath a twisted office chair in an expanding pool of blood that was quickly turning pink in the rain. His wide-open eyes stared up at the sprinkler nozzle soaking him.

When they arrived in front of the infirmary, they stopped. A broken chair lay in a small splash of glass below the window that looked from the infirmary into the hallway. One wooden leg remained lodged in the reinforced glass, spearing between horizontal blinds on the inside of the room. Mitch prodded one of the doors with the end of the club. It swung open a couple of inches then returned to neutral with diminishing whoosh-thunk, whoosh thunks. He wondered why someone tried to smash their way into an unlocked room.

He looked at Ray. "My guess? They came here first, hoping for drugs, what not. Anything worthwhile will be gone. I doubt anyone will come back. You'll be as safe here as anywhere else." He held out the club. "Take it. Use it. Don't hesitate. If you think, it'll be too late."

Realization spread across Ray's face. He took the club reluctantly it seemed, the weight of it dragging his arm toward the floor. "You're leaving, then?"

"I'm going to try. I need a portal, whether you believe me or not." Mitch shrugged a genuine apology. "This thing in my head."

"Tyler will come after you."

"It's not Tyler I'm worried about. It's Cole. When it comes down to it, when the tinnitus peaks, he'll open a portal for me and I'll take it. Then he owns me." He shook his head. "I'd prefer to avoid that, if possible."

Ray said, "I don't know what you're talking about." He widened his stance and tightened his grip around Christopher's waist, taking all of the guard's weight with a soft grunt of exertion.

"But, if you have to go, you better get to it." There was no reprimand or accusation in his voice. "I've got Christopher."

Mitch hesitated, unsure why he felt the need to explain to this office geek, this person he wouldn't have known on the outside. Maybe deciding to act, rather than passively accepting his affliction, made optimism possible and gave him something he wanted to share.

"I'm going to find Liv," he said. A sudden rush of excitement made him smile. He left her world believing he'd never see her again. But within a week, assuming his idea worked (and she made time for him), he and Liv would be sipping coffee in a Starbucks while he tried to explain his absence. It wouldn't be an easy conversation. It might not go anywhere. The thought of having it scared him, but surely that was better than submissively accepting whatever the tinnitus and Cole told him he had to live with.

Ray asked, "How?"

The sprinklers clicked off as abruptly as they turned on. Mitch's eyes flicked to the nozzles in the ceiling, grateful the water was no longer cascading off his head and shoulders. He looked at Ray. "A Days Inn, south of Jacksonville." He grinned stupidly as a fresh cloud of nervous butterflies fluttered through his body.

He long suspected there were multiple portals, rather than one that moved from place to place. Lindsay said as much and Cole proved it, which logically meant he did not have to slip through the first portal to which the tinnitus dragged him. He could pass it by, until the tinnitus latched onto a different one. If that was true, and he saw no reason to believe otherwise, he could choose which portal he used.

"Why there?"

"I'm going to use the same portal I used when I entered Liv's world the first time. No reason it won't take me back to her world again."

Ray looked incredulous. "How do you know it will work that

way? It might send you somewhere else entirely. It might only work once. What if it *does* work like you expect? Cole might guess where you'll go." He shook his head in disbelief. "I was right. You are insane."

Might was unlikely.

Cole would know exactly where he'd go. Not only that, Cole would come looking for him. Mitch shrugged. "I'll be out. He won't have any leverage. What's he going to do? Move her world to the top of his hit list? It's already there. Anyway, he can't kill it overnight. It takes a while. Liv and I will—"

The tinnitus slashed like a white-hot sword. His eardrums pulsed painfully. Mitch's eyes filled with sparkling white dots. He winced.

Ray said, "What if the room is occupied?"

"It won't be. The same force that draws me to a time and place, pushes away people who don't slip." Cole's words, but Mitch had seen it happen eleven different times.

"It might not be there. What if they've torn the hotel down?" Ray shook his head and swore. "How do you plan on getting out of here?"

"I'm not entirely sure," Mitch answered vaguely. "I've got an idea, maybe, if I can beat the cavalry."

"You mean the anti-riot team? I doubt they're too far away."

"I better get going, then. Wish me luck." He jogged away and Ray called after him, "Good luck."

Mitch raised a hand and waved without looking back.

CHAPTER 39

RAY WAS NO longer certain if Mitch was insane or delusional. A guy couldn't be that dedicated to an idea without believing it to be true, could he? But, believing it to be true didn't necessarily make it so. Lots of people, from conspiracy theorists to Muslim extremists, believed all kinds of weird things that weren't true.

When Mitch disappeared, Ray sighed heavily. In all likelihood, that would be the last he ever saw of Mitch Reilly. He took a firm grip on Christopher's waist and shouldered through one of the swinging doors into the infirmary, half-carrying, half-dragging the unconscious guard behind him.

He paused just inside the door, standing in a puddle of water, his feet cold and wet in his canvas shoes. The door swung shut behind him in decreasing whoosh-thunks. The back-and-forth motion painted the room in stripes of diminishing white light and created a small breeze that wafted the acidic stench of puke into the damp air, making him cough.

The door stopped swinging. A thin knife edge of light sliced between the horizontal slats that were tangled around the chair leg jutting from the window. The dark room was filled with large, black shadows that made no sense. Something resembling a dinosaur stood behind one of the shadows, a velociraptor maybe, with its long neck and long snout and mouth filled with razor-like teeth. Ray remembered a movie he'd watched a few years back in which the predator had waited in perfect stillness before pouncing in an invisible blur of speed.

"Shit," he muttered. He was freaking himself out. The infirmary was no different than a strange hotel room the moment after you clicked out the bedside lamp. It took a minute before the blackness turned to shades of gray and all the weird shapes became familiar items—furniture on the floor, small appliances on the desk. The blinking red light in the ceiling was only a smoke detector, not Sauron's all-knowing eye.

Ray raised his arm in a slow arc, up from his thigh, brushing the back of his fist along the wall beside him. He found the light switch and bumped it up and down several times. Nothing. Maybe the lights shorted out when the sprinklers came on, or maybe they were just another thing the rampaging inmates had somehow broken.

While he waited for his vision to adjust, he raised his arm to his face, covering his mouth against the wet stench of vomit. It was an awkward, uncomfortable position with the club in his hand and he quickly dropped his arm and concentrated on inhaling through his mouth. Behind him, footsteps in the hallway grew louder, peaked, faded. The heavy infirmary doors muffled the yelling and the screaming and the sounds of destruction, making him feel isolated and vulnerable.

Someone in the room groaned. Loudly. Distinctly.

Ray stiffened.

His ears went ultra-sensitive; he thought he could hear his own heartbeat. Christopher exhaled and inhaled ragged gusts of hot air across his neck. Water dripped from the ceiling, plinking when it landed in the puddle in which he stood. A large, fat drop landed on the back of his neck, as cold as the tip of a fillet knife. Ray started and almost screamed. Clothing rustled behind the black rectangle in front of him. He heard a second, longer groan.

The velociraptor hadn't moved. Of course it hadn't, because dinosaurs didn't exist. Something other than a man-eating killer had made those sounds. Ray blinked several times and concentrated. The shapes in the room became more distinctive. The small dark cubes to his right were nothing but armchairs casting suddenly recognizable shadows on the walls. He saw a cot to his left. File cabinets lay on the floor. The strange shadows on the walls solidified into cabinets, with doors hanging askew. The large black rectangle was only a desk and the velociraptor was a gooseneck lamp, the snout aiming down onto a leather writing surface.

On the floor, two legs pointed out from behind the desk, feet pointing up like the hands of clock at ten and two. He stared at them. They remained motionless. Whoever was back there was unconscious, in a drug-induced coma, judging from the empty pill bottles scattered on the floor. He'd probably puked on himself.

After several seconds, Ray's hitching breath smoothed. Embarrassed at his sudden fear, he chuckled. The noise sounded unnatural in the silent room and he broke the laugh off abruptly.

Now that he could see, he realized he wasn't in an infirmary after all. It was more of an office than medical center. Tony Carter made it clear inmates never, ever left Level Three. He probably exaggerated. In the case of a serious medical condition Ray guessed an inmate might end up sedated, guarded, restrained, and then transported to a local hospital. Anything less, and a doctor would gather what he needed from this office, enter Level Three to treat his patient, and then return to the safety of his Level Two office to complete his administrative tasks.

Ray sighed and mumbled a frustrated, "Now what?" unsure what to do with Christopher. For lack of a better plan, he shuffled sideways, dropped the club on the cot and with a grunt of relief, dropped Christopher's upper body onto the mattress. The springs squeaked. The stink of wet wool filled his nose, better than barf he decided, but not pleasant. Squatting, he scooped up the young guard's legs and placed them on the cot. He straightened and shook his arm and rolled his shoulders, releasing the strain in his tired muscles.

Someone snorted, hawked and spit.

Ray yelped in startled surprise. His heart rattled erratically, high in his chest. The unexpected burst of adrenaline combined with tired muscles made his arms and legs feel weak and rubbery. A familiar voice he recognized but couldn't place said, "Who's there?"

A Squat—his Neanderthal silhouette and guttural voice made that much clear—straightened to his full height in the depths of a corner. He wore a hat or bandana, part of which dangled down the side of his face. He stepped out of the shadow and said, "Well, what do you know? It's the Killlller. Without his bodyguard."

It wasn't a hat or bandana, of course. It was the fist of long black hair for which Joshua Parker was known. The buttons of his coveralls were undone to his waist. His belly pushed against the orange fabric, creating a wide, bulbous V. Black chest hair, thick as a shag carpet fluffed out the opening. Both lapels were stained black, two large palm prints that smeared down to nothing as though he had dried his palms of… what? Water? Blood?

Hopefully not blood.

Keeping his eyes on him, Ray slowly bent at the knees and patted the mattress, searching until he found the club. His fingers traced its length. He wrapped a clammy hand around the handle.

Use it. Don't hesitate. If you think, it'll be too late.

He said, "You and me, we have no problems." He hoped Parker didn't hear the wobble in his voice.

"No?" Parker's face twisted into a snarl that was supposed to be a smile. "You might not have a problem, but I do. You killed two young First Gens. I don't forget. I've been waiting for a while."

Ray stepped back, wondering what Mitch would have done at this point, and knew he would have stepped forward not backward, probably swinging the club instead of holding it down the length of his leg. He would have known several seconds ago (as Ray knew now), that there'd be no talking his way out of this situation. No way of avoiding it.

Parker charged.

Ray recoiled, backpedaling fast without thinking, raising the club, probably too late but still worth a try.

Before he had a chance to defend himself, his feet went out from under him on the wet, slippery floor. He waved his arms, found nothing, and landed on his tailbone hard enough to slam his teeth together with a loud clack. A fraction of a second later the back of his head slammed into the floor. The breath left his mouth in an exhaustive grunt and phosphorous stars filled his vision and white pain exploded throughout his body. Dimly, he heard Parker laugh, the sound high and drawn out and insane.

"You're dead, Albright. You just don't know it."

Ray swallowed and gulped and his chest heaved. He saw Parker's leg swing back, saw it slash forward in a fast, smooth arc. He rolled his head to the side and took the kick near his ear instead of the center of his face, and even though the Squat wore light Glades shoes, the soles had collected grime and other debris, and the kick scraped his skin raw.

A second kick landed on his jaw, pounding his cheek into his teeth, lacerating his tongue, filling his mouth with blood. He wondered if he'd ever see Dawn and Angie again, or if he'd see them within the next couple of minutes, because Parker wouldn't stop. It wasn't in a Squat's nature. An unexpected feeling of humiliation filled him. He hadn't saved Christopher. He hadn't gone down swinging. All he'd done was curl up in a ball on the floor.

Light from the hallway flooded the room.

A deep voice with a slight Scottish accent said, "I've been looking for you, Joshua."

"Get lost," Parker said. "This doesn't concern you."

"Oh, but it does." A pause. "Albright, can you hear me?"

Ray tried to nod. "Yeah." It came out as a slobbery slur.

"Can you stand?"

Moving slowly, Ray got his elbows underneath him. He paused, let the fireworks flashing behind his eyes settle down, then pushed himself to a sitting position. Eyes closed, he probed the back of his head, wincing when his fingers found a huge, wet goose-egg. After a slow three count, he opened his eyes and struggled to his feet, one hand running up the wall for balance. He wobbled, and the Scottish voice said, "Easy now," and Ray grabbed more wall with splayed fingers. Slowly, his equilibrium returned. He spit a mouthful of blood on the floor. He looked at Colin McTavish. "I'm okay. Dizzy."

McTavish nodded without looking at him. His eyes were on Parker, who stared back, his body vibrating with tension. McTavish bent at the knees and grabbed the club Ray dropped when Parker charged. He said, "What are you doing here, Albright?"

Parker said, "This has got nothing to do with you, McTavish." His jaw and chest jutted out and his hands were balled fists at his side. "Albright needs to be taught a lesson."

McTavish ignored him.

Ray said, "I wanted to get Christopher some medical attention. You see what these animals did? They cut his hand off." The lacerations in his mouth and his swollen tongue muddled his voice, making it sound like he had a mouthful of marbles. "They cut his fucking hand off!"

McTavish flicked a half-second glance at Christopher's inert body, his face uninterested. "Hardly surprising. This Squat piece of shit is always causing trouble." He held the club out, in Ray's direction. "Take it. Higher-ups want to see the problem go away."

Parker's eyes widened. "You can't—"

"Watch me," McTavish bellowed, the force and volume pushing Parker back a step.

Ray tentatively reached for the baton, uncertain of this new situation. What did these two guys know that he didn't yet understand?

"Put him down for good. Nobody's going to miss him." McTavish grinned beneath his bushy, Fu Man Chu. "I guarantee nobody will investigate."

Comprehension came in a rush. "Oh," Ray said. He heard of this sort of thing happening. An inmate named Sawyer still hadn't recovered from a recent assault. Word was, Glades staff didn't like him (specifically the deputy warden), and Tyler had arranged a dreadful beating.

"Me or you," McTavish said. "It makes no difference. Either way, he's not walking out of this room. But, I'm betting you want some payback?"

Ray did.

He wanted Parker to know what it felt like to take a beating. He wanted the Squat to know what it was like to be intimidated and nervous and scared. He wanted to be able to say he'd done what he thought Mitch would have done and swung the club without hesitation. Most of all, he wanted his humiliation and embarrassment to go away. How many people had Parker terrorized? Society was filled with guys like him, bullies who intimidated with size and aggressive voices, who imposed their will on others simply because they could. It would be nice to see one of them humiliated and embarrassed for a change. It would be a lesson. A message to others like Parker.

Ray took the baton. The weapon sent a burst of power surging up his arm. He moistened his lips and tightened his grip. He raised the club, brought his arm back. Already he could hear the soggy, satisfying crunch of the impact. Already he could see Parker falling, the bright scarlet stain on the club, the blood dripping off the end.

Parker whined in a tone Ray had never heard before from a Squat, "We got no problems, Albright. You just said so."

Ray hesitated. Was he really going to beat this Squat with a club because he was embarrassed about falling in a puddle of water? It felt a lot like shooting two kids on the court house steps. When Mitch told him to use the club, he meant defensively. He wouldn't have swung it in this situation. Ray felt certain of that. He closed his eyes. His arm dropped. "I can't," he whispered.

McTavish said, "I'm not surprised. Shooting a couple of Squats who did your family isn't the same thing, is it? I never thought you belonged in a cage with the rest of us animals." He stretched out a hand and took the club. He nailed Ray in place with steely eyes. "After that thing with Rufus, you kept your lip buttoned. That's a very good policy." He paused. "You don't have any idea what's going to happen in here, do you, Albright?"

Ray swallowed, felt his Adam's apple bob nervously. He knew exactly what was going to happen when he left the room. He said, "If someone asked, I wouldn't even venture a guess."

McTavish tilted his head at the door. "Get out. You don't want to be here. Take Christopher if you—"

Three loud bangs, what could only be gunshots, interrupted him.

Ray jumped in startled surprise.

McTavish acted like he hadn't heard them. He said, "Find a place to hole up, Albright. Take Christopher if you want—I don't know why you're helping a screw—but don't try and get out of Level Two. Whoever just tried is dead now." He grinned. "Squats, with luck."

Parker growled at this, and he lurched forward and then stopped when McTavish raised the club.

Ray said, "How do you know?"

"I'm a lifer, Albright. I've been there and back a time or two. What happens, the riot-squad musters inside Level One. They gather intel and assess, because it's a fluid situation for the first sixty minutes. After that it becomes predictable. If the door between Level One and Level Two opens while they're working out a plan, they got marksmen with Colt M4s on the other side. The theory being, anyone who tries going through the door at this point, shouldn't be there. Which makes it open season, no different than if someone tried going over the wall. Those guys get tired of shooting at paper, let me tell you. They enjoy a real target."

"Jesus, this place," Ray whispered. Louder he said, "What then?"

"They'll pop off some tear gas and follow it in with tooled-up Glock 21s, laser sights, and strobe lights. You want to make sure they know you're not a threat. They won't give a con much latitude." He cut hard eyes at Parker. "Now, go. I got business to take care of."

Ray bent at the knees, thrust his arms beneath Christopher's and locked his hands together across the unconscious guard's chest. With a grunt, he straightened. The exertion sent a fresh wave of dizziness spinning through his head. McTavish watched impassively. Maybe helping a guard was one step too far, a step the lifer would never take. Ray wasn't about to hang around and ask.

He backpedaled out the infirmary doors, Christopher's heels scraping along behind, uncertain where to go next. Behind him, from the infirmary, he heard loud voices and then a soggy whump. The shrill screech of pain and terror that followed made him smile for a millisecond before guilt erased it completely. He walked backward toward the door between Level Two and Level One, shoulder checking occasionally. When he had a clear view, he spotted three bodies—it seemed McTavish was right. Hopefully Mitch would proceed with caution, if he wasn't already out.

With no fresh ideas, he picked an office at random and dragged Christopher inside. He settled the guard as comfortably as he could on a leather arm chair, then dropped into a second chair, breathing heavily with exertion and pain. The back of his head throbbed. He was dizzy and his mouth was dry. He wanted to sleep. Hopefully these weren't symptoms of a concussion—he didn't think he'd hit his head that hard when he fell in the infirmary. With luck it was nothing more than a medley of pain, stress, depression, and all the other emotions and physical sufferings he'd experienced in the last couple of months.

When they came, they came precisely the way McTavish described—tear gas first, gun shots (presumably Glock 21s and a few more dead inmates), second. Other than raising his hands well above his head, palms wide open, Ray did not move a muscle. By the time the two paramedics entered the room, he was face down on the floor with his fingers linked behind his head.

Slobbering blood and drooling saliva past the lacerations on the inside of his mouth, he explained Christopher's injury, as if it wasn't obvious, and told the paramedics how he and another unknown inmate cauterized the young guard's arm. Ray saw no upside in mentioning Mitch's name. If Mitch somehow escaped, drawing extra attention to him seemed unwise. Then he explained how he had fallen and struck his head on the concrete floor.

One of the paramedics shone a flashlight into each of his eyes while the other snapped on latex gloves. The paramedic with the gloves gently parted his hair and probed the growing goose egg. He asked, "What happened to your face?"

"Don't remember," Ray slurred. He could blame his amnesia on the bump on his head. He wasn't putting himself anywhere near Joshua Parker. By now the Squat would be dead, he guessed. The club would have no fingerprints and McTavish would be long gone, ten of his friends swearing up and down how he'd never left their sight.

"Tell me where it hurts."

"My face. My head is throbbing. My back kind of sizzles, from my neck all the way down to my shoulders."

"Okay," the paramedic said. "We're going to put a collar on you. You're going to the hospital on a backboard." They wrapped a stiff plastic collar around his neck, fastening it in place with Velcro straps, making it impossible for him to nod or turn his head. When Ray objected, the paramedic who'd said nothing to that point, responded in a deep voice, "Are you a doctor?"

"No."

"Are you a paramedic or a nurse?"

"No."

"Dentist? Any medical training? Anything whatsoever?"

"No."

"I bet you have a lawyer, though."

"Of course."

"Imagine my surprise. Every convict has a lawyer. I'm not about to assume liability because you don't want to go for a ride in an ambulance. Be quiet. Let us do our jobs."

"Take it easy, Dale," the first paramedic said conversationally, like he didn't care one way or another if Dale "took it easy."

"I'm tired of the bitching."

Ray heard tape peeling off a roll, and then two hands descended toward his forehead with a wide, white ribbon of tape stretched between them. Dale, the grumpy paramedic, stuck it to Ray's forehead and fastened the ends to the backboard on either side of his head. A second strip went around the hard collar, just below his chin. Secured to the backboard, they lifted him up, and then put him back down on a stretcher. They rolled the stretcher out to an ambulance and two minutes later Ray was staring up at a row of six lights attached to the vehicle's ceiling with six Phillips screws, listening to the paramedics discuss the overtime they were banking, seven trips already that day, and they were only one of several ambulances making the round between Glades and the hospital.

The pain Ray complained about in his neck and back disappeared during the ride. Now all he could feel was the wooden backboard. Every bump in the road traveled up the ambulance's suspension, into the board and applied pressure to his head, shoulders, and tailbone. An itch developed between his shoulder blades. He couldn't squirm enough to scratch it, never mind reach for it. He needed to use a bathroom.

Ray was incredibly uncomfortable but, strangely, content. He was in better shape than the dead bodies on the floor in Glades. Unlike Christopher Tanner, he still had both arms. And, he was outside of Glades, somewhere he never expected to be again.

CHAPTER 40

THE MOMENT MITCH turned around, the tinnitus backed off and his thoughts cleared. He expected it would happen that way. Experience.

He had one thought in mind—getting out of Glades. In all likelihood, that would happen on Cole's terms within the next few days. As much as Mitch liked the idea, escape was still a tenuous hope. Even after the complete disintegration of order and procedure within Glades, the biggest obstacle remained unchanged. He was inside a facility expressly designed to keep him exactly where he was.

Despite that, he still felt like he was looking at a unique window of opportunity. It was worth exploring, if it meant he'd be gone before Cole returned. Imagining the expression of loss and anger on Cole's face when he realized his latest recruit had disappeared, was incentive enough for Mitch.

He ran for the dining hall. His single idea was as solid as a rotten fish net and dependent almost entirely on factors outside of his control. These were good reasons to avoid explaining his plan to Ray, who would have talked away a bunch of time, analyzing the idea to death, but if there was any way of making it work, Mitch had to perform his part now, before the anti-riot team arrived.

He guessed the cavalry had procedures designed to handle situations such as this, but a prison riot was not a cookie-cutter event. How they proceeded would depend on the circumstances— was there a hostage situation? Were there fires or barricades? What percentage of the inmate population was involved? It might take them sixty minutes, possibly as many as ninety to muster, figure out all the variables, and tailor their SOPs accordingly. Once they did, they'd come in hard. Tear gas, possibly flashbangs, definitely guns. Things happened fast in this world. They didn't fuck around.

He figured he had a conservative forty-five minutes. After that, his small window would slam firmly shut. He'd be Cole's, fully and completely.

He ran past fights, the bodies on the floor, and the sounds of wreckage coming from the various offices. The guy who challenged him earlier in the common room saw him coming and stepped in front of him, a wide malicious grin on his face. He said, "Fucking cracker, I told you we ain't done."

Mitch adjusted course, arrowing toward him.

Reflexively, the guy retreated half a step, and his eyes widened at the sight of two hundred plus pounds charging directly at him, then Mitch's hands landed on his shoulders. Barely breaking stride, he slammed his forehead into the guy's face, momentum and force coming together perfectly, and the guy crumpled with a piercing wail, spouting blood from his crushed nose.

Mitch slowed when he entered the dining hall, scanning the large room quickly. It was empty, as he expected it would be. Rampaging inmates weren't going to hang around a Level Three area they were routinely allowed to access, not when Level Two was suddenly open. Inmates who weren't actively rioting would be in their cells or out in the yard, as far from the havoc as possible, making sure they showed up on camera, or were seen by guards on the other side of the chain-link, so as not to be clumped in with the rioters. They didn't want to add time to their sentences.

Unsurprisingly, Mitch saw no sign of Shane Wilford.

The most logical thing the screw could have done when the Level Three doors unlocked, was scan out, make his way through all the various doors to the safety of Level One, and give the cavalry as much information as possible when they arrived. After that, the riot was no longer his problem. However, not more than ten minutes ago, Mitch left him in the dining hall with a freshly broken leg, virtually incapable of moving under his own steam.

Mitch thought Wilford's escape to Level One without assistance was highly improbable. It presented him with two viable scenarios, as far as he could see.

Wilford was still inside Glades, either hiding or captive. If he was captive, if some inmate with a grudge had grabbed him, Mitch didn't envy the screw's next couple of hours, on top of which, he'd never find him in time to capitalize on the riot's frantic, unorganized personality. Not within forty-five minutes.

If Wilford wasn't a captive, he couldn't have gone farther than the kitchen under his own power. The kitchen offered more places to hide than the wide-open dining hall. In the dining hall the fat, unpopular screw would have stuck out as visibly as a pimple on a prom queen. If he was in the kitchen, he'd be dead and missing an arm and a keycard, or he'd be hiding as best he could and praying the cavalry arrived before a Squat decided to see if anything of value remained in the kitchen.

All Mitch had to do was find him. When he did, he'd tear a page out of Cole's playbook and present Wilford with two choices. He would help the screw to safety—Mitch was thinking locker room—or he'd tow the fat ass out of his bolt hole and drop him into the middle of the dining hall, making sure several enraged Squats found him.

He liked the locker room idea. He'd find street clothes there, perhaps a wallet with some cash. On the other hand, it was a risky spot because if any screws remained inside Glades, the locker room seemed a reasonable place for them to gather. He decided to worry about that problem if and when it arrived. If he got that far, he'd be supporting Wilford, the overweight slob, and he'd tell everyone he wasn't trying to escape, he was simply helping the screw to safety.

The kitchen was in shambles. Evidently, the looting had been good. The exhaust fans hummed and beneath the sheet metal grills, the gas hissed. For the first time in several minutes he heard the music again—Mariah Carey telling everyone what she wanted for Christmas, which Mitch enjoyed because, with all the conjecture and supposition of the afternoon, he didn't see any harm in throwing one more assumption into the mix: she was singing directly to him. Mariah as a Christmas gift, wrapped up in her tight red dress, was an exceedingly pleasant thought.

He shook the idea out of his head. This was no time to daydream. He stood in the center of the room and did a slow three-sixty. Where would Wilford hide? The kitchen was huge, large enough to store both frozen food and dry goods for eight hundred inmates, plus counter space to prepare the meals. Deep sinks and wide stainless-steel troughs led to industrial-sized dishwashers. A walk-in cooler in the back, right-hand corner reminded Mitch of how he ended up in Glades in the first place. A second cooler sat in the same place on the left side of the room, the door partially ajar. Presumably, one was a freezer for meat and frozen goods, the other a chiller for vegetables and consumables with expiration dates. Between the coolers, a closed garage door dominated much of the back wall. Two regular-sized doors with the familiar hand scanners, were set into the wall on his right.

Mitch doubted Wilford would have dragged himself from the dining hall into a meat locker. With no idea how long he'd need to hide, the screw would not have chosen the inside of a freezer. The thick rolls of fat around his waist wouldn't protect him long in temperatures near zero degrees.

Mitch didn't find the screw hiding in the kitchen proper, tucked under the counter beneath pots and pans and cleaning supplies.

Only one place remained. The second cooler, the one meant for perishables. Mitch thought this ironic, given the screw he was searching for was intensely disliked; his life expectancy would be minutes if he were discovered by most of Glades' population.

Mitch opened the door the rest of the way and slapped the light switch above the handle several times. The only light came from behind him and the worn green linoleum absorbed it all, reflecting nothing into the depths of the chiller. He looked at the ceiling. There wasn't a single bulb in the overhead fixture. Glass lay below it, sprinkled like chips of ice amongst the cans of food littering the floor. The impression that jumped to mind was someone had thrown the cans at the light bulbs.

Much of the food—heads of lettuce, bushels of carrots, cabbages and the bins in which they'd been stored—lay in a high mound in a back corner. Brussels sprouts pebbled the floor. Seeing as there weren't any deer or goats or horses housed inside Glades to eat the hateful little bastards, the floor was the best place for them. A five-gallon pail of Mayonnaise had fallen, or more likely been pushed off a shelf, and exploded, spraying the white goop in a fan, splattering the shelves and the opposite wall. On the green flooring, disks of pickles looked like warts on an ogre's face.

Peering into the depths of the chiller, Mitch swore. No Wilford. Escape had never really been much of an option. He'd known that from the beginning. Now that it was gone entirely, the dread he'd managed to contain, sprang to life. His heart rate spiked, leaving him feeling faint, making his fingers and toes tingle uncomfortably. The sparkling white lights dancing around the circumference of each eye, brightened slightly.

What kind of immoral tasks would Cole ask of him?

He took a moment and breathed in deeply and breathed out

slowly. Then, he stepped back, ready to swing the door shut...
and spotted something unusual. Sometimes it happened that way;
a person could stare at a room all day long and not see it, and
then a sideways glance out of the corner of an eye, and a whole
new picture developed. The long, narrow shape of a screw's baton,
perhaps six inches, poked out from beneath one of the plastic
food tubs and spilt groceries. He wouldn't have noticed it, except
the incongruity of the perfectly symmetrical shape amongst the
rubbish stacked in the corner, caught his eye.

He tilted his head and narrowed his eyes and studied the pile
that suddenly looked much more deliberate than he first imagined. Could the cruel guard have hidden himself, buried himself,
under the tubs and groceries? It wasn't inconceivable. Given his
size and his history, Wilford probably had the strength, even after
suffering the trauma of his shattered leg. He unquestionably had
the motivation, given the hatred every inmate in Glades bore him.

Mitch said, "Wilford, can you hear me?"

Nothing.

"I'm coming in, Wilford. I'm going to start kicking stuff out
of the way. Hopefully, I won't hit that broken leg."

Nothing.

"Okay. Maybe you're unconscious. Can't hear me. That's possible. But if you're trying to trick-fuck me, and I find you, I'm
going to drag you into the dining hall by your good leg. You can
take your chances with the Squats instead of me."

Nothing.

Mitch wiped his hand down his face. He still hadn't shaved
the goatee and it felt more like a beard every day. For a second
or two, he wondered if he had guessed incorrectly. Maybe there
was another reason for the baton to be buried under a shelf in a
chiller, hidden for the most part, by tubs and food. Offhand he
couldn't think of one, but maybe.

"Is that you, Reilly, you shit-stain?" As weak as Wilford's voice was, it was still filled with venom.

Mitch smiled grimly. "Yeah, it's me and you need to listen up. I'm going to give you two choices. You need to decide which one you like best. You need to decide immediately. Time's pressing, and I'm not about to waste any of it on you."

PART 4

"Mother Nature is a mad scientist."

Kramer (*Seinfeld*)

CHAPTER 41

LESS THAN SEVEN hours after his ambulance ride to the hospital, Ray watched a Super Eight parking lot on the opposite side of the road from the dumpster behind which he crouched. He had no way of knowing how long he'd been there, but the heat of the day had dropped a degree or two and he no longer noticed the pungent stink of garbage.

His escape from the hospital had been comically simple. On a day he would later consider the most abnormal of his life, fortuitous timing and unnatural good luck had coalesced and he walked out of the hospital without attracting attention. If they'd driven him to the hospital one hour earlier or one hour later, Ray suspected he would have been handcuffed to the bed and guarded by someone who carried a weapon and wore a badge. As it turned out, for a brief period of time, it seemed he was nobody's priority.

At the hospital, the nurses were focused on a steady influx of new patients. The doctors concerned themselves with guards and inmates who were more seriously injured than him. After handing him off, the paramedics had more return trips to make. Presumably, they all forgot about him.

At Glades, the anti-riot team was dealing with inmates inside the prison, the ones destroying property and attacking everybody in sight with makeshift weapons. They didn't care about inmates on the outside. Guards were in charge of inmates inside a prison. Occasionally they watched them on the outside too, but typically it wasn't their job, especially when there weren't enough to go around on a good day. Apparently, it didn't cross anyone's mind to post one or two in the hospital. Possibly, everyone assumed someone else had taken on that responsibility.

Various other groups who might have been tasked with the security of those being sent for medical care, were victims of the short-lived confusion and miscommunication Colin McTavish mentioned, and the complacency that came with Glades' perfect record—zero escapes. Everyone loved the wall with the impossible-to-climb roll of polished aluminum at the top. Evidently, no one had seen the Levels of Security protocol as a vulnerability, particularly when an inmate was freely escorted out of the prison.

The paramedics had parked Ray in a bay sectioned off from other patients with hospital-green curtains, and then they disappeared. A nurse asked him a bunch of questions, told him a doctor would see him shortly and then she disappeared. He stared at all the dimples and pin-holes in the hung ceiling, listening to a constant buzz of conversation, the continual chuff of hurried footsteps, the steady drone of moans and whimpers from patients. Someone coughed like he'd inhaled a burr the size of a tumbleweed. A nurse asked someone else for his particulars—name, age, emergency contact number.

Surrounded by people but ignored and therefore virtually alone in the busy hospital, Ray unstuck the white medical tape, undid the Velcro on the hard collar, and unfastened the snaps and buckles securing him to the backboard. He needed a bathroom, and he wasn't about to wait for people who'd forgotten he was there. With a relieved groan, he rolled onto his feet. He poked his head between the green curtains, spotted a lavatory and bee-lined to it, locking the door behind him. When he faced the mirror, the reflection looking back at him made him jump with surprise—no wonder the paramedics had hustled him to the hospital.

Both eyes were black. One side of his face was swollen, cut and scraped, covered in dried blood. More blood was crusted into his hair, splats like paint on his orange coveralls, some of which had come from the cuts on his face and the back of his head, he guessed, but much of it would have been Christopher's. He looked far more damaged than he really was.

He washed his face gingerly, wincing at the stinging touch of his fingers. The water went from dark pink to clear. Then he went to work on his hair, raking his fingers through it until the blood disappeared, slicking it back like he routinely combed it that way, still too short to be considered a style, but better than the matted mess it was minutes before. When he straightened, forcing his shoulders down and back, he looked like a different person, even to himself. He certainly didn't resemble the individual the paramedics wheeled into the hospital.

That's when it finally hit him...

Other than the orange coveralls, there was nothing about his appearance that told someone he belonged in the hospital. That would likely change soon. A nurse would notice an empty bed. Eventually a doctor would check on him. Someone at Glades would start asking questions about the inmates at the hospital.

Mitch spoke about windows of opportunity. Ray realized this was his. He snagged a white lab coat hanging off a hook on the back of the door, fastened all the buttons and walked out of the lavatory, and then out of an exit on the opposite side of the hospital from the Emergency wing.

Initially his only thought was getting away from the hospital as fast as possible. Then he started thinking about getting out of town. After that, he wondered where he should go. The ideas came fast. He scrapped them just as quickly. They all hinged on cash and transportation.

Cash was an impossible problem. Transportation was doable, perhaps, but not by any conventional means. He couldn't hot-wire a vehicle. He had no mechanical knowledge and, outside of the movies, he suspected nobody knew how to do that sort of thing in the first place. Hitch-hiking was out. People seldom stopped for hitch-hikers, on top of which, a hitch-hiker on the side of the road was as visible as an inmate in a bus depot. The authorities would have eyes all over the transportation hubs and again, he had no cash for a ticket.

So, where did that leave him?

Across the street from a Super Eight, with one idea.

It wouldn't work at a high-end hotel. It wasn't a rule or anything, like a law, but more often than not, when someone drove a fancy car like a Mercedes or BWW, they stayed in a fancy place like a Hyatt or a Wyndham. They parked underground, or took advantage of a valet service, or drove vehicles with sophisticated security systems. The vehicles were never left unattended. There wasn't space in front of an expensive hotel for an empty, idling vehicle. It would get in the way. It would inconvenience the taxis with the conference guests. It would block stretch limousines carrying wedding parties and limit the movement of busses with the airline crews. A steady stream of people in tuxedos and gowns would have to walk around it, in order to get to their banquets. A concierge would notice it. Tow trucks were on speed dial.

On the other hand, at a low-cost chain, out near the interstates, vehicles were routinely left unattended. They were usually non-descript vehicles, a more basic means of transportation, compared to a Mercedes, and the drivers were more budget conscious. They stayed at these hotels for a different reason—it wasn't a rule or anything, but usually all they wanted was a good night's sleep. They checked in, maybe ate a meal at a nearby fast food restaurant and then left early in the morning. They parked under the hotel's awning and then went into the lobby for their key. In a place like Florida, they often left their vehicle running, for the AC presumably, or for the heat in the northern states, or to give themselves the impression the check-in procedure would happen quickly. It was a psychological thing. There was no need to shut the vehicle off when the spot under the awning was transitionary in nature and the car would be moved almost immediately. Usually within four or five minutes, if the clerk at the counter did her job well. Nobody felt any apprehension. The car was perfectly safe, only a short distance from the check in desk and in sight the entire time.

Ray had followed that exact procedure himself many times, sometimes with Dawn in the car and sometimes when he was travelling on his own. Never once had he checked in and then exited the hotel, expecting to find his car had vanished.

Tonight would be a different story for someone. When the right vehicle showed up—something with a few miles on the body and a few miles on the clock—Ray planned on stealing it and heading to a Days Inn on the south side of Jacksonville. He didn't believe in Mitch's magical doorway. Not by a long shot. But, he didn't think he had much to lose. Where else was he going to go? If a different world existed, it was his best way of avoiding a firing squad. And, a tiny percentage of hope existed in the back of his mind, if for no other reason than Mitch believed in the doorway and Roger Olson believed in it as well, and the two men didn't agree on anything.

A quiet, feminine voice said from behind him, "Who are you waiting for?"

A surge of surprised adrenaline hit Ray like water from a fire hose. With a yelp, he whirled in place, raising his hands to show he wasn't a threat. He scanned the alley frantically, searching for this unknown stranger, the first person he'd encountered since his escape from the hospital. He found a pale white face, partially hidden behind a drop-down fire escape. For the next two or three seconds, he could only gulp air and wait for his heart rate to fall. When he regained his breath, he said, "Where did you come from? You scared me."

"Who are you waiting for?" she repeated softly.

"Nobody." He kept searching but only found one face hidden in the alley's shadows. "What are you doing back there?"

"None of your business."

She spoke in a loud whisper but he still had a sense of her age—younger than Dawn, older than Angie. He recognized the tone, the universal-young-girl-voice that Angie tried occasionally but had yet to perfect, that unique mixture of apathy and aggression, of insecurity and confidence. As annoying as it was, he would have enjoyed the chance to experience it with his daughter.

He shot a glance across the street, guessing with no way of confirming, that at least twenty minutes had passed since the last car pulled into the Super Eight parking lot. Without looking at the girl in the shadows he asked, "Do you know what time it is?"

A moment of silence, then, "Ten-forty."

"That late?"

The riot started at noon. By midafternoon he was strapped to the backboard on his way to the hospital. Early evening found him walking toward the south side of town, where rows of hotels and fast food restaurants stood ready to serve traffic off the interstate. Time was ticking away. The next car had to be the one. No more excuses. Unfortunately, he'd never stolen a vehicle before and his nerves kept getting in the way. Every potential vehicle that parked under the Days Inn awning was wrong, for some nebulous reason.

He let his attention return to the girl in the shadows. She hadn't moved, and he wondered what someone so young was doing out so late, then he wondered how old she really was. It was difficult to tell these days in the best of situations, never mind in an alley in the middle of the night. He said, "How old are you?"

"Why?"

"What's your name?"

"None of your business."

He sighed. "Don't you have somewhere to be?"

"Don't you?"

"Not at all. It's why I'm sitting on my thumb in an alley in the middle of the night." He was re-thinking how much he may have wanted to experience this aspect of Angie's teenage years. Was this how it would have gone with her? Every question answered with a question? Every situation a challenge that bordered on a fight? He remembered something his Grandmother used to say in her wobbly, old lady voice… "A young girl needs to be placed in a deep freeze the day she turns thirteen and left there until she becomes a young woman."

"It's your wife, right? Or girlfriend? She's coming here with another man and you're—"

"You watch too much television," Ray interrupted.

"What?"

"Life is not a trashy reality show starring Ashley or Kim. Why don't you go home, before your parents start wondering where you are?"

"I do what I want," her whisper like a snake's angry hiss.

"Can you do it somewhere else?"

Behind him, the street brightened. He wasn't sure what he said to anger her, and he wasn't going to spend time worrying about it. He turned his attention back to the hotel. A car slowed and pulled in and stopped beneath the awning. A Camry. Maybe. He wasn't great at recognizing makes and models, especially mid-range sedans that looked almost identical from manufacturer to manufacturer.

The driver followed the familiar pattern. He climbed out, slammed the door, and strode around the front of the car. He entered the lobby, his suit jacket flapping in assertive haste.

Without giving himself time for second thoughts, Ray broke into a jog. He crossed two lanes of hot asphalt with barely a glance left or right, doing his best to keep one of the pillars that supported the awning between him and the lobby window. If he couldn't see the check-in counter, nobody in the hotel could see him.

Even from a few feet away, he couldn't tell if the Camry was running. Only exotics and sports cars were meant to be heard. Family sedans were designed for silence. Moving in a low shuffle, he reached the driver's door. Not more than four car lengths away, the clerk watched CNN on a television hanging from the wall while the driver read paperwork on the counter. Ray's fingers curled under the door handle. A soft vibration told him the car was running. He lifted the handle and with a quiet thunk, the door unlatched. A thrill of excitement raced up his spine. He opened the door wider.

The dome light illuminated like a spotlight on a Glades guard tower.

Ray's heart staggered. How could he have forgotten something as basic as a dome light? Not that he could have done much about it. For three-quarters of a second, he waited in a frozen squat with the door open, dome light burning, and then he heard a dim shout.

He shot a quick look over the car's roof, saw the owner staring across the lobby toward him. The man's hand fell into a pocket and came out fast with a phone, or what Ray hoped was a phone. Even at this distance, he thought he'd recognize a gun. He could have slid into the seat, slammed the car in gear, and sped away before the owner tackled him...

...but he panicked—he'd never stolen a car before—and he ran. He leapt across the low hedge to the left of the Camry like an Olympic hurdler and by the time he reached the edge of the highway four paces later, he was flat out. Behind him the driver yelled a second time. Ray didn't waste time looking over his shoulder to see if the man was pursuing him. He headed for the alley in a sprint, unsure why he decided to go in that direction, other than it was familiar. He ducked behind the dumpster and looked back at the hotel, bent over with his hands on his knees, panting heavily. After a career behind a desk, he'd thickened around the middle; he was no kind of runner.

The driver stood beside his car gesturing wildly with one arm, holding the phone to his ear with the other, most likely on the line to the cops. Ray had to move; they might already be on the way. But, where to go from here? And, how? A feeling close to terror chased every logical, analytical thought out of his mind.

"You tried to steal that car!"

Her voice was outraged and impressed at the same time. Ray wasn't expecting it and once again the bottom of his stomach fell away and he jumped in surprise. "You need to stop doing that."

"You tried to steal that car."

"Yeah. I did. I need to get to Jacksonville. Now, can we drop it?"

She shrugged and Ray knew, after the outrage he'd heard seconds before, that her sudden casualness was an act. She said, "Sure. I don't care."

"What's your name?"

"You asked me that already."

"You didn't answer."

"Eva."

"Okay, Eva. My name is Ray. I don't know what you're doing here, but I'm guessing that guy across the street just called the police. If you don't want them to find you, it might be time to scoot. If you know a safe, quiet way out of here, maybe you could show me?"

"What happened to your face?"

"I slipped in the shower."

"So, don't tell me." She tilted her head and sucked her lower lip and gave him a direct stare out of eyes circled with heavy, black eyeliner. Her hair shone, making her pale face unnaturally white in contrast. There was a small dot just above her upper lip that Ray couldn't identify. After a couple of seconds, she said, "You're not going to rape me, are you?"

"What? No. Of course not." *Too much television.* "Are you insane?"

"Let's go." She turned and walked deeper into the alley. She wore a long black coat and black boots. A worn backpack drooped off one shoulder. A patch on the outside panel read, "Han Shot First."

He hurried after her, afraid he might lose her in the darkness, wondering why a teenage girl would have a forty-five-year-old movie badge sewn on her backpack. She moved with assurance, following an obviously familiar path. After a couple of zig-zags, they walked out of the alley onto a quiet, commercial street. Overhead lights shone down onto dark store fronts—a drug store, an auto parts store, a liquor store with bars on the windows.

Eva looked back at him. "This way." Under the lights, the unidentifiable dot above her upper lip became a tiny jeweled stud. Ray walked beside her in silence, content to let her lead while he tried to figure out his next step. His mind remained frustratingly blank.

"Why do you need to go to Jacksonville?" Eva asked.

"Where are we going?"

"There's an all-night Thai place up ahead, and a 7-11. They've got a phone and an ATM. Why do you need to go to Jacksonville?"

"You ask a lot of questions."

"Yeah, but why?"

"I've hit a rough patch. I'm hoping to meet a friend there. He's going to help me out. Why were you in that alley?"

"Shortcut. Then I saw you and I wondered…" Her voice faded away. "I guess you don't have a bank card. That's why you tried stealing the car?"

"Good guess," he said. "A shortcut to where?"

After a short hesitation she said, "Home?"

She sounded tentative. Ray thought she was lying. He wiped sweat off his forehead with the inside of his arm. The temperature may have dropped a couple of degrees, but the remaining heat had changed. It had thickened and grown heavy and humid. It was like a late August afternoon in Chicago, when the towering cumulonimbus clouds piled up, and everybody knew a huge evening thunderstorm was imminent. Gusts of warm, sticky wind blew down the street carrying the occasional lazy, fat raindrop. He could no longer see stars.

Eva said with full seriousness, "Three weeks ago I hit a rough patch."

Ray almost laughed, but instinctively choked it back. She'd overreact if she thought he was laughing at her. But really, how rough could she have it? Aside from her weird personal style, she looked healthy and clean and she seemed as well adjusted as any teenaged girl. He said neutrally, "Is that right?"

"My dad kicked me out of the house. I don't get along with his girlfriend. He said it was her or me, and it wasn't going to be her. Skank. She's only seven years older than me." Her voice was filled with indignation.

Ray felt her words like a physical blow, thinking about Angie again, how bad it would need to be for a father to kick his daughter out of the house. He chastised himself for making premature assumptions. He didn't believe Eva was without responsibility. Teenage girls were perpetually moody, overly dramatic, and entirely self-involved, but when she said she'd hit a rough patch, she hadn't been kidding. "I'm sorry to hear that. Where do you stay?" He thought she was too clean, for lack of a better word, than a typical alley vagrant.

"I'm not homeless," she said, accurately reading his mind. "I work at the donut store. I get cleaned up at school. When I don't have a place to stay, like at a friend's," she gave him a quick, mischievous grin, "I sleep in my dad's car. It's a Bentley. It's big. I took his spare key. He loves that car. He'd go crazy if he knew I was using it like an apartment."

If Eva's dad loved his car as much as she said (and it was a Bentley so he undoubtedly did), he had to know his daughter slept in it. He must not have objected as much as she thought, otherwise he would have parked it in a garage, or changed the security code on the car's electronic locks or woken her up in the middle of the night and chased her away. Somehow that made Ray feel better about the situation, like maybe father and daughter weren't completely estranged and would eventually reconcile, despite the man's young girlfriend. He smiled back at her. "Very resourceful, you are."

Her eyes widened. "You know Yoda?"

"Probably better than you. It came out way before you—"

"Nope. No way," Eva interrupted, vigorously shaking her head. "They might be old, but they're classics. I've seen every one of them more times than I can count. I've watched *Battlestar Galactica* and *Star Trek* too, even the really old ones with William Shatner, but *Star Wars* is the best." She paused, sucking her lower lip. The mischievous grin returned. "You know what would drive him nuts? If I took his car. I can drive. I could drive you to Jacksonville. I could be there and back before he woke up. He wouldn't know where the extra mileage came from. Crazy town."

He didn't answer immediately. Suddenly, possibly, he had a means of reaching Jacksonville before Mitch's portal disappeared.

If he encouraged this young girl's revenge fantasy, if they managed to steal a vehicle without getting caught, if they drove three plus hours to Jacksonville, somehow avoiding potentially dozens of cops, and then, if they were fortunate enough to find a certain Days Inn containing a magical doorway...

He shook his head. This wasn't a plan. There were too many variables. It would never work. Ashamed of himself for even entertaining the idea he said, "Yeah, I expect that would drive him crazy."

The problem was, he still didn't have a single feasible idea of his own and time was running out. Eva's offer—suddenly it was an offer rather than a meaningless statement—seemed like his one and only option. "Why would you make an offer like that, Eva? You don't know me. I'm a complete stranger."

She sucked her lip. After a moment's thought she said, "I don't know, actually. It just feels right."

Ray wasn't proud of what he did next, but he was desperate. He said, "Are you serious? Do you want to do it? Drive me to Jacksonville? It wouldn't be a big deal for you, just a few hours each way. You wouldn't even have to get out of the car. I know you might have to think about it, but if you're serious, we've got to leave soon."

Without hesitation she said, "I don't have to think about it."

"Are you sure? Why would you do this?"

"The night feels weird." She shrugged. "The idea came into my head, like clear blue. It's the first thing that's felt normal all month."

"Clear blue?"

She shrugged a second time.

CHAPTER 42

HE VOLUNTEERED TO drive.

Eva said no, she didn't think her father would like a stranger driving his car, so Ray watched apprehensively from the passenger seat as she took the wheel. She held it tightly with both hands, leaned forward in her seat, and sucked her lower lip. She stayed that way for a while, concentrating. As her confidence grew, she started talking, telling him how some kids at school thought she was a geek for joining the science club, but she didn't care because she loved that shit (waiting a beat for him to say something, possibly reprimand her about her language, Ray guessed), then continuing on about Beverly Dryden and a couple of her bitchy friends saying stupid things like, "Is the Force with you today, Eva?" which she didn't consider an insult, but when they brushed past her in a flurry of giggles, she still felt like crying.

Ray listened without comment and prayed she didn't drive them off the road with her sudden bursts of speed and jerky corrections.

She thought there had to be extra-terrestrial life out there in the universe somewhere, maybe not like *Star Wars* or *Aliens*, but something, and how was this belief somehow crazier than the typical fantasy girls bought into, reading romance books, or watching rom-coms? Her opinion: her beliefs weren't any more farfetched, and she'd given it a great deal of thought lately. More than usual she said, probably because, "I've been having stress dreams. You know about those? Every night I get chased through some haunted black wasteland into a different world. They're seriously fucked up." She gave him another fleeting, defiant glance. "Stress, right? Being kicked out of the house and Lana and everything?"

Her use of the term "different world" raised the hairs on the back of Ray's neck.

Eva repeated more loudly, "Stress, right?" as if she suspected something else caused the dreams, wasn't sure what that might be, and wanted an adult's assurance that stress was indeed, the most likely cause.

He bobbed his head and made non-committal noises. He didn't want to say her dreams meant nothing, not when she was chauffeuring him to a meeting with a guy who claimed he routinely travelled between worlds. Instead he said, "Who's Lana?"

"The skank."

He should have known.

Traffic was light, illogically light after a riot in which at least one inmate had escaped. Ray couldn't understand why. It didn't make sense. The occasional car rushed past in the opposite direction, leaving a misty cloud in its wake and filmy gauze on the windshield but nobody came up fast behind them, flashing red, white, and blue lights. Helicopters wouldn't have surprised him an hour ago. Now he guessed the worsening weather prevented an air search. There should have been reports on the radio. Instead, the stations Ray found quickly filled the speakers with static. Mitch didn't specifically mention this phenomenon when he explained slipping. Typically, radio stations transmitted thirty or forty miles, not three or four. Ray doubted the weather alone was responsible for the poor reception.

Where was everyone?

Where were the roadblocks?

Rain that once sounded muted in the well-insulated luxury vehicle now sounded like a fast march on a snare drum. The windshield wipers slapped the water off in fast swipes. Strong gusts of wind buffeted the car, making his stomach do slow, languid rolls. A raw taste thickened in the back of his throat and sticky sweat pebbled his forehead. The last time he was car sick he'd been ten years old. To this day, the hot stench of burnt diesel took him back to traffic jams on the way to summer camp, ninety degrees outside and no AC in the car.

Physically, he felt truly awful. Worse, his earlier nervousness had turned into unexplainable foreboding that had nothing to do with Eva's driving. He looked at her and wondered if she felt as miserable as he did.

"How do you feel?" he said. "Is this weather making you nervous?"

"Why? I'm not doing that bad, am I?"

"Sometimes I get nauseous when I ride shotgun," Ray lied. "You're doing well."

"Good," Eva said, sounding pleased and proud. "I just got my license. Usually I don't like driving in crappy weather. Tonight, I feel great. Better than I have in a long time. I should have stolen my dad's car a long time ago."

He watched her for several seconds. She drove with assurance. Her inexperienced hands had settled on the steering wheel and she sat easy in the big leather seat. There was a small, contented smile on her face. Her answer didn't surprise him. She radiated confidence, like everything was as it should be. How did this improvement happen so quickly, especially given the deteriorating weather? Especially when, as they approached Jacksonville, his own sense of impending menace worsened. He looked out the side window…

…and hooded eyes streaked with red veins stared back at

him. Ray recoiled so violently into his seat, it felt as though he tripped and landed on his butt. He grunted and his teeth clicked together and he closed his eyes and when he reopened them, he was no longer in the car. He pushed himself to his feet and ran, pumping his arms, casting fast glances over his shoulder into the rain and mist, searching for the maniacal cackles that chased him, corralling him down narrowing paths toward a shallow grave he somehow knew had already been dug…

"By the way," Eva said, "where exactly in Jacksonville are we going? Did your friend give you an address?"

Her voice made him jump in the comfortable leather cocoon of his seat. He blinked several times. What was going on in his head? Thoughts such as these were not the product of simple trepidation. They were nightmares come disturbingly alive. He kept his eyes away from the windows, focusing instead on the interior of the car. He took a deep breath and exhaled slowly. His hands were tight fists. He forced himself to wiggle all his fingers like a writer warming up in front of a keyboard. "His name is Mitch. The hotel is on the south side of Jacksonville. That's all he said."

"Not much to go on," Eva said, calmly.

Not much?

Nothing at all. And, assuming they found the right hotel, the chances of Mitch being there was a stretch Ray's imagination could scarcely manage.

"It doesn't matter. We'll find it," Eva said, with assurance. "I'm in the zone."

"You're in the zone?"

"The blue zone." She giggled. "It's like, there's a sound in my head and it's cool and blue and it's pointing the way." Her brow puckered into a curious frown. In a less certain tone she said, "I think if I get away from the sound, it won't be nice anymore. I think it would hurt. It would be a stabbing red." She shook her head and mumbled, "Crazy town."

A sound is guiding her now?

Goose flesh pebbled Ray's arms. "Is the sound actually there, right inside your head? Or, do you just imagine it's there?"

She sucked her lower lip and seemed to give the question some serious thought. After several seconds she said, "It's there. Right between my ears. I'm not imagining it. It's like the time I went to a Taylor Swift concert. It was so loud. Later, when it was over, there was a humming in my ears. It was just noise, though. Annoying. This is noise too, but it's okay. It's blue."

There was no longer a reason for skepticism. Mitch hadn't lied or exaggerated. He wasn't delusional. The similarities between his and Eva's experiences were too comparable to be coincidental. If that weren't enough, Ray now thought the force that pulled Mitch toward a portal was warding him off in various ways—the dreadful weather, the nightmare come alive, and the pukey feeling in his stomach and head. If his belief was accurate, and he was confident it was, it would explain the vacant roads, the lack of pursuit, and Eva's growing confidence. Mitch alluded to all this when he told his story in the Glades' yard and now Ray was experiencing it firsthand. He wasn't supposed to be out here on this night. Eva, on the other hand was driving in the direction in which she was destined.

Shit.

There were different worlds out there, parallel to the one he had known his entire life. Once again, he breathed in deeply and breathed out slowly, forcing himself to relax. It was a great deal to grapple with.

In a voice devoid of inflection, designed to calm himself more than Eva, he said, "The sound you're hearing is called tinnitus. My friend suffers from it too. It guides him, just like it's guiding you. The sound will grow louder over the next hour. It won't hurt as long as you follow it. If you turn around, the volume will increase and the pitch will change and it will hurt."

"It would turn red." She glanced at him out of eyes filled with fear and excitement. The jewel above her lip glittered in the dash-board lights. "How does it hurt?"

"I don't know exactly," he said, in a way that wouldn't frighten her, like a father would, and then immediately felt like a fraud. Eva wasn't his daughter. "Mitch said it felt like needles stabbing his ears."

"So, as long as I follow the Blue, it won't hurt and it will take us to the Days Inn?"

"It'll take you to a portal. You know what a portal is, right?"

"Duh. I'm not stupid."

"Mitch said he had to get to this motel and that's where he'd find the portal."

"And, that's the end? The Blue will stop?"

"It's not the end, it's the beginning. But, yeah, the portal will open up between our world and a different, parallel world and the Blue will go away. Until next time."

"Won't people be there? Won't they see?"

Ray remembered asking similar questions and now he was answering them as though he had first-hand experience. To his ears, he sounded like a lunatic. He closed his eyes and shook his head. The abrupt motion washed him in a wave of vertigo. He said, "The portals aren't out in the open. And, they repel people who don't know about this sort of thing."

"Then what happens?"

"My friend walks through, out of this world, into the other. He starts his life again in a new place."

"What if he doesn't walk through?"

Your condition will deteriorate. You'll go crazy or lose your mind.

Ray decided he'd told her as much as he would. "I don't know, Eva. He always walks through."

She said nothing for several miles. "You're trying to get away from your rough patch, right? You're going to go through with him."

"That's the general idea."

"Could I go too?"

With the limited information Ray had, he suspected she'd have an easier time walking through than he would. He said, "When Mitch came to this world, he came with someone else. I don't see any reason why you couldn't leave the same way. It's what I plan to do."

And, if Mitch isn't there, if he's asleep in Red 350, or locked in the box, or lying in a morgue with .223 round in his head, I'll walk through the portal with Eva, because she's like Mitch and she is driving in the direction in which she is destined.

She said, "That's not what I mean. I want to go through with you, Ray."

He said nothing.

"Ray?"

He blew out a long, quiet sigh. "Your life is here, Eva. Your friends, your job. Even your family. Your father will miss you, believe it or not. My guess, in a few months or a year, he'll realize you're more important than his girlfriend. You might think you want to leave it all, but do you really?"

She said, "If I go through, will you stay with me? At least for a little while?"

CHAPTER 43

WHATEVER THE BLUE was, it worked for Eva. She found the motel without consulting the Bentley's navigation system and wheeled the big vehicle into an empty spot like she drove a semi-truck for a living, rather than the novice she was. She turned the car off and for two or three seconds, they sat in the dark, while rain tattooed the roof and the wind sought a way inside.

She asked, "Now what?"

"It's going to get weird. Weirder." Ray wasn't sure how he knew this, but he was confident he was right. A headache had joined his nausea. He was tempted to open the window for a face full of cold, wet air, but the memory of the monsters had taken root and he was convinced the roiling clouds were alive and waiting to pounce. Without optimism, he searched the console between the seats for a bottle of aspirin. He doubted he'd find any and if he did, he was positive they'd be ineffective. That's how the night was working. Turning around, getting as far from the Days Inn as possible, was the only cure. He guessed half a mile in any direction would be enough for the symptoms to ease, as long as the hotel was behind him.

There were no aspirin, turning around wasn't an option—he'd come here for a reason—so procrastinating in the car was pointless. "Last chance," he said. "I'll get out, and you can drive home."

"I don't fit into this world," she said with complete assurance.

Ray heard the conviction in her voice. The first time Mitch slipped from one world to another, he was fifteen. He said, even at that age, he knew he didn't have a choice. It was as inescapable as death. Was that true for Eva as well? At that moment, she didn't sound like a typical teenager who hated school and felt ostracized by her peers. She sounded like a woman who knew deep down, instinctively, that something about this world would always be wrong for her.

She said, "You didn't answer before. Will you stay with me?"

Just that quickly, she sounded like a young girl again. He stared at a spot between his feet and did a mental shrug. At sixteen Eva was presumably capable of making her own decisions and, ultimately, he wasn't her guardian.

In a thin, forlorn voice she said, "You don't have to if you don't—"

"You won't see this life again. Ever," he said.

"I know."

"Emotional decisions aren't smart decisions."

"I know."

"It sounds like you've made up your mind." He patted her hand, and she snatched at his and held on tightly. A calm, easy feeling filled him for the first time that night. The headache lessened, his stomach settled and the dizziness disappeared. "I'll stay with you. Don't worry."

Blinking rapidly, she gave her head a short, abrupt nod. In a husky voice, she asked a second time, "Now what?"

Ray had no idea. The vacancy sign hanging in the window flickered and blinked, but there was no movement in the foyer behind the red swirl of neon. He counted three other vehicles in the parking lot—a couple of four-door sedans and a seventeen-foot cube van with the familiar U-Haul logo painted on the side. The sides of the van collected wind like sails and shook the big vehicle on its suspension. As far as he could tell, through the driving rain and churning mist, the hotel on the opposite side of the road was similarly deserted. A slow night in the tourist trade. He saw no clues and no indication where they had to go next. But, he had a feeling Eva would know.

"Is the Blue still working?" he asked uncertainly.

"Uh-huh."

"It's up to you, then. Use it and find the right room."

"It's louder now. It hurts." She sucked her lower lip. "We're going to get drenched."

"Yeah," Ray answered, thinking the rain was the least of their problems. According to Mitch the tinnitus worsened just before the portal opened. Worsened in a hurry. If Eva experienced it in the same way he did, and it was beginning to hurt, their time was short. Ray put some "adult" into his voice. It seemed she expected grownups to be the ones in charge. "You have to lead, Eva."

She gave his hand a quick squeeze then, just as quickly, released it and opened the car door. "Let's go."

The moment she let go, the night flooded in, thick and full of malice. It struck like a punch to the stomach. He turned to his right, flung his own door open and retched all over the parking lot. He rolled out of the car into the teeming rain, landing on his hands and knees, drooling and dry-heaving.

In an instant, he was saturated. A black fog surrounded him, swirling and filling him, until his head swam with unexplainable childhood nightmares and the endless doubts of adulthood. Every thought fused and became genuine and authentic and it was all there in front of him in the shape of a black Cadillac Escalade. The SUV bore down on him rapidly, doubling then tripling as it drew closer. The powerful engine roared. He held his hand up to shield his eyes from the headlights pinning him in place like two huge spotlights.

His mind screamed at him to move and he rolled sideways.

Sand and grit bit into his palms. His knee dug into a stone on the pavement. Lightning bolts of pain made his eyes water. The twin headlights became one. Somehow, he could still see the Cadillac's wreath, growing like a malignant weed on the massive front grill.

The SUV hit him with a sickening, life-ending crunch. He felt no physical pain but he saw the light leave Dawn and Angie's eyes all over again. Weeping, he reached for them. They were only an arm's length away, but no matter how far he stretched, he couldn't touch them.

Something warm landed on his shoulder. The painful images instantly dispersed, becoming the memories his mind had grown used to and his soul had yet to accept. His head stopped throbbing and his heaving stomach quieted. He looked over his shoulder through blurry, tear-filled eyes. Eva stood beside him with her hand on his shoulder, her face covered with uncertainty.

She shook him. "Get up."

"Don't let go," he said.

"I guess my driving wasn't so good."

"You're the best sixteen-year-old driver I know." With Eva pulling his arm and generally getting in the way, he staggered to his feet. He scrubbed his hands together, brushing off the parking lot grime.

"I'm scared. It doesn't feel normal here."

Her little hand fumbled around his. Ray folded it in his own and gave her fingers a gentle squeeze. She seemed to need his touch as much as he needed hers. "Normal is a long way away."

The rain fell and the wind whipped. Water streamed off his head and glued his shirt to his body. He leaned on the car for a second or two, catching his breath. Then he wiped the back of his hand across slimy lips and ran his tongue across his teeth, cleaning them. He turned his head to the side and spit the bitter, sour taste away.

"The Blue is really loud."

In the back of his analytical mind, Ray wondered how she heard the colors. Hopefully, in an hour or week, he'd be able to ask how they came to her. For now, there was no time for explanations. He said, "We've got to hurry."

She took a couple of tentative steps then sped up, towing him by the hand. She followed a slightly zig-zag path, tightening her grip and making small whimpers of pain each time she went off course. "The Red is so close. It cuts."

"I know. If we're going to get through this, you have to tough it out."

CHAPTER 44

THE MAN IN the driver's seat of the seventeen-foot U-Haul cube van thought the only thing that made sense on tonight's "mission" was the bean-bag gun he carried. According to his earlier briefing, their quarry was neither armed nor dangerous. He was simply an individual of extreme interest. For that reason, a non-lethal weapon was a good choice. Everything else however, like the camouflage paint on his face and the shotguns his two colleagues carried? Ludicrous. His opinion of course, but since the Squat perched on the crate between the front seats insisted, and since he was the one running the show, Robert Ward's opinion was irrelevant.

The camouflage paint and combat gear weren't the only unusual things tonight. Ward couldn't remember the last time he'd suffered through so much as a head cold. He may have had the flu once when he was a kid, but he wasn't sure. He never got sick. Tonight though? His head was spinning like a tornado and his stomach boiled and, every time the tall, skinny dude with the missing tooth opened the door and climbed out the back of the van—eight separate times now—the feeling worsened.

Ward told himself to concentrate.

Low threat or not, he needed to be on full alert. That was a big part of the job. Wishing he was at home eating pizza with his family, drinking beer, arguing about what to watch on television, was not appropriate for the time and place. For some strange reason, the pull toward home was incredibly intense tonight. Strange because he couldn't remember the last time he wanted to spend time with his stoner of a son, diva of daughter or, "… a muffin is NOT a cake…" thirty pounds overweight, wife.

Unusual?

Oh, yeah.

And, there it went again—his concentration. Gone. As if it had blown away in the hellish wind out there, in a storm like he'd never experienced before, the sky at sunset a harsh black and purple bruise, the rain sheeting down like Mother Nature herself had tipped an ocean on its side.

Most unusual of all was having to take orders from the Squat. Ward didn't care for that one bit. The Squat looked at him and his colleagues with a disdainful curl on his lip before introducing himself as Deputy Warden Tyler, saying it like his title demanded instant and unquestioning respect.

A glorified prison guard giving him orders?

Fuck's sake.

The Squat had a night vision scope pressed to his eye and ceaselessly scanned the darkness surrounding the Days Inn with slow, left to right sweeps. He slurped noisily on an endless succession of hard candies. His long tan rain coat covered a suit and a clip-on tie, the tie dangling loose from the left side of his collar, to give the impression he'd rushed away from his cushy office job to join them at the last minute. He was too busy and important to change into more appropriate attire.

Ward's heavily biased opinion, of course.

For the last two hours, they'd driven from one hotel lobby to another, the Squat growing edgier every time the skinny dude called Carter came back saying, "Nope, he's not here." Carter hadn't yet climbed out of the van on this, their ninth stop—Tyler hadn't given the order—and Carter hadn't shown any initiative and volunteered.

Tyler was busy with the scope, busier than the previous eight times they'd stopped. That should have put Ward on high alert, except he'd grown so bored and resentful he'd convinced himself nothing-at-all would happen. And, he was having a difficult time thinking about anything other than how close he was to barfing and the damned awful crunching sound Tyler the Squat made when he crushed his candies between his teeth.

Ward said, "We're running out of hotels. How much longer are we gonna do this?"

The Squat lowered the scope. "Do you have somewhere to be, Mr. Ward?"

Anywhere but here. "As a matter of fact—"

"Robert," the soldier in the passenger seat interupted, caution in his voice.

Ward locked gazes with the Squat. The protuberant eyes looking back at him from below the sloping forehead didn't blink. Ward let the silence stretch. He wouldn't apologize, no matter what this puffed-up prison guard wanted or expected. Still, he wordlessly thanked his colleague for the interruption. What was wrong with him? He couldn't question the leader. He couldn't voice his opinion on camouflage paint, hard candies, or anything else for that matter. He didn't know where Tyler's authority came from, but Ward's direct supervisor told him the Squat was running the show, at least until the action started.

Deputy Warden Tyler finally broke eye contact. He frowned. After a second or two he said in a friendly, conversational tone, "Everyone, pay attention."

Ward's annoyance eased. What kind of pep talk would someone so inflated with his own importance give? He took a quick look around the van. Both his colleagues straightened and looked at the Squat, apparently as curious as Ward himself. Carter didn't move, he just sat there with his head hung down toward his knees. Every time he'd returned from one of his excursions to a hotel lobby, he appeared sicker than the last. If he felt as bad as he looked, Ward sympathized.

Tyler started speaking. All traces of friendliness had been replaced with condescension. "Somebody way above my pay grade, and therefore way above yours, has tasked us with apprehending Mitch Reilly. Because I'm familiar with Mr. Reilly, and because you know nothing at all about the man, I was put in charge of tonight's mission. That must sting." He paused long enough to look at them all in turn. "I don't care. My sole interest is apprehending Reilly. Like it or not, whether you feel this mission is beneath you or not, if taking orders from a First Gen is one of your particular irritants, too bad. I don't care."

A second pause, longer this time.

Ward's curiosity vaporized. Annoyance returned in full force. His spine stiffened and his fingers stroked the grip of the Glock 19 at his waist.

Tyler continued his motivational speech, seemingly unaware of how close he was to being shot several times in the face at close range. "I don't care if you feel sick. I'm not feeling one hundred percent myself, but I'm not bitching about it. I expect you to settle down and focus. The racket you're making, the way this vehicle is shaking, our mission could hardly be called stealthy." He finished disdainfully, "I was led to believe you were professionals."

Ward would never have admitted it out loud, but on that score, Tyler was correct. The team's professional standards were lacking tonight. He'd seen these men sit motionless and silent for hours at a time. He suspected they felt like he did: restless and ill. Without a doubt, something unusual, other than having to take orders from a prison guard, was taking place tonight. Something else was throwing them off their game. Even his sudden hunger to shoot the arrogant Squat was unusual. It seemed an extreme reaction, no matter how little he liked the man.

Ward reluctantly took his hand off his pistol and put it on the steering wheel. He told himself to focus. He forced himself to concentrate. When this night was over, he vowed he'd have strong words with his supervisor about having to take orders from a prison guard who was not qualified to lead missions requiring combat gear. In the meantime, he had his bean-bag gun and a job to do.

CHAPTER 45

THE CONTEMPT IN the U-Haul cube van didn't bother Deputy Warden Tyler in the least. Eight hundred angry inmates projected the same kind of animosity in his direction every day. He managed it easily. He found three disrespectful, so-called soldiers less bothersome than an itchy pimple on the back of his hairy ass. The slight headache he had, and the mild nausea were larger irritants than Robert Ward and his colleagues. He gave each man a final hard glare and then turned back to the windshield, raising the night vision scope to his eye.

Tyler liked the scope. It gave everything a soft green glow. It made him feel like he was a step ahead of everyone, like he knew things nobody else knew. He swept his gaze across the Days Inn parking lot. He ignored two unremarkable family sedans and focused instead on a big, solid-looking Bentley that pulled in a minute or so after he'd arrived in the cube van. It was a nice car, an expensive car. Not the kind of car a person normally saw in a Days Inn parking lot. Cars like that parked themselves downtown, at Hyatts or Wyndhams. It wouldn't be Mitch Reilly.

Or would it?

After a second's thought Tyler shook his head. Probably not. Feasible, of course—at this point all things were possible—but he doubted Reilly would have gotten off a bus and then sought and somehow stole a luxury vehicle.

What he did know was this: Reilly had climbed on a bus in Tampa after buying a one-way ticket to Savanah, using cash he stole from the worthless sack-of-fat, Shane Wilford. He got off the bus at a satellite stop south of Jacksonville, well short of his final destination, presumably in an effort to confuse pursuit. Tyler knew that much after interviewing Wilford, the bus driver, and checking station CCTVs.

What happened next was a mystery.

After looking at the situation from several different angles, Tyler figured there were only two remaining options for Reilly to act upon.

Option one—Reilly gets off the bus before it reaches a major transportation hub. He steals a vehicle. He drives away, hoping to vanish before the authorities start looking for him in a stolen car. A plausible scenario, given the challenges the atrocious weather would create for cops and pilots and anyone else involved in a manhunt.

Or, option two—Reilly gets off the bus before it reaches a major transportation hub. He checks into a no-name motel, hoping to become invisible while authorities waste time searching obvious destinations and choke points. He uses Wilford's cash sparingly for food until the immediate urgency of the manhunt dies down.

Option One meant Mitch Reilly was a ghost. US Marshalls would take over the search and Tyler would end up in a closed-door conference with Mr. Barnett. It wasn't his fault Reilly escaped, but he had little doubt Barnett would see it that way.

Any chance of apprehending Reilly hinged solely on Option Two, which is why they were canvassing hotels within a six-mile radius of the satellite stop—the limit Reilly could reasonably have traveled on foot in the two hours since he got off the bus. There weren't many hotels and, unfortunately, as the so-called soldier in the driver's seat pointed out in such an insubordinate fashion, they were running out. If Reilly went to ground in a backyard shed or a doghouse for instance, he was a ghost once again.

Tyler said, "Carter, you're up." He ignored the unenthusiastic sigh and the resigned, "Yeah," that came from the back of the cube van. He re-focused the scope on the Bentley. With a hard, lemon-flavored candy rolling lazily around in his mouth, he wondered how many more wrist watches and gold chains he'd have to liberate from various Inmate Possession Bags before he could afford a Bentley. He wondered if that would be an option in the future. How displeased would Barnett be? Perturbed or livid? Would he fly into one of his blinding, white-hot rages? If he was really furious, would he follow through on his threat and tell the Glades' inmates about the young boys?

Tyler clenched his jaw in a sudden surge of fear, loudly crushing the candy into tiny flavor-saturated fragments. No amount of money would keep him safe if he became an inmate in his own prison. Colin McTavish would eat him alive inside ten minutes.

The door on the driver's side of the Bentley opened and a young girl stepped out, shoulders hunched against the rain. An instant later the opposite door opened and the passenger tumbled out of the car onto his hands and knees. The girl circled the front of the vehicle and stood beside the person on the ground, obviously unsure of what she should do. She put her hand on his shoulder, as if trying to comfort him. The individual sat up on his haunches and stood a second later. He staggered back a couple of steps until he was leaning on the Bentley's front fender.

Tyler lowered the scope. His eyes narrowed in concentration. What had he just seen? The man's profile and the way he moved seemed familiar. After checking eight hotels—what amounted to tossing darts blindfolded in the dark—had he finally discovered something significant? Or, was simple desperation creating mirages? He said quietly, but with force, "Mr. Carter, stop. Don't move. There's something…" His voice faded to nothing.

The so-called soldiers stiffened into alertness.

Tyler pressed the scope tightly to his eye and waited. A second or two later, the man leaning on the Bentley raised his head and scanned the parking lot from left to right. Tyler recognized Raymond Albright. Inmate 66-780, if he remembered correctly, and he usually did.

He rocked back on the crate. "What the hell?" he muttered. Barnett told him to keep a protective eye on Mitch Reilly. For that reason, finding Reilly was the night's priority. Tyler had all but given up hope, but when a second inmate, Reilly's cellmate no less, shows up within six miles of Reilly's satellite stop, it couldn't be considered a coincidence.

"Mitch Reilly is here," Tyler snapped at the so-called soldiers. He pointed out the windshield at the two figures walking through the rain toward the hotel. "Follow them. They will lead you to him. He is your only priority. Now, go." He raised his voice. "But go very slowly and with extreme caution. Reilly is smart and he is slippery. He will surprise you."

CHAPTER 46

EVA LED RAY through the parking lot on the back side of the hotel, past two battered green dumpsters partially hidden behind a wooden fence, one gate hanging askew. The smell of wet garbage lay heavy in his nostrils. All the lights were dark back here, as if the hotel's night crew had come on shift and forgotten to hit the switch. Or, as if something unexplainable had blown out every bulb at the same instant. Ray had never seen rain like this, water falling hard enough to bounce off the ground. A rush of trash and debris floated toward storm drains in fast rivers. A cardboard coffee cup jammed in a grate and water backed up, forming a small lake that glowed with a silver sheen. Petroleum washing off the asphalt most likely gave it the unnatural color, but Ray wouldn't have bet on it. Not tonight.

They came to a staircase at the center of the building. Unhesitatingly, Eva climbed and Ray followed, their fingers twined. The metal treads rang beneath their combined footsteps and the wind whistled through holes in the risers. Small flakes of paint chipped off the banister under his right hand. After six switchbacks, they reached the top level and could climb no higher. A sign with the numbers 300 to 330 pointed left. A second sign pointed to the right. 331 to 360.

Her face a frown of concentration, Eva turned right.

Their feet squelched on the outdoor carpeting lining the balcony. Hanging baskets filled with flowers hung on chains off the roof line, the colorful petals beaten down, ragged and pitiful in the rain. The pots scribed crazy orbits in the wind. Water spouted out the bottom of them as though from a faucet.

She stopped outside room 350.

A fleeting grin touched Ray's mouth. He knew he didn't have to ask, but he did anyway. "This is it?"

Eva took a couple of steps to the left, winced and quickly stepped back. "It's Blue here. Red over there. Should we knock?"

"I don't think we need to." He curled his fingers around the knob. The brass was cold in his palm. He gave it a twist. The knob refused to move. He tightened his grip and tried a second time. Nothing. He tried in the opposite direction. To his complete astonishment, it still didn't budge. He wiped a frustrated hand down his face and ignored Eva's questioning gaze. He had no answers, only a rising sense of dread. If they couldn't get through the door he'd end up back in Glades. Worse, if Mitch was to be believed, a neurological strand in Eva's mind would stretch like a pink elastic band, until it turned white and snapped, scrambling her brains in a small but significant manner. They had to get through. Everything about the night told him he was in the right place, so why wouldn't it open? It made no sense.

And, then it did.

Eva was in the right place. He was not. He was not supposed to be here. The night kept telling him so. "You try, Eva."

She flicked him a doubtful glance.

He nodded.

She sucked her lip for a second or two and then reached out tentatively with her free hand. She grabbed the knob and twisted. With a soft click, the door unlocked. She mumbled, "Crazy town."

Ray gave his head a small shake. Water dripped off the tip of his nose. More water ran down his neck, cold rivers against the suddenly sweaty skin of his back. With his heart beating faster than normal, unsure of what he'd see and far from convinced Mitch would be inside the room, he toed the door fully open with the end of his Glades-issued shoe.

CHAPTER 47

WHEN THE DOOR to his hotel room swung open, Mitch thought…

How did Cole find me so quickly?

Never before had the tinnitus accelerated at such a pace. The seven-day early warning system with which he'd grown up had compressed itself into thirty-six hours. Less. Now, when he only needed two more minutes, one hundred and twenty insignificant seconds, to get out of this fucked-up world, away from the Squats and Glades and all the fucked-up situations he'd tripped over since the cop pulled him over in Step's truck, Cole had found him.

How?

Fear powered him up from his perch on the corner of the mattress. He spun in place.

It wasn't Cole.

It wasn't Glades personal or US Marshalls standing in the door. It was Ray Albright. Ray and a young girl with wavy brown hair, a red jewel piercing her upper lip and two rings of black eye makeup, smeared wide from the rain. Mitch recognized her but with the tinnitus shrieking, and strobing white light circling each eye, he was unable to pinpoint from exactly where. He sank back to the mattress with a heavy exhalation. An embarrassed smile jumped onto his unshaven face. "You sacred me. I thought I locked the door."

"You did," Ray said, sounding more amused than contrite. He paused. "Room three-fifty? Like in Glades?"

"That shouldn't surprise you."

"It doesn't. Not really. Not anymore."

"The worlds are similar. There's splash over."

"It's good to see you," Ray said. "I wasn't sure you'd make it. How'd you get here?"

"I found Wilford. I gave him two choices. Me or the Squats."

"He chose wisely." Ray smiled. "What's with the track suit?"

"He had three pair hanging in his locker." Mitch pulled out the elastic waist band, showing off the orange coveralls he wore beneath the track pants. "He had a couple of hundred bucks in his wallet. I took that too. I bought a bus ticket."

"Risky."

"Yeah and no. There was a lot going on in the prison. A lot of confusion. You saw Control. They destroyed it. There were fires. They couldn't lock the place down. Not right away; there wasn't a single inmate where he was supposed to be. Some were in the hospital, or on the way in ambulances. Some were dead. Logically, a head count wasn't going to happen soon, and it wasn't going to be too accurate when it did happen." He hiked his shoulders. "I didn't think I'd be missed right away."

"You're lucky, Mitch. Twenty minutes after you left me, maybe less, the riot-team shot three Squats trying to get into a Level One area."

"I found Wilford fast. He scanned me out…" A little ashamed, Mitch let his voice fade.

"What?"

"I slammed his face into a wall. He wasn't mobile. It wasn't like he could resist. He went down. He's probably going to need another gold tooth. I stuffed one of his T-shirts into his mouth, tied him up with one of his ridiculous track suits. Then I hauled him into the back corner of the shower room. Unless they were specifically looking for him, he wouldn't have been too easy to see."

"And, you feel bad about it?"

Mitch didn't hear any recrimination in Ray's voice, but for some reason he felt like he needed to explain. "I feel guilty about not feeling bad. Wilford had some payback coming."

Ray nodded. "Yeah. He did." There was a long silence. "I didn't believe you."

"Nobody does. That's why I don't discuss it. Don't worry about it." Mitch waved the apology away. He looked from Ray to Eva then back again. "Who's your friend?"

"My name is Eva." She introduced herself without looking at him. Her attention was entirely focused on the luminous swirling square hovering chest high against the back wall. She whispered, "Is that it?" She immediately answered her own question. "That's the portal."

Mitch said, "Yeah, that's it." He gave Ray a questioning look.

Ray said, "The door was locked for me. She opened it no problem. She hears the tinnitus, like you. It brought us here. It's her first time. You know, she's never…" His voice faltered. He looked over Mitch's shoulder.

Mitch followed his gaze. The portal had grown in the forty-five seconds Ray and Eva had been in the room, increasing from the size of a hardcover book to that of a serving tray. Within its confines, black storm clouds churned. Specks of red and white light flashed like lightning, or malevolent eyes, inside the growing rectangle. Mitch said, "She's never slipped, Ray? After everything you've seen tonight, it's still hard for you to say?"

Ray's face had turned drywall-white. He shuddered and took a halting step backward. In a shaky voice he answered, "Yeah, it is. Sue me."

"Don't look at it. It'll suck all the positivity out of you."

Ray tore his eyes away from the portal. He gave the room a fast appraisal. "Nice place."

Mitch guessed he was deliberately searching for something that would serve as a distraction—the hotel room was unremarkable in its normalcy. Generic furniture, uninspired artwork churned out of a printing press by the thousands in a Chinese factory. Two queen-sized beds were pushed against the wall to the right. The duvets were printed with horrible mustard-yellow flowers. A single lamp burned brightly on a narrow bureau to Mitch's left. On the same bureau, a flat screen television flickered in silence—a crowd of actors wearing black suits, furrowed brows, and intense frowns rushed from place to place waving handguns.

This was the room through which he'd entered Liv's world thirteen months ago, so in that one respect, this was a better place to wait than most. "I'm not here for the ambiance," he said.

"What happens now?"

Mitch opened his mouth and worked his jaw, trying to clear his ears. He wiped his hands down his face, drying the water leaking from the corners of his eyes. He thought quickly, trying to decide the best way to explain something that was as terrifying the twelfth time as it was the first. "You cut it kind of short, so pay attention. There won't be time to explain it twice."

Ray said, "Go."

"You want to get in and out fast. To do that, you have to concentrate. Especially you, Ray. I'm not sure how the process will work for you. You might not see the opposite portal right away. If Eva is like me, she'll see it immediately." He cut Eva a look, uncertain if she was paying attention. The portal seemed to have hypnotized her. He snapped his fingers several times. "Eva, listen up."

Her gaze jerked toward him, her eyes wide, her cheeks damp with tears. "My ears," she said in a moan.

"It's going to get worse in a hurry," Mitch said flatly. The portal had grown to three quarters the size of a normal door; there wasn't time to repeat himself or reassure her with meaningless platitudes. "The sound will get deafening. You'll see an explosion of light. When that happens, go. If you stumble, start crawling. Just keep moving. As long as you cross from light to dark, you'll be fine. Inside, you can think again. Stay calm. Look for a gray rectangle. When you see it, don't think about anything else. The only thing that matters is that door, and how much you want to get there."

The first time he slipped, he found the vaporous gray shadow in seconds. Perfectly rectangular in shape and stationary in the wind, its presence was abnormal. Mother Nature loathed straight lines. Once he found it, his only thought was getting through it. A short time after that, his feet landed on the surface of a different world. The process wasn't difficult—horrifying and sickening certainly—but he deliberately made it sound harder than it was. He wanted Ray and Eva focused, with only one thing on their minds. He looked back and forth between the two of them. "Got it?"

Ray's face was a study in concentration. After a beat, he nodded. "Got it."

Eva didn't look at him. Mitch wasn't sure he'd reached her. The time for pleasantries had passed. He barked, "Eva—"

Ray interrupted. "Eva? Did you hear him?" He spoke gently and slowly. "Do you know what you have to do?"

* * *

Eva didn't much like Mitch. He was abrupt. Bossy. He snapped his fingers at her. She didn't care for that. He looked scary and desperate, like a homeless guy she would have crossed the street to avoid. Dark, half-moons hung under his bloodshot eyes. Stress lines scratched across his forehead and framed his mouth. His hair had been buzzed close to the scalp, like Ray's, but it was growing faster in some places than others. It looked like someone cut it with a weed whacker.

Ray on the other hand, had been friendly with her from the start. He didn't judge her and he didn't talk down to her. Neither had he lied, although she sensed he softened some of the things he told her. Somehow, that deepened her trust in him. She wiped her cheeks dry with the heel of her hand. She smiled wanly, the best she could manage, and said, "I heard him. Get into the portal. Concentrate on the gray door. I got it."

Her eyes slid sideways to Mitch. "I got it. Okay?" She gave him her most contemptuous stare, the one she reserved for her father, when he said something stupid like, "Maybe you and Lana could go shopping together?" As if the skank, in her tall boots and tight yoga pants, would go to Game Haven with her and thumb through their enormous selection of Bronze Age comics.

Everything around her was Red except the portal. It was irresistibly Blue. The tinnitus speared her ears. The smells of the room—dust and mildew, plastic and cleaning products—filled her nose. A peculiar stench, air singed by electricity, made her decidedly queasy. Her eyes left Mitch's scruffy face. The mystery of the portal terrified her, but it magnetized her as well. It erased her confusion about her place in the world. Any doubts about where she needed to be, were gone.

She tilted her head and watched it grow.

* * *

Mitch recognized Eva's expression. That dead, teenaged stare spoke entire sentences about her opinion of him and his intelligence. He heard the scorn in her voice, the derision only a teenage girl can manufacture with such perfection. He didn't care one way or another about her opinion, but the look worried him. In his limited experience, when a teenage girl didn't like an adult, they did exactly opposite of what was expected of them. If Eva hadn't been paying attention, didn't "get it," she would be in trouble.

Ray would be fine. Even though he'd never slipped (and wasn't really meant to), fear and adrenaline would get him across to the new world. Eva though...

The growing rectangle was only a hand's breadth from the floor. On the beds, the hideous flowers bloomed and began spinning like pinwheels, the petals flashing and throwing off yellow sparks. In the far corner, the arm chair dripped molten pleather and against the window, the curtains melted in wide smudges of acrylic color.

Mitch breathed in and breathed out. He rose to his feet with a grunt and squared his shoulders. He stood beside Eva, Ray on the other side. Together in a line, they faced the portal on the back wall of the room. He reached for Eva's free hand. If he held one and Ray held the other, they could help her across the Space Between in tandem.

Tinnitus screeched like an out-of-tune violin. The ring of striated light around both eyes ignited into a white phosphorous cloud. Red and black dots swam across his vision. Two thunderous booms filled the motel room, followed an instant later by a third. The shockwaves pulsed into the room and pressed on his eardrums. He staggered and flung an arm out for balance and thought...

...*This is different.*

Eva shrieked and collapsed. She simply dropped and hung there, dangling from Ray's hand like a dead thing. Mitch missed her free hand all together. He whirled around, ignoring a fresh wave of dizziness the rapid motion caused.

His eyes went wide with surprise.

CHAPTER 48

WOODEN SPLINTERS RAINED from the door frame to the carpet. The door knob was gone, as were the hinges, three gaping holes in their place. The door wobbled and then toppled into the room, struck the edge of the bureau and landed on the floor with a crash. Blue gunsmoke wafted into the room and dust plumed out of the carpet, both clouds assaulting Mitch's ultra-sensitive nose. The lamp teetered, hung motionless for a fragment of a second, then fell. The bulb burst with a sharp pop. The flat screen television shook on its plastic stand but the picture didn't change and the actors, who'd been joined by a female agent, also with a gun in hand and the same impossible intensity, carried on as if nothing abnormal were happening.

Three men stormed into the hotel room, black combat gear glistening with rain water, faces striped in nonsensical green and black paint. They fanned into a ragged line, dropped to their knees and raised ominous-looking weapons, one with a massive, cylindrical magazine attached below the barrel. A fourth individual followed the soldiers into the room and came to stop between two of the kneeling men. He dropped his hand to the grip of a Taser in a holster on his belt. He swiped his tongue across chapped lips.

Tony Carter.

Mitch swung a fast glance over his shoulder. He shouted, "Go.

It's open. Go." He slid sideways a step, putting himself between Carter and the portal, protectively shielding Ray and Eva from the soldier's guns. They'd need two or three seconds longer than he did—unfamiliarity bred hesitation—and he didn't want the soldiers or Carter slowing them down.

Carter's lips moved inaudibly over the echoes of the shotgun blasts and the chiming tinnitus. If Mitch had to guess, he would have said Carter was telling him not to move, or something equally as foolish, but nothing the screw had to say at this point was important. The portal tugged at Mitch as though he were connected to it by an insistent rope. The cold air plucked at him like invisible hands. It was time to go. Liv was only one concentrated thought away. He turned his back on Carter, ready to take three fast steps out of this world…

…except…

Ray and Eva were still in the room!

Eva was back on her feet, her mouth open in an unheard scream, her eyes huge in her unnaturally blanched face. She had Ray by the hand, clearly trying to tow him toward the portal, but something—Carter, the soldiers, possibly the portal itself—had frozen him in place like a concrete statue. His face was slack, mouth open, eyes glazed.

Mitch planted both hands on Ray's back and gave him a tremendous shove.

* * *

Ray stumbled forward two steps and then his paralysis broke. He gave his head a single, dogged shake. With a firm grip on Eva's hand, he leapt toward the portal and together they crossed the line on the carpet where reality ended and the Space Between began.

Wind whistled, every gust frigid across his tightly shorn scalp. His saturated clothes stiffened in the sudden cold. Little puffs of white cloud disappeared as fast as he exhaled. His teeth chattered and he shivered uncontrollably. His head swam with vertigo. He felt as though he were standing on solid ground but only liquid blackness existed beneath his feet. He inhaled air tinged with something putrid and scanned the darkness for a door.

He couldn't see it.

His gaze jumped from random points of light, to smears of wispy vapor, to blinking red dots that might have been the bloody eyes of unholy creatures. He couldn't see anything that resembled a door. Raw panic nibbled the edges of his concentration. They were going to end up trapped in the dark, forever in this dead space. "I can't find it, Eva!" His voice rose until it verged on a shriek. "I can't find it."

* * *

Mitch was a blink away from following Ray into the portal when something in the back of his brain, perhaps some primal survival instinct ten thousand years old, made him check over his shoulder.

Carter was lurching toward him with zombie-like determination, his Taser in his outstretched arm.

The weapon rattled.

Mitch recoiled and rotated. The Taser's wires floated through the air, harmlessly missing his neck by inches. He swiveled back ninety degrees, transferring his weight and momentum, back foot to front, and drove his fist into the side of the lanky screw's head. The same kind of shot almost put Wilford on his ass.

It worked better on a guy who weighed one third the ex-footballer's weight.

With a surprised moan, Carter dropped like a sack of sticks. He didn't get up.

A new voice said, "Mr. Reilly."

Mitch shook his aching fist and flexed his fingers. He looked up from Carter's prone figure and saw Deputy Warden Tyler framed in the door. Wind whipped his raincoat around his ankles. Behind him, the rain dropped out of the sky in an unfathomable fury. Tyler's sloping, ape-like face twisted into a smile. His onyx eyes glowed with feverish rage. "You've complicated my life. I promise you're going to regret it."

With a terrible sense of déjà-vu, Mitch backpedaled—barely a month before he pretended to use Lindsay as a shield while he searched for the portal with his feet. Just like last time, he guessed he had a few seconds. The soldiers hadn't shot him on sight. Which meant they were here to arrest him, which further meant Tyler wanted him alive. Probably on Cole's behalf. But, an arrest took a measurable amount of time. Three to five seconds at least, beginning with his willingness to stop moving, to accept his capture, to allow the soldiers to handcuff him and drag him back to Glades.

None of which Mitch had any intention of doing.

Three to five seconds. He was safe-ish.

As if reading Mitch's mind, Tyler's smile widened. "Shoot him, Mr. Ward."

The gun with the massive cylindrical magazine thundered. The shotgun slug slammed into Mitch's chest. The tinnitus reached an unbearable pitch, a silent scream of rage as intense as he'd ever experienced. The pain was seismic, like being struck by a semi. It folded him in half at the waist. All the air left his lungs in a single, enormous blast. He catapulted toward the wall behind him, where the portal hung like a chilling work of art. The back of his legs hit something solid, tripping him. His upper body flopped inelegantly into the Space Between but his legs hooked the bottom edge of the portal so that his calves and feet remained poking into the Days Inn.

* * *

From her knees inside the Space Between, Eva pushed with a flat palm against an area where she imagined the floor might be located. Her hand hit nothing, but in the context of helping her stand, the unyielding darkness supported her. Another quick movement and she regained her feet, although, once again it didn't seem as though they were planted on anything solid.

Ray shouted, "I can't find it, Eva! I can't find it."

She squeezed his hand, letting him know she'd heard him. Her heart beat quickly and her breath came faster than normal, but they weren't symptoms of someone who was frightened. Rather, they were the natural reactions of a person completely in control of a tense situation. The pain that came with the tinnitus had disappeared, making coherent thought and concentration possible. Mitch's instructions lived in the back of her mind, but she didn't need them. Instinctively, she knew what to do.

She sucked in her bottom lip and did a slow scan, turning her head from left to right in a smooth, concentrated arc. When she hit the two o'clock position she saw it—a light gray shadow with a top, a bottom, and two long, vertical sides. A perfect, unmistakable "door" floating in space. Without anything to scale against it, the rectangle might have been the size of an aircraft hangar miles from where she stood, or it might have been much closer and therefore much smaller. There was no way to tell. It didn't matter. That's where they were going; she was as certain of that as anything she'd ever known. She re-tightened her grip on Ray's hand. "There," she said, pointing with her opposite hand.

* * *

Ray followed the line off her index finger. He found the opposite portal easily this time and wondered how he could have possibly missed it himself. The next part came easily. He barely needed to concentrate, he wanted out of the Space Between so desperately. He stared at the rectangle and without any sense of movement, he and Eva were there.

Hand in hand, they stepped into a sprawling room. He blinked against the late afternoon sunlight shafting through grubby ceiling-to-floor windows. Dust mites swam lazily in the air. Empty pallets were stacked against one wall. Wooden shipping crates lined another. An old warehouse? Possibly a loft? He wasn't sure and he didn't take the time to examine his surroundings too closely. He turned in place on the scuffed plywood floor and stared across the Space Between, into the Days Inn.

Everything happening in the motel had taken on a two-dimensional quality, as though Ray were watching the flat screen television in the room, except the people he saw weren't actors. They were real, and they were closing in on Mitch.

He saw Mitch trip and fall and lay motionless. He saw Deputy Warden Tyler crouch and extend his arm, presumably reaching for something on the floor.

* * *

Mitch pulled one leg toward his chest, planted his foot on the lower edge of the closing portal and pushed away from the room. He dragged his opposite leg across the portal's lip, out of the motel, deeper into the darkness between the worlds. The effort sent fresh blooms of pain spiraling through his body.

He felt as though he was lying on his back, but if the portal hadn't been there as a vertical reference, he could just as easily be lying on his stomach or standing on his feet. His chest ached. Every breath burned, but pain meant he was alive. How was that possible after being shot in the chest? With probing fingers, he searched but found no blood, no yawning wound. The soldier must have hit him with a rubber bullet or a bean-bag. They must have wanted him alive after all.

He began his own slow scan. He didn't see the opposite portal immediately but he did have a clear view into the Days Inn, through the gap between his splayed feet. Deputy Warden Tyler peered back at him through the portal, lips pulled back from his teeth in a ghastly grin. He extended his arm and touched something to Mitch's foot.

The Space Between made the Taser's rattle, now working in stun mode, sound like it was operating at half speed. The electrical shock it delivered wasn't diminished in any way. Like a mirror falling off a wall, Mitch's every thought shattered into bright pieces of glass, each shard a broken thought.

He needed to do something, something important but he couldn't pin down exactly what.

In one large fragment, Cole appeared behind Tyler's right shoulder and stood there like the patriarch in a family portrait. His eyes bored into Mitch's. He spoke. The portal warped and slowed and slurred his game-show baritone, but Mitch understood him well enough.

"I know where you'll go," Cole said. He flicked his wrist.

A Green Earth loyalty card flew into the Space Between. It twisted lazily for a moment, swirling near Mitch's eyes before the wind sucked it into the darkness.

Cole broke eye contact and turned his glare on Tyler. His respectable mask fell away, the façade of control disappearing as it had in the suicide room. "Well?" he shouted. "Go get him!"

Tyler's mouth unhinged. At first, he said nothing. Then he stammered, "But—"

"But nothing. From the beginning I said this project was vitally important to me, did I not? I made Reilly your responsibility. My exact words were, 'Keep a very careful eye on him,' yes?"

Reluctantly, almost as though he had no choice and his

body was acting independently of his mind, Tyler reached into the Space Between, first as far as his elbow and then deeper, all the way to his shoulder, grasping for Mitch's ankle. "He's too far away," Tyler wailed.

"I can see that." Cole raised his eyebrows questioningly. "What are you waiting for, Mr. Tyler?"

* * *

The "television screen" Ray watched continued to shrink and Mitch continued to float in the wind. In the dwindling motel room, Deputy Warden Tyler argued with a third individual Ray assumed was Cole. Who else could it logically be, given the situation? Then, incomprehensibly, Tyler scissored one leg up and over the lower edge of the portal. He dipped his shoulders and lowered his head and pushed his upper torso into the Space Between.

Mitch didn't react.

"Oh, no," Ray said in a dismayed whisper. If Mitch couldn't move for whatever reason, Ray would have to go get him. He couldn't allow Tyler to take him back to Glades. Not to mention whatever horrors Cole had in mind.

Ray thought fast. Presumably the slipping process worked in reverse. All he had to do was "think" his way back to the original portal, grab Mitch and return to the empty warehouse. Three or four concentrated thoughts at the most. He swore again, louder this time. He closed his eyes and shook his head at his own foolishness and then he lifted one leg and straddled the lower edge of his own shrinking portal.

Eva's eyes widened. She grabbed his arm. "No, Ray. No. You said you wouldn't leave me."

"I've got to do this, Eva. I've got to go get him."

Tears flooded her eyes. She clutched his arm with both hands and despairing intensity. "You don't have time. It will kill you."

"I'll only be gone a second," Ray said, the tremble in his voice betraying what he knew to be a lie.

* * *

Tyler cut an imploring look over his shoulder, bulgy black eyes popping in panic, rivulets of terrified sweat at his temples. The top edge of the portal fell like a guillotine. The sides collapsed and the bottom rose. "There's no time," he moaned.

"I know," Cole answered. "Too bad I made Reilly your responsibility."

A head full of splintered thoughts didn't prevent Mitch from knowing what would happen next. He'd seen something similar a few weeks before. He decided it would be a good idea to close his eyes. While he made that decision, the portal crushed Deputy Warden Tyler in half with a sickening, wet crunch. The evil sound joined all the other evil noises inhabiting the darkness. A great geyser of blood spurt from Tyler's mouth, quickly dispersed into individual particulates and then vanished. The two halves of his body tumbled away, the top half trailing a slash of scarlet viscera and blood, the bottom half kicking and thrashing as comically as a cartoon character on Saturday morning television.

The hazy disengagement disappeared in tandem with the portal. Mitch's eyes fluttered a couple of times and suddenly he could think again. He found the opposite portal at once, or rather, he saw Ray scrambling over the portal's lower edge, re-entering the Space Between.

Eva wailed, "You don't have time. It will kill you."

She was right. What was Ray thinking? If he wasn't careful

the portal would pinch him, just like it pinched Tyler. They didn't have time to waste in the Space Between.

Mitch saw himself there and the process worked like it always did; like slipping from one world to the next occurred instantly.

Except, it didn't happen that way.

In the concentrated thought that was (and was not) an instant, Mitch realized with dismay that his twelfth crossing (and presumably his previous eleven), took a quantifiable amount of time. In the infinite space between worlds, "instant" has no reference. When the start line vanishes and the finish line is neither close nor immeasurably far away, "instant" is relative.

As Cole explained in the suicide room, slipping didn't happen in the space of a thought. It only felt that way.

* * *

Ray allowed Eva to pull him back into the warehouse. Panting with diminishing adrenaline, he ran the geometry through his mind. The portal was shrinking but he didn't believe it was shrinking *too* quickly. Mitch still had time to cross, squeeze through and join him and Eva, at which point the nightmare of the previous several months would end. Overwhelming relief wrapped around him like a warm blanket. If he never slipped again, it would be too soon. With luck the Space Between would quickly fade in his memory and become nothing but a bad aftertaste. He gave her a shaky smile. "Thank you, Eva—"

Her stricken face interrupted him. She muttered, "I'm sorry." Refusing to meet his eye, she pointed behind him.

Confused, he swiveled in place and met Mitch's eyes, Mitch looking back at him from inside the Space Between through a window the size of a serving tray.

"No," Ray yelled. He lunged for the portal and curled his

fingers around both vertical sides. He pulled in opposite directions with all his strength. Inexorably, the gap narrowed. One
hand slipped. A fingernail snagged and tore on the warehouse
wall. He ignored the eye-watering pain. He grabbed one vertical side with both hands, threw his weight into it and pulled in
the opposite direction. His muscles screamed in protest and sweat
beaded his forehead.

The portal shrank.

Mother Nature was like that. Day followed night without
variation. Winter came after autumn. And, when an aberration occurred in the universe, man-made or otherwise, she
repaired it. Sometimes it took centuries. Other times, like now,
it took seconds.

In a hollow, tired rasp, Mitch said, "You're gonna hurt yourself, Ray."

Panting, chest heaving, Ray dropped his arms. His shoulders
slumped. Hot tears welled in his eyes. He chewed his lower lip
and looked to the side and said nothing because the moment he
spoke he knew the tears would fall and he didn't want that to be
Mitch's last memory. And, then despite himself, he looked at his
friend and blurted out, "I couldn't get to you in time. I'm sorry.
I'm so sorry."

* * *

"No apologies," Mitch answered. He found the Saint Christopher
medallion on the chain around his neck. There was never a time he
believed the medallion would bring him good luck. Today's Gong
Show bore that out. But, it was a tangible connection to Liv and
that gave the medallion more value than a good luck charm ever
would. He wanted her to know in one way at least, he'd never truly
left her. He gave the chain a hard tug. The clasp broke. Looking

at Ray's tear-filled eyes he said, "Do me a favor?" With the Saint Christopher dangling from his fingers, he reached through the notebook-sized window. "Get this to Liv. Green Earth."

He dropped the medallion into Ray's hand and snatched his own hand back. The square of light into a different, better world vanished and as it did, Mitch remembered the sad vision he experienced when he slipped out of Murphy's Pub, the vison in which two people he didn't recognize, a balding middle-aged man and a young girl with brown hair and too much makeup, walked into Green Earth without him.

CHAPTER 49

THEY SAT IN silence, side by side on a bench. Across the street, in the left-hand window of a small store, a sign advertised exciting new hemp products and tasty, gluten-free snacks. The right window displayed a selection of Birkenstock shoes. Above the door in the middle of the building, a large (seemingly), hand-painted sign read, "Green Earth."

With his elbows on his knees, his fists supporting his chin, Ray gazed across the street. He held the broken chain with the Saint Christopher medallion in one clenched fist. For some reason, his mouth was dry and his heart beat fast. He couldn't understand his nervousness. It didn't make sense. Why did meeting Liv make him feel like he was meeting Mitch all over again? Why did it bring back the previous month, in bright, vivid color—Glades, the riot, the drive to the hotel the night they slipped, and worst of all, Mitch's disappearance into the Space Between? Despite the Florida heat, Ray shivered. He clamped his jaw against a rush of hot emotion.

He hadn't forgotten Mitch's instructions that night in the Days Inn, but when the time came he couldn't move. He tried. His feet refused to budge, as if the Space Between had placed a hand on his chest and held him back. He shouldn't have been surprised. The night had warned him over and over again—*you aren't supposed to be here.* By the time Mitch shoved him, it was too late, the delay long enough to trap Mitch between the worlds. Ray's guilt was as deep as ever, although now it punished him like a blunt instrument instead of cutting him like a scalpel.

He sensed Eva's questioning eyes on him. He ignored her and studied the health food store, as if it would give him a better sense of who Liv was and somehow make it easier to explain what happened in the Days Inn. Despite his racing heart, he yawned. Would insight arrive more quickly if he wasn't quite so worn out? Ray wasn't sure. He knew he and Eva couldn't continue living as they were. Every single day was hand to mouth, although the week after they slipped had been the toughest.

They went hungry. They went without sleep. They went without showers. Eva managed to find a job before he did, as a chambermaid at a no-name, beach motel. Not much money, but the owner paid cash at the end of each day and didn't care if she and Ray used the shower and bathroom facilities, as long as the room was recently vacated and not freshly cleaned. Previous occupants often left their keys behind, on the dresser or bed. In those cases, Eva pocketed them and they'd sleep in the motel. In the beginning, they used her paltry salary—less than minimum wage, Ray suspected—to buy essentials such as toothpaste and shampoo, as well as underwear and socks. They hit a Goodwill store for a couple of changes of clothes, and a backpack for Ray to carry it all. Eva still had her ratty pack with the Han Solo patch.

Shortly after she started work, he found daytime employment at a marina where rich people maintained their yachts during the winter. He learned the misery of pressure washing barnacles off the bottom of boats and repainting them with antifouling paint. At night, he scraped and scrubbed dishes at an all-you-can-eat, Chinese buffet. After he found that job they always had something for supper.

They didn't talk about the future, neither short term nor long.

Neither of them wanted to face several large truths. First, living in a motel, moving from room to room every night, wouldn't be an option for much longer. Vacancy rates on the beach were relatively high in December. Come spring he and Eva would no longer get away with a free place to stay.

Second, cash jobs were difficult to come by and temporary in nature; sooner or later they'd need more money than they currently made. They also needed identification, especially Ray, who didn't have to slip in a year's time.

Ray's biggest concern, however, something he hadn't voiced, was Cole. What if he discovered Eva was like Mitch? Cole collected those who slipped and used them to kill worlds. Ray didn't find thoughts such as these crazy anymore, and it seemed the only way of protecting Eva was somehow defeating Cole. The big question was, how? How did a mortal such as himself, bring down an element that had existed since the dawn of time? Was it even possible?

He didn't know.

He doubted he'd ever find an answer.

He doubted there was an answer.

For now, at least, there were manageable problems. For now, there was Green Earth.

Eva coughed quietly. He looked at her and her eyebrows rose in question. A couple of days after they slipped she stopped using the heavy black eye makeup and she'd removed the ruby above her lip. Devoid of the temporary accessories that defined her youth, and without the worry and laugh lines that would eventually underline her age, her face became clean and fresh. Ray preferred her new look, although he realized his preference was that of a conservative, middle-aged man and not one of a much younger individual.

She said, "Why are we just sitting here?"

Ray didn't answer immediately. He had to walk across the

street and introduce himself to a woman he'd never met, then explain the circumstances in which he'd known her boyfriend. He'd tell Liv she could expect a visit from an entirely demonic individual named Cole, and that she might "see" him as someone from her past. Somehow, he had to convince her that Mitch missed her and had tried to make it back to her, and that he regretted leaving in the first place. When she looked at him like he was insane—which she indisputably would—he'd hand her the only proof he possessed and explain how the Saint Christopher came to him, how Mitch saved him and Eva from a psychotic prison warden and something evil called the Space Between.

And, Eva wondered why he was hesitating?

She coughed a second time, loudly and deliberately.

The tiniest, briefest of grins touched Ray's lips. Maybe there was something to be said for the rashness and impatience of youth. Eva would have walked directly into the store without pause or consideration, without a clear idea of what she'd say or how she'd handle the situation. She'd wing it.

He felt his first conversation with Liv needed a gentler approach.

Hence the nerves?

Possibly.

He sat up and rolled his shoulders, trying to ease the ache, wondering if the muscles he'd hurt trying to hold the portal open would ever be the same. He pushed himself to his feet. Staring at the store front hadn't given him any fresh insight. "No good reason, I guess," he answered.

"Should I come with you?"

When she gave up the makeup and ruby, he asked her why. She shrugged and mumbled something about, "… time for a change…" He didn't enquire further. He guessed it was less about change and more about growing up several years in a few short weeks. One thing that hadn't changed was her fear of being alone.

"Do you want to?" he asked. It was important she learned to make her own decisions. Little events like this popped up regularly, reminding him of her probable future: in a year's time, Eva would have to slip. He would no longer be able help her with life's choices. This knowledge filled him with numb despair. She was as lost to him as Dawn and Angie.

She sucked her lower lip, and eventually nodded. "I didn't like him. But this isn't fair."

"I know," he said. He looked across the street and sighed. "It's going to get harder before it gets easier. Let's go." He stood, reached for her hand.

She brushed it aside. "I'm not a baby."

Ray said nothing. He had learned to accept these inconsistencies in her manner and mood without annoyance or judgment. They were illogical and indecipherable and it kept the peace when he didn't question her. They were an odd couple. They couldn't be considered friends because of their age difference and the element of guardianship in their relationship. But, he wasn't her guardian. Nor was she his daughter, wife, or girlfriend, so he had no idea how to define their bond. He decided to accept it as it was, just as he accepted so many things over the last several months. It was what it was, and it was beyond explaining.

Side by side they walked across the street.

He paused at the entrance to Green Earth and then pushed open the door. A bell rang merrily. Somewhere in the distance a radio played a song Ray recognized but couldn't name. He liked the husky, moodiness of the singer's voice. It suited the store. It was a Blue Rodeo kind of place. Leonard Cohen or Bob Dylan. Definitely not pop or top ten. A pleasant mix of spices and incense perfumed the air. The walls were covered in shelves, every shelf filled with bottles of pills and containers of supplements and jars of vitamins. Beneath his feet, the warped and scarred hardwood flexed and squeaked, making more noise than the doorbell had upon his entrance.

A lady walked out from behind a rack of "natural ingredient" snack bars, the kind that tasted like sawdust. She was tall and slim, athletic in sneakers and stretchy black pants. Not much shape to her. Ray had no problem imagining her running a marathon. Light, straw-blonde hair hung to the top of her shoulders. She pushed it away from her face in what was clearly a habitual gesture. She wore a small understated pearl in each ear lobe. She smiled and asked in a friendly voice, "How can I help you?" Her lightly glossed lips shone. The entire look unaccountably reminded Ray of a bright, spring morning when texture and tone and balance and color were all just right and the photographers come out with their high-definition cameras. If first impressions meant anything, he thought he understood why Mitch was taken with this lady.

He swallowed a lump in his throat and blinked several times, clearing his eyes. He said, "You're Liv. We have a friend in common."

Epilogue

HALF A BLOCK away, hidden in the shade of an awning over the entrance to a designer kitchen boutique, the element Mitch Reilly once knew as Cole, watched two people enter Green Earth. Cole recognized the man. His name was Raymond Albright. Albright didn't routinely travel, slip in Reilly's parlance, so knowing the man's name was nothing but trivia to Cole. The young lady though… He didn't know her but became curious after seeing her at the Days Inn. Who was she to Reilly and Albright?

When Reilly didn't make it out of the Space Between, it seemed logical his friend from prison would seek out the girl-friend and break the sad news. If not logical, then even odds, at least. Cole thought staking out Green Earth might be worth his time, to assuage his curiosity about the young lady, if nothing else. If Albright showed up at the health food store, perhaps she would accompany him.

After a month in sunny Florida with no sign of either Albright or his young travel companion, Cole came close to giving up sur-veillance. It was so boring. All Liv did was go to school, work, run, and attend yoga class. If that was all a person had to look forward to, humanity should have stood up and applauded when he killed off a world. Couldn't she have mixed her routine up, just for interest's sake? Maybe worked as an assassin Saturday night and lead the church choir on Sunday? Something. Anything. But she was squeaky clean.

Cole asked himself, how long did one reasonably wait for something that wouldn't necessarily happen? Then again, he had nothing pressing. Hurricane season was several months away. An uprising in the Middle East was building steam but events in that area of the world were always uprising. The sand-monkeys needed so little management. Cole enjoyed recruiting them.

He committed himself to one more week.

It came and went.

He waited a further four days without any sign of Albright or the mystery girl.

And, then on the fifth day, almost a full six weeks after they traveled, he saw them sitting side by side on a bench across the street from Green Earth.

From the shadows Cole watched and waited and for a long time they did nothing other than sit and chat. And then, abruptly, Albright stood. His back straightened and his shoulders squared into a posture of determination. He spoke a few indistinguishable words with the girl before she too rose to her feet. When Albright reached for her hand she brushed it aside, making Albright shrug. He looked right and left then strode across the street toward Green Earth. He hesitated for half a second before pulling open the door and entering the store. The young lady followed him inside.

Cole tapped a contemplative index finger on his lips. Who was she? Where had she come from? Instinct and countless years of experience told him she was a puzzle worth solving. If his suspicions were correct and she was a traveler, the entire operation could be salvaged or, at least, mitigated. He still teetered on the verge of apoplectic when he thought about losing Mitch Reilly. Who could have anticipated the Taser would slow the man down and dull his senses long enough for him to miss the door into the new world? Cole shook his head. After a millennium of centuries, he still had things to learn. The universe was truly an amazing place.

In ten months, certainly no more than twelve, he'd know for sure if the young lady with Ray Albright travelled.

Ten months.

No time at all.

A drop of water in an ocean. A single breath in an entire lifetime.

Ten months. He could wait that long.

The end

Two points...

First, in the scientific world, cosmic inflation and the multiverse are valid theories. I loosely defined them at the beginning of this novel in part to help explain what may appear to those who read my previous novels, as a haphazard grasp of time and events on my part.

I say "loosely" because both these (and associated theories and concepts) are incredibly complex. I could only sum them up in the simplest manner possible and present them in such a way as to best serve the story. Remember, *A Different World* is fiction. As for the facts, the full truth of the matter, people much smarter than me are debating, agreeing, disagreeing, and researching but as of yet, there is no known proof one way or the other if cosmic inflation occurred, thereby creating the multiverse.

Second, once again I've taken liberties with geography. High school was a long time ago. I don't remember paying much attention in geography class and I'm not proficient with Google Maps. I apologize to those of you who take issue with the locations of hotels, distances, etcetera.

Thank you for your continued interest.
Kevin